*The Club Series* book five

# THE INFATUATION

*Josh and Kat Part I*

---

## Lauren Rowe

Published by SoCoRo Publishing
Layout by www.formatting4U.com
Photography: Kelly Elaine Photo

# Chapter 1

*Josh*

Oh my fucking God. What's wrong with Jonas this time? I'm so worried I'm jumping out of my skin. I look out the window of the limo, wracked with the same sense of dread I always feel when Jonas calls me with that barely contained panic in his voice. Of course, I dropped everything and immediately caught the next flight to Seattle, just like I always do—but this time, unlike every other time, I don't have a clue what's happened to freak Jonas out. And that, in turn, freaks *me* out.

"Hey," I call up to the limo driver. "Can you change the channel to something a bit more mellow, please?" The song blaring in my ear is "I'm Too Sexy" by Right Said Fred, definitely not a song that's gonna calm my jangling nerves.

"How's this?" the driver says, switching to another station on the radio. The song playing now is "Mad World" by Tears for Fears.

"Yeah," I say, smirking to myself. "Leave it here. Thanks."

When I saw my brother's incoming call on my phone earlier this evening, I figured Jonas had gotten back from his trip to Belize with the "most amazing girl ever," the one and only Sarah Cruz, the magical, mystical unicorn he hacked into U Dub's server to find, sight unseen, and that he was calling to slobber all over the phone about how "amazing" she is. But the minute I heard his voice, I knew he wasn't calling to babble happily about his Belizian getaway with his new crush—I knew something was wrong. Very, very wrong.

"Are you okay? Is Sarah okay?" I asked him, my stomach twisting into knots.

"Yeah, I'm okay. The trip was incredible—Sarah's incredible," Jonas replied. But before I could exhale with any kind of relief, he said something that sent me reeling: "It's The Club, Josh. It's total bullshit—a fucking scam. I think Sarah's in danger—like, maybe *serious* danger."

What the fuck? I couldn't process what that statement could possibly mean.

Mad World, indeed.

It's been well over three hours since Jonas called and said those bizarre words, and I still haven't figured out what the fuck he meant by them. *The Club's a scam*? Well, no, it isn't, Jonas. I happen to know through my own personal experience it's one hundred percent *not* a scam. I can personally attest that I filled out my application, paid my money, and got exactly what I asked for, to the letter, in multiple cities, over the course of one very awesome and cathartic month. So what's the fucking scam?

The more likely scenario is that Jonas didn't get what he asked for because, whatever it was, it was literally impossible to deliver. Knowing him, he probably asked for something only some magical combination of the circus, the philosophy department at Yale, and *American Ninja Warrior* could have delivered. And that's what he thinks of as a *scam*? Maybe this is a wanton case of "it's not them, it's *you.*"

Shit. When I told Jonas about The Club in the first place, I should have told him, "Dude, when you fill out your application, less is more. Just go for the big one or two things you're dying for and leave it at that. You can only do so much in one month, trust me—don't get too ambitious." I shake my head. Jonas is so fucking bad with women, I swear to God—and he always has been. They fall all over themselves the minute they see him, of course—everywhere he goes women practically throw their panties at him. But then he opens his fucking mouth and starts quoting fucking Plato and talking in riddles and looking like a fucking serial killer and they run away, screaming in bloody terror. (God only knows how he tricked this Sarah girl into sticking around for so long. Hell, maybe she has a thing for Plato, too, for all I know.)

But for the sake of argument, let's say The Club is some kind of scam (which it's not); how the fuck could that possibly mean this new girl of Jonas' is in some kind of danger—let alone "serious" danger? I can't wrap my brain around any of it. The only thing I can think is that Jonas must have met Sarah in The Club? But that makes no sense. When I asked Jonas about his membership not too long ago, he said he'd applied but had gotten hopelessly distracted by his quest to get laid by his mystery law student.

I'm just so fucking confused. I look out the window of the limo, listening to the song for a long minute.

Frankly, I'm really worried that all this rambling is a sign that Jonas is having some sort of psychotic break again. And if that's what's really going on, why now? As far as I know, my brother's been in full beast mode lately. I mean, shit, just last week when we negotiated the acquisition of all those rock-climbing gyms, he was in tiptop form, kicking ass and taking names like the beast he is. He was a sight to see, actually—he sure out-beasted me by a fucking mile. Of course, he couldn't stop talking about this Sarah chick the whole three days I was with him—which is so unlike him, at first I wasn't sure if he was punking me—but I didn't see that as any cause for alarm. In fact, I was happy for him.

But now, I'm wondering if his obsession with her was a sign that things weren't completely right in his head.

Actually, I was a tad bit worried when he called me in the first place, barking at me to find some random girl who'd sent him an email. (Any time Jonas gets ultra-obsessed about something, it's usually not a good sign for his mental health.) But, much to my relief and surprise, the magical, mystical Sarah Cruz turned out to be well worth his effort, a truly fantastic girl. The minute I met her during our mutual limo ride to the airport, I thought, *Now here's a girl who's gonna bring out the very best in my brother.* She's absolutely adorable. And I can certainly understand the physical attraction, too, I don't mind admitting.

So what the fuck happened in the four days between that limo ride and today that made Jonas' wheels fall off his cart?

Downtown Seattle is whizzing past me outside my car window.

I exhale and shake my head.

I'm so fucking worried right now, I can't think straight. I just wish I understood what's going on with Jonas. And The Club. And Sarah? I shake my head again. What the fuck did Jonas mean she might be in serious danger?

My phone buzzes with a text and I look down.

"Hey, Josh!" the text says. "Looooooooooong time no see. How ya doing, baby? LOL!"

I chuckle in surprise. Now there's a name I never expected (or particularly wanted) to see on my phone again: *Jennifer LeMonde*. I admit I was dazzled by the girl's pedigree (and slamming body) when we dated for four or five months when I was twenty-three—chalk that up to youth and being stoned out of my mind half the time—but once the initial heat and the novelty of her Grammy-winning daddy and Oscar-winning mommy wore off, not to mention the weed, I quickly realized Jen was very likely the least interesting girl in the world. And that's when I decided once and for all to pull my shit together and lay off the weed and fulfill my family obligations in earnest. And I've stayed on track ever since, other than during the occasional short vacations of total debauchery I've allowed myself over the years (which I'm not sorry about, by the way). Honestly, my little sojourns into hedonism have helped me stay the course, something I've been bound and determined to do, not just for me, but for Jonas, too. I mean, let's face it, Jonas and I can't both be on the verge of a nervous breakdown at all times, and Jonas long ago called dibs on that role.

"Hey, Jen," I type. "It's been a long time. What's up?"

"Have you seen what's going on with Isabel lately? OMG!"

"Yeah. Hard to miss. Good for her. I'm thrilled for her," I type.

I'm being sincere. From what I remember of Isabel from seven years ago, she's a really sweet girl. I'm honestly thrilled all her dreams of stardom are coming true.

"The studio rented Isabel a freaking castle in San Tropez all next week to celebrate her movie opening at number one!" Jen writes. "Dude. It's literally a castle! Made me remember that time our whole group partied together in Cannes—remember that? Or, actually, come to think of it, you probably don't! LOL!!!!" She adds a whole bunch of wineglass emojis and a marijuana-leaf emoji and a smiley face wearing sunglasses. "So, anyhoo, Isabel's getting a huge group together to party in the castle in France (did I mention it's a freaking castle???!!!! OMFG!!!!) and she wanted to know if maybe you and Reed wanna join us for a mini-reunion? It'll be just like old times! LOL!" She adds what appears to be a dancing cat, a reference I'm not sure I understand.

I stare at my phone for a moment, shaking my head. I'm not

even remotely tempted. "Sorry. I'm in Seattle for a family emergency," I write. "Gonna be tied up here for a while helping my brother. Plus, I'm an old man nowadays, Jen. You wouldn't even recognize me. I'm practically chasing damn kids off my lawn. Been working pretty hard building my family's business since you last saw me. But, hey, feel free to contact Reed directly to ask him if he's interested. I'll send you his number. And please tell Isabel congrats on all her success for me," I continue. "I'm genuinely thrilled for her. Just saw she won some People's Choice Award or something? Ha! Awesome. She's America's Sweetheart."

"I know! She totally is! LOL! She's blowing up! She's gonna do Jimmy Fallon in NYC when she gets back from France! OMFG! Can you believe it? She's so excited."

"Saw her face plastered on a billboard on my way to LAX today. She looks great. Tell her nice boob job, btw. Her surgeon did excellent work. Unless that's photoshop?"

"Not photoshop. The real fake deal. Brand new, actually. She'll be geeked you noticed. Did you notice her nose, too? (The polite answer is no. Haha!)"

"She looks great, top to bottom. Tell her I said so. But she was always beautiful."

"Aw, come on, Josh. You're making me remember what a sweetheart you are. I wanna see you soooooo bad! Are you sure you can't swing it? Pwetty pwease? I'll make sure you have a REALLY good time." She adds a winking emoji.

I smirk. This is patently ridiculous. Jennifer LeMonde can't possibly give a rat's ass about me, any more than I give one about her. We dated for, what, five months when we were in our early twenties. Not exactly a soul connection. Obviously, this is more about Isabel pining for Reed like she always has than about Jen and me. My guess is Isabel asked Jen to lure Reed to France by any means necessary, including using me as bait.

When I don't immediately reply to Jen's last text, she sends another one right on its heels. "What if I promise not to wear my bikini top the entire time we're there? 'When in France,' right? I remember how much you loooooved my pretty titties." She adds a bikini emoji and a pair of lips. "And they're still all-natural, baby!" Winking emoji.

"Sorry. Can't. Family emergency, like I say," I write. But what I'm thinking is, *I'm thirty fucking years old, Jen. You really think I'm gonna travel halfway around the world just to see a pair of tits (even if they are, admittedly, the most perfect pair of tits I've ever seen)?*

"Bummer." Sad-face emoji. "Saw you and your brother on the cover of some magazine the other day, creamed my panties just looking at you. Talk about the Wonder Twins. Day-am. You boys should be in movies."

"Thanks."

"Well, okay. Text me if something changes. I'll be crossing my fingers you change your mind."

"Family emergency, like I say," I type. "Sorry."

"Well, if France isn't gonna work out, we'll have to get together another time really soon. I've been thinking about you a lot lately. About how much fun we used to have." She adds a lips emoji. "I'd make it worth your effort if you come see me, Josh." Another winking emoji.

I roll my eyes. Was she always this annoying? I just told the girl I've got a family emergency and that my brother needs me—and she invites me to fuck her rather than ask me if everything's okay? Not to mention I told her I've been working hard to build my family's business and she didn't ask me for any details? Par for the course, though. Our "relationship," such as it was, certainly wasn't based on anything deep.

The limo stops and I glance up from my phone. I'm in Jonas' driveway. Damn. For a second there, I'd actually forgotten where I was headed.

I exhale audibly. Whatever's waiting for me on the other side of Jonas' front door isn't gonna be good—I can feel it in my bones.

# Chapter 2

*Josh*

The minute I walk through Jonas' front door, my brother bounds toward me like a Labrador retriever, dragging his new chew toy (Sarah) with him as he goes.

"Hey," I say, putting down my duffel bag and giving Jonas a big hug. "Well, hello, Sarah Cruz." I give her a hug, too. "Fancy meeting you here."

"Get used to it," Jonas says, obviously thrilled to be saying those words.

"So what the hell's going on?" I ask, steeling myself for whatever fucked up shit's about to come my way.

Jonas moans. "It's so fucked up, man."

My stomach twists. I sit down on the couch, readying myself. "Tell me."

Jonas sits down next to me and runs his hand through his hair, obviously getting ready to launch into some sort of monologue, but before he gets a word out, the bathroom door on the far side of the spacious room opens abruptly and a blur of golden blondeness moves into my peripheral vision. My eyes dart toward the movement—I wasn't aware there was anyone else here besides Jonas, Sarah, and me—and then I absentmindedly look back toward Jonas.

But all of a sudden, my brain processes the startling golden perfection my eyes just beheld and my eyes dart back to the astonishing figure striding toward me. Oh my fucking God. *Who the fuck is this creature?*

The girl walking toward me is literally the most spectacularly beautiful woman I've ever laid eyes on in my entire life, without exception (and this is coming from a guy who briefly dated Miss

Universe and currently fucks a Victoria's Secret model whenever we both happen to be in L.A.). This girl's... oh my God. She's the precise sum of parts I'd order at the Build-a-Girl store if there were such a thing. Holy fuck. And she's headed right toward me, smiling at me like she can read my exact thoughts.

She's got to be a model. Or an actress. Of course, she is. What else could she be, looking the way she does? Shit. Damn. Fuck. Oh my God. Holy fucking Christ.

Miss Perfect sashays right up to me, without hesitation. "I'm Kat," she says, putting out her hand. "Sarah's best friend."

She's got sky-blue eyes. Her long hair is a heart-stopping shade of golden blonde—and it's obviously totally natural. And, oh my God, this can't be happening—*she's got a subtle little indentation in her chin, too—the slightest cleft.* That's always been my Achilles' heel—ever since I made out with Jessica Simpson at Reed's twenty-first birthday party so many years ago.

"Josh," I say, taking her hand. "Jonas' brother."

"I know," she says, smirking. "I read the article." She motions in the direction of the coffee table.

I glance down to see which article she's referring to, and I'm bummed to discover it's the one that made Jonas out to be some kind of deep-thinking poet with a Midas touch with investments and me out to be nothing but a giant, throbbing dick with cotton between my ears.

"I sure hope you're more complicated than that article makes you out to be," Kat says, her blue eyes sparkling.

I look at Jonas, hoping maybe he'll step in and say something to help a brother out, like, oh, I dunno, how 'bout, "Oh, that reporter was just trying to sell magazines." Or, maybe, "We thought we were doing a serious interview about Faraday & Sons and it turned into a fluff piece for *Tiger Beat.*" But Jonas doesn't say a damned thing on my behalf. Of course, he doesn't, the motherfucker. I guess now that he's got his dream girl all locked up he's content to let me twist in the wind in front of a woman who looks like mine?

"If the article is to be believed," Kat goes on, smirking at me, "Jonas is the 'enigmatic loner-investment-wunderkind' twin—and you're just the simple *playboy.*"

I laugh. So this girl's not only gorgeous, she's sassy, too? Oh, how I like me a sassy woman.

"That's what the article said?" I ask, even though I know that's exactly what the article said.

"In so many words," she says, arching one of her bold eyebrows.

"Hmm," I say, returning her raised-eyebrow gesture. "Interesting. And if someone were writing a magazine article about you, what gross over-simplification would they use?"

She bites her lip. "I'd be 'a party girl with a heart of gold.'" She glances at Sarah and they share a smile.

Oh man. This girl's too much. My skin is buzzing like I've just downed a double shot of Patron. "How come I only get a one-word description—*playboy*—and you get a whole phrase?" I ask.

She shrugs. "Okay, party girl, then."

"That's two words," I say.

Kat raises her eyebrow, yet again. "In this hypothetical magazine article about me," she purrs, "they'd spell it with a hyphen."

Oh, well, fuck. My dick just stretched and yawned and said, "Do I smell coffee and doughnuts?"

She smirks. She knows she's caught a fly in her web. But then again, I'm guessing flies in her web are just par for the course for her.

"So what's going on here, Party Girl with a Hyphen?" I ask. "I take it we didn't all congregate here to party?"

"No, unfortunately," Kat says breezily. "Though, hey, we did have some of your tequila earlier, so thanks for that." Her mouth tilts up, and I have the palpable urge to kiss it. "No, I'm just here to support Sarah," she says, "and, well, I think I might be some kind of refugee in all this, too." She looks at Jonas and frowns. "Although I think maybe Jonas is being slightly overprotective having me stay here. I'm not sure yet."

"You're a *refugee* in all this?" I ask, suddenly on full alert. "What the fuck's going on, Jonas?"

Jonas grunts. "Sit down," he says.

I sit down, my stomach churning. I can't for the life of me guess what he's about to tell me. How are Sarah *and* Kat involved in whatever the fuck's going on? I can't even fathom the connection.

Jonas takes a deep breath and launches into a story that immediately makes my brain hurt. *Sarah worked for The Club? And she was Jonas' intake agent—the one who reviewed his application*? Holy shit! Well, well, well, Little Miss Sarah Cruz isn't quite the naive little law student I thought she was, after all. But, hang on, Jonas is still yammering. There's more? *Sarah emailed Jonas after reading his application? And that's when he got a boner to find her?* Oh my God. This is too much. What the fuck did little Miss Cruz say to Jonas in that email of hers? And what the hell did he say in his application that caught Sarah's attention in the first place?

Oh my God. There's even more to the story. Jonas is still talking. I can't fucking believe it. Some woman in a purple bracelet showed up to meet Jonas at a check-in before he'd ever met Sarah and—hang on, I thought Jonas said he never actually became a member of The Club—and then that same woman turned up at another guy's check-in wearing a yellow bracelet?—and Jonas knows all this because Sarah and Kat went to spy at both check-ins! Whoa, whoa, whoa. *Sarah went to spy on Jonas at a check-in with a woman in The Club?* Holy shit. And, even after that, she's nonetheless sitting here right now, looking at Jonas like he walks on water? Now that's an open-minded woman. I wonder if Kat's as open-minded as her kinky little law-student friend.

I glance at Sarah and she flashes me an endearing look that could only be described as "adorkable." I laugh out loud. Well, shit. If this girl's kinky, then I must be shy and intellectual. Oh man, Sarah's a total dork, through and through, God love her—no wonder my dork of a brother digs her.

". . . so I was thinking we could try to trace The Club through emails," Jonas is saying. "Do you still have any of the emails from when you were a member?" he asks.

*Gee, thanks, Jonas.* Is my brother *trying* to keep me from getting laid by the most beautiful woman I've ever seen?

I glance at Kat, my cheeks instantly turning red, and I'm surprised to find her eyes blazing at me. *Oh.* Nice. Kat's not grossed out by the revelation that I'm a past member of The Club, she's *intrigued. Lovely.*

I clear my throat. "I don't know if I kept any of their emails," I say. "It's been about seven months since my membership and I don't typically keep emails past three months."

"Shit," Jonas says. "Would have been nice to have something to trace."

Jonas goes on to explain that he and Sarah came home from

Belize to find Sarah's and Kat's apartments trashed and their computers stolen—which proves, according to Jonas, that The Club will stop at nothing, including physical violence, to keep both women from divulging the supposedly indisputable fact that The Club is actually nothing more than a global prostitution ring.

I don't reply, partly because I'm simply trying to process Jonas' reasoning, but also because Kat is so fucking hot, it's hard for me to think straight in her presence.

I wonder if Kat's got a boyfriend. Please, God, don't let her have a boyfriend. Oh shit, what if she's married? I glance at her finger. No wedding ring. Thank God. Does she live here in Seattle? Yeah, she must—Jonas said she and Sarah spied on Jonas and that other guy at their check-ins in town. Huh. If Kat lives here, the odds are slim she's a model. I wonder what she does for a living, then. Does she—

Oh.

Jonas is staring at me like he expects me to say something. Shit. I have no idea what he's been saying for the past few minutes.

"Huh," I finally say, trying to look deep in thought. "Interesting."

Jonas exhales a shaky breath, clearly containing some sort of rage at my response. But what the fuck does he expect? I can't track each and every one of his ramblings under the best of circumstances, let alone when a woman like Kat is sitting fifteen feet away from me, looking at me like she's thinking about sucking my dick.

And, anyway, it's obvious to me Jonas is probably grossly misinterpreting the situation or, at the very least, overreacting to it (shocker!). Even if Sarah and Kat saw some chick wearing a yellow bracelet after she'd fucked Jonas a few nights earlier wearing a purple one, that doesn't necessarily mean the sky is falling, does it? It could simply mean some women in The Club are assigned more than one color. Why is that such a fucking revelation? Some people have extremely varied tastes, after all.

Or maybe one of Jonas' exes found out he's been dating Sarah and went ballistic, trashing Sarah's apartment in a fit of jealous rage (and then doing the same thing to Sarah's best friend's place, too)? Even if that seems like a far-fetched scenario, it's probably no crazier an idea than some hitman coming after Sarah and Kat simply because they happened to observe some woman wearing two different colored bracelets.

Jonas is glaring at me again, obviously waiting for me to say something.

I clear my throat. "Wow," I say. But he's still waiting, and so are Sarah and Kat. "I'm not sure, bro," I add. "I met some really great girls." It's a true statement—I honestly did meet some really great girls in The Club—but, nonetheless, even as I say it, I cringe at how douche-y it sounds.

I glance at Kat and, yep, she's put off.

Oh, really? So she's intrigued when she finds out I *joined* a high-priced sex club, but put off to learn I actually *enjoyed* my short time in it? Ha! This one's a handful, I can already tell.

"How long was your membership, Josh?" Sarah asks.

"A month," I reply.

"And you... completed your entire membership period... successfully?"

Oh my God. Sarah can barely get the words out. This girl really is adorable—and, yep, clearly, there's not a kinky bone in her body. A total goody-two-shoes, through and through, which is funny considering she processed sex club applications for a living.

"Oh, yeah. Definitely," I say, looking at Kat and smiling broadly. Maybe I shouldn't smile, but I can't help it—I'm enjoying how every little thing I say about The Club pulls an animated reaction from Kat of one kind or another.

Plus, shit, I'm just being honest here: My month in The Club was fucking awesome—just what the doctor ordered after Emma ripped my heart and stuck it into a blender. Fucking yourself back to happy truly shouldn't be underrated, I gotta say—it was exactly what I needed at the time. Plus, in an unexpected twist, a handful of the women I hooked up with that month stayed with me in my hotel room for hours after we'd fucked and listened to me pour my guts out about my shattered heart. I normally never would have been such a blathering pussy-ass, of course—I'm not Jonas, for fuck's sake—but I guess there was freedom in knowing I'd never see any of those women again. And so, I let my guard down completely and let it flow—and at the end of that whirlwind month of fucking and fantasy-fulfillment and unexpected gut-spilling, I actually felt like myself again, ready to move on and stop acting like a brokenhearted little pussy.

I've never told anyone about my month in The Club, except to suggest to Jonas that he join—(if anyone needs to fuck himself to happy, it's my brother, that's for fucking sure)—but now that it's out in the open in front of Sarah and Kat (and especially Kat), I'm not gonna crawl into a hole and act like I'm embarrassed by it. I was single. It was fun and uniquely cathartic. As far as I'm concerned, I have absolutely nothing to be ashamed of when it comes to my time in The Club. Might some of those girls have been hookers? Well, now that I think about it, sure—how else could The Club have supplied everything I asked for in my application, to the letter? But I can't believe *all* of them were straight-up hookers. Some of them might just have been looking for a very wealthy boyfriend with a big ol' dick.

"There's no way all those girls were prostitutes," I say, but even as the words come out of my mouth, I realize I don't actually believe them. The truth is, even as I filled out my application, I didn't care *how* The Club supplied what I asked for—just as long as they did. So, okay, if it turns out the women I fucked in The Club were all prostitutes, then fine, they were well worth the money, and then some. Clearly, I needed to do something to move on from Emma—and fucking my way back to beastliness with a bunch of super cool, nonjudgmental, hot-as-hell women was a helluva lot cheaper (and a lot more fun) than a month's worth of therapy. "They were super cool, all of them," I say, matter-of-factly. Fuck it.

Sarah crinkles her nose. "They were *all* super cool, huh?" she asks. "Well, Julia Roberts was 'super cool' in *Pretty Woman*, too."

I chuckle. Oh my God, I absolutely love this girl. "True," I say. I flash Jonas a look that says, "She's a cutie, bro," but his eyes are as hard as fucking flint right now.

Shit. Here we go. I know that look. It means my brother's about to lose his fucking shit.

"How many women could you possibly have gone through in a month?" Kat suddenly blurts from across the room.

Oh, hello. I lock eyes with Kat and, yup, it's written all over her gorgeous face: she wants me. Oh, fuck yes, she does. I can't help but smile as my cock begins tingling at the blatant desire on her face.

"I mean . . ." Kat says, but she doesn't continue.

I keep staring at her, making her squirm, daring her to say more and show her cards, but she doesn't.

She bites her lip.

"A couple," I finally say slowly. Oh yeah, this is gonna be fun.

Sarah lets out a little moan that wrenches my attention away from Kat's gorgeous face. "Josh, did you ever use your membership to meet a 'super cool' girl in the Seattle area?" she asks, her face darkening with anticipatory horror.

I wanna laugh at the expression on Sarah's face. Oh my God, she's so fucking cute, this woman.

I nod. "Once," I say. I scowl, but my scowl is for Sarah's benefit—mainly to match her look of obvious horror at the thought of Jonas and me having been unwitting Eskimo brothers with some random, nameless woman in Seattle. As far as I know, Jonas and I have never fucked the same woman, and I'm certainly not fond of the idea, but if it happened by sheer chance with a woman neither of us cares about or intended to pursue for something more serious than a one-night stand, it really wouldn't be the end of the fucking world.

"Brunette. Piercing blue eyes—like the bluest eyes you've ever seen—fair skin," Jonas says, rattling off the description of his Seattle girl like he's doing the play-by-play at a Seahawks game. "C-cup. Perfect teeth. Smokin' hot body—" He looks at Sarah apologetically. "Sorry, baby."

"It's okay." Sarah says—and, damn, it sure sounds like she means it. Well, that settles it: Sarah's totally awesome in my book. If there's one thing I can't stand, it's a jealous woman.

"No," I say. "That doesn't describe my Seattle girl." Honestly, I don't actually remember my Seattle girl specifically—my whole month in The Club is a bit of a blur—but by Jonas' description, it's abundantly clear we didn't hook up with the same woman. "When I filled out my application," I continue, glancing at Kat, "I requested only—"

I stop talking midsentence, thanks to the look on Kat's face: the girl's sitting on the edge of her seat, looking like she's literally holding her breath at whatever I'm about to say. Ha! What the fuck does Kat think I'm about to say?

That's funny. The truth is I was about to say something pretty innocuous—but obviously, the girl's imagining something pretty fucking titillating, or maybe even really fucked up. Well, far be it for me to disappoint her depraved imagination. In fact, I can plainly see by the revved-up expression on Kat's face, it's in my extreme interest to let this girl's imagination run wild.

"Thank God, bro," I say, making a big show of my relief. "That would have been just like having sex with *you.*" I mock-shudder at the thought.

Jonas flashes me his usual look of annoyance. "We're totally off track here," he barks out. "The only thing that matters is that these bastards have fucked with Sarah and Kat, and we have no way of knowing whether they're done fucking with them or if they're just getting started."

I lean back on the couch and sigh. Yep. My gut tells me Jonas is overreacting to this situation, probably spurred on by somehow trying to impress Sarah. "Oh, I don't know," I say, putting my hands behind my head.

Oh shit. Oops. I just unleashed Jonas' crazy as surely as if I'd opened the door to a rabid dog's cage.

"*Sit down, Jonas,*" I say emphatically, over and over, in response to Jonas' tirade, but he won't listen to me. "Let's just talk about this for a minute, rationally."

"Oh, *you're* gonna tell *me* how to be rational?" Jonas seethes. "Mr. Buys-a-Lamborghini-on-a-Fucking-Whim-When-His-Girlfriend-Breaks-Up-With-Him is gonna tell *me* to be rational?"

I roll my eyes.

Nice, Jonas. First my stupid-ass brother outs me for joining a sex club and now he's gonna give me shit for what a pussy I was after Emma drop-kicked me and cheated on me with that Ascot-wearing prick? Talk about a cheap shot.

Up 'til now I was feeling pretty entertained by my asshole-brother, maybe even sympathetic, but now I feel like throttling him. But because I'm the sane and rational twin in this fucked-up duo, I somehow manage to keep my shit together, like I always do. "I'm just saying I don't know; that's all," I say, gritting my teeth. "I'm not saying I disagree. Big difference. Just sit the fuck down for a minute. Jesus, Jonas."

But, of course, Jonas doesn't immediately shut the fuck up or calm the fuck down or do anything even remotely resembling sane rationality. Why? Because he's Jonas, which, I guess, gives him a lifelong pass to act like a fucking lunatic while I sit here holding his shit together for him, even though on any given day it takes almost all my strength to hold my own shit together, thank you very much.

It takes ten minutes of talking to Jonas like the man-child he is, but I finally get him to sit down and breathe deeply.

"Okay," I say, taking a deep breath. Jesus God, give me strength. "Let's think. What's the point in taking down the entire organization? I mean, really? Just *think* about it, logically. That sounds like an awfully big job—and maybe overkill. Think about it, Jonas. Yes, we've got to protect Sarah and Kat, of course . . ." I smile at Sarah and then at Kat. "*Of course.* And we will. I promise. But beyond that, why do we care what The Club does?"

Jonas shifts in his seat. He's considering.

That's good. I'm clearly making headway. I take another deep breath.

"Why kill a fly with a sledgehammer when a flyswatter will do?" I continue. "The Club provides a service—and very well, I might add, speaking from experience. So, yeah, maybe things aren't exactly as they appear, maybe they oversell the fantasy a bit—but so does Disneyland. I mean, you can go ride a rollercoaster anywhere, right?—but you pay ten times more to ride that same roller coaster at Disneyland. Why? Because it's got Mickey Mouse's face on it."

Jonas' eyes could cut diamonds right now.

"Maybe all these guys who join The Club want to ride a roller coaster with Mickey Mouse's face on it—and they're happy as clams to pay a shitload to do it. They don't even *want* to know they could ride the same roller coaster *without* Mickey's face on it for two bucks down the street."

I'm trying to make Jonas see another side to things, something he's never been particularly good at doing, but I've clearly just tripped yet another Jonas-landmine—I've barely gotten my last words out when the dude begins literally sputtering with outrage, so Sarah steps in to speak for him.

"Josh," Sarah says, putting her hand gently on Jonas' forearm. "Your premise is faulty. When you buy a ticket for Disneyland, you *know* you're signing up to ride a Mickey Mouse roller coaster. Not everyone signs up to ride a Mickey Mouse roller coaster when they join The Club—but that's what they give them, anyway."

Okay, now I'm completely confused. What the hell is she talking about? Why would anyone join The Club, except for the sole purpose of riding a Mickey Mouse roller coaster? That's all The Club is or could ever be—a vehicle for mainlining cotton candy—no more or less—an unhealthy but delicious diet of pure sugar to be consumed once in a blue moon for a short period of time, even though you know it's total crap for a growing boy. I mean, shit, only a fucking moron would think he could consume cotton candy as his diet's main staple, right?

I wait for Sarah to explain further but, apparently, that's all she's gonna say. She sits back down on the couch and primly folds her hands in her lap.

"What do you mean?" I ask.

Jonas exhales. "She means not everyone is totally fucked-up like you and me." He clears his throat. "Or, at least, like me—you seem to have been cured of your fuckeduppedness by that stupid book."

I burst out laughing at that one. Good times.

"She means some people are, you know, *normal*," Jonas continues. He sits down on the couch next to Sarah and puts his arm around her, obviously displaying some sort of solidarity with her. Wow, he must really like this girl, because what he just said is the stupidest thing I've ever heard him say.

"What the fuck does that even mean?" I ask. "*Normal?*"

Jonas doesn't answer. (Of course, he doesn't—because there's no defending the idiocy of his comment.)

"Okay, fine, let's say there are *normal* people out there... Why the fuck would any *normal* person join The Club?"

"To find love," Jonas says quietly. "That's what normal people want. That's what The Club promises to the normal ones. And it's a scam."

I burst out laughing again. Oh my God, that's the funniest thing I've ever heard in my entire life. But Jonas and Sarah don't look the slightest bit amused. I glance at Kat, hoping to find one other sane person in this room besides me, and, thankfully, the Party Girl With a Hyphen doesn't disappoint—she flashes me a sexy little smirk that says she thinks Jonas and Sarah are being ridiculous, too. I match her smirk with one of my own and she flashes me a wide smile that bares her perfect, white teeth.

"It's true," Sarah says, like she's defending truth, honor and the fucking American way.

"Seriously?" I say. I take a beat to study my brother's face. But, yeah, he's dead serious. "Did *you* join The Club looking for love?" I ask. I swear to God, if he says yes, then I know for sure this adorkable Sarah Cruz girl has cast a fucking spell on him. Either that, or he's truly had a psychotic break.

Jonas looks at Sarah like he's asking his master for permission to speak, and Sarah nods. Well, that answers that question—she's cast a spell on him. He kisses the back of her hand. "No, I didn't," Jonas says.

"Well, neither did I," I say, trying to ignore how pussy-whipped my brother's acting right now. "I can't imagine anyone ever would. That's pretty far-fetched—even if someone's *normal*." I shoot an apologetic look at Sarah. Even if my brother's acting like a flop-dick right now, that's no reason for me to be disrespectful to Sarah. Obviously, she's passionate about this ridiculously naïve notion of hers. "Sorry, Sarah," I say.

Sarah nods and shoots me a half smile.

"I'm pretty sure I joined The Club because I was having some kind of mental breakdown," Jonas says softly. "*Again*."

Whoa, whoa, whoa. I shake my head with whiplash. *No.* Those are the exact words I didn't want to hear coming out of Jonas' mouth tonight. I'm not equipped to babysit Jonas through another mental breakdown. No fucking way. I've been doing it my whole fucking life and I don't wanna do it anymore. Shit. And he seemed to be doing so well lately. What have I been missing?

"Though I didn't realize it at the time, of course," Jonas continues. He looks at Sarah. "I joined The Club because I didn't understand what was really going on with me, what I really wanted—or what I needed. I was spiraling, man."

My heart is thumping out of my chest. Shit, shit, shit. I don't know what the hell to say. I thought Jonas was kicking ass and taking names lately, I really did. Work has been better than ever—the whole company is a fucking behemoth right now, thanks primarily to Jonas and his incredible instincts for deals. And he's in the best shape of his life, too.

True, the guy's been kind of a weird hermit for a while now—obsessed with nothing but climbing and working out and finding new investment opportunities—and, true, I've often thought Jonas should get out more, maybe go to a fucking party now and again, fuck some random woman he meets in a fucking bar, for Chrissakes. But that's just not Jonas. He's always been the sensitive one, attaching a deeper meaning to everything, including sex.

Actually, I suggested Jonas join The Club for a month in the first place because I figured a little meaningless sex might do the guy a world of good, exactly the way it did for me (and he's clearly not capable of getting random pussy for himself, that's for sure, though God only knows why, given what he looks like). And now I'm finding out my poetic brother viewed joining The Club as some sort of "surrender to insanity"? Well, shit.

I run my hand through my hair, desperation descending upon me. I feel like I could cry like a baby right now, even though I haven't cried since I was ten years old. I seriously cannot do this again. I've carried my brother's sanity on my back my whole fucking life, even when I've barely been able to hold the weight of my own. And I'm tired. I cover my face with my hands for a moment, trying to pull myself together.

There's a long silence in the room.

"Well, all righty, then," Kat finally says.

I glance up at her and she smiles warmly at me.

And just like that, I regain my footing. "Holy shit, Jonas," I mumble, rubbing my hands over my face. "I'm all in when it comes to protecting Sarah and Kat, okay? Whatever it takes—you know that, right?"

"I know." Jonas exhales. "Thanks."

"I just think maybe you're overreacting about—"

"Fuck, Josh!" Jonas leaps up from the couch and glowers over me like he's about to strangle me—but I don't flinch. The dude wouldn't hurt a fucking fly and we both know it. "These motherfuckers threatened my girl and her best friend. Do you understand? They crossed the fucking line!"

I stand and open my mouth to speak, but Jonas cuts me off.

"I'm not letting them near her." He pulls Sarah up off the couch and into him. "I'm gonna protect her—which means decimating the fuck out of them. Do you understand me? *Decimating them.*"

"Whoa," I say. "Calm down." Every hair on my body is standing on end. What the fuck is happening right now? He's spiraling into some sort of panic attack and I don't fully understand why.

"I'm not gonna let it happen again, Josh," he blurts. "I couldn't survive it this time—I know I couldn't. I barely survived it before. You didn't see what I saw... the blood... it was everywhere. You weren't there." He shuts his eyes tight. "You didn't see her. I'm not gonna let it happen again. I can't do it again."

I feel like he just punched me in the teeth. Why the fuck is he saying this to me, especially in front of Sarah and Kat? I'm well aware I was sitting at a fucking football game, cheering happily, while Jonas watched our mother being fileted like a fish. No one needs to remind me of that fact.

"Jonas... Oh my God," I say.

"I thought *you'd* understand, of all people." Jonas' voice is thick with emotion. "I don't want to do this alone, but I will. I'll do whatever I have to do, don't you understand? I can't let anything happen to her. Not again. Never again."

This is insane. I can't believe Jonas is comparing this situation to what happened to our mom. Motherfucker. He's crossed a line here. He's fucking crossed a motherfucking line. "Ladies, could you give us a minute?" I say, gritting my teeth. "*Please*."

Jonas juts his chin at me and squeezes Sarah like he's worried I might fucking attack her or something.

"Jonas," Sarah whispers, brushing her lips against his jawline. "Talk to your brother, baby. He's on your team." She touches his face. "Your brother's on your side. Just listen to him. He dropped everything to come here for you. Listen to him."

Jonas lets go of Sarah's hand, grabs her face with both hands, and kisses the hell out of her. Clearly, his kiss is a giant "fuck you" to me, but I don't understand what I've done to deserve it.

When Jonas pulls away from kissing Sarah, he looks fiercely at me, his nostrils flaring, glaring at me like he's daring me to say a fucking word. But I'm not even tempted to speak. There's nothing I could possibly say that wouldn't involve the words "crazy" and "fuck" and "you."

"One can easily forgive a child who's afraid of the dark," Jonas says, visibly trembling. "The real tragedy of life is when men are afraid of the light."

I roll my eyes. Fan-fucking-tastic. Another Plato quote from my crazy-ass brother. Fuck me. This is gonna be a long fucking night.

## Chapter 3

*Kat*

As Derek kisses my lips, he runs his fingertips along my thigh underneath my pencil skirt. I return his kiss with equal enthusiasm and run my fingers through his hair. Heck yeah, I do. Derek the ex-SEAL-bodyguard is way, *way* hotter than Kevin Costner ever was (and Kevin Costner was pretty freaking hot back in the day). I lean back onto the arm of my couch, pulling Derek's lips with me as I go and coaxing Derek's body on top of mine. Holy shitballs, this man's clearly got a hard body beneath that Men's Wearhouse suit. And that's not all that's hard about Derek, either—the bulge behind his slacks feels like it was forged in a steel factory. Good lord.

It's all I can do not to bust out singing Whitney Houston's "I Will Always Love You"—not because I will always love Derek Insert-Last-Name-Here, obviously. I only met the guy less than twenty-four hours ago, and, as far as I can tell, he's got the personality of a baseball bat. No, that iconic song is on the tip of my (extremely busy) tongue right now because *oh my effing God* I'm about to fulfill a fantasy I've had since I first witnessed a certain juggernaut of cinematic artistry at the tender age of nine.

My mom rented *The Bodyguard* from Blockbuster Video on a Friday night (plus video games for my dad and four brothers to keep them distracted while we two girls watched our movie), and by Sunday afternoon, I'd watched that damned movie at least six times from start to finish (and that was a full year before we got our first DVD player, which means I actually had to *rewind* that freaking thing every time I wanted to re-watch it, so that tells you how committed I was to Whitney and Kevin's once-in-a-lifetime love).

And all through the years since that first *Bodyguard* marathon, through puberty and high school and college, whenever I've been dumped or no one asked me to a dance or I've had PMS or gotten a crappy-ass grade in a class (that last one being a fairly common occurrence), I've watched Kevin and Whitney as a sort of therapy, I guess, kind of like digging into a cinematic pint of Ben and Jerry's.

So it's no wonder that now, as a twenty-four-year-old woman with an unapologetic sex drive and an unwavering dedication to you-only-live-once, having hot sex with my very own real-life bodyguard is right at the top of my sexual bucket list. I mean, come on. Not all sex has to be about some kind of deep soul connection—sometimes, it can simply be about making a lifelong sexual fantasy come true.

"Katherine Morgan?" Derek the Bodyguard asked yesterday when I opened the front door of my apartment and beheld his no-nonsense hotness for the first time. I leaned against the doorjamb and smiled broadly, pleasantly surprised about the gift the universe had just plopped into my lap (or, more accurately, the surprise Sarah's new boyfriend, Jonas, had just plopped into my lap).

"Yes, I'm Katherine Morgan," I replied to Derek yesterday, extending my hand and flashing him my most flirtatious smile. "But please, call me Kat." I knew a bodyguard would be coming to my house, of course—Jonas had already said as much earlier that morning—but only in my wildest dreams did I imagine he'd look like Derek.

"Miss Morgan," Derek said, seemingly impervious to my charms. "My name is Derek Something-or-Other, and I've been assigned to protect you." He looked at his phone. "By a Jonas P. Faraday?"

"Yeah. Jonas mentioned he'd be sending someone. Thanks for coming."

"I'll be watching over you during the daytime," Derek continued matter-of-factly. "And my partner, Rodney, will take the night shift." He motioned across the street. "That's Rodney over there, just so you know what he looks like."

I walked out of my apartment and peered across the street in the direction Derek was pointing—and there, sitting in a nondescript sedan, was Father Time. When Rodney saw me looking at him, he curtly waved, started his engine, and drove away, and I suppressed the urge to laugh with glee that Derek had been the one to show up on my doorstep to take the first shift.

"Come in," I purred to Derek, brushing past him into my apartment.

"Sure. Just to do a sweep of your surroundings and give you a safety de-briefing. After that, I'll keep watch from across the street to give you privacy." His tone was strictly professional—very Kevin-Costner-at-the-beginning-of-*The-Bodyguard.* Not the least bit flirtatious.

Things looked grim for my chances of singing Whitney's tune right about then—and honestly I might have dropped the whole thing if it weren't for what happened next: Derek's eyes unmistakably darted down to the curve of my breasts in my tight-fitting blouse and then down to my hips in my slim-fitting business skirt and then back up to my lips—*at which point they flickered with unmistakable desire.* And that's when I knew Mr. Professional Bodyguard maybe wasn't quite as all-business underneath that dark suit as he seemed—and that maybe, just maybe, it was only a matter of time before Derek the Bodyguard would be whispering things like, "No, Kat, I can't protect you like this" and "Not on my shift" and "I was hired to protect you, not to help you shop" into my ear.

"Come in, Derek," I said, waltzing back into my apartment from the walkway. "You wanna cup of coffee?" I asked breezily, even though coffee wasn't at all what I was thinking about.

Derek grinds his hard-on into me and kisses me, jolting me back to the delicious present on my couch. His hand skims my thigh under my skirt and I widen my legs to let him know I'm not at all shy here, big fella, that this isn't my first time at the sexy-times-rodeo and he need not be quite so respectful of my *vagina* (which I've noticed he hasn't even attempted to touch).

Derek reacts to my implicit invitation by floating his hand up toward the increasingly wet crotch of my panties. *Yes. That's right. Go for it, Bodyguard. Do it. I've got the chorus of Whitney's song all cued up for you, baby.* But, damn, his hand stops at the inside of my thigh and then trails across my hipbone and around to my ass.

Damn.

I press into him with increased enthusiasm, and—

My cell phone buzzes on the coffee table, repeatedly, with an incoming call.

Crap. I'm supposed to be at work right now, actually. I had an early breakfast meeting with a client (the owner of a new boutique) about the social media campaign I'm planning for her—and afterwards, I swung by my apartment on my way back to the office "to grab an umbrella." Or so I said. Yes, it had started to pour—this is Seattle, after all—but we have plenty of extra umbrellas and plastic ponchos at the office. What I was actually doing with the whole "I gotta grab an umbrella" ruse was creating an excuse to lure my new bodyguard (who'd been shadowing my every move all morning long) into my apartment to see if I could seduce him into seducing me.

My phone stops buzzing and I refocus my attention onto Derek's lips.

I kiss him a bit more enthusiastically and he follows my lead, running his hand over my blouse, right over my nipple. *Good. That's good. Come on, Derek. Let me be your Whitney.*

I wonder who was calling. Was that my boss? Or maybe Hannah Banana Montana Milliken? Or maybe it was Sarah, calling to tell me some new juicy tidbit about her new boyfriend (who supposedly loves her but won't say the actual words)? Or maybe, just maybe, it was the boyfriend's Hottie-McHottie-pants brother, Josh Faraday?

I smile at the thought, even as I'm kissing Derek.

Josh sure didn't try to hide his attraction to me the night before last at Jonas' house.

"Don't worry about me, guys," Josh yelled to Jonas and Sarah as Jonas barreled to his room with Sarah slung over his shoulder. "I'll just party the night away with Party Girl with a Hyphen."

"Oh no, you won't, Playboy," I shot back at him. "You'll have to find another Mickey Mouse roller coaster to ride tonight."

Of course, I was wildly attracted to him, too—who wouldn't be?—but I'm not sure how I felt about his whole "Mickey Mouse rollercoaster" analogy. And, regardless, there's nothing I love better than taking a cocky guy down a peg. It's kinda my specialty, actually.

I was trying to stun Josh into humbled silence with my little zinger, but Josh wasn't even remotely fazed. He swaggered over to me and leaned his lips right into my ear, making the hair on the nape of my neck stand up and my crotch tingle. "So that's how we're gonna play this, huh, Party Girl with a Hyphen?" he said. "We're gonna play it cool? Okay, babe, fine with me—we'll play it however you like," he whispered, his warm breath teasing my ear. "But we both know where this is headed. Mmmm." And with that, he sauntered out of the room, whistling as he went, and never looked back.

I must have stood there for a solid five minutes, my mouth hanging open and my crotch pulsing in my panties. Day-am.

My phone buzzes sharply with a voicemail on the coffee table next to my couch.

Who the heck is trying to reach me so insistently?

Derek's tongue is swirling around mine and his hard-on against my thigh is becoming urgent. Well, whoever's calling, they'll just have to wait. I press myself into Derek's erection, goading him on, and he reacts by kneading my ass with his strong hand. Hmm. That ass-kneading thing isn't really working for me, actually. There's just no finesse to it. It's like the dude's wearing freaking oven mitts. Or maybe the problem is that Derek just isn't that great a kisser?

Oh, shit, I've still gotta come up with my social media campaign for that chain of barbeque restaurants. Damn. Maybe Hannah will help me brainstorm? Yeah, I'll take her to lunch tomorrow and see if she'll pretty-please help me out. We haven't been to The Tavern in a while. They've got such great salads—

Oh, jeez. I'm thinking about salad while kissing my hot bodyguard? What the hell? Come on, Kat! Kevin Costner. Whitney Houston. Bodyguard. *Focus.*

My phone buzzes again, just once, with an incoming text. Oh jeez. Someone's really trying to reach me. I push on Derek's chest. "Hang on a minute," I say. "Lemme check my phone real quick."

Derek sits up and wipes his mouth, his eyes blazing.

I grab my phone and look at the display. The missed call was from a number I don't recognize. A "323" number. Isn't that L.A.? I peek into my texts and the new text is from that same unrecognizable number, too: "Kat, this is Josh Faraday," the text says. My heart skips a beat. "Call me immediately. Please. It's urgent that I talk to you."

Derek kisses me and kneads my ass again.

Could it be the Playboy is calling me with an "urgent" invitation to dinner? Sarah told me Josh asked for my phone number last night, intending to ask me to dinner after Jonas kicked him out of his house, but Sarah told him I was already out to dinner with my new bodyguard. Sarah said Josh looked deflated and said he was gonna hop a flight back to L.A.—but did he change his mind and stay in Seattle?

I push on Derek's chest again and sit completely upright. "Excuse me, Derek," I say, wiping my mouth with the back of my hand. "I've got to make a quick call."

Derek exhales, clearly frustrated, but I don't care. It's suddenly quite clear to me I'd rather be out on a date with Josh Faraday, world-class Mickey-Mouse-rollercoaster-rider or not, than trying to screw a bodyguard wearing oven mitts who couldn't kiss his way out of a paper bag.

I practically sprint into my bedroom and close my door behind me, my heart leaping out of my chest.

*Josh Faraday.* Now *there's* a guy who makes visions of blowjobs dance in my head. The minute I laid eyes on the man, I felt like I'd been struck by a sexual lightning bolt—and I'm positive he felt it, too. He didn't even try to hide it.

But I've got to be careful. Josh is obviously a player of staggering proportions, and I'm not a girl who likes to be chewed up and spit out by any man. If anyone's gonna do the chewing up and spitting out, then it's gonna be me. And I'm not so sure I could manage getting the upper hand with a seasoned player like Josh Faraday.

Every article I read about the Faraday brothers when I was snooping around in Jonas' office the other night (and there were a lot of them) made at least passing reference to Josh's oversized appreciation for beautiful women. But, of course, I would have figured that out without the benefit of those articles. One quick Google search of the guy revealed he burns through supermodels and reality TV starlets and actresses and daughters of moguls like a Weedwacker. I mean, seriously. The dude's face is plastered all over the Internet with strikingly beautiful women at black-tie events and fundraisers and concerts and parties all over the frickin' world. Jeez. I love to have fun, too, God knows I do—but I'm just a pharmacist's daughter living in Seattle and working at a PR firm. My idea of fun is going to a karaoke bar with my friends on a Saturday night—not the Cannes Film Festival with Isabel Randolph. Holy shitballs.

And the way he referred to the women in The Club as Mickey Mouse rollercoasters was kinda Douchey McDouchey-pants I gotta say. I'm certainly not one to judge anyone, guy or girl, for enjoying sex and having a whole frickin' lot of it—more power to all my horny sistren and brethren—but before I volunteer to be one of Josh Faraday's many, many rollercoasters, I'd sure like to know what I'd be getting myself into. Holy shitballs. That's an understatement. I'd give literally *anything* to read that boy's application to The Club and find out his dirty little secrets.

But first things first: why'd he call? Well, no sense wondering. I'll just call him back and find out. And, heck, maybe as a condition to saying yes to dinner (if, indeed, that's what he's aiming for), I'll ask him to email me his Club application. Why not? It sure seems like Sarah reading Jonas' application from the get-go worked out pretty damned well for them.

I take a deep breath. Okay, yes. That's my strategy. I'll say yes to dinner *if* he sends me his application. Bold. Ballsy. Kind of obnoxious—but awesome. Yes.

I'm about to press the "call back" button next to Josh's text, when I remember his voicemail message. I'd better listen to it first before calling him back.

"Kat, this is Josh Faraday," Josh's voice says—and the tightness of his tone makes my stomach clench. That's not the tone of a man calling to ask a girl out on a date. "Please call me right away," he says. "It's urgent. Thank you."

Now I'm confused. What on earth could—

I gasp.

*Sarah.*

Oh my God. Was Jonas right? Was Sarah actually in grave danger, just like he predicted? I can barely breathe as I push the "call back" button on my phone.

Josh picks up my call immediately. "Kat?" he says, his voice tight.

"What happened, Josh?" I blurt. "Is it Sarah?" I sit down on the edge of my bed, swallowing hard. This is gonna be bad. This is gonna be really, really bad. I know it is. I suddenly feel like I'm gonna throw up.

Josh exhales loudly. "Sarah's been stabbed."

"No," I blurt.

"She's at the hospital now. Jonas just called me." His voice wobbles. "She was attacked in a bathroom at school."

"No." Tears instantly flood my eyes. "*Sarah*."

"I'm trying to get a flight back to Seattle—not having any luck. I need you to get Sarah's mom and get over to the hospital as soon as possible, okay?"

"Oh my God. Oh my God. Sarah."

"Kat. Listen to my voice. I need you to get Sarah's mom and get over to the hospital as soon as possible. Can you do that for me?"

I take a deep breath and wipe my tears. "Okay."

"Good girl. I'll get there as soon as I can."

I can't control my emotions anymore. I lose myself to sobs. "Sarah. Oh my God. No."

# Chapter 4

*Kat*

There's a raging storm outside Sarah's hospital window, but the rain is no match for my tears. Oh my God, this is the worst day of my life. Sarah's my best friend. My partner in crime. My rock. We finish each other's sentences. We laugh 'til we pee. She's more than my best friend—she's my *sister*. We tell each other everything—or, at least, *I* tell Sarah everything. I'm not sure it works the other way around. But I've never cared about that because that's just Sarah. She's this weird mixture of shy and reserved and confident and insecure and hilarious and crazy all at once. There's just nobody like Sarah Cruz. She's the absolute best.

And some bastard out there *purposefully* hurt my girl? Just the thought is making me bawl all over again. How could anyone even think of hurting Sarah of all people? The girl wouldn't hurt a fly. And someone tried to *kill* her just because she figured out their stupid sex club is actually a prostitution ring? Who the fuck cares? *That's* worth killing the best girl in the world over?

I look across the hospital room at Sarah, asleep in her hospital bed. She's bandaged and hooked up to tubes and wires and monitors. She looks tiny and pale.

I just can't believe this is happening.

Sarah's mom is seated next to Sarah's bed, asleep and draped over her daughter's bed. And in the corner of the room, there's Jonas Faraday, the so-called "boyfriend" himself, sitting in a chair that looks way too small for his large body, his muscled arms crossed over his Seattle Seahawks T-shirt. The poor guy looks horribly pained, even in his sleep—distraught, I'd even say. Gazing at him right now, it's suddenly perfectly clear I've completely misjudged him. I had my doubts about his intentions toward Sarah, and I told him so, but looking at him now, he sure looks every bit the devoted and loyal boyfriend. Shit. I wish I'd been nicer to him at his house yesterday morning. The guy gave me a computer and I acted like a total bitch. Classic Kat.

I look at Sarah again and tears squirt from my eyes for the millionth time today.

Sarah always says I've got a heart of gold, but she's wrong. She's the one who cares so deeply about making the world a better place, not me. She's the one who's always thinking about helping people, not me. Compared to Sarah, I'm a downright bitch. And not just a bitch, a horribly reckless bitch. What the fuck was I thinking, trying to seduce my *bodyguard*? Jonas hired Derek to *protect* me, not fuck me. Jonas was right all along—the bad guys really were out to get Sarah and maybe me, too, and what did I do? I made the whole thing about me getting my rocks off. I'm so freaking predictable—and so freaking ashamed of myself, I feel physically ill.

But wait a minute. It takes two to tango. Derek was the one who was supposed to be a *professional*, right? How the hell did he plan to protect me while pounding me? My life was quite possibly at stake and he was macking down on me! *Oh my God.* Is my life at stake now? I feel like I'm gonna barf. I throw my hands over my face. This whole situation is crashing into me like a ton of bricks.

My phone buzzes in my purse with a text and I pull it out. *Josh Faraday.* I wipe my eyes. I feel oddly comforted seeing his name on my screen.

"Are you at the hospital?" Josh writes.

"Yeah, I'm in Sarah's room now," I reply. "The doc says Sarah lost a ton of blood and she's definitely in a lot of pain, but she's gonna be okay, thank God. She'll probably go home tomorrow. She got really lucky. The blade didn't hit anything critical."

"SO AWESOME. Huge relief. OMG. Is my brother there? He hasn't answered any of my texts or calls. I'm worried."

I look across the room at Jonas again. His face is twitching in his sleep like he's having a nightmare. Just as I'm about to look away from him, his entire body jolts like someone just leaped out from behind a bush and yelled "Boo!" Aw, poor guy. He's actually kind of breaking my heart right now.

"Yeah, he's here," I write. "He's asleep."

"When he wakes up, could you tell him I couldn't get to Seattle tonight? All flights are grounded due to weather."

As if on cue, thunder crashes outside the hospital window. "Yeah, if he wakes up while I'm still here, I'll be sure to tell him," I write.

"Thanks."

There's a long beat. Is that the end of our text-conversation? I drop my phone in my lap and stare at Sarah for another long moment, listening to the driving rain outside the window, my thoughts drifting to the thousands of times Sarah's been the best friend a girl could ever hope for.

I've just decided something. I'm done being Classic Kat. From this day forward, I'm New Kat—a responsible and levelheaded girl. A girl like Sarah. Smart. *Careful.* A look-before-leaping kind of girl, especially when it comes to men. New Kat takes things slow. New Kat has her head on straight. New Kat doesn't just jump into the sack or throw her heart away willy-nilly. New Kat isn't tempestuous and crazy. Nope. She's just like Sarah. Well, pre-Jonas Sarah, that is. I don't know what the heck's happened to Sarah since she met Jonas—nowadays, she's acting like me. But that's beside the point.

My phone buzzes with another text. "How are you holding up, Party Girl?" Josh asks.

I take a deep breath and tap out an honest answer to the question, tears streaming down my cheeks. "Not good. The Party Girl doesn't feel at all like partying right now."

"I know what you mean. The Playboy doesn't feel at all like playing right now, either." He adds a sad face to the end of his message.

Well, as long as I'm being honest, I might as well go all in. "I've never cried so many tears in all my life, Josh," I write. And, of course, the act of writing that message makes me cry even harder. "This is the worst day of my life."

I've no sooner pressed send on that message than my phone buzzes with an incoming call from Josh.

I bolt out of my chair and into the hallway to answer. "Hi," I say softly into my phone, my cheeks suddenly hot. I don't like crying in front of men, even over the telephone. It always ignites their superhero instincts—and I'm not a girl who needs to be saved.

"When I get there," Josh says softly, his voice low and masculine, "you can cry on my shoulder all you like, Party Girl."

There's a long pause. I'm having a physical reaction to that statement, not to mention the masculine tone of his voice.

"Thanks," I finally say. "I'd like that."

There's another long pause. "So how's that bodyguard working out for you?" he finally asks. "Do you like him?"

"Do I *like* him?" I repeat, my pulse suddenly pounding in my ears. Does he suspect I was trying to get into my bodyguard's pants when he called earlier today?

Josh exhales. "I mean does he make you feel *safe*? Is he doing a good job of protecting you?"

"Oh." I exhale. "Well, actually," I say, "I've got two bodyguards—one for day, one for night. The nighttime guy is here at the hospital now—in the waiting room. I feel pretty safe with him. But I'm gonna ask for a replacement for the daytime guy."

"You don't feel safe with the daytime guy?"

"No."

"Why not?" There's a strange edge to his voice. He inhales sharply. "Did he make a pass at you, Kat?"

Holy Jealous Boyfriend, Batman—except, of course, that Josh Faraday isn't my boyfriend. We've never even been on a flippin' date.

"Shit," Josh breathes before I can reply to his initial question. "What's the bastard's name?"

"Josh," I manage to say. "No, he didn't make a pass at me." I think that's technically true—I'm the one who made a pass at Derek. "But if he had," I continue, "it wouldn't be any of your business." I let that sink in for a minute. "Derek just didn't take things seriously enough for my taste, that's all," I say evenly.

"*Derek*, huh?" Josh says, his voice edged with testosterone.

"What the hell, Josh?" I say. "You sound like a caveman. Don't worry about it. I'm asking for a new guy. Problem solved." I'm suddenly pissed. He has no claim on me. I can do what I want. "I'd better get back into the room," I say stiffly. "I came out into the hallway to take your call."

He exhales. "Listen, Kat. I don't want you being alone 'til we figure this shit out. Not for a minute. Okay? Jonas obviously had a sixth sense here—he was totally right. We've got to take this seriously."

"Yeah. Okay. Got it. Thanks. But like I said, Rodney's out in the waiting room, and I'll get a new guy tomorrow."

"You promise?"

I exhale with exasperation. I'm not sure I like this caveman crap from a guy I'm not even dating. "I'm getting a new guy because it's what I wanna do, not because you told me to do it."

"Jeez. Touchy. I'm just looking out for you."

Tears flood my eyes. "I'm sorry. I'm a wreck right now. Ignore me. I didn't mean to be bitchy. It's been a really hard day, Josh."

"Oh, I'm sorry. I know," he coos. "Of course, it has."

I sniffle into the phone. "I'm sorry."

"No worries."

We're silent for a long moment.

"Okay, well, I gotta go," I say. "I came into the hallway to take your call. If Sarah wakes up, I wanna be there."

Josh exhales. "Kat, listen . . ." But he doesn't finish the thought. "Yeah, I gotta go, too. Don't forget to tell my brother I'm stuck down in LA, but I'll get there as soon as I can. Please tell him, okay? I'm really worried about him." His voice breaks. "He's been through a lot, Kat—something like this was the last thing he needed."

"It's okay, Josh," I say softly. "Hang in there, okay?"

I hear him breathing, but he doesn't reply.

"I'm sure this is rough on you—being down there when your brother's wigging out up here."

He doesn't reply for a long beat. "Kat, you have no idea."

"Hang in there."

There's another long beat.

Josh clears his throat. "It sounds like Sarah's gonna be good as new, so crisis averted. Jonas will take her to his house tomorrow and nurse her back to health and he'll be happy as a clam. I'm sure the minute I walk through his door tomorrow, he'll kick me the fuck out again, just like he did last night."

I chuckle. "He kicked you out last night?"

"Yeah. I guess he wanted some *privacy*, if you know what I mean."

I can hear him rolling his eyes across the phone line.

"Well, from what I heard before you got to Jonas' house the other day, consider yourself lucky you didn't hear them. Yeesh."

"Really?"

"Oh my God. They sounded like they were dying in there."

He laughs. "Don't tell me any more. I make it a point not to think about my brother having sex."

I laugh, wiping the tears out of my eyes as I do.

"I've never seen Jonas like this about a girl. Ever," he says. "I actually think this might be the real thing for him."

"Really? Wow. Sarah said the same thing."

"Awesome. I'd hate for Jonas to get his heart broken. He doesn't put it out there very often. Looks like he's fallen hard for this girl."

I never thought for a minute about *Jonas* getting his heart broken—I've been too concerned about Sarah getting hers smashed to smithereens.

"Trust me, if anyone's heart's gonna get broken here, it won't be Jonas'," I say. "Sarah's all in."

"Well, good. I hope it works out for them. They're awesome together."

"Yeah, they are."

"Okay, well . . ." he says. "Hopefully, I'll get my ass back up there tomorrow on the first flight out, just in time for him to kick me out of his house again." He chuckles. "So when I'm up there with nothing to do, maybe we'll have a chance to hang out—maybe grab some dinner or drinks?"

"Maybe," I say casually, but my heart's racing. I'm sure he can hear me smiling over the phone line.

"Mmm hmm," he says. "Okay, Party Girl with a Hyphen. I forgot we're playing it cool. That's fine. We both know how this ends—but, sure, we can play it that way."

"I have no idea how this ends," I say, my crotch tingling at the flirtatious tone of his voice.

"Oh, well, then, far be it for me to spoil the ending for you." He pauses. "Well, I better go. Hang in there, Party Girl. I'll be there soon and you can cry on my shoulder all you like."

"Thanks. Maybe I'll see you soon, Playboy."

"Oh, you can count on it."

## Chapter 5

*Josh*

"Dude, pull your head out of your ass. *Please*," I say. "She's not gonna stay at her mom's house forever."

"I'm going fucking crazy," Jonas mutters, gripping his steering wheel like a madman. "I'm about to fucking blow."

I exhale and look out the passenger window of the car, trying to collect myself. My brother is a fucking lunatic. There's no way around it. I truly thought dragging Jonas rock climbing all day would take his mind off Sarah—and, specifically, the fact that she's decided to stay at her mom's house to recuperate instead of Jonas' (and also hasn't been very communicative while she's been there, either)—but I was wrong. Dead wrong. Not only did Jonas continue obsessing about Sarah throughout our climb today, he did it while I was trapped on a fucking mountain with him with nowhere to go. Jesus Christ. If I'd known Jonas was gonna drive me nuts during our entire climb, I would have just sat on his couch, watching basketball and drinking way too much beer. At least then I could have left the room occasionally to bang my head against the wall. Or, at the very least, numbed myself with way too much alcohol.

All I wanna do right now is call Sarah and say, "Whatever's going on between you and Jonas, please just give the guy a fucking call and tell him whatever the fuck's on your mind, good or bad, because until my high-strung brother hears from you and confirms whatever it is you're thinking, he's gonna be a fucking nightmare to be around." But, obviously, I'm not gonna do that. The girl was stabbed. She's probably scared and freaked out and maybe a little bit confused right now. She's got plenty on her plate worrying about her own mental health without having to worry about Jonas' too. I've got to just let this thing take its natural course—and pray to God it goes Jonas' way. Because after everything Jonas has had to endure in his life, I really don't want his dream girl to shatter his heart, too.

"Jonas, I know it's hard for you," I say, "but you've just gotta let the girl sort her shit out. She's been through a huge trauma. She probably just needs a little break. Be patient with her."

"I don't do patient."

"No shit." I roll my eyes. "But it's only natural she'd want her mom after what she's been through. I'm sure most people with a mother would react the same way."

Jonas literally snarls at me.

I roll my eyes at him again. "Oh my fucking God. Jonas, I'm as motherless as you are. Obviously. I didn't say that to twist some knife into your heart. I'm just saying we don't know what it's like to turn to a mother in a time of crisis—but other people do. Normal people."

"But why isn't she even talking to me?" Jonas says. "I understand her wanting her mom. But something's off. I can feel it. And it's fucking killing me."

"Just give her a little space," I mumble, but my tone isn't compassionate. I've been with Jonas all fucking day. I'm all out of compassion. "Sarah wanting to be with her mother is no reflection on how she feels about you. Stop thinking everything's about you all the time. You make me want to open my car door and hurl myself onto the freeway just to get away from you."

Jonas grits his teeth as he glares out the windshield of his car. "Maybe I should drive over there?" he finally says. "Tell her how I feel?"

"No, Jonas."

He grips the steering wheel again. "Or send flowers with a note?"

"Flowers? Jesus, Jonas. *No*. Just leave her alone."

"Maybe I should, I don't know, go park my car across the street from her mom's house and sit there for a while?"

I laugh. "What the fuck? You mean like a stalker?"

"No, not like a *stalker*. Like a *boyfriend*."

"Like a... Ha!" I can't control my laughter. "That's your idea of what a boyfriend does? You're gonna go be John Cusack in *Say Anything* with the beat box over your head, standing in the rain?"

"John Cusack didn't stand in the rain."

"Sure he did."

"No."

"Well, either way," I say. "That'd be totally stalker-ish. It was stalker-ish when John Cusack did it in the first place. I don't know why everyone thinks that was so fucking romantic. It was just *weird.* Fucking desperate. Women hate desperate."

Someone cuts Jonas off and he honks his horn. "Motherfucker." There's a long pause. "Well, I can relate," he says.

"To what?"

"To John Cusack." He exhales. "I'm desperate."

I shake my head. What the fuck am I gonna do about my fucking brother? He doesn't say a word about any particular woman since Amanda, not a fucking word, and now he won't shut the fuck up about this one? I can't decide whether I like hermit-Jonas or desperately-in-love Jonas better. "You sent a couple bodyguards over to her mom's house, right?"

"Yeah."

"Well, then. She's safe. That's all that matters. Leave her alone."

Jonas sighs audibly. "But if I drive over there, she might at least notice me sitting out there. And then she'd know I'm thinking about her."

I can't help but chuckle. I've never in my life met someone like my brother. Probably a genius IQ, no exaggeration. He's easily twice as smart as I am. Triple as smart. And yet he's so fucking stupid he makes me want to wring his neck at least a hundred times a day. "What would be the point of you sitting there in your car, watching the house, Jonas? Explain this to me."

Now it's Jonas rolling his eyes at me like I'm a complete moron. "Because then maybe she'd come out."

I laugh. "And then what?"

He shakes his head but doesn't answer me.

"Dude, Sarah's healing from being stabbed multiple times and having her head busted wide open like a walnut. And you want the poor girl to hobble outside in her little nightgown and fuzzy socks and pat you on the head and say 'Good, doggie'?"

"I didn't... No. I just . . ." His anguish is palpable.

"You know what she'd *really* say? She'd say, 'Gosh, Jonas. Ever thought of sending a *text*?'"

He grumbles. "Okay, so what if I—"

"Jonas, *no.* Stop. No stalking. No calling. No flowers. No boom box. No luring the poor girl across the street in her nightgown and slippers. Do you want to push this girl away forever?"

His face flashes with earnest concern. "No. Of course not. Quite the opposite."

"Do you want her to think you're a total pussy?"

He clenches his jaw. "No."

I shake my head. "Then just give her some fucking space. Please. Just listen to me. When am I ever wrong about women?"

He opens his mouth and then closes it.

"The answer is 'Never.' *I'm never wrong.* I'm some sort of woman-whisperer, dude—trust me. You want a woman to want you? Then you gotta know when to leave her the fuck alone. Just chill the fuck out and give the girl some time to figure her shit out. I guarantee you, if you back off and let Sarah take things at her own pace, let her figure out what she's feeling and what she needs, she's gonna call you and say, 'Come get me, Jonas. I want you.' Mark my words, bro."

"But what if I just—"

"No! Just let her call you when she's ready to talk. And in between, send her a few texts to let her know you're thinking about her—nothing too heavy. She's probably all doped up on pain meds and feeling like shit and sleeping most of the time, anyway. And her mom's probably bringing her homemade chicken tortilla soup or whatever. You can't compete with that magical-mom shit, bro. No one can. That's why everyone says, 'There's nothing like a mother's love.' I realize we don't know what the fuck they're talking about, but the rest of the world does. I'll bet you a thousand bucks if you listen to me and give her some space, she's gonna call you within three days and say, 'Come get me.'"

Jonas grunts. "Why would I take that bet? I'd be betting against myself."

We've arrived at Jonas' house, thank God. I've never wanted to get out of a car more in my entire life. Jonas pulls into his driveway and kills the engine on his car. He turns to look at me, his eyes blazing. "Josh, you don't understand."

"I think I do."

"No. I have something really important I need to tell her. Right away. Something she needs to understand."

"Whatever it is, it'll have to wait."

He shakes his head furiously. "Josh, listen to me. I need to tell her something—something I've never said to any other girl—even Amanda." He swallows hard. "*The most important thing there is to say.* I'm gonna say it to Sarah."

I can't believe my ears. My brother's gonna tell this girl he *loves* her? Wow, he's never even said those words to me. Jesus, I'm light years ahead of Jonas in my emotional evolution, and I've only said those words to one girl in my entire life. (And it didn't work out so well.)

"Wow, Jonas," I begin to say, but he cuts me off.

"So don't fucking tell me to be *patient*," he roars, out of nowhere. He abruptly gets out of his car, slams his car door like he's trying to tip the car onto its side with me in it, and stalks toward his house.

I watch Jonas as he marches away, imagining myself hurling Chinese stars into his back. Oh my fucking God. I can't take it anymore. I'm trying to be compassionate with this motherfucker. Just like I've tried to be my entire fucking life. But it's hard to be compassionate with a guy when he's a total and complete dick.

# Chapter 6

*Josh*

Oh, yeah. So good. *Yes*. I pump my shaft with increased intensity as the steaming hot water of the shower rains down on me. I can't stop imagining her face, her unbelievable face. Oh my God. She's a gift from God, created just for me. Those eyes. Those gorgeous blue eyes. That subtle little cleft in her chin. I imagine myself pressing the tip of my cock into that little cleft in her chin right before sliding my full length into her sassy little mouth.

Oh God. I can barely breathe. I'm about to blow. I'm so close. I work myself even more furiously. My cock feels like a rocket about to lift off. Oh fuck. Yes. It's beginning to ripple.

And her lips. They're perfect, just like everything else about her. I imagine those lips wrapped around my hard cock, sliding up and down, devouring me. I run my finger over my wet tip, imagining it's her swirling tongue.

"Oh shit," I say out loud. I open my mouth wide and a blast of hot water floods it. My knees are buckling. I'm twitching. I'd pay a million dollars if my hand could be her warm mouth right now—two million if it could be her tight little pussy. The Club is full of hookers, it turns out? Fine by me. Some women are well worth the money. If Kat asked me to pay her to fuck her, I surely would. No questions asked. I'd give anything, *anything,* to see Kat looking up at me with those big blue eyes, her lips wrapped around my cock. I imagine her eyes glittering the same way they did when she found out I'd been a member of The Club. That's the look that told me the girl is up for anything—with the right guy, anyway.

I'm the right guy for you, baby. Fuck yeah, I am. You've never been fucked like this before. That's right, baby.

I fondle my balls with my free hand while my pumping hand continues working my shaft. Oh shit. My knees are buckling. This is so good. Any second now.

I picture her on top of me, riding me, her blonde hair falling down over her shoulders and cascading over her perky little tits. Erect nipples. Cleft in her chin. Blue eyes. Tight little body. Oh my God. She throws her head back. She's having an orgasm. She's screaming my name.

My skin prickles for just an instant, like I've got a chill even under the steaming hot water, and then an epic orgasm slams into me, making me spurt a massive load all over my hands. I shudder with my release and lean my head against the marble shower wall.

"Kat," I say out loud, like she's lying next to me in bed. "Oh my God."

That's the first time in a really long time I've stuck with the fantasy of one woman while jacking off. I usually start out thinking about whatever woman I've been seeing lately, whatever sex act we might have recently performed, and then, at some point, move on to that raven-haired dental assistant I always fantasize about, even though she's married and never gives me the slightest whiff of a come-on, or the college professor I used to fuck during office hours during my second year at UCLA, or, occasionally, the platinum-blonde Swiss foreign exchange student in high school who de-virginized me when I was a wee little freshman, the one who taught me exactly where to touch her and how to get her off. And then, right at climax, without fail, whether I like it or not, my brain inevitably slams me with Emma's angelic face, the face that fooled me for so long into thinking she was The One.

Hot water is gushing down my back.

"Kat," I say again, reliving the vision of her riding me, her face awash in ecstasy.

She's the most gorgeous girl I've ever seen.

Holy shit.

I want this girl.

I want her bad.

And I'm stuck here with my goddamned brother.

## Chapter 7

*Josh*

When I enter the family room after my shower, Jonas is nowhere to be found, which is good because, after his little tantrum in the car, I still feel like punching him in his pretty face. I grab a beer from the fridge, plop myself down on Jonas' pristine white couch, and turn on the basketball game.

Shit. I should be with the Party Girl with a Hyphen right now, pouring on the charm, making her realize this story's ending is inevitable—not babysitting my high-maintenance brother. But I can't leave him right now, especially to go chase a girl (even if that girl happens to be a particularly gorgeous one). He's just too wound up. I'd never forgive myself if he lost his shit completely and did something stupid.

I take a giant swig of my beer. Seriously, though. I don't blame Jonas for freaking out about Sarah, despite what I said to him before. What the fuck's going on with her? Is she fucking with him? I mean, in theory I understand why Sarah opted to stay with her mom instead of recuperating at her temperamental boyfriend's house. Jonas isn't exactly anyone's first choice as a relaxation buddy. But why has Sarah been so fucking non-communicative with the poor guy while she's resting up? Is she doing what I always do—keeping the other person guessing? If so, why? He's obviously waiting with bated breath to hear from her—she must know that. And yet she's not calling him back? She's just been engaging in superficial text conversations with the poor guy, tearing a page right out of my book. I hate to admit it, but things don't look good for my brother's chance at a happy ending here.

I shake my head and exhale. Please, God, let this girl call him and tell him she wants him, once and for all. Please, God, let her do the equivalent of holding a boom box over her fucking head. Because if Jonas shatters again, then it's gonna be me who'll have to pick up his infinite pieces—again. And at some point, there's not gonna be enough superglue in the world to hold that motherfucker together anymore.

I take another long swig of my beer.

Well, shit. I should just call Sarah for him and ask her what the fuck's going on. I down the rest of my beer. Hell yeah. That's exactly what I should do. Nobody fucks with my brother. She seems like the coolest girl in the world, I must admit—but right now she's fucking with him. No doubt about it. And that's not cool.

No. Obviously, I can't do that. She's not fucking with him. I'm just being an idiot. She was stabbed. She's being hunted by a global crime syndicate. Jesus. Maybe placating Jonas' feelings isn't high on her priority list right now.

Poor Jonas. My stomach twists. What the fuck am I gonna do with him?

I run my hand through my hair, my stomach twisting into knots. I exhale loudly.

Well, I gotta do something.

A smile dances on my lips. Maybe I should try to get some inside information from her hot best friend? Now there's a call I certainly don't mind making.

I pull out my phone and I'm assaulted with a naked selfie from Bridgette, her legs spread-eagle, her fingers shoved up her hairless crotch, a huge smile on her face. The note accompanying the photo reads, "Come and get it, Faraday!"

I roll my eyes. What the fuck have I been doing, messing around with Bridgette? She's stunning to look at, but she's such a fucking train wreck, it's not even worth it.

"Your waxer missed a spot," I text to her in reply.

Her reply is immediate. "Ha, ha. Are you gonna come hit this or not?"

"Not. I'm in Seattle with my brother. Family emergency."

"Oh damn," she writes. "I was in the mood for some huge Faraday peen. I don't always do peen, but when I do, I make it huge Faraday peen."

"The most interesting woman in the world," I write, though it's the furthest thing from the truth.

"I guess I'll have to find some other huge peen to satisfy me, then," Bridgette writes.

"Good luck with that. Once a girl's had Huge Faraday Peen, no other peen shall do."

"Well, then, I guess I'll just have to get me some pussy. You know I'm a big believer in affirmative action."

"Whatever floats your boat, Bridge. Enjoy."

"So when will you be back in LA?"

"A couple days at least," I write. "Just depends on how long my brother needs me." Of course, I have no desire to fuck Bridgette when I get back to LA, whenever that happens to be. I've long since lost interest. But we're so rarely in the same city at the same time, given both of our travel schedules, I've never felt the need to make a formal declaration of my lack of interest.

"Okay. See ya around," she writes. "Say hi to your big dick for me."

I stare at my phone for a long minute. Really? That's it? '*Say hi to your big dick*'? I tell the woman I've got a family emergency and that the length of my stay in Seattle depends on how long my brother needs me and she doesn't even ask me what's up? Or if my brother's okay? Well, that's Bridgette for you in a nutshell: a sociopathic narcissist, through and through.

I'm done. I should have done this a long time ago. I've spiraled into total douchebaggery since Emma, and I'm fucking sick of myself.

"Hey, Bridgette," I type. "I'm gonna take a break from meaningless booty calls and sociopathic narcissism for a while. Well, forever, actually. It's been super fun. Thanks for the memories. Best of luck." I press send. A total dick move, but I don't care. She's not even gonna ask me if everything's okay with my family? Didn't I just tell her I'm in Seattle for a fucking family emergency? Jonas is literally my only family, other than my uncle, and she knows it—I told her about Jonas once when she told me about her sister going into rehab—and she's not even gonna ask me if he's okay?

"Sure thing," she writes back immediately. "I'm going to Milan next week and then to Barbados for a shoot. I'll text you next time

I'm in LA, just in case you change your mind, which we both know you will. *Küsse*, Faraday."

I'm tempted to write something like, "Erase me from your contacts," but I refrain. I'll just leave it. I said what needed to be said. And it felt pretty damned good, too. I just turned down one of the most objectively beautiful women in the entire world. (Well, physically, anyway—I think her heart is filled with battery acid.) That's got to be a sign I'm headed in a new, healthier direction.

There's a clattering noise in the kitchen and I look up. Jonas is freshly showered, doing something in the kitchen, looking like a bull in a china shop. "I'm making myself some kale-apple-beet-spinach-carrot juice," he shouts at me. "You want some?"

I hold up my beer. "No, I've got my vitamins right here, bro, thanks."

He doesn't reply.

I feel electrified. I should have told Bridgette I wasn't interested in her a long time ago. It's time to clean up my act. My little vacation in The Club was perfectly understandable, and I'm not at all sorry about it, but after that, I just kept going in vacation-mode in my real life, too. I don't need to see a shrink to figure out I've been wallowing in self-pity since Emma, afraid to get back in the dating pool with real women. But it's been almost a fucking year since Emma kicked me in the teeth and then didn't even have the courtesy to break up with me officially before running off with that ascot-wearing cocksucker. It's seriously time for me to move on and stop acting like a douche. That's it. No more mainlining cotton candy for me—it's time for me to start feasting on some meat and potatoes again.

"Hey, you know what?" I call to Jonas. "Yeah, gimme some kale-apple-whatever-whatever juice. Sounds great, bro."

I swig my beer, letting my mind wander. Today marks a new era for me. No more women who are only in it for courtside seats at Lakers games or backstage passes to concerts—women who don't even ask me if I'm okay when I've had a family fucking emergency.

Kat's beautiful face flickers across my mind, but I force myself not to think about her. This isn't about Kat in particular. This is about me checking back into reality. Moving on. Getting my personal life back on track. This is about me getting off the Douche Train.

I tap out a text. "Hey, Party Girl with a Hyphen. I've got a quick question for you."

She answers immediately. "Hey, Playboy. Did you make it back up to Seattle okay? How are you doing? Is Jonas hanging in there?"

Well, holy shit. After my text exchange with Bridgette, Kat's genuine interest in how we're doing feels like a thunderbolt cracking the sky. Is this just a coincidence or a sign from God?

"Jonas is a fucking wreck," I reply. "A total asshole to be around. That's why I'm texting you, actually. Do you know if Sarah's been avoiding Jonas?"

"Not to my knowledge. Why do you ask?"

"It seems like she's giving him the cold shoulder, maybe—but, of course, she's also recently been stabbed by a hitman, so it could be that. But, seriously, Sarah hasn't asked to see Jonas since she left the hospital. That seems a bit odd. I'm worried he's about to get crushed. He's really, really into her, Kat—like, seriously out of his mind for this girl."

"I'll see if I can get some info," Kat writes. "But Sarah's my best friend, so it's not a lock I'll be able to tell you whatever I find out."

"I understand. But I'm kinda desperate for any little crumb you can feed me. Any intel you could throw my way would be greatly appreciated. I'd owe you one."

"Well, I will say this—as far as I know, Sarah's absolutely crazy about Jonas."

"Good to hear."

"So how are you doing, Playboy?" Kat writes. "Are you okay? Must be hard trying to keep Jonas on track all the time. From what I saw at Jonas' house, you have your work cut out for you."

Yeah, there's no question about it: this text exchange with Kat is a sign from God. I can't remember the last time a woman asked me sincerely how I'm doing.

"Thanks for asking," I write. "I'm okay. I just decided to stop being a total douche so I'm doing pretty good."

Jonas sits down next to me on the couch and hands me a juice concoction that looks like it was squeezed out of an alien.

"Thanks," I say.

He doesn't reply, but instead turns up the volume on the basketball game.

"You've decided to stop being a douche? So you were a douche and now you're magically not one anymore?" Kat writes.

"Correct," I write.

"Any particular thing that's inspired your decision to make douchebaggery a thing of the past?"

"Nope. Just had to be done."

"Hey, you wanna start working on our business plan?" Jonas asks, swatting my thigh. "I've got a thousand ideas."

"When the game's over," I say to Jonas. "There's only ten more minutes left." I look at my phone again. "Hey, can you talk rather than text?" I type to Kat, suddenly yearning to hear her voice.

"Not right now. I'm just now leaving a client meeting with my boss. We're heading back to the office in her car."

"What do you do?"

"I work at a PR firm. We just met with a client about a social media campaign for a chain of barbeque restaurants."

"How'd it go?"

"Good. They loved everything I came up with, except for my proposed slogan. (Damn it!) But I'm gonna work on it with this awesome girl from my office when I get back to the office. No worries."

"Hey, I've got a great slogan you can use. My gift to you."

"Awesome. I'll take any help I can get. Hit me."

"I've got your pulled pork right here, baby!"

"LOL. OMG. That's actually kind of brillz. This chain is all about being brash and blue-collar and funny. They might actually like it."

"Oh no. That wasn't my slogan idea. That was just me trying to sweet talk you, PG. The slogan idea is this: 'Hey, if you like barbeque, then we'd appreciate it if you'd eat at our restaurant. Thank you.' What do you think? Pure genius, right?"

"OMG. I'm literally laughing out loud right now in my boss' car. You're a PR whiz, PB."

"I've got all kinds of mad skillz, PG. I'm a wise and powerful man; you should know that up front."

"And a total douche—oh, wait, except that you're not now. Scratch that." She attaches a winking emoji.

"Exactly. You only live once, right? Best not to waste valuable time being a total douche."

"Hey! I say that ALL THE TIME," she writes.

"You say 'best not to waste valuable time being a total douche' all the time?"

"Haha. No. I say, 'You only live once.'"

"So do I. YOLO. It's kind of my thing."

"Oh, God, no! Not YOLO. Don't say YOLO! Oh, the humanity!"

"Douchey?"

"Yes. Don't do it!

"What about 'go big or go home.' Can I say that? Because I say that all the time, too," I write.

"Yes. And you may also say, 'I can sleep when I'm dead.' Those are fine. Just not YOLO," she writes.

"What about 'Work hard, play hard'? I say that one all the time, too."

"You like spiffy little catchphrases, huh?"

"Hey, at least I'm not running around quoting Plato all the time."

"What's wrong with Plato?" she writes.

"Hang around my crazy-ass brother for a day and you'll see."

"LOL. Okay."

"Oh, I just thought of another one I say all the time. 'Under-promise and over-perform.'"

"Oh, words to live by," she writes.

"I do. Religiously."

"Interesting."

"So is that it?" I write. "I can say all that stuff, just not YOLO?"

"Correct. Just not YOLO. EVER. Though you CAN say the actual words 'you only live once.' Just not 'YOLO.'"

"So many fucking rules. Jesus."

"Dude, I don't make the rules. I just enforce them."

I laugh out loud.

"And for God's sake don't get a YOLO tattoo!" she writes. "Promise me!"

I burst out laughing. "I make no such promise."

"Don't do it!"

"How about a YOLO tattoo on my ass? Can I do that?"

"LOL! The absolute worst possible scenario! DO NOT DO IT! TOTALLY AGAINST THE RULES!!!!"

I can't stop laughing. "There's something you really should know about me, PG: I like breaking rules."

"Do what you must, but you've been warned. A YOLO tattoo is social suicide."

I laugh again. "Okay. Good to know. So what other really uncool things should I avoid like the plague besides a YOLO tattoo on my ass? Help an old man out."

"How old are you?"

"Thirty," I write.

"Holy shitballs! Where's your walker?"

"How old are you?"

"Twenty-four."

"Aw, just a kitten."

"Meow."

"This is good. I need help from a whippersnapper like yourself to keep me in the cool. What else should I absolutely avoid, according to these rules of yours?

"Not MY rules. They're just THE rules."

"Okay. What else is against THE rules?"

"A barbed-wire tattoo around your bicep fo shizzles. Don't do it."

I laugh to myself. I couldn't agree more with that one. "Okay," I write. "I promise I won't get that no matter how drunk I am."

"And don't get a tribal band around your bicep, either, unless you're from the Islands. Are you an Islander, Josh?"

"Nope. Duly noted."

"Or dragon. Cliché."

I laugh. "Really?"

"Yup. And God help you if you get a girlfriend's name tattooed onto your arm. Just ask Johnny Depp. He had to get 'Winona Forever' lasered to 'Wino Forever.' Lasers are painful, Josh. Not good. Don't do it."

"Yeah, I could see how that could be a bit of an oops."

"A little gold hoop in your left ear. Don't do it."

"Jesus. The Rules are as long as my fucking arm. Anything else?"

"Nope. Avoid all that redonkulousness and you'll be super cool."

"So you're allowed to use the word redonkulousness and I can't say YOLO?"

"Correct. Again, let me repeat. I do not make THE rules. I merely enforce them."

I laugh out loud again.

"Whoa, did you see that?" Jonas says, swatting my knee.

I look up and catch the instant replay of a smooth-as-silk pass and dunk on TV.

"Sweet," I say. But I don't care about the game right now. I'm having too much fun playing with a certain little kitten. I look back at my phone.

"Hey, my boss is about to get off her phone call, so I better go," she writes.

"Josh," Jonas says. "Game's over. You ready to do some Climb & Conquer?"

"I gotta go, too," I write. "My captor has summoned me. Hey, you've still got those bodyguards around the clock, right?"

"Yeah."

"Good. Stay safe. Have a good one, PG."

"You, too, PB. Have fun with your captor."

"Thanks. He's always an adventure, for sure."

"Who are you texting with?" Jonas asks.

I look up. Jonas has already opened his laptop. He's staring at me.

"Just a girl."

Jonas gives me a knowing look. "No sexting when you're sitting on a couch with me. Ew."

"Fuck you. Come on. Climb & Conquer, baby. Let's do this. I'm chomping at the bit to get our baby launched, put out the press release. Hey, when are we gonna tell Uncle William we're both leaving the company, by the way?"

"Soon," Jonas says. "I just gotta figure some shit out first. With both of us leaving . . ." He lets out an anxious breath. "I don't want Uncle William to feel like we're deserting him."

"I know, but it is what it is. I'll be seeing him next week at the board meeting," I say. "Why don't I tell him then?"

"No, just wait," Jonas says. "Lemme figure out the game plan first, get my strategy into place, write the press release. I really wanna tell him in person together."

Jonas looks so wracked with anxiety, I don't have the heart to argue with him. "Okay, bro, whatever you say." I pat his cheek. "No worries. But I really should go to that meeting, regardless. Are you gonna be okay if I leave and go to New York next week?"

"Of course. You don't have to babysit me. I'm a grown-ass man."

"I know."

There's a long pause.

"But thanks for babysitting me," Jonas finally says. He exhales. "Thanks for coming when I called."

"I always will."

We smile at each other.

"Okay, Climb & Conquer," Jonas says. "Our baby. Let's figure out how to give her legs."

"And then wings." I rub my hands together. "It's gonna be fucking awesome, bro."

"Fuck yeah, it is. I've got the whole thing planned in my head. Now to flesh it out and make it real."

Jonas launches into an animated monologue about his vision for our new company, but as excited as I am about the whole thing, my mind keeps wandering. I keep thinking about Kat, her golden blonde hair swooshing across her naked shoulders, those big blue eyes of hers staring at me as she rides me. Or sucks me off. Or as I fuck her nice and slow, my hands cupping her breasts. Shit. Just thinking about her is making me hard again.

"Hey, are you listening to a word I'm saying?" Jonas asks. "I'm bursting at the seams to tell you this stuff and your eyes are glazed over."

"Sorry. Got distracted. I'm totally listening now. Shoot."

Jonas looks at me sideways. "Does this have anything to do with whoever you were texting a minute ago?"

"I can neither confirm nor deny," I say. "But if it *does*, it's because she's so fucking hot, no mortal man could resist her."

Jonas laughs. "You're talking about Kat, aren't you? She's exactly your type, man."

I grin broadly. "Never mind. Come on," I say, rubbing my hands together. "Climb & Conquer. Let's do this shit. I've never been more excited about anything in my entire life."

## Chapter 8

*Kat*

My phone beeps loudly with an incoming text. Shoot. I thought I'd turned off the ringer when Cameron and I sat down at our table. I reach into my purse. *Oh.* My stomach fills with butterflies—it's a text from Josh Faraday. My eyes dart across the spacious restaurant, just in time to see Cameron slip into the men's restroom. I look back down at my phone, grinning like a fool.

"Free at last, free at last, thank God almighty, I'm free at last!" Josh's text says.

I chuckle and tap out a quick reply. "What happened?"

"Can I get a 'fuck yeah!' from the gorgeous blonde in the front row?"

"Who me?"

"Yeah you! Do you see another gorgeous blonde in the front row?"

I laugh out loud. "Fuck yeah!" I type. "What am I 'fuck yeahing' about?"

"Sarah just called Jonas and asked him to 'bring her home.' Jonas just flew out of here like a bat out of hell to get her!"

"Fuck yeah!" I type. I can't wipe the huge grin off my face. I look across the restaurant again, toward the bathrooms, but there's no sign of Cameron yet. I steal a quick glance toward the bar area and lock eyes with my bodyguard Rodney. He nods and I smile.

"Jonas kicked me out the minute Sarah called, the ungrateful bastard," Josh writes. "Thank God! Because now I'm freeeeeeeeeee!"

My phone buzzes with an incoming text from Sarah.

"Jonas is coming to get me!" Sarah writes. "Woohoooooooo!"

"Woohoooooooooooooo!" I type.

"Woo fucking hoooooooo!" Josh replies immediately.

Oops. I'd meant that last woohoo for Sarah. "Woohoo!" I type again, this time to Sarah. "So happy for you, girlio! Are you feeling better?"

"A million times better," Sarah writes. "I think I was depressed. Or high on painkillers? Or both. But I feel like me again. Woot! Can't wait to see Jonas. I've been going through Jonas withdrawals."

"Go get him, honey. I'm actually on a date with Cameron right now. Remember him from the sports bar when we spied on Mr. Yellow?"

"OMG! Kat! You mean the baseball player guy? Kerzoinks! Hottie! Those eyes! That smile! That jawline! Gah!"

"I know. I gotta go. He's in the bathroom."

"Okay, I gotta go, too. Jonas will be here any minute. I'll call you tomorrow. Have fun with Mr. Razor Commercial. Bwahahahahahaa."

"I will. Have fun with Thor. Bwahahahahahaaaaa. I love you, girl."

"I love you, too." She sends me a string of bright red hearts and I return them, relief and elation flooding me. *Sarah's back.*

I go back to the thread with Josh. "Sarah just texted me," I write. "She's doing a happy dance about Jonas. Woohoo!"

"Just in time. Jonas was seriously about to lose his mind. I had to talk him down from standing outside Sarah's window with a fucking boom box ten different times."

"Haha! Sarah would have loved that," I write.

"Why the hell do girls love that movie?"

"Because it's romantic."

"It's lame."

"ROMANTIC."

"By any chance do you have a VAGINA?"

"Why, yes, I DO."

"Well, then, that explains why you don't know that movie is LAME."

I laugh out loud. "ROMANTIC."

"No. Standing outside a girl's window holding a boom box isn't ROMANTIC. It's LAME," Josh writes.

I scoff at my phone. "By any chance do you have a PENIS?"

"Why, yes, I DO."

"Well, then that explains why you don't know that movie is ROMANTIC."

"It's not romantic. It's DESPERATE."

"Sometimes love can feel DESPERATE," I write. "And why are we writing selected words in ALL CAPS?"

Cameron slips into his chair across the table from me and I abruptly put my phone down on the table.

"Sorry I took so long," Cameron says. "There's a kid over there celebrating a birthday so I stopped to say hi and sign an autograph."

"That's so sweet, Cameron. No worries. I was actually texting with my friend Sarah." That statement's not technically a lie, is it? Even though I've fudged the timeline a wee bit?

"Oh, how's she feeling?"

"Much better."

"Good."

He picks up his menu. "Have you decided what you're gonna order?"

"Not yet," I say. "I haven't even looked at the menu yet. Sorry."

"No worries."

My phone vibrates with an incoming text, but I exercise superhuman strength and leave it sitting on the table next to me.

"I'm really glad we were finally able to get together, Kat."

"Me, too. Thank you for being persistent. Sorry I had to cancel on you."

He shoots me a sparkling smile. "*Twice*."

"Twice. Yeah. So sorry about that."

As bad luck would have it, I cancelled on Cameron the first time because my place had been broken into by The Club, and the second was because Sarah had been attacked.

"All's well that ends well. We're here now. But I must admit I was beginning to wonder if your dad is Tony Soprano or something."

I laugh. "I don't blame you for wondering."

He laughs. "Glad we're here now."

"Me, too."

I bite my lip.

What the hell is wrong with me? Cameron is gorgeous. And charming. And charismatic. And he just made a cute joke about my dad being a mob boss, for crying out loud. That was funny, right? *And I like funny.* So why am I not feeling this? I felt it when I met him in that sports bar (just before Sarah dragged me out of there after Stacy the Bitch read her the riot act in the bathroom).

Cameron purses his lips as he studies the menu.

He's a total catch. I just need to get my head in the game. I look at my menu. "So what looks good to you tonight?" I ask.

"You mean besides you?"

I smile, but I'm forcing it. All I want to do right now is read whatever text is sitting on my phone from Josh Faraday.

A waiter approaches the table.

"Hello, folks," he says. "How are we doing this evening?"

"Great," Cameron says. "How are you?"

With Cameron's attention diverted to the waiter, I quickly pick up my phone and sneak a peek.

"Well, I used all caps for the word VAGINA because that word is most definitely all-caps worthy. How it spiraled out of control from there, I have no idea. I think we should STOP. So, hey, PG. I'M IN THE MOOD TO CELEBRATE!" Josh's last text says. "Let me take you to my favorite restaurant in Seattle. They make the best MARTINIS in the city. You'll SCREAM WITH PLEASURE. Oh, and you'll like the MARTINIS, too. Snicker."

My stomach somersaults. Oh my God. Of all the nights for Josh Faraday to ask me out. This can't be happening.

"And for you, miss?" the waiter asks.

I look up from my phone. The waiter is looking at me, his eyebrows raised. My eyes drift to Cameron's face. He's looking at me expectantly.

"What would you like to drink, miss?" the waiter prompts.

"Uh. Yes. Thank you." I clear my throat. "A dirty martini, Grey Goose, two olives, please. Thank you."

"Great. I'll get your drinks and come back for your food order."

"Thanks," Cameron says.

The waiter walks away and Cameron picks up his menu again.

"What are you drinking?" I ask. "I didn't hear your order."

"Just water. I don't drink," he says.

"Oh," I say. "I didn't realize. I can cancel my martini if—"

He laughs. "No worries. I'm used to it."

"You don't drink because you're sober, or . . .?"

"I don't drink during the season."

I'm relieved. "How long is the season?"

"Including spring training and post-season, if you're lucky, about eight months."

What the fuck? The guy doesn't drink for eight months of the year? "Good lord," I say. "No drinking for eight whole months? It's like you're pregnant once a year." I shudder with mock horror. Or maybe it's just straight-up horror, actually. That sounds like a fate worse than death to me.

"Yeah, pretty much."

"Do you get weird cravings, too—like for pickles and ice cream?"

He laughs. "Thankfully, no."

"I really wouldn't knock drinking as part of a healthy lifestyle," I say. "Vodka comes from potatoes. Potatoes are vegetables. Hence, vodka is a vegetable." I snort.

Cameron grins politely, but he doesn't laugh. He looks back down at his menu. "I'm thinking the surf and turf. You?"

Ooph. Brutal. Where's our chemistry? Is it hanging out with Waldo? I feel like I'm pulling teeth here. Surely, Cameron must feel the same way. "Yeah, surf and turf sounds good," I say. Oh my God, my phone is calling to me like a siren. I've got to respond to Josh's invitation. "Hey, you know what, Cameron? I'm so sorry, but I just need to finish something . . ." I motion to my phone. "I'll be quick. I promise."

"Okay," he says tentatively.

"Sarah again," I say.

"Oh, yeah, take your time." By the compassionate tone of his voice, it's obvious he thinks being there for my best-friend-Sarah-who-was-stabbed-in-a-bathroom is something admirable. And, bitch that I am, I'm happy to let him think it if it means I can get away with texting Josh for a little bit longer.

"I'll just be a minute. And then I'm all yours."

He flashes me a beaming smile. "I like the sound of that."

"I'm really sorry, PB," I text to Josh quickly, my heart pounding. "I'd love to celebrate your freedom with you with the best martini in Seattle, but I just sat down for dinner. Can I take a rain check?"

"HOLY FUCK PUT YOUR FORK DOWN!" he immediately replies. "I'M COMING TO GET YOU RIGHT NOW! Where are you?"

I bite my lip to keep myself from giggling. "No can do. I've already ordered," I write.

"Well, then, that's an easy one. How about I join you? Are you with friends? Make sure you order whatever you want. Dinner's on me."

My stomach twists. Shit. I stare at my phone for a long beat, trying to decide how to word my reply. "I'm not with friends," I write. "I'm on a date." I press the send button, wincing. But I can't figure out another way to phrase it.

"NOOOOO!" he replies immediately.

I bite my lip again, but it's no use. A giggle escapes my mouth. I glance up at Cameron. He's studying his menu intently.

"It's a first date," I reply. "We were supposed to go out the night I met you at Jonas', actually. And then it got rescheduled and we were supposed to go out the night Sarah was attacked. And now we're here. Finally."

"Kat, the universe clearly doesn't want you to date this guy. Get up and leave now! What do you need the universe to do before you start listening—send a fucking bus crashing into the restaurant?"

I laugh out loud.

Before I can reply, Josh sends another message. "Tell him you have to leave. I'll send a car for you right now. It'll be there in five minutes. Tell him NOW."

I make a face at my phone. On what planet would I ever ditch Cameron like that? I'm a bitch, but I'm not that big a bitch. That might be how things happen in movies (and, admittedly, in one of the many fantasy-pornos that plays inside my head) but that's not how nice people in real life act. "I'm not gonna do that," I write to Josh. "Cameron's a nice guy. And I've already cancelled on him twice."

"So what. He deserved it. He's a tool."

"He's not a tool. Far from it."

"Yes, he is. Obviously."

"He's not."

"Yes, he is. You wanna know how I know?"

"Enlighten me."

"Because you're on a date with him and you're more interested in texting me."

I smile broadly. *Touché,* Playboy.

"Ergo, he's a tool," Josh writes.

I shouldn't do it—I know I shouldn't—but I can't help myself. "He's not a tool. He's a professional baseball player."

"Oh, really?"

"Really," I text.

"Oh. Minor or major league?"

"Major."

"Bah. He's probably some benchwarmer, Kat, trying to impress you. He's some utility player or relief pitcher who sits around waiting for someone to pull a hamstring so he can get in the game. That's why he said 'professional baseball player' instead of saying his team or his position."

"Well, a boy in the restaurant just asked him for his autograph. Do kids ask for autographs from players who sit on the bench?"

"No," he writes. "Not usually."

I smirk.

"Is he on the Mariners?"

"I don't know. I didn't ask."

"The guy says he's a professional baseball player and you don't ask him for what team?"

"No, I just said, 'That's cool.' I was playing it cool, acting like I didn't care. That's a bit of a strategy of mine with guys, if you must know. A girl should never seem too eager, especially with a pro athlete." I attach a winking emoji.

"Ah, clever. The ol' 'I don't give a shit you're a major league ball player' strategy. Clever. Works every time, I'm sure."

"Well, it certainly worked this time, anyway."

"Grrrrrrrrrrrrrr."

"LOL."

"Well, does he live in Seattle?" Josh texts.

"Why are we talking about my date?" I write.

"I need to know what I'm dealing with. Does he live in Seattle?"

"I'm pretty sure he does. His phone number is 206."

"What's his name?"

"Cameron."

"CAMERON?"

"Correct."

"Oh Jesus. Motherfucking fuck. Does he have dark hair? About six foot two? Looks like an ad for aftershave?"

"Yeah! That's him. That's what Sarah said! She said he looks like an ad for razors."

"Motherfucker! That's because he IS an ad for razors. Literally! He's Cameron Schultz, Kat! Goddammit!"

"Yeah! Schultz! That's his last name. Now I remember. You know him?"

"No, I don't know him personally. I know who he is because he's a fucking ALL-STAR! Kat, you're on a date with the fucking shortstop for the Mariners!"

"Oh. That's cool. Haha! Maybe I should have asked more questions."

"Kat, this is my worst nightmare right now. You know that, right? I literally had this very nightmare last night," Josh writes.

"Why is this your nightmare?"

"You know why. But I'm not gonna feed your ego and say it. I can play the 'I don't give a shit' game, too. It doesn't just work on professional ball players, it also works on gorgeous women who are used to men falling all over them."

"Okay, well, as long as neither of us gives a shit, I guess I'll go, then. I'm on a date with an All-star baseball player, in case you didn't know."

"WAIT! No. I take it back. I GIVE A SHIT! I'm coming to get you. Where are you?"

I giggle. "Screw you, dude. I'm having fun. I'm on a date with Cameron Fucking Schulz. I'm sure he's about to re-enact his latest razor commercial for me. Sexy!"

"Put your fork down. My Party Girl with a Hyphen's not allowed on a date with Cameron Fucking Schultz. Hell no. Especially when I'm in the mood to celebrate my freedom. Tonight's MY night, Party Girl, not that dickweed's. Tell him to step the fuck aside and let a real man show you a good time."

Those butterflies in my stomach just turned into bald eagles. I can't think what to say in reply, so I just stare at my phone, freaking out.

"Kat, tell him you've had a family emergency. Or that you feel sick. I don't fucking care what you say. Just end the date. I'm coming right now. THIS IS MY FUCKING NIGHT AND YOU'RE MY GODDAMNED PARTY GIRL WITH A HYPHEN!"

My entire body feels electrified. "OMG. You're nuts. No."

Cameron clears his throat and I look up from my phone. Oh crap. Cameron's staring at me intently. My cheeks blaze with sudden heat.

"I'm sorry, Cameron," I say. "I'm being rude—absolutely horrible." I put my phone down. But then I pick it right back up. "I'm... Lemme just... I just need to say goodbye."

"No worries. She needs you. I understand. You're worth the wait." His eyes darken.

"Thank you," I say, blushing. "Just a minute more, I promise. And then I'm all yours."

He picks up his water, salutes me, and winks. "I'm gonna hold you to that."

"Please do," I say, but my voice lacks its usual flirtatiousness. I bury my nose in my phone again. "Careful, Josh. You're gonna make me sleep with Cameron just to spite you."

"NOT FUNNY, KAT."

"I'm not being funny. I've never slept with a pro athlete before. It's on my list."

I've no sooner pressed send on that last text when my phone buzzes with an incoming call from Josh.

I decline the call and put my phone back on the table, smiling at Cameron.

"Sorry about that," I breathe. The phone buzzes with another incoming call and I decline it again. "She's just really needy right now," I say, despicably spiraling into full-blown, pathological deception. "Post traumatic stress or something, poor thing." Oh my God, I'm morally bankrupt. Heinous. Reprehensible.

*Turned-on.*

"Why don't you just go give her a quick call?" Cameron suggests. "Make sure everything's okay. And then we'll start fresh, you and me."

I nod. "Yeah, good idea. Thanks. As long as you don't mind." My phone buzzes with another incoming call and I decline it. "I'm just gonna step out front, real quick, call her, see if everything's okay, and then I'll put my phone away for the rest of the night. I promise."

The waiter comes to the table with my martini and sets it in front of me. "Are we ready to order?"

My phone buzzes with another call and I decline it.

"I don't think we're ready to order yet—" Cameron begins.

"No, no, I'm ready," I say. "I'll only be gone a minute, I promise."

He smiles at me.

I quickly place my order with the waiter, take a huge swig of my martini, and then another, and sprint outside, gripping my phone with white knuckles as I go. I'm scum right now. A lying, deceitful, insincere piece of shit. But I can't help it. I feel like a junkie hankering for her next fix—and Josh Faraday is most definitely my next fix.

The chilly night air feels like a slap to my face—which is good. Maybe it'll slap some sense into me. I'm being an absolute nightmare right now. A female-asshole, which is a massive step above bitch. Oh my God, I need to stop this. I'm on a date with Cameron. He's hot. He's a professional athlete. He's sweet—like a Boy Scout. Jeez, the man's pursued me through *two* cancellations of our dinner date. I've got to go back in there and give him my undivided attention. He deserves that much. And I will. Just as soon as I talk to Josh for a teensy-weensy second.

I press the button to call Josh.

"Oh my fucking God!" Josh shouts in my ear the minute the call connects. "Just the *thought* of you sleeping with Cameron Fucking Schultz is turning me into my goddamned brother. I'm coming to get you. Tell me where you are. You're not allowed to be on a date!"

I laugh. "Oh, please. I've seen your Instagram account, Josh. You're not exactly a monk."

"Don't believe everything you see. I just got propositioned by a bisexual supermodel the other day *and I turned her down.*"

I laugh. "Well, give the man a medal."

"Tell me where you are."

"No."

He's silent for a long beat. I can practically hear his gears turning. "Are you gonna turn this guy down or what?" he finally asks, his voice intense.

"Wouldn't you like to know?"

"Oh my fucking—"

"Josh, you're assuming he's gonna make me some kind of offer. There might not be anything to turn down."

"Ha! Kat, gimme a fucking break. Of course, the guy's gonna make you an offer."

"Not 'of course.' We might not hit it off. You never know."

"Kat, Jesus. Don't act like you don't know you're literally the most gorgeous girl on planet earth. You're physical perfection and any man who meets you is gonna want to sleep with you and he's gonna pull out all the stops to seduce you."

I'm speechless. He just said things that would rock any girl's world—and he said them like he was rattling off state capitals.

"So, are you gonna turn him down or not?"

"You think I'm the most gorgeous girl on planet earth?" I ask, my mouth still hanging open.

He exhales with exasperation, like I'm asking a stupid question. "Of course. You're insanity—a fantasy come to life. You must know that."

My heart is suddenly pounding in my ears.

"You're drop-dead gorgeous," he continues, his voice shifting from matter-of-fact to something distinctly sexual. "Anyone who sees you is gonna want you. It's fucking primal. Anyone would want you."

"Anyone?" I ask, clearly asking if that word includes Josh.

"*Anyone.* Jesus, Kat. *Of course*. That little cleft in your chin?" He makes a sound like I just licked his dick. "I've got a hard-on just thinking about it. God help me if I ever get to touch it, I'm gonna lose my fucking mind."

I swallow hard.

"And on top of all that, you're funny and sassy, too. You're the whole package, Kat. A fucking eleven."

Holy shitballs, I wanna have sex with this man. If we were alone right now, my clothes would already be off and my legs spread. A thought pings my brain like a pebble against a window: *What did you ask for in your application to The Club, Josh Faraday?*

"So, where are you?" Josh says softly, like he's luring a rescue puppy with a hunk of sausage. "I wanna celebrate my newfound freedom tonight with my Party Girl with a Hyphen and I won't take no for an answer."

I can barely breathe. "I can't, Josh," I finally say. "I'm not gonna do that to Cameron. I'm a bitch, but I'm not that big a bitch. We'll celebrate tomorrow."

"Aw, come on, Kat. If you're willing to meet me tomorrow night, that means you already know you're not gonna be on a date with Cameron Schulz tomorrow night, which means you already know you're not gonna sleep with him *tonight*, which means there's no point in going through the motions with him anymore. Under the circumstances, the kind and efficient thing to do, therefore, is to stop wasting everyone's time and come hang out with the guy you actually want to sleep with tonight. It's the kindest thing you could possibly do, Kat—don't you wanna be a kind person?"

"And you're assuming the guy I actually want to sleep with is you?"

"Of course. It's no big secret."

I scoff. "You're awfully cocky."

"No, I'm *confident*—and with very good reason."

Oh man, that last comment sent a shiver down my spine. "I wouldn't be so confident, if I were you," I say. "I haven't spent five uninterrupted minutes with Cameron, thanks to you—with a little time, we might really hit it off. You never know. Maybe I *will* be sleeping with him tomorrow night. Hell, maybe I'll throw caution to the wind and sleep with him tonight."

Josh's voice shifts to something animalistic. "*Kat, fuck that shit right now.* I'm the sane twin compared to my brother, but I'm still a fucking Faraday—you can't say that fucking shit to me. Do you understand me?"

Oh, his voice is so fucking sexy right now, I'm wetting the cotton crotch of my undies.

His voice turns into a low, intense growl. "You like torturing me. Is that it? It gets you off?"

I'm so freaking wet. Oh my God, I want him. "Yeah, actually. It does."

"Oh my fucking God," he replies. "Go back in there and tell him you've got to go. Tell him you got a better offer from a man who's gonna make you scream tonight."

My heart is racing. The cool air on my face is doing nothing to calm my raging arousal right now.

"Come on, Kat. Do it now. Right now. I've got such a big fucking hard-on for you right now—and I know exactly how to use it."

"You'd make me scream, huh?"

"Oh yeah. You bet. All night long, baby."

"Coming from a guy who joined a sex club, I'm not sure if that's good or bad. Would you make me scream your name or scream for the police?"

He laughs. "You'll just have to roll the dice and find out, baby. Either way, you'll thank me."

I let out a shaky breath and shift my weight. I feel like every drop of blood and fluid in my body has flooded into my crotch all at once.

"You know how this story ends every bit as much as I do, Party Girl," he coos. "Let's cut out the middle bullshit and get to the good stuff. Because, trust me, the good stuff is really, really good."

"I don't have any idea how this story ends."

"Yes, you do."

"No, I don't."

"Well, I do. And, believe me, it's *so fucking good* it's gonna make you drip down your thighs."

My clit flutters. So, it turns out Josh Faraday's a dirty-talker, huh? He just gets better and better. I take a deep breath. "It's gonna be that good, huh?"

"So. Fucking. Good. Oh my God. Best you ever had."

If I weren't on a public sidewalk right now, my fingers would already be inside my panties. "What'd you ask for in your application, Josh?" I purr.

He exhales. "You'll just have to roll the dice and find out, Party Girl. Come on, Kat. YOLO. I've got a boner the size of the Space Needle for you right now. I jacked off in the shower yesterday, thinking about you. Don't make me do it again tonight. What a waste of an epic boner. Come on."

Oh man, he's making me so aroused, I can't think straight. "What'd you write in your application, Josh?" I ask. "Tell me and maybe I'll tell Cameron I feel a migraine coming on."

"I don't negotiate with terrorists," he says. "Just tell me where you are."

I laugh, even though I don't want to do it.

"YOLO, Kat," he whispers like he's trying to put me into a trance. "*YOOOOOLO.*"

I laugh again and shake my head, bringing myself to my senses. "Are you gonna tell me what you asked for in your application or not?"

"Not. You just have to roll the dice. That's half the fun of fucking someone new. Come on."

I'm pissed as hell he won't tell me. Didn't I just say I'd ditch Cameron if he told me? That'd be an exceedingly bitchy, heartless thing to do to the guy—and I'm still willing to do it *for him*—even though Cameron is a goddamned Major League baseball player, too. Well, now I'm pissed.

"Come on, Kat. *YOLO*," Josh coos, clearly still thinking he's got a chance of getting what he wants.

"Nope. I'm not gonna be a total bitch to Cameron. And I'm not gonna sleep with you without knowing what I'm getting myself into. So forget it."

"Tell him you've gotta go. Right now."

"No. We've already ordered our food—really expensive, nice food. Surf and turf."

"Wow. Big spender."

"Stop it. He's nice—a really sweet guy. He doesn't even drink."

Josh bursts out laughing. "What? Oh my God. He just gets better and better."

I'm smiling so big, my cheeks hurt.

Oh man, Josh is laughing his ass off like I've just said the funniest thing in the world. "Fun guy," he finally chokes out. "Oh yeah, you're having a blast, Party Girl." He laughs again. "No wonder you're talking to me instead of sitting with him. You couldn't get away from him fast enough."

"A guy doesn't have to drink to be fun. I think it's awesome Cameron doesn't drink—it shows he's got discipline."

"Pfft," Josh scoffs. "No, you don't think it's awesome. You were mortified when he told you, admit it."

I audibly shrug. He's right, of course. But wild horses couldn't make me admit that to him right now. "Why don't we just see each other tomorrow night?" I purr.

Josh exhales. "I can't. I'm headed to New York tomorrow on the early flight on business. And then I gotta be in LA for a couple days on a deal. I won't be able to get back to Seattle for at least a week."

I make an "oh well" sound. In all honesty, I'm wildly disappointed, but I'm not gonna let him know that. "Well, then, I guess we'll be seeing each other in a week or so," I say primly. "If ever."

He makes an exasperated noise.

"Assuming you've sent me your application to The Club by then, of course," I add. "Since that's a required prerequisite of me going out with you."

He makes a scoffing sound.

I ignore him. "Oh, *and* assuming I'm not impregnated by Cameron Schulz by then—which is entirely possible."

Josh makes a caveman roar that shocks the hell out of me. "Fuck this, Kat!" he booms. "*Tell that boring, sober motherfucker to fuck off right now*. I mean it. No more bullshit. I'm coming to get you. Tell me where you are."

I can only imagine how shocked my face looks right now. I must look like that emoji with wide eyes. I didn't expect that kind of volcanic reaction. Jeez. It came out of nowhere. He always seems so laid back. I open my mouth, but nothing comes out.

"Are you there?" Josh barks.

"Yeah."

"Enough with the bullshit, Kat. Playtime's over. You don't wanna be with Cameron Fucking Schulz tonight and you know it. You wanna be with *me*. Now tell me where you are because I'm coming to get you."

Kerzoinks, as Sarah would say. Sounds like he's got something of a jealous streak. Ha! Well, he's in for a rude awakening. Because Kat Morgan doesn't do jealous-boyfriend bullshit. Ever. Wait. What am I thinking? Josh isn't even my boyfriend! We're not even dating! Why would he think, even for a minute, he's in any position to tell me what to do?

"Hmm," I say calmly, like he just asked me for directions to the nearest gas station. "I don't think so, Playboy. Caveman shit doesn't really work with me, you ought to know."

He's either fuming or coming on the other end of the line—I'm not sure which. By the noise he just made, it could be either.

"You know what *I* think's gonna happen right now? I'm gonna hang up the phone and go back into the restaurant and have a nice meal with a very sweet guy who politely asked me out to a very nice restaurant, and rescheduled *twice* despite his very busy schedule, and who's treated me with nothing but respect all night long—and who, it turns out, happens to be the starting shortstop for the Mariners. Who knew?"

Josh makes another raging caveman noise. "Kat. I'm not kidding. Stop fucking around and tell him—"

"So I guess I'll see you soon, whenever you're in Seattle next—*if* I'm not already desperately in love with Cameron Schulz and carrying his love child by then."

"*Kat.*"

"What?"

"Fuck."

I don't reply.

"Come on," he says. "Stop it."

He's clearly used to getting whatever he wants, when he wants it.

"Travel safe, Josh. I really do hope to see you soon."

"*Kat.*"

I'm about to hang up, but his tone is so emphatic, I feel compelled to stay on the line. "*What*?"

He exhales. There's a long beat as he collects himself. "YOLO, Kat," he says earnestly.

I bite my lip. Oh, he's good. He's really good. A giggle escapes my mouth, even though I don't want it to.

Oh man. I want him. He's one hundred percent right. But I've got a problem. I make it a rule never to sleep with a man on a first date if I'm interested in him as potential boyfriend-material. It's a rule I *never* break. I'm not quite sure if all my interactions with Josh add up to the equivalent of a first date or not, but I don't want to risk it. But, regardless of my stupid rule (because if ever there was a time to break my rule, it's now, with Josh), if Josh is leaving on a flight to New York first thing tomorrow, then tonight's not our night, anyway. Something tells me when I finally get to take a big ol' bite out of this particular man's ass—and I'm not being figurative there—I'm gonna wanna go back for seconds and thirds and fourths and fifths. I exhale a long, shaky breath. It's been so freaking long since I've felt even a glimmer of what I'm feeling right now, I don't want to fuck it up by being Classic Kat.

"I gotta go, Playboy," I say. I exhale again and my tone shifts to complete sincerity. "Josh, seriously. It'd be too heartless, even for me, to blow off Cameron after how sweet he's been to me. I can be a bitch, you should be warned, but not that big a bitch."

Josh is silent on the line for a long beat. "Shit," he finally says. "Okay. Then. Fuck. I guess I'll see you next week, then."

"I'm looking forward to it."

He exhales with resignation.

"Hey, make sure you get my email address from Sarah in the meantime."

"Why?"

"So you can send me your Club application. It's required reading before I'll go out with you."

He audibly rolls his eyes. "Not gonna happen."

I laugh. "You're used to getting whatever you want, when you want it, aren't you?"

"Damn straight."

"Well, guess what? *So am I.*"

He laughs. "Mmm hmm. Well, sucks to be you, Party Girl. I guess you've finally met your match."

"Mmm hmm. We'll see."

He chuckles. "We'll see."

"Travel safe, Josh," I say earnestly. "I gotta go have dinner with *Cameron Schulz,* the shortstop for the Mariners." I wait a beat, but he doesn't reply. "I hope to see you soon, Josh," I add sincerely.

"Tell Cameron his batting average sucks dick right now and that whiff at the plate last night against the Yankees was a fucking embarrassment."

"I'll be sure not to tell him you said so."

"Bye, Kat."

"Bye, Josh. I'll look forward to your email with your application attached."

"Not a fucking chance, Party Girl. Not a fucking chance in hell."

I laugh. "We'll see about that."

"Yeah, good luck with that."

"I don't need luck. I've got you right where I want you, Playboy."

"Mmm hmm. I think it's the other way around."

"That's what I *want* you to think."

He laughs. "Sure thing, PG. Keep telling yourself that. Bye, Kat."

"Bye, Josh."

I hang up and turn off my phone. For a long beat, I stand in the chilly night air, staring at the traffic whizzing by on the street, my crotch throbbing mercilessly and my heart leaping out of my chest. He's right. He's got me right where he wants me—not the other way around—just like every other woman he burns through, I'm sure. Clearly, the man has his pick of every bisexual supermodel and starlet in Hollywood, and I can see why. Well, maybe I'm the first woman who's gonna teach this Playboy that not all women will say "how high" when a rich, handsome, charismatic studmuffin like Josh Faraday commands, "Jump."

After a moment, a wide smile spreads across my devious, bitchy, turned-on, intrigued, conniving little face. If Josh wants me, he's gonna have to work for it—something he's clearly not used to doing. I'm dying to read his frickin' application, that's true, but at this point, that stupid application is more than just an application to a sex club. *It's a brass ring.* If this is gonna be a battle of wills, then I'm gonna be the one who wins it.

My smile widens.

Kat Morgan knows two things in this life: men and PR. And, by God, when it comes to Josh Faraday, victory will be mine. Along with his supremely bitable ass.

## Chapter 9

*Kat*

"Hey!" I shout, knocking on the door of Jonas and Sarah's hotel suite. "Vegas, baby!" I begin pounding maniacally on the door like I'm the Energizer Bunny on speed, which is actually a perfect analogy because I feel high with excitement—out of my mind with unbridled glee. I'm in the Promised Land, baby! My own personal Mecca! And on Jonas' generous dime, no less. Ha! My hotel room is freaking spectacular—I could never in a million years afford to stay in a hotel like this on my own—plus, as Josh would say, I'm free at last, I'm free at last, thank God almighty, I'm *finally* free at last of my round-the-clock bodyguards (with Jonas' permission). Who knew having two grumpy old guys trail your every move for a week and a half could become so freaking suffocating? No wonder Whitney finally fucked Kevin—she just needed to de-stress from having some grouchy guy following her around twenty-four-seven.

And the most exciting thing of all? Sarah's finally feeling back to her old self again, and then some. When Sarah called yesterday to say, "Pack your bags for Vegas, Kitty Kat—we're going *Ocean's Eleven* on The Club's motherfucking ass!" I practically peed my pants.

"I'm in!" I shrieked (even though I had absolutely no idea how I could possibly contribute a damned thing to going *Ocean's Eleven* on The Club's motherfucking ass).

"Woot!" Sarah replied.

"Woot!" I shouted back.

"Will it be just you, me, and Jonas?" I asked, trying to sound breezy and nonchalant.

"Who else would be joining us?" Sarah asked coyly.

"Oh, I dunno," I answered. "No one in particular. Just wondering."

Sarah laughed. "Well, a certain *hacker* will be joining us, if that's who you're referring to," Sarah said, teasing me.

"Oh, that's good," I said. "Yeah, we'll definitely need one of those."

"Mmm hmm," Sarah said. "Fo shizzle pops."

There was a very, very long beat, during which I held my breath and bit the inside of my cheek with anticipation until Sarah burst out laughing.

"Oh, Kitty Kat. Of course, the Playboy's gonna be there, too. Wherever Jonas goes, Josh goes, too—that's something as reliable as gravity."

I exhaled like I'd just surfaced from being held forcibly underwater.

I hate to admit it, but I've been going out of my mind thinking about Josh this whole week while he's been in New York—I can't remember the last time my Rabbit's gotten this much action in a single week.

Thankfully, Josh has made it clear he's been thinking about me, too, though he's obviously playing his cards close to his vest, the smooth bastard. On the one hand, he's sent multiple texts this past week, just enough to let me know he's thinking about me, but, on the other hand, his texts say absolutely nothing. No teasing. No innuendo. No semi-inappropriate photos. Not even any questions about Cameron Fucking Schulz. And, notably, no reference whatsoever to his application, despite my explicit demands for it. Just the occasional, "Hey, Party Girl" and "Whatcha doing, hot stuff?" or "Did you have a nice dream about me last night, PG?"

Of course, I know Josh's game—I've played it a time or two (or three) myself: he's forcing me to make the first move—breaking me down, making me question his interest. Bush league. He clearly doesn't understand whom he's dealing with here.

Well, two can play the "I don't give a shit" game. Hmmph. All week, I've answered each and every one of Josh's texts with pleasant but brief and noncommittal bullshit. "Hey yourself," I've replied. Or "Oh, nothing, just looking for something interesting to read—hint hint," or, on occasion, "None of your freaking beeswax, PB." If Josh thinks I'm gonna chase him like every other girl obviously does, he's sadly mistaken. And so, to put it mildly, our recent communications have been textually unsatisfying—while subtextually dripping with heat—and the whole situation is making me want to jump his freaking bones.

Bastard.

I continue pounding on Jonas and Sarah's door, my excitement about to boil over.

"Hey!" I shout again. "Vegasssssssss!"

The door to Jonas and Sarah's room opens abruptly and Sarah's beaming face greets me.

"Woohoo!" I shriek, throwing my arms around her.

Sarah clutches me like her life depends on it and the two of us jump up and down, screaming, for a solid minute. When we finally unravel our bodies, I enter the spacious suite, instantly in awe.

"Wow," I say, marveling at the splendor of our surroundings. Wall-to-wall marble floors. Sleek leather and glass furniture. Light fixtures that look like works of art. And, the *coup de grace*, floor-to-ceiling windows overlooking The Strip.

"Wow, Jonas," I say. "You really knocked yourself out. I bet, like, rock stars and Prince Harry stay in this place, especially with that private elevator to get up here. It's amazing."

Jonas is standing by the fully stocked bar, looking hella hot in his jeans and tight T-shirt, if I do say so. "I wanted to show my precious baby an extra good time," Jonas says, "seeing as how this is her first trip to Sin City."

*My precious baby*? I glance at Sarah and she's positively giddy. Is it possible the manwhore has changed his manwhoring ways at the magic touch of the right woman? I've read about that mythical phenomenon in fairytales, but I've never seen it happen in real life—or, at least, it's never happened to me.

"Oh, Jonas," Sarah coos, blushing. "You're so sweet."

Jonas' face bursts with immediate color. Aw, he's absolutely adorable right now. I just wanna pinch his cheeks. I can plainly see why Sarah's so smitten with him—this boy's a puppy!—I don't know why I didn't see it before.

"Thank you for paying for my flight, Jonas," I say, smiling. "And my room."

"You're welcome. You got checked in okay?"

"Yes, thank you."

Sarah flashes an adorable smile at Jonas and he returns it.

Oh good lord, these two are smitten. "Did you see this view?" I say, grabbing Sarah's hand and pulling her to the floor-to-ceiling windows at the far end of the room. "Just wait 'til you see The Strip at night. The lights are gonna blow you away." I sigh. "God, I love Vegas."

"I've seen The Strip in movies," Sarah says, "but I bet it's really cool in person."

I glance at the bar and spy a bottle of my favorite champagne chilling on ice. "Oh, champagne!" I squeal. This day just keeps getting better and better.

"I'll get you a glass," Jonas says, moving gracefully toward the bar.

There's a loud knock at the door to the suite. "Open up, you beast!"

Oh my God. Every hair on my body stands on end. *He's here.* Shit. I wish I'd checked my makeup before heading up to Jonas and Sarah's room. Gah. "Do I look okay?" I whisper to Sarah. I bare my teeth. "Do I have anything in my teeth?"

Sarah grins broadly. "You look perfect," she says. "He'll be putty in your hands."

Jonas opens the door and there he is, the Playboy himself, dressed in a designer suit perfectly tailored to his muscled frame, standing next to a much smaller, kind of nerdy-looking guy in a V-neck T-shirt and goatee.

Holy shitballs. My chest constricts at the sight of Josh's utter deliciousness.

Was he always this hot?

I've ogled countless photos of Josh on the Internet since I first met him at Jonas' house two weeks ago, but absolutely no two-dimensional simulation of the man comes even close to capturing his magnetism. He's oozing raw masculinity, even in that expensive suit. In fact, the sophistication of his clothes somehow emphasizes the brute swagger hiding underneath the fabric. Oh my fucking God. This man is sex on a designer stick.

"You ready?" Sarah whispers.

I nod. "Let's do it."

She grabs my hand and we bounce happily over to the guys.

Oh shit, I'm trembling. What the hell's gotten into me? I never act this way. I feel like a schoolgirl with a crush.

"Hey, Party Girl with a Hyphen," Josh says, his eyes sparkling wickedly.

"Well, hey yourself, Playboy," I say, sounding remarkably collected, I must say. "It's a crazy, fucked up world when a Playboy and a Party Girl cross paths in *Vegas*, huh?" He bursts out laughing and I join him. "It's good to see you again," I say. Wow, I sound like I hardly give a shit. Sometimes I amaze even myself.

Josh wraps me in a huge hug and kisses me on both cheeks and I practically melt into his strong arms. Oh my God, his cologne is divine. Was he wearing that cologne the first night I met him? It's deadly.

I kiss him softly on the cheek and the sensation of his skin under my lips makes my skin sizzle and pop.

He puts his hand on my cheek and brings his lips to my ear. "You look gorgeous, Party Girl," he whispers.

"Uh," I say. Oh my God. I can't even think. Is it possible he's gotten even *better-looking* than he was two weeks ago?

Josh grins. "You ready to find out how this story ends, Party Girl?" He rubs his thumb along my cheek.

Before I can reply, the hipster guy standing next to Josh makes a weird noise, like a horse rejecting a saddle, and I suddenly realize I haven't introduced myself. I train my full attention on the hipster-nerd-guy and extend my hand, ignoring the fact that my cheek is still tingling where Josh just touched me. "Hi, I'm Katherine Morgan," I say. "But everyone calls me Kat."

"Oh. Huh. Hi. See. I'm ... Nice... fleb beet you."

"What?" I laugh.

"Hennessey. But... calls... Henn. Me. Calls. Henn. Everyone. Me."

Jonas bursts out laughing from behind me and the hipster guy's face turns beet red. Oh my gosh, this hacker dude's the most adorable human I've ever met. I'm already in deep, irreversible like with him. Without even thinking about it, I wrap him in a huge hug and kiss his cheek. He looks like he could break into beat poetry at any given moment. Adorbs! I want to take him home and put him in a rhinestone jacket and feed him treats. "I'm so excited to meet you, Henn," I say. I kiss him on the cheek again and his face turns the color of a vine-ripened tomato.

"Kat, stop treating Henn like a Chihuahua," Sarah says. "Henn, tell her to stop assaulting you."

I laugh and release the poor guy. "Sorry, Henn," I say. "I'm impulsive. I should have warned you. Sometimes, I just can't control myself." I glance at Josh on that last comment and his eyebrows drift up, every so slightly.

Henn nods and mumbles something adorably incoherent.

"Time for alcohol!!" Josh booms. "I always say, 'If a guy doesn't drink, he must be a total fucking tool.' Or, at the very least, he's just fucking *boring*." He shoots me a smart-ass grin and strides to the bar. "Don't you agree, Kat?"

I twist my mouth, trying desperately not to smile. "Not necessarily," I say. "Sometimes, it just means a guy is *disciplined.*"

Josh scoffs. He refills my champagne glass and then Sarah's and grabs three beers from the fridge. "Oh yeah," he says, snapping his fingers like he's just remembered something important. He opens the first of the bottles and hands it to Jonas. "I've also heard from several *extremely* reliable sources that guys who don't drink also make limp-dick-shitty-ass lovers."

"Really?" Henn asks.

"Yup."

"Well, jeez," Henn says. "Hand me a beer, then. *Pronto*. And a couple shots."

Josh hands Henn a beer, his eyes still trained on me, his expression clearly saying, "Don't fuck with me, little girl—you're out of your depths."

I look away. Holy shitballs, Josh Faraday is sexy as hell.

The five of us move to the black leather couches in the sitting area and make ourselves comfortable—and I gotta say when Josh Faraday makes himself comfortable, it's a sight to behold: he leans back, spreads his strong legs, and unapologetically adjusts his dick in his pants.

"I'm shocked you splurged on this place, bro," Josh says, glancing around the room. "So un-Jonas-like of you."

"Would you stop telling me what's Jonas- or un-Jonas-like of me already? Apparently, you have no idea what I'm like."

Josh laughs. "Apparently not."

I bite my lip. *Sexy man. Sexy man. Sexy man.* I can't think straight.

Henn opens the browser on his computer and logs into some application-program-thing.

"Okay, folks. I've got an update on the Oksana sitch you had me working on."

"Fantastic," Jonas says, rubbing his hands together.

We all crowd around Henn's laptop—and when I bend over to get a good look at Henn's screen, Josh rests his hand on the small of my back. Oh my God, his touch is drawing every ounce of blood from my brain into the three square inches of flesh under his palm. Holy Hotness, Batman, I can barely process what Henn's saying right now. It seems to be something about someone named Oksana Belenko.

"Sounds like an Olympic ice skater, doesn't she?" Henn says, but I'm barely listening. Josh's hand has moved from the small of my back to the curve of my hip. Holy shitballs. Nuclear energy is wafting off Josh's body just a few inches from mine.

"Boom shakalaka," Henn says, showing us something on his screen.

"See? Fucking genius," Josh says. His hand returns to the small of my back, where it begins making little swirling motions.

"You sure that's our girl?" Sarah asks.

Henn explains why he's sure he's got the right Oksana.

"So that means we've got a confirmed physical address?" Sarah asks.

"Yep."

"Wow," Sarah says. She pauses, the gears apparently turning inside her head. "So it sounds like Oksana supplies the girls for The Club—" She looks at Josh. "Or, if you'd prefer, the Mickey Mouse roller coasters."

Sarah and I simultaneously burst out laughing and Josh straightens up, abruptly removing his swirling hand from my back.

"It was an *analogy*," he says, looking genuinely annoyed.

"We know, Joshie, we know," Sarah says, winking at him. "But it's still funny." She looks at me and makes a ridiculously cute cartoon-face and I burst out laughing again. God, I love Sarah. Relief floods me yet again to have her safe and sound.

"Yeah, Oksana's like this frickin' old-school *madam,*" Henn says. "Probably not the brains behind all the tech stuff."

"She's probably got a business partner who handles the tech side of things," Jonas says.

"Definitely," Henn agrees. "And whoever that person is, he or she knows exactly what the hell they're doing. Because there's no finding these guys by accident. And even then," Henn continues, sipping his beer, "their storefront is just a shell. Their real shit's gotta be buried way down in the Deep Web. And that's a scary place."

"What's the Deep Web?" I ask.

Henn grins broadly at me.

"Is that a stupid question?" I ask, blushing.

"Oh no, not stupid at all. I'm just so used to hanging out with computer geeks all day long, I forget normal people don't know about this stuff." He smiles at me again. "I'm glad you don't know what it is. It means you're probably a well-adjusted, happy person."

I laugh. "I am, as a matter of fact."

"I can tell," Henn says. "Happiness is a very attractive quality in a person."

"Thank you," I say. My eyes flicker to Josh and I'm shocked to see he's already staring at me—looking at me like he wants to fuck my brains out, actually. My skin sizzles and pops, yet again.

Josh clears his throat. "So, guys, before Henn launches into The Grand Story of the Deep Web, how about we all do a shot of Patron? We're in Vegas, after all—when in Rome."

"Sounds like a fabulous idea to me," I say. "Do we have Patron in the bar?"

"Of course," Jonas says. "I made sure of it. My brother is nothing if not predictable."

Josh strides purposefully behind the bar, grace in motion, flashing me a come-hither stare as he goes.

I feel like he's pulling me on a string. "I'll help you out, Playboy," I blurt, bounding over to the bar.

"Why, thanks, Party Girl," Josh says.

I stand next to him in the bar and lean into him, involuntarily drawn to his sheer physicality. He leans his muscled body into mine and whispers softly in my ear. "You ready to cut the middle bullshit yet, Party Girl—see how this story ends?"

"That depends. Are you ready to give me your application?"

He laughs. "I told you—I don't negotiate with terrorists."

"Well, then. I guess not."

## Chapter 10

*Josh*

"You're freaking me out, Henn," Kat says.

She's responding to Henn—he's just finished explaining the difference between the Surface Web (the "Internet we all know and love" where anyone can "Google a sushi restaurant") and the Deep Web (the "ink-black waters below the surface" where "jihadists and drug warlords and fucking human traffickers" operate)—and it's obvious from Kat's facial expression she's completely horrified by what she's just heard.

"How have I never heard of this before?" Kat asks. "Have you heard about this, Sarah?"

Sarah shakes her head, exactly the way Goofy would. I can't help but chuckle at the sight of her. The more I get to know this girl, the more I love her. She's smart and sweet and a total ass-kicker, on the one hand, and yet the dorkiest, goofiest girl I've ever met on the other. I don't think I've met anyone quite like her before—and I've especially never met anyone better suited for my brother.

"Kinda freaks you out when you hear about it for the first time, huh?" Henn says.

"Totally," Kat agrees. "It reminds me of when I found out there are trillions of invisible microbes on my skin at all times."

"Please don't talk about that whole microbes-on-your-skin thing," I say. "That always creeps me out."

Kat bursts out laughing and I join her. It's easy to laugh when Kat does—the girl laughs like a dude.

Henn continues his tutorial, explaining in detail how he only uses his hacking-superpowers for good. "I leave no trace, take nothing, do no harm," Henn says, "unless I'm being paid to leave a trace, take something, do harm, of course. But I only do that kind of thing when I'm positive I work for the good guys."

"But how do you know you're working for the good guys?" Jonas asks, clearly skeptical. "Everyone thinks their cause is righteous. Hence, the concept of war."

I'm about to jump in and defend Henn, but he clearly doesn't need my help.

"Well, yes, of course." Henn looks right at Kat and flashes what I imagine he's hoping is a charming smile. "But let me show you how I tell the good guys from the bad guys." He looks right at Sarah. "Sarah, are you a good guy or a bad guy?"

"A good guy," Sarah says.

"And there you go."

Sarah shrugs like it makes perfect sense. "And there you go," she says.

Jonas is clearly not impressed. "But who would ever say they're one of the bad guys? Who would even *think* that about themselves? People are brilliant at justifying their actions to themselves—trust me, I should know."

"Well, *yeah*," Henn concedes. "But I don't always *believe* people when they say they're one of the good guys. In fact, I rarely do. If I *believe* them, the way I just believed Miss Cruz here, then that's good enough for me."

"Aw, you believe me, Henn?" Sarah asks.

"I do. Indubitably."

"Why, thank you."

"Of course."

"Sometimes, it's a no-brainer," Henn continues. "Like when a job comes from Josh, for example, I always know I'm fighting for truth and justice and the American way, no questions asked. Because a guy can set his moral compass to Josh—he's *always* one of the good guys, through and through."

*Thank you, Henn.*

Now *here's* a guy who's got a brother's back, unlike Jonas. I glare at my stupid brother, sending him a nonverbal "fuck you" for the way he let me twist in the wind in front of Kat the other day—but Jonas is too engrossed in staring at Sarah like a lovesick puppy to notice me.

"Thanks, man," I say to Henn.

"Just speaking the truth," Henn replies.

"Well, well, well," Kat says, arching that bold eyebrow of hers. "It turns out the Playboy's a good guy, after all—Mickey Mouse roller coasters notwithstanding."

I smile broadly.

She bites her lip.

Oh man, I can't wait to fuck this gorgeous woman. It's gonna be so fucking good.

"So, Henn," Jonas says. "If The Club lives in the Deep Web, how the fuck do we find them and take them down?"

Henn proceeds to explain his strategy for implanting malware onto Oksana Belenko's computer. In essence, Sarah's got to pay a personal visit to "the pimpstress extraordinaire," as he calls her, obtain her email address, and then send Oksana an infected email on the spot, which Oksana's got to open in Sarah's presence. Sounds kind of hairy to me, actually—I agree completely when my brother insists on accompanying Sarah on her mission.

"But they think I'm *playing* you, remember?" Sarah protests in a huff. "Why on earth would I bring you with me if I'm *scamming* you?"

"I don't know," Jonas says, crossing his monstrous arms over his chest. "Use that big-ass brain of yours to come up with something they'll believe."

Sarah sighs in frustration.

"It's non-negotiable, Sarah. We're doing this together or we're not doing it at all."

Sarah huffs. "Why would I bring you to meet her? It makes no sense."

Jonas looks at me, obviously inviting me to come up with a suggestion, but I've got nothing.

"They think I'm *playing* you," Sarah says slowly, like she's thinking out loud. "Why would I bring you with me?"

"I don't know, but it's non-negotiable."

"I heard you the first time, Lord-God-Master." Sarah crosses her arms over her chest. After a moment, she picks up her champagne flute and ambles to the floor-to-ceiling windows on the other side of the room. Nighttime has descended on the city while we've been talking and The Strip's dazzling display of neon lights is sprawled out before us.

"Wow," Sarah says, staring out at the expanse of lights. "It's beautiful."

We all get up and take in the view alongside her, drinks in hand.

"Let's take a photo, Sarah," Kat says. The two girls smile for a selfie on Kat's phone, followed by Jonas and Sarah, at Kat's urging.

"You two look good together," Kat says to Jonas. "*Really* good together."

At Kat's words, Jonas looks like a fucking kitten being stroked. Aw, Jonas. Shit. It's times like this I remember my brother's gone his whole life without a single person other than me telling him how fucking awesome he is.

"Don't post those pics anywhere, Kat," Henn warns. "We don't want the bad guys knowing we're on their turf."

"I won't post them; don't worry. I just want to remember being here in Vegas with my best friend for her first time." Kat wraps Sarah in a warm hug. "Thank God you're okay. I was so worried about you. I love you so much."

"I love you, too." Sarah says, nuzzling into Kat's blonde hair.

I can't take my eyes off Kat and Sarah right now—especially Kat. Yeah, she's gorgeous, but I already knew that. Yeah, she's sassy as hell. But, watching the way she's so tenderly kissing and hugging Sarah, it's suddenly dawning on me she might also be… dare I say it… *sweet*? Huh.

Sarah whips her head up and gasps. "I've got it," she says.

"You've got what?" Kat asks, brushing Sarah's dark hair out of her face.

Sarah disengages from Kat, suddenly animated with an idea. "We use their *greed* against them."

"That's my girl," Jonas says. "I knew you'd think of something."

Sarah leaps over to Jonas and throws her arms around his neck, something she seems to do a lot, I've noticed. "This is gonna work."

"Of course, it will," Jonas says. "We're an unstoppable team."

Henn looks at his watch. "Okay, get your plan figured out and we'll launch first thing tomorrow. I'm gonna work all night on my malware. I want to make sure whatever we send them is ironclad." He grabs his laptop, clearly excited to get to work.

"Well," Kat says, her hands on her hips. "While Henn's hard at work cooking up a fancy virus, I guess the rest of us will have to find *something* to do in Las Vegas. Hmm." She taps her finger on her temple like she's solving an algebra problem. "What on earth could we possibly do in *Las Vegas*?" She raises her eyebrow at me, clearly inviting me to provide a suggested solution to the riddle.

"You like to gamble, Kat?" I ask.

Her face lights up. "I love it."

How did I know she was gonna say that? "What's your game?"

"Blackjack."

"Lame," I say.

"Excuse me?"

"The real fun is craps."

"I've never played," she says. "It seems complicated."

"Nah, it's easy. I'll spot you a grand and teach you how to play."

Her eyes pop out of her head. "I'm not gonna take your money."

I love that she just said that—I can't remember the last time a woman said anything even remotely like that to me, actually—but, of course, it's out of the question.

"No, you've got to roll the dice for me, Party Girl," I say matter-of-factly. "You've got first-timer's luck *and* lady luck on your side, and they only let you roll when you've got a bet on the table."

"Well, then, I'll bet my own money."

She tosses her golden hair behind her shoulder in what appears to be a misplaced gesture of defiance. Oh God, she's such a sexy little thing.

"Kat," Jonas says. "Let my brother pay for your fun."

*Thank you, Jonas.*

Finally, for the first time ever, my brother has actually stepped in to help me with a woman. I open my mouth to thank him for his unexpected assistance, but the fucker keeps talking.

"There's nothing Josh Faraday loves more than throwing his hard-earned money away on mindless entertainment," Jonas adds.

I laugh. I knew it was too good to last. "*That's* your idea of helping me, bro?"

Jonas shrugs.

"You'd be doing me a favor, Kat," I say, turning away from my useless brother and fixing my eyes on Kat's ridiculously beautiful face. "Betting on a first-time roller is the dream of every craps player—it's as exciting as it gets. *And I love excitement.*"

Kat grins and bites her lip, her eyes blazing. "Okay, Playboy," she says. "I'm in. You had me at 'excitement.'"

Oooooooooh, I like this girl. My skin is beginning to tingle.

"But we're all going out together, right?" she asks, looking at Sarah.

"Of course," Sarah says.

"Where should we take these lovely ladies to dinner?" Jonas asks me.

My dick is beginning to tingle along with the rest of me. "It just so happens I know the perfect place," I say.

"Of course you do," Jonas replies.

"Do you ladies think you can handle a night out with the Faraday brothers?" I ask, but the only lady I'm looking at is Kat.

Sarah and Kat squeal with excitement, and Sarah throws her arms around Jonas' neck for the hundredth time today. "Thank you, Jonas."

I stride over to Kat. "Hey," I say softly.

"Hey," she replies, her blue eyes blazing at me.

"You ready to earn that nickname of yours, Party Girl with a Hyphen?"

Her eyes flicker at me. "I was born ready, Playboy."

I hold her gaze for a long beat. She truly is the most spectacularly gorgeous woman I've ever beheld. I have the sudden, irresistible urge to kiss her. I lean in, slowly.

"Just as soon as you resend me that email that must have gotten lost," she says, pressing on my chest and halting my forward progress. "The damned thing must have gone into my spam folder when you sent it earlier this week."

"Gosh, Kat," I say. "I didn't send you an email this week."

"No?"

"Nope."

"Why not?"

"Because I don't have a *vagina*."

"Oh, really? Huh. That's too bad."

"It's too bad I don't have a *vagina*?"

She smirks. "It's too bad you didn't send me that email. I was really looking forward to reading it."

I smile at her. She might be the most gorgeous creature I've ever beheld, but she's also the most stubborn. Jesus God. "You're not gonna get what you want this time, no matter how sexy you are," I say. "So you can stop banging your head against the wall. Wouldn't want you to bruise that pretty forehead of yours."

"You obviously don't know me at all. I don't back down," she says. "I only get more determined."

"There's a first time for everything."

She squints at me. "We'll see."

"I guess so."

She stares me down. When I don't look away, her cheeks flush. She clears her throat. "Why don't you ask Henn to come with us to dinner?" she says. "Since we're obviously just gonna have a friendly dinner and nothing more, the more the merrier, right?"

"Great idea," I say. "Henn, you wanna join us for dinner?" I call to him sharply, but I don't take my eyes off her. My cock is rock hard. I'd pay any amount of money to have her sitting on it right now.

Henn doesn't reply.

"Yo, Henn?" I call to him, devouring Kat with my eyes. "You wanna join us for dinner, man?"

"Oh, Josh," Henn says. "How many times do I have to tell you? You can wine and dine me all you like, but you're never gonna get me into bed."

Kat chuckles.

I step close to her and brush her cheekbone with my fingertip, and she abruptly stops laughing.

She parts her lips and lifts her face like she wants me to kiss her. My cock is straining for her.

I lean down and brush my lips as close as humanly possible to hers without actually making contact. "Laugh it up, Party Girl," I whisper. "But Henn's not the one I'm gonna wine and dine and get into bed tonight." I pull back from her face and wink.

## Chapter 11

*Josh*

"Hard four!" the dealer yells.

"Woohoo!" Kat shrieks.

"You're on fi-yah, sistah!" Sarah shouts. She shakes her ass into Jonas' crotch, and he gropes her ass and hips.

The dealer pushes a stack of chips at Kat and she leans over the craps table to collect them—which, of course, gives me the perfect opportunity to ogle her backside. Jesus. That sequined mini-dress of hers is barely longer than a men's dress-shirt, and holy shit, she's working it *hard.* Endless, toned legs. Sky-high heels. Long, tousled blonde hair cascading down her back. And a tight little ass to cap it all off. In summary, the girl is smoking hot. Gorgeous. Sexy. Beautiful. I can't come up with enough praise to do her justice. She's physical perfection.

An old dude in a Hawaiian shirt on the other side of Kat leans into her shoulder. "What number ya feeling, Blondie?"

Kat picks up the dice. "I'm not sure," she answers. "I'm just gonna bet the pass line this time—I'm not getting a vibe."

"Oh, I'm feeling a six for sure," Sarah says confidently, wiggling her ass into Jonas' crotch again. "I'm feeling hella *sixy* right now, baby."

Jonas presses himself into Sarah and wraps his arms around her. "Oh, my precious baby's feeling *sixy,* is she?"

"Yes, sir, baby-sir," she says. "Sixy as hell."

Jonas throws a couple thousand bucks in chips onto the table. "On six," he says to the dealer, his free hand running up and down Sarah's torso. "Always bet on Sarah Cruz."

"Hard or easy six?" Hawaiian Shirt Guy asks Sarah, clearly hanging on her every word.

"Easy," she answers.

Jonas nibbles her neck and pulls her hips into him forcefully. Jesus. Who the fuck is my brother right now? I've never seen him act like this with a woman, ever. He's acting like... *me.*

"Oh my," Sarah says, laughing. "Easy six... and hard... *Jonas*."

Jonas bursts out laughing.

Kat and I look at each other, grimacing.

"I don't know whether to swoon or barf," Kat whispers to me and I chuckle.

"I'm definitely leaning toward 'barf,'" I reply.

"Easy six," Hawaiian Shirt Guy yells to the dealer, jumping on the Sarah-train.

"Me, too," I say, throwing a couple orange chips onto the table. "And for the lady, too," I add, throwing a thousand-dollar chip to the dealer for Kat.

"Josh, no. You already gave me plenty of gambling money. I'll use the money you gave me."

"Nah, put that away, PG. I've got a feeling—trust me."

In a sudden flurry, every other guy at the table follows suit, throwing their chips onto six, all of them betting on Sarah's intuition.

Kat picks up the dice. "Jeez, talk about pressure," she mutters. She tosses the dice onto the table.

*Easy eight.*

Everyone at the table cheers. It's not a six, true, but it's not crapping out, either, which means we're all still alive.

The dealer quickly distributes winnings on the roll.

"Bets?" the dealer invites.

"Yeah, add this to my six," I say to the dealer, tossing yet another pumpkin to him. "Plus another one for the lady," I say, tossing yet another orange thousand-dollar chip onto the table.

Kat looks at me with wide eyes. "No, Josh. *Stop*. No more."

I wink. "Humor me," I say. "I have a feeling."

Kat presses her lips together, but she doesn't argue. She holds the dice out to Sarah.

"*Vaya con dios,*" Sarah says with solemnity. She blows on them.

"Come on, Blondie," Hawaiian Shirt Guy says. "Roll us a six."

Kat rolls. *Five*. Everyone at the table cheers. We're still alive.

"Add this to the lady's bet on the six," I say, throwing the dealer another orange. “And put this on mine.” I throw him three more orange chips.

Kat takes a deep breath, blows on the dice, and rolls again. *Jackpot.*

The entire table erupts. Kat and Sarah leap into each other’s arms, jumping up and down, while Jonas and I look on, laughing hysterically and shaking our heads.

When Kat disengages from Sarah, she sees the mammoth stack of chips headed her way from the dealer. “Oh my effing God,” she says, her face suddenly turning to ash. She scoops up her winnings with shaking hands, suddenly looking like she’s gonna puke. “I’ve gotta stop rolling now,” she says, her voice tight. “That’s it for me.”

“You can’t stop,” I say. “Your roll’s not finished.”

“I can’t... I’ve gotta stop. I can’t gamble anymore. Oh my God.”

“Good call, Kitty Kat,” Sarah says. “Quit while you’re ahead. Speaking of which.” She turns around, puts her arms around Jonas’ neck for the millionth time tonight, and whispers something into his ear.

Jonas’ entire body jolts. He abruptly pushes all his chips over to Kat’s already mammoth stack, grabs Sarah’s hand, and yanks her away from the table like he’s pulling a blowup doll. “See you guys later,” he calls out over his shoulder.

“See you, bro,” I shout. “Have fun.”

And just like that, the lovebirds disappear into the crowded casino.

“Wait, Jonas!” Kat yells. “Your chips!” But he’s long gone. “Jonas gave me his chips,” Kat says, her eyes wide. “Oh my God. He gave me his chips.”

“Because he wanted you to have them.”

“But that’s got to be—” She does a cursory count of the chips in front of her. “Holy shitballs! Almost fifteen thousand bucks! Plus what I won on that last roll, thanks to your extra bets—oh my effing God. I’ve got like twenty thousand bucks here, Josh.”

“Congratulations.”

“But . . .”

“Kat, whatever Sarah said to Jonas to make him shove those chips at you was obviously far more enticing to him than any amount of money.”

Kat's mouth is hanging open. Obviously, this is a life-changing amount of money for the girl.

"Take it, Kat. You just made everyone at this table a crapload of money, including me. That's how Vegas works, baby. You earned it."

The dealer shoves the dice at Kat. "Still your roll, miss," he says.

She shakes her head. "You roll for a while, Josh. I'll just watch." She plops a tall stack of orange chips in front of me on the ledge of the table.

"What's this?" I ask.

"The money you gave me to gamble with at the beginning, plus the oranges you just threw onto the six for me."

"Come on, Blondie. It's still your roll," Hawaiian Shirt Guy says, clearly getting annoyed.

"Josh, I can't." She looks at me for help, her face tight.

"She's done," I say forcefully—even though I know it's unthinkable for a hot roller to quit mid-roll. Hawaiian Shirt Guy starts protesting, but I glare at him, making him shut his fucking mouth. I tip the dealers a thousand each and scoop up my chips. "Come on, Blondie," I say, staring down Hawaiian Shirt Guy. "Let's go celebrate our good fortune."

We begin walking toward the cashier, our hands overflowing with our bounty.

"I can't keep all this," Kat says. "This is an insane amount of money."

"Don't overthink it."

She holds out her chips. "Really, I can't. Take it before I give in to temptation."

I tilt my head at her. "You got a car payment?" I ask.

She nods.

"Will this pay off the loan?"

She snorts. "And then some."

"Then that settles it. It would be fiscally irresponsible for you *not* to accept this money. Don't be fiscally irresponsible, Kat."

She looks unsure.

I chuckle. "Seriously, Kat. That's chump change to Jonas, and you just made me a ton of money. See?" I hold out my chips to prove it. "I'm *rich*!"

She purses her lips. "Well... are you gonna expect something in return?"

"Nope. No strings attached."

Surprisingly, her face flashes with disappointment, not relief.

*Interesting.*

"Although, of course," I quickly add, "I *do* expect to get something from you tonight—something that's gonna be so fucking awesome, you're gonna thank me profusely and beg me to do it again and again. But you're gonna give it to me because you wanna do it so fucking bad, it hurts—not because you're paying me back for a few stupid gambling chips."

# Chapter 12

*Kat*

"Whatcha drinking?" Josh asks me when the bartender approaches us for our order.

"A dirty martini. Grey goose. Two olives," I say.

"I like your style, Kat." He smiles at the bartender. "Make it two—plus two shots of Gran Patron, please."

When the bartender leaves, Josh turns a heated gaze on me. "Jesus, Kat. You're so fucking beautiful, you're causing me pain."

"Wow. Thank you. You're so fucking beautiful, you're pissing me off."

He laughs. "You're so fucking beautiful, you make me wanna punch a wall."

"Well, you're so fucking beautiful, you make me wanna hurl all over you."

"Wow. Really?"

"Yup."

"Damn. I must be *really* fucking beautiful."

"Or I've got a particularly weak stomach," I say. "Which, actually, I do."

He pauses briefly. "You really are fucking beautiful, Kat." He reaches out, slowly, like he's not sure if I'm gonna stop him or not, and gently touches the tip of his finger to my chin.

I close my eyes. "Holy Who-Knew-a Chin-Could-Be-an-Erogenous-Zone, Batman," I say.

One side of his mouth hitches up. "I've wanted to touch this little cleft in your chin since the minute I first laid eyes on you," he says, his voice low and intense.

I take a deep breath. My flesh feels hot under his fingertip.

His hand migrates to my cheek. He pulls me toward him.

I stiffen, halting my forward progress. "What'd you ask for in your application, Josh?" I whisper.

He leans back sharply. "Seriously?"

I nod.

"Fuck. You're the most stubborn woman in the entire fucking world."

I shrug. "I warned you. I only get more determined."

The bartender puts our drinks in front of us and Josh raises his shot glass.

"To you, Kat. May you soon realize the folly of your ways and stop being so fucking stubborn."

"Thank you, Josh. And to you, as well." I raise my glass. "May you soon realize I never back down so you might as well give me what I want now so we can move quickly to the inevitable conclusion of this ridiculous showdown."

We clink our shots and down them.

"You don't really give a shit what's in my application, do you?" he asks. "You just wanna *win.*"

"Sure, I care. I'm absolutely dying to know. And now that you're being so secretive about it, I wanna know even more." I wag my finger at him. "You should have used reverse psychology on me, Josh. I might have dropped the whole thing if you hadn't been so freaking weird about it."

He scowls. "I'm not being weird about it. It's just... not *relevant*."

I exhale. "What if sleeping with you means waking up in a dog collar, chained to a donkey? That seems like something I should know."

A wide grin spreads across his face.

"Why are you smiling like that?"

"Because you just tacitly admitted you want to sleep with me. Otherwise you wouldn't care if I like donkeys and dog collars."

I scowl at him. "Okay, how about this? I don't need to see the actual application. Just tell me verbally what you said in it. That's my final offer."

"Oh, that's your 'final offer,' huh? You think you're running this negotiation?" He takes a long sip of his drink. "Nope. I don't negotiate with terrorists. Ever."

I throw up my hands. "You're really frustrating, you know that? The harder you fight me on it, the more I wanna know."

"And you gotta know before you'll even *kiss* me now? Not just before you *fuck* me?"

"Correct. The stakes have officially risen."

He exhales with exasperation. "Lame. Just one kiss, Kat. You don't need an application to give me a simple kiss."

"It won't be a simple kiss."

"It won't be a simple kiss," he concedes, nodding. "That's true. Because after one kiss, you're gonna wanna fuck me." He grins. "You won't be able to control yourself."

I roll my eyes, though he's undoubtedly right: if I kiss this man, it's gonna take a grand total of forty-three seconds before I jump his bones. I know it as surely as I know my own name.

"Your demand is patently unfair, you know," he continues. "Because *you* don't have an application to give to *me*. You're asking me to bare my perverted soul to you without getting anything in return. Sex doesn't count because you want it as much as I do."

"Fine, then. I'll lay my perverted soul bare to you, too. I've got nothing to hide. Ask me anything you want—right here and now."

He motions to the bartender. "Another couple shots, please. Gran Patron. Limes. Thanks."

"I'm serious," I say. "I'll show you how truth and honesty works. Let 'er rip."

"Okay." He sits back, assessing me with smoldering eyes. "Admit you're soaking your panties for me right now."

I shift in my seat. "No."

"No, you won't admit it—or no, you're not soaking your panties for me?"

"No, I'm *not* soaking my panties for you."

"Bullshit. It's written all over your face. You're soaking them clean through." He rolls his eyes. "I thought you were gonna model truth and honesty for me. Ha! You're so full of shit." He swigs the last of his drink.

I lean forward and grin. "I'm not full of shit. I'm telling the God's truth. I'm not soaking my panties for you—*because I'm not wearing any panties*."

## Chapter 13

*Josh*

Oh fuck. She's the devil.

My dick is doing fucking jumping jacks in my pants.

I can't breathe.

What the fuck is wrong with this woman? Is she insane? Her dress is barely longer than a fucking T-shirt. Is she trying to give the entire world an unimpeded peek at her pussy? All of a sudden, I can't remove my eyes from her crotch or stop imagining what's hiding just beyond the sequined hem of her itty-bitty dress.

She re-crosses her toned, bare thighs and flips her blonde hair, and I tear my eyes away from her lap.

"Do you always go commando?" I ask. But then I roll my eyes at myself. *That's* my lame response? Who the fuck am I right now—*Jonas*?

"No," she says, laughing. "I typically wear underpants. A teeny-tiny G-string, to be exact." She blows me a kiss and winks.

Oh, she's a fucking sadist.

"That's what I was wearing tonight, actually—a teeny, tiny, black lace G-string—mmmm—but I took it off in the bathroom right before we sat down at the bar." She opens her beaded clutch purse and pulls out a tiny black swatch of lace. "Looks like you're not the only one who likes a little *excitement,* Playboy." She winks again.

Holy fuck. My pulse is suddenly pounding in my ears. I lean forward, right into her gorgeous face.

"Goddammit, Kat. That's it." I pull out my credit card and throw it onto the bar. "This bullshit competition is over. Get up. I'm taking you upstairs right now."

She laughs and doesn't move a muscle. "Great. Can't wait to read your application before we get started."

"Kat. *No*."

"I've told you my terms, Playboy—and I'm prepared to do *anything* I have to do to get what I want." She whirls her undies around on her finger. "*Anything at all*."

I exhale, exasperated. "Dude, you're a freaking suicide bomber, you know that? You want me as much as I want you—but you're willing to blow yourself to smithereens in order to *win*."

She re-crosses her legs, yet again. "Gosh, is it breezy in here? Wow. It feels kinda breezy in here." She mock-shivers and lets out a sexy growl. "God, I wish I had an application to a sex club to keep me warm right now. Brr."

"You're evil," I say, my voice low and intense. "Pure fucking evil. You're a fucking *jihadist*."

She smiles broadly. "Oh, I like that word. I *am*." She laughs. "Oh, God. I really am."

My cock is throbbing. "Half the fun of being with someone new is not knowing what you're getting yourself into in advance. Maybe you wake up chained to a donkey; maybe you don't. It's like opening a present on Christmas. You don't get to ask, 'What's in the box?' before you rip into it—you just rip into it, baby."

She shrugs and re-crosses her legs, yet again. "Interesting theory. Let's agree to disagree."

"I feel like you're licking my balls and punching them at the same time," I say.

She bursts out laughing. "Oh my God. You're hilarious."

"And you're demonic."

"I am. I really am."

"Obviously."

She shrugs. "Sorry. I can't help it. It's the way I am. I have four brothers. You show weakness with four brothers, you're dead."

"You have *four* brothers?"

She nods. "You'd be shocked what I've had to do to survive and thrive in a house with four guys. Holding off on kissing you 'til I get my way, even though all I wanna do right now is kiss the hell out of you—including sucking on that delectable lower lip of yours, by the way, mmm, that's a sexy lower lip—is freaking child's play. So give up now because I *will* get what I want. Just ask my brothers. *I always win*."

I'm rendered speechless for a moment. "Well, joke's on you because I also grew up with four brothers," I finally manage to say. "All of them contained in the sole person of Jonas Faraday. You'd be shocked what I've had to do to survive and thrive in a house with a brother with four personalities. Holding off on kissing you 'til I get my way, even though all I wanna do right now is kiss the hell out of you—including biting that goddamned lower lip of yours and doing unmentionable things to that goddamned cleft in your chin—is freaking child's play."

She parts her lips but doesn't speak.

"Do I give off a Jeffrey Dahmer vibe or something?" I ask, leaning forward into her personal space.

"Not at all." She leans back and sips her drink. "Maybe that's why I'm so damned curious. Your seeming normalcy makes me wonder even more why a guy like you felt the need to join a sex club."

"I didn't *need* to join a sex club—any more than I *need* to go to Tahiti or Monaco."

"Or Disneyland," she adds, snickering.

I roll my eyes. "Or Disneyland. Correct. Joining The Club was a *vacation.*" I sip my drink calmly. "Which means it's soundly in the realm of 'none of your fucking business.' I don't owe you a play-by-play of my vacations. And, news flash, I'm not gonna let you run my credit report or call my ex-girlfriends, either."

She takes another long sip of her drink. "Oh, that's a great idea about calling your ex-girlfriends, Playboy. I didn't think of that. You can email me their contact information along with your application."

I smirk. "You do realize, in theory, you could wake up gagged and chained to a donkey after fucking any guy, right? The fact that I joined The Club doesn't make me any more or less of a pervert-weirdo-serial-killer-donkey-fucker than the average guy."

"Maybe, maybe not. I'll know for sure after I read your application. And by the way, I didn't say anything about waking up *gagged.* You just added that part." She raises one of her eyebrows at me.

I feel my cheeks blazing, despite my best efforts to keep a neutral face.

"Sarah sure enjoyed reading Jonas' application," she says. "Maybe I'll like yours as much as she liked his."

"Ah, so that's what this is about. Jonas and Sarah."

She shrugs, but her body language tells me I've hit the nail on the head.

"But Jonas didn't *willingly* give Sarah his application, you might recall—he sent it to an anonymous intake agent. If Jonas had met Sarah in real life the way I've met you, he never would have given her his fucking application, not in a million years, I guarantee it. Sarah only had it because Jonas had no choice in the matter—and she misappropriated it for her personal use." I sip my drink slowly. "Shame on her."

"But that's my whole point. Jonas wouldn't normally have given it to her—and yet that's exactly why they clicked so hard and fast. All cards on the table. Nothing to hide. No way to hold back, even if they wanted to. I think there's something to that kind of forced honesty."

Oh, she's good, but I'm not gonna fall for her manipulations. "Sure you wanna try it—it's a one-way street. No downside for you."

We sip our drinks again, eying each other.

"Yeah, but most likely a *huge* upside for you," she says. "Think about it like that."

She makes an excellent point, I must admit. But I'd never tell her that. "Did Sarah show you Jonas' application, by any chance?" I ask.

"No. She wouldn't even summarize it verbally for me. And she wouldn't tell me what she wrote to him in response, either."

"Yeah, neither would Jonas. Not a word."

"Damn. I'm dying to know."

"Me, too."

"Well, whatever they said to each other, it sure seems to have worked out well for them." She looks earnest. "It seems like maybe they're on to something with all that... forced honesty."

Well, shit. If I knew she was right—if I knew participating in some sort of bizarre honesty-game would turn out to be some sort of unparalleled aphrodisiac, I'd be all in. I really would. But I don't know if she's right. For all I know, my application could easily have the opposite effect than she's anticipating. It could make her run away, screaming. And, regardless, at this point, I'm probably doomed no matter what it might say. She's pinning so much expectation on the damned thing, it can't possibly live up to whatever kinkfest she's imagining it to be. No matter what it says, it's gonna be anticlimactic now.

And, more importantly, is it gonna open up an entire dialogue I have no intention of having? What I wrote in my application is a fucking time capsule—a moment in time I have no desire to revisit or fucking explain. My stomach twists. Yeah, it's settled. No matter what, I'm *not* gonna give this goddamned terrorist my fucking application.

"Do you usually practice 'complete honesty' with guys before you'll even *kiss* them?" I ask.

"No. I can't remember ever practicing 'complete honesty' with a guy, period," she replies. "Have you ever practiced complete honesty with a woman?"

"Complete?"

"Yeah."

"No. I came very close once. It didn't work out very well."

She twists her mouth.

"But enough about that." I drain my drink. "I don't negotiate with terrorists, like I said. So make your unreasonable demands all night long if you want—you're not getting what you want."

She exhales. "I tell you what. Just *tell* me what your stupid application says—and we'll call it a day. Tell me and then kiss me and then... who knows what might happen next?" She looks at me suggestively.

"Nope."

Her pucker turns to a pout.

"I don't negotiate with terrorists."

"So you keep saying."

"You don't even care about my stupid application. You're just trying to *win.*"

"I could say the same thing about you. At least I'm being reasonable."

"You're being reasonable?"

"Yes. I backed down from my original demand and said you could just *tell* me what's in it. *And* I've offered to answer any questions honestly tonight. But you? You're just sticking to your guns, not budging an inch."

"All right. Show me how it's done." I lean forward, my eyes blazing. "Play the honesty-game."

"Fine. Ask me anything."

"Admit Cameron Fucking Schulz bored you to fucking tears."

She twists her mouth—and then she nods.

I laugh. "*I knew it.*"

"I went back into the restaurant after we talked and after two minutes with the guy I wanted to gouge my eyes out."

"Hey, maybe I like this honesty-game, after all." I chuckle. "So how'd he take it when you turned him down?" I ask, picking up my drink gleefully.

I'm expecting her to laugh with me or at least break into a wide smile. But she doesn't. Instead, she furrows her brow, takes a long sip of her drink, and levels me with an unflinching gaze. "I didn't turn him down."

## Chapter 14

*Josh*

She continues staring at me, her blue eyes sparkling with defiance.

"You *fucked* Cameron Schulz?" I blurt.

Her cheeks flush. "Back at his place." She maintains my gaze, her eyes blazing. "He has a very nice house, bee tee dubs. Just what you'd expect of a professional baseball player."

I don't know whether to cry or scream. Or charter an airplane to Seattle and kick Cameron Fucking Schulz's ass. Oh my fucking God. I glance around the bar, my heart racing, clenching and unclenching my fists.

She fishes a crunchie thing out of the bowl in front of us and pops it into her mouth. "And I'm not sorry or ashamed about it. He was sweet and I got to check off one of my fantasies. (I'm big on fantasies, bee tee dubs. It's kinda my *thing*.) So, yeah, I count the entire experience as a win-win."

I open and shut my mouth like a fish on a line.

"News flash, Playboy. Not all sex has to be deep and meaningful. Even for the members of the species with *vaginas*."

I'm still speechless.

She drains her drink.

"What fantasy did you get to check off?" I finally say. Oh my God, I feel physically ill just saying the words.

"Well, gosh, that's kind of a personal question." She laughs. "But since we're being completely *honest* and all, I'll tell you. One of my all-time fantasies has always been to have sex with a professional athlete—though admittedly, in a manner much more exciting than it went down with Cameron." She pops another crunchie into her mouth. "I slept with a guy on the football team in college who was drafted by the Lions his senior year, but he went pro *after* I slept with him so I don't think that counts as having sex with a pro athlete. Do you think it does?" She pops another crunchie thing into her mouth and washes it down with her martini.

I press my lips together, incapable of saying a goddamned thing. I'm feeling a strange mixture of arousal and rage and complete repulsion.

"Oh, please," she finally says. "You think sex *always* has to be something deep and meaningful and profound? Pffft."

I make a face.

"Well, then. Why should it be any different for me? Just because I have a *vagina*?"

I lean back in my chair. "So you say. I'm not sure I believe it."

She laughs.

"Just tell me right now, Kat. Do you really have a vagina? Because I swear to fucking God, if you're hiding a dick and balls under there, I'm gonna lose my fucking shit."

She laughs. "I'm not a dude. I promise."

"Because you're acting like a dude right now."

"Nope. Rest assured, I do indeed have a *vagina* and ovaries and fallopian tubes. Oh, and boobs, too, which I've been told multiple times are 'absolutely perfect,' bee tee dubs. But I can certainly understand your confusion about my genitalia, because I'm actually an *honorary* dude, probably from growing up with four brothers and all."

I can't formulate a response. My head is reeling.

"And, to be clear, I don't have *only* meaningless sex. I absolutely love meaningful sex, too, but I'm not hung up about it either way. I do what I want—oh, and I'm very *selective*. I'm just saying when I *do* have meaningless sex, it's because I want to do it—and, therefore, I'm not at all sorry or ashamed about it. My choice."

I mull that over.

"So I take it you've never had meaningless sex, then?" she asks. "That's so sweet."

"This is a really bizarre conversation. Excuse me," I say to the bartender. "Two more shots of Patron, please."

"Have you ever wished you could have meaningless sex, Josh?" she persists.

I roll my eyes. "I've had meaningless sex, Kat."

"But it was somehow supposed to be simultaneously meaning*ful* for the woman you were screwing, is that it?"

"No. Of course, not."

"Well, there you go. Works both ways. Have you ever had *meaningful* sex?"

"Of course. I strongly prefer it, actually. But I find it's much, much harder to come by."

She nods. "I agree. I prefer it, too—and, yes, it's much, *much* harder to come by."

We stare at each other for a long beat.

The bartender places our shots in front of us.

"To you, Kat—to the honorary dude who's blowing my mind right now."

"To you, Josh—to the playboy who's maybe not quite as much of a playboy as I originally thought."

We knock back our shots.

"Whew," she says. "I can't feel my toes."

"So do you possess any other dude-like qualities besides unapologetically engaging in meaningless sex with sports stars?" I ask.

"Well, my brothers say I laugh like a dude, but I don't know about that."

"You do. Totally."

"I hardly ever cry."

"Okay. That's a plus."

"I'm not easily offended, but when I am, watch the fuck out, because I've got a fucking temper, motherfucker, and I will cut you."

"Whoa. Good to know. Anything else?"

"Well, I can burp the alphabet. And I don't flinch when men fart around me—the sound of men farting is just white noise to me at this point, like a sound machine that lulls me to sleep."

I laugh. "Wow."

"Yup."

"What about girlie stuff? Tell me some of that stuff so I don't start imagining you hiding a dick and balls under there."

"Well, let's start with the biggest girlie thing of all: I have a *vagina*."

"That's definitely a biggie. Glad to hear it."

"Oh, and here's something. I like saying the word *vagina*. Vagina, vagina, vagina. I say it a lot. *Vagina*."

"Actually, I think that's another dude thing. Vagina, vagina, vagina. See? I like saying it, too. *Vagina.*"

"Or maybe that's a *girlie* thing about *you*."

"Hmm. I never thought of it that way. *Vagina*. Hmm. I dunno. You may be right."

"Have you noticed people never say that word?" she says. "Why is that?"

"Because they're pussies," I reply.

She laughs.

"What else?" I ask. "Tell me something really girlie about you that'll prove you've got a *vagina* under there, once and for all."

"Okay. Well, I'm a sucker for sequins and fringe."

"You and Neil Diamond. That proves nothing."

She laughs. "Good point. You're right. Okay. Let's see. Pink is my favorite color." She looks up at the ceiling, thinking. "I love getting pedicures and doing yoga and drinking white wine. Oh, and eating cupcakes. That's all pretty girlie."

"Especially if you do all of it while wearing sequins and fringe," I say.

She laughs. "I have Hello Kitty sheets on my bed. And I'm not talking about my childhood room at my parents' house. I currently have Hello Kitty sheets on my bed in my apartment."

"Whoa."

"Kitty Kat," she says by way of explanation. She winks.

"I figured."

"Let's see. Well, my all-time favorite movie is *The Bodyguard.* My close second after that is *Pretty Woman*. And the bronze goes to *Magic Mike.*"

"Okay, okay. That's it," I say, holding up my hands. "I need nothing further. I'm now one hundred percent convinced you've got a *vagina*."

"Whew. What a relief. I was beginning to worry my dick was really, really tiny."

I laugh.

We sit and stare at each other for a long moment. I'd pay an inordinate amount of money to know what she's thinking right now. Right after paying an inordinate amount of money to fuck her.

"You said sleeping with a pro athlete is *one* of your fantasies?" I say.

"Correct. Well, it *was*." She snickers and makes a "check mark" motion with her finger in the air.

I grimace.

She laughs. "But, actually, my pro-athlete fantasy is a bit more elaborate than what I did with Cameron. And it involves an NFL player, actually—not a baseball star—so maybe that checkmark was a wee bit premature."

"Wow. Your fantasy is pretty specific, huh?"

She nods. "MVP of the Super Bowl, to be exact—in the locker room after the big game."

"Interesting. Are all your fantasies that specific?"

She nods. "You have no idea."

"You've got a lot of fantasies?" I ask.

"I do. Lots and lots." She sips her drink.

I'm finding it a bit hard to breathe. "All of them *specific*?"

"Most of them."

"Tell me some of them," I say. I can feel my cheeks blazing.

She leans forward. "I'll tell you *all* of them—*just as soon as you tell me what you wrote in your application.*"

I smile. "Here we go again. No."

She exhales. "Okay, then. No fantasies for you." She licks her lips. "Too bad. You would have liked them."

I squint at her.

"Answer a question for me, Josh."

"Maybe. Maybe not." I sip my drink.

"Did you sleep with someone while you were in New York?"

I choke on my drink. Jesus. This woman's gonna be the death of me.

Under any other circumstances, I'd lie right now. But after what she told me about Cameron, that's obviously not an option.

I take a long, deep breath. "Yeah."

Her eyes light up. "*I knew it*. Such a hypocrite."

"I'm not a hypocrite. I slept with a girl I used to know a long time ago. We both just happened to be in New York at the same time, by sheer coincidence. Completely meaningless."

She smiles. "Ah. Blast-from-your-past sex—definitely *not* a fantasy of mine." She shudders. "That can be dangerous."

"Dangerous? How so?"

"It can bring up old feelings—and usually only for *one* person, which is *never* good." She shudders again.

I scoff. "There were no old feelings to bring up. We dated for, like, four months seven years ago, and I don't think we had sober sex more than twice."

She purses her lips. "How'd you guys wind up hooking up after all this time?"

I exhale. "It's a long story."

"I've got time."

I have no desire to tell this story. I exhale and run my hand through my hair.

"Come on, Playboy. Spill it."

I roll my eyes. "My good friend Reed happened to be in New York last week because one of his bands was doing *Saturday Night Live.* Coincidentally, Reed's ex-girlfriend Isabel and her best friend—the girl in question—had just come back from a week in France and stopped in New York so Isabel could do this TV interview thing. The girls figured out Reed and I were both in New York by total coincidence—thank you, Instagram—so they invited us to go to the show taping with them. After the show, we all went out for dinner and drinks and I... got... shit-faced... and made an impulsive and extremely stupid decision." I feel sick. I wouldn't normally be saying a word of this to anyone, let alone a woman I'm interested in sleeping with. Why am I saying all this?

Kat sips her drink quietly. "So your friend Reed's in a band?"

"That's what you want to know after everything I just said? You wanna know if my friend Reed's in a band?"

She shrugs. "To start with, yeah."

"No, Reed's not in a band—he owns a record label. He also co-owns a dance club here in Vegas. Maybe I'll take you there tonight."

"Oh, I'd love that. I *love* to dance. Who's the band that played on *Saturday Night Live*?"

I pause. "That's really what you're curious about? You're not gonna ask me about *her*?"

"Oh, I'm getting there, trust me. I'm just playing it cool."

I laugh. “Ah, stealing a page out of my book.”

“It’s a good page.”

“Red Card Riot.”

“*That’s* the band on your friend’s label? Wow. I love them.”

“Yeah, they’re awesome.”

She screeches the chorus from Red Card Riot’s monster rock hit, “Shaynee.”

“Great song,” I say.

“Have you met them?” she asks.

“No, the guys in the band didn’t come out with us in New York. I think they had some groupies to ‘meet and greet.’”

“I’m sure they did. They’re huge right now—your friend Reed must be thrilled.”

“Yeah. He’s always had quite the knack for spotting talent. A bit of a Midas touch.”

She takes a sip of her drink and then levels me with an unflinching gaze. “So do you plan to see her again?”

“Okay, here we go.”

“I told you I’d get to it.”

“And you did.”

She pauses. “So do you plan to see her?”

“No.” I snort. “Never. Like I said. It was completely meaningless.”

She chews the inside of her mouth.

“Do you plan to see Mr. Baseball again?” I ask, my heart pounding.

“No.”

“Really?”

“Really.”

“He wants to see *you* again, though, right?”

She nods.

“You’re not gonna say yes when he asks?”

“He’s already asked twice. And I’ve already said no both times.” She presses her lips together. “I told him very clearly it wasn’t gonna work out. I was nice about it, but clear.”

I make a caveman sound.

“What does that grunt mean?”

“It means I’m plotting his murder in my head.”

"Why? He didn't do anything wrong."

I grunt again.

She smiles. "You're *jealous*?"

"Of course, I'm jealous. Fuck yeah, I am."

"But I just told you I'm not gonna see him again."

"So what. I can't get a certain visual out of my head and it's making me crazy."

Her smile broadens.

"You like that I'm jealous?"

She thinks for a minute. "Usually, I'd say no—that I hate jealous bullshit. But, yeah, I'm liking it." She bites her lip. "So does Miss Blast from Your Past wanna see you again?"

I nod. "She seems to think we've got some sort of... *soul connection*." I make a face. "But I've already told her it's not gonna happen."

"Hmmph."

"What does that mean? Are you *jealous* of Miss Blast from My Past?"

"Honestly?"

"Of course. Isn't that what we're doing here—playing the honesty-game 'til we both wanna bang our heads against a wall?"

She laughs. "Um... I'm more like *envious*, I think, but, no, not *jealous*. I don't get jealous when I'm not in a relationship." She glares at me, clearly telling me my jealousy about Cameron Schulz is premature. "Now, if you were my *boyfriend* and I found out you'd fucked another woman, then, yes, I'd be so jealous I'd burn your fucking house down. And then I'd cut off your balls, roast them over the burning embers of your house, smash them between two graham crackers with a Hershey bar and make testicle-s'mores out of them, which I would then gobble up as I stood over your writhing, whimpering body on the ground."

Holy shit. I'm so shocked, I can't even laugh. But Kat does—in fact, she belly laughs and throws back her head, completely enthralled with herself.

"And do you wanna know *why* I'd burn your house down and make myself s'mores out of your balls, my dearest Josh?"

I shake my head. "I'm too scared of you to even venture a guess."

"Because if you were my *boyfriend*, I would never, ever cheat on you, I can promise you that on a stack of bibles. *Never.* I've never cheated and I never will. And here's why: because I never agree to be someone's *girlfriend* unless I'm one hundred percent willing to give the guy my whole heart. And as the relationship progresses, if I'm feeling like cheating, then I don't stay. It's scorched earth maybe, but a man never, ever has to wonder where my feelings stand." She picks up her drink. "It also means that, if you were my boyfriend and you cheated on me, then you'd undoubtedly be breaking my heart."

I place my palm on my chest, steadying myself. I look down at the bar, collecting myself. This girl just knocked the wind out of me.

"But since you and I aren't even dating, then, no, I'm not *jealous*." She takes a long sip of her drink. "Because I can't justify getting jealous when a man's not mine to begin with."

"I've never met anyone like you, Kat," I manage to say.

"Thank you," she says. "I've never met anyone like you, either."

"You're like some bizarre, undiscovered species of fish that washes ashore after a nuclear disaster and freaks everyone the fuck out," I say.

She laughs. "Wow. That's your idea of a compliment?"

"I'm normally much smoother than this, I assure you. You bring out the Jonas in me."

She laughs. "Jonas seems pretty damned smooth, actually."

"Not usually. Just with Sarah all of a sudden. She brings out the Josh Faraday in him, I guess."

She grins and I can't help smiling back at her like a fucking dope.

There's a very long beat, during which we're smiling at each other, not saying a damned thing. Finally, Kat bites her lip and touches my hand, sending electricity throughout my entire body.

"For God's sake, Playboy," she purrs, "just tell me what's in your application so we can get this show on the road. Please?" She squeezes my hand and licks her lips. "I'm suddenly feeling extremely... *impatient*."

Oh man, she's good. She's very, very good. But she's also shit out of luck. There's no fucking way I'm giving this girl my application. Period. And certainly not in exchange for the honor of fucking her. Hell no, when she finally fucks me, it's gonna be for no other reason than she's dying for it, not because I gave her some stupid application.

I drain the rest of my drink. "Nope." I clap my hands together. "Getting this show on the road is entirely up to you, Party Girl. All you have to do is kiss me, just once, and then I'll know you've conceded your demands and have finally decided to find out the good old-fashioned way if I'm gonna chain you to a donkey or not."

She smirks. "No, no, no, my dearest Playboy; you've got it backwards. What's actually gonna happen is *you're* gonna kiss *me*—thereby signaling to *me* you agree to my demands and will give me what I want."

We stare each other down.

"I'm not gonna give you my application, Kat. It's none of your fucking business."

"Oh, I think you are."

"Nope."

She puckers. "I'm a really good kisser, Playboy." She raises an eyebrow. "At least, that's what Cameron Schulz said."

I squint at her. "You're evil."

"I am."

I motion to the bartender. "Check, please." I glare at her for a long beat. She looks so fucking sure of herself—and so fucking hot, I doubt this girl's experienced disappointment once in her entire life. "Okay, Party Girl," I say. "The time for chitchat is over. I'm not gonna give you what you want—which means you're not gonna fuck me." I make a sad face and she matches it. "So I guess that means there's only one thing left for us to do," I continue.

"And what would that be?"

"Dance, of course."

Her face lights up. "Oh, I *love* to dance."

"Well, of course, you do. You're the *Party Girl With a Hyphen*, for fuck's sake."

She grins.

"It's time for you to earn that nickname of yours, babe." I touch the cleft in her chin one more time and then put out my hand. "Let's go, baby. Time to paint Sin City red."

# Chapter 15

*Kat*

Josh slams the taxi door shut and we bound toward "the hottest dance club in Vegas," hand in hand. A line of immaculately dressed people waiting to get into the club wraps around the side of the building and down the block, but, apparently, lines don't apply to Josh Faraday—because he grabs my hand and pulls me past the throngs of people and straight to the front doors.

"Hey, Barry," Josh says to a very, very large black man standing at the front door of the club.

The man beams a huge smile at Josh. "Joshua Faraday," he says, bumping fists with Josh. "I didn't know you were coming out tonight."

"Yeah, it was super last minute. Is Reed in town, by any chance?"

"Yeah, he just flew in this afternoon. Have you texted him?"

"A few minutes ago, but he hasn't responded yet. Will you let him know I'm here? We'll hang out by the downstairs bar for a bit so he can find us." Josh motions to me. "Oh, sorry. Barry, this is my lovely date for the evening, Kat."

"Hello there, Kat," Barry says in his deep voice. He puts out his hand and I take it.

"Nice to meet you, Barry," I say.

"Careful, Barry. Don't look her in the eyes. She'll hypnotize you with that fucking gorgeous face and try to trick you into telling her your darkest secrets."

I look at Josh, flabbergasted, but Josh and Barry are laughing easily together.

"I dunno, Josh. Seems like there are much worse things that

could happen to a guy than getting royally fucked over by this one here."

"Amen, brother," Josh says.

"Uh . . ." I say, at a loss for words. I think Barry just complimented me, but I'm not sure if "thank you" is an appropriate reply.

Before I can figure out what to say, Barry opens the velvet rope and motions for us to pass into the club. "Have fun, kids. Go easy on him, Kat. He's a good guy." He chuckles. "I'll tell Reed you're here."

The minute Josh and I enter the club, I slip into some sort of hedonism-induced coma. I've been to my share of nightclubs, but I've never seen a temple to pure excess quite like this. Almost-nude women "bathe" throughout the club in clear Plexiglas bathtubs filled with flower petals; lithe, rippling acrobats in skin-tight bodysuits hang from the ceiling on trapeze swings, twisting and gyrating like the performers Josh and I saw earlier tonight with Jonas and Sarah at *Cirque Du Soleil*; seizure-inducing lights and lasers are bouncing around every square inch of the place; and screens scattered throughout the club flash shocking pornographic images in rapid-fire succession, so fast my brain isn't sure what my eyes just witnessed. It's sheer spectacle. Obscenity. Titillation to the extreme. *And I love it.*

Josh pulls me to a long, sparkling bar and flags down the bartender.

"Martini?" he shouts into my ear above the thumping music.

"Shots!" I yell. "So we can get onto the dance floor right away."

"Good idea!" Josh shouts back and turns toward the bar.

Oh man, I'm ready to dance. Even standing here at the bar, my body's already begun involuntarily herking and jerking to the bass-heavy beat.

A phenomenally good-looking guy in a suit sidles up to Josh and taps him on the shoulder. Josh turns toward the unidentified tap and, when he sees the guy, his entire face lights up. The two men hug with what looks like extreme affection and as they break apart the guy kisses Josh on his cheek with a giant, enthusiastic swak.

Josh motions to me, talking into the guy's ear, and Mr. Handsome smiles and waves at me, though I can't hear a thing above the thumping music.

Josh leans into my ear. "Reed's part-owner of this club."

"Nice to meet you Reed," I say, but it's clear he can't hear me. He just smiles and waves again. Wow. He's a really, really good-looking man. I lick my lips. I guess hotties travel in packs. *The Brotherhood of the Traveling Hottie McHottie-pants*, I think, making myself laugh.

The bartender places the shots in front of us on the bar, and Josh distributes them among the three of us.

Josh leans into Reed's ear and says something and they both burst out laughing. Reed nods and slaps Josh's back.

Damn, I wish I had superhuman hearing right now. But all I can hear is the blaring music. Appropriately, the song playing right now is "I Can't Feel My Face" by The Weekend, a song about a guy who, of course, can't feel his face, presumably because he's drunk or high. On what, though, it's not clear. Booze? Lust? Whichever it is (or both), I'm right there with him. Fo shizzle-pops.

Josh and Reed are still talking in each other's ears and laughing, so I begin dancing in place to the music, marveling at just how little I can feel my face. Or toes. Or brain. I'm verging on drunk, actually. And it feels hella good.

"Thanks, bro," I hear Josh say. "I owe you one."

"You bet."

Josh turns his gaze on me and smiles like a wolf. He leans into my ear and snakes his arm around my waist.

"You still going commando?" he asks, right in my ear. His hand migrates down to my ass.

"I guess you'll have to find out for yourself," I say. "Right after you kiss me and concede to my terrorist demands," I say.

He laughs. "You mean after *you* kiss *me* and give up your fucking *jihad*."

I shake my head and retract my lips completely into my mouth, signaling my lips are unkissable until he gives me what I want.

He laughs and grabs my hand. "Come on, Madame Terrorist. It's time to dance."

# Chapter 16

*Kat*

Holy hell.

If dancing is any indication whatsoever of a man's sexual prowess, then Josh Faraday is a sex god. Oh my God, the way he swivels and rocks those hips makes me yearn for him to grind them just like that on top of me while wearing nothing but a cocky smile. Holy shitballs. This man can *move*.

The song playing is "Want To Want Me" by Jason Derulo and Josh knows every word. He's singing the song to me, serenading me—and with so much charm and swagger, I can't help but laugh with glee. I can't remember having this much fun dancing with a guy—with my girlfriends, sure. But with a guy? A *hot* guy? No. Usually, when I'm dancing with a really hot guy, I'm so concerned about coming off as sexy and desirable to him, I forget to just let loose and have fun. But Josh makes it impossible to feel anything but totally uninhibited. Oh my God, I'm laughing too much to even try to be sexy. I throw my hands above my head and wiggle my hips and giggle uncontrollably, mirroring Josh's confident movement, and he laughs his ass off at every little thing I do. And the crazy thing is, having fun like this is making me so wet, I'm worried I'm gonna drip down my bare thigh in this shorty-short dress.

As the song reaches its conclusion, Josh looks up toward the balcony and locks eyes with Reed. He gives Reed a thumbs up and Reed returns the gesture. When Josh's eyes dart back to me, he levels me with a smile that makes me feel like he's planning to put me in an oven with some onions and potatoes.

The song abruptly changes to a hip-hop song I don't know. But, clearly, Josh does—because as the rapper begins spitting out lyrics,

Josh mouths every single word along with him. Oh my God, Josh is freaking hilarious right now. He's thugging out to the song, going all in, shaking his ass and owning it. Oh man, I've never seen a concoction of maleness quite like this before. He's raw and smooth and funny and hot and goofy all at the same time. He's redefining sexy for me, right here and now. He's just... wow.

I listen intently to the lyrics of the song, trying to plumb the depths of my dance-club memories, but nope, I don't recognize it. I pull out my phone, activate my Shazam app—and just when the song title displays on my phone—"Kiss Me" by Lil Wayne—Josh begins singing along to the chorus. "Kiss me," Josh raps, grinding his hips like he's auditioning for *Magic Mike*. "Kiss me."

I laugh. What a sneaky little bastard. And a hilarious one.

He inches closer and closer to me, still rapping and grinding his hips ferociously, until, suddenly, and with great dramatic flair, he grabs me, pulls me into him, and grinds his body into mine with enthusiastic thrusts to the beat of the music. "Kiss me," he says to me, his lips on my ear, his intoxicating cologne wafting into my nostrils. His strong hands encircle my waist and grip my back as he presses his undulating body into mine. His lips migrate to my cheek, where they trail the length of my jawbone. His tongue laps at my neck.

Oh muh guh. Playtime's over. Shit just got real.

His hard-on presses into me, thrusting, grinding, making my knees weak—and, holy shitballs, there's no mistaking the size of that hard bulge, even through the man's pants. Good lord. Josh doesn't need to chain me to a donkey—he's got it covered on his own.

He parts my legs with his thigh and grinds his hard dick right into my clit, over and over, still rapping and groping me as he does.

I throw my head back.

*Yes.*

My clit ignites inside my panties. I'm beginning to warp and ache. My skin is beginning to prickle.

"Kiss me," he says into my ear, gyrating his body against mine. Oh my God. He's taking my breath away.

His mouth skims my ear and lands on my cheek and then my neck. I run my fingers into his hair, pressing my breasts into the hardness of his chest and my crotch into the bulge of his pelvis. Oh God. He nuzzles the tip of his nose against mine, teasing me. His lips are an inch away from mine, skimming, teasing, hovering as close as humanly possible without actually making contact, his erection continuing to grind into me as his mouth taunts me.

The song is thumping in my ears.

The lights on the dance floor are entrancing me.

My body is moving in time with his.

He smells so frickin' good, I wanna ingest him.

I feel dizzy.

Weak.

Frenzied.

I lift my leg and encircle his hip with it, aching to take him inside me. He shifts position and presses himself even more feverishly against me, sending his hard-on right up against the exact spot that makes me burst into flames.

Yeeeeeeeeoooowwwwwwww. *Yes.* Right there. I press into him harder, moaning, and he rubs that hard bulge ferociously against me, still rapping the words to the song.

His hand navigates under the hem of my dress and brushes against my bare ass cheek, causing goose bumps to erupt all over my body.

Without the slightest hesitation, he fingers my ass crack, presumably trying to figure out if I'm wearing a G-string, and when he finds the string, he slides his fingers all the way down it, down, down, down, and then forward, straight to the crotch, where his fingers begin exuberantly stroking the soft, extremely wet fabric of my panties.

My knees buckle and he holds me up, his fingers continuing to stroke. He kisses my ear and then my neck, yet again, rapping into my ear. "Kiss me," he purrs.

His lips migrate to mine and hover, yet again, just over my lips, inviting me to bridge the gap and slip my tongue into his mouth—inviting me to lay my weapon down.

But I don't.

"Terrorist," he breathes.

Without warning, his fingers slip underneath the fabric of my G-string and plunge right into my wetness.

Holy fuckburgers.

I cry out in surprise and extreme pleasure, pressing myself into his fingers and gyrating to the pulsing music.

"You're so fucking hot," he whispers in my ear. "Stop torturing me."

I don't reply, but he can plainly feel how badly I want him, too. I'm absolutely dripping for him.

I moan loudly right into his ear and lick his cheek, and his body responds against mine with obvious excitement. I run my hands through his hair, grinding myself into his fingers like I'm riding on top of a big, hard cock. I inhale sharply. I can't breathe. My body is warping. "Oh God, here it comes," I say into his ear. "A big one. Oh God. Josh, yeah. Don't stop. Just like that."

A huge orgasm slams into me and I stiffen in his arms, my loud moans swallowed by the blaring music as my body clenches around his fingers, over and over.

"Oh shit," he says. "Yeah, baby. Do it."

When the clenching and warping and rippling stops, I can barely stand. I nuzzle my face into his neck and he holds me close, supporting my entire body weight in his arms. He presses his body into mine as he holds me, and our bodies sway together to the loud, thumping music.

A new song begins. "In Da Club" by 50 Cent.

He suddenly pulls back from me and puts his hands on my face. His chest is rising and falling sharply. His gaze is intense.

By the look on his face, I'd guess he's trying to decide if fucking me counts as losing the bet. Or, at least, that's what I'm trying to figure out. Did we decide *kissing* or *fucking* ends our stalemate? I can't remember now.

Sweaty bodies are bouncing and swaying all around us on the dance floor, but we're standing stock still, looking at each other, trembling with pent-up desire. I tilt my face up to his and close my eyes, inviting him to swoop in and kiss me already. But he doesn't take the bait.

"*Fuck*," he says.

I open my eyes.

He's glaring at me like he's enraged at me.

He releases my face, grabs my hand, and begins dragging me across the packed dance floor. It takes effort to snake through the sea of bouncing people, but finally we're off the dance floor, working our way through the crowded club. The restrooms are in sight—but there are long lines of people waiting to get into both sets. Is that where he was intending to take me? Or was he headed to the exit? Or maybe to the bar? Any of these destinations is equally possible, given our current location in the club.

He stops walking.

"Fuck," he says, gripping my hand. He looks up at the ceiling for a brief moment, apparently gathering himself. "Goddammit."

50 Cent raps his famous line about being into *sex* rather than *lovemaking* and I can't help but sing along at the appropriate moment.

Josh chuckles. "You're hell on wheels, Kat. Jesus Christ."

Out of nowhere, Reed appears next to us, swatting Josh on his shoulder. "Hey, man."

"Oh, hey, bro." Josh glances at me, a wistful smile on his lips. "Thanks for the song."

"Did it work?" Reed looks at me. "Did you kiss him?"

I shake my head. "Nope."

"*No*? Uh oh. Are you losing your touch, Faraday? I thought it was a foolproof plan."

"Hell no, I'm not losing my touch. I'm wise and powerful; you know that. This woman's not normal. She's made of fucking steel or something—the most stubborn woman alive."

"Oh, she's *stubborn*, huh?" Reed says. "So she's the female version of you?"

Josh laughs. "Hey, maybe that explains why I find her so goddamned attractive." He squeezes my hand.

Reed laughs. "So, hey, man, there's someone I want you to meet." He looks over his shoulder, zeroes in on some guy across the room, and motions to him. "I just signed this amazing guy to the label—a rapper-singer-songwriter-multi-instrumentalist. Oh my God, he's so fucking incredible, man, I'm crapping myself that we got him. A year from now, mark my words, he's gonna be the biggest thing in music."

A blonde guy with tattoos walks up with a beautiful, dark-haired girl on his arm.

"Guys, this is Will Riley—'2Real'—one of the most talented songwriters and performers you're ever gonna meet, no exaggeration—and his girlfriend, Carmen."

"Aw, thanks, Reed," Will says. "Hey, guys."

Carmen smiles sweetly and waves at us in greeting—and she instantly reminds me of Sarah.

"This is my buddy, Josh Faraday, and his apparently *stubborn* friend, Kat."

"Hey, Josh," Will says. "Hey, Stubborn Kat. That sounds like a character from a comic strip—like some sort of bad *Garfield* rip-off."

Josh laughs. "Oh no! Stubborn Kat won't get off the couch and it's already noon."

"Damn it, Stubborn Kat! She won't chase the ball of yarn," I add. "No matter how many times you throw it for her."

"Chase a mouse?" Reed says. "Hell no. Stubborn Kat just painted her claws."

"Damn that, Stubborn Kat," Josh adds.

"Stubborn Kat won't do *anything* you want her to do—as *usual*. Aw, gosh, Stubborn Kat!" Will says.

We all laugh hysterically.

"So, hey, guys," Reed says, "I'm throwing a little party in the penthouse suite right now. The guys in Red Card Riot just got into town for their show at the Garden Arena tomorrow night, and they're ready to blow off some steam tonight. Plus, we're celebrating Will coming on board. You two wanna join the party?"

Josh looks at me for confirmation and I nod furiously.

"Yeah, absolutely."

"Hey, isn't Henn in town with you?"

"Yeah."

"Well, call that little fucker and tell him to join us."

"I doubt he'll come. He's working on an important job tonight."

"Well, shit, man." Reed looks at his watch. "It's almost two. Call him and see if he's done for the night. It's not a raging party 'til Peter Hennessey breaks out his dance moves."

Both guys laugh hysterically.

"Oh man," Josh says, shaking his head. "One of the simple pleasures in life. I'll call that little fucker right now."

## Chapter 17
*Kat*

When Josh and I walk through the door of Reed's penthouse suite, along with Reed, Will, and Carmen, we join a raging party already in progress in the most magnificent hotel suite I could ever imagine. The interior is fit for a sheik—twice the size of Jonas and Sarah's suite—plus, French doors at the far side of the massive main room reveal a private terrace and swimming pool outside.

I glance around, my heart racing. Insanely attractive people are milling around, lounging, laughing, swigging drinks, smoking pot, making out—and I'd say half of them are at least vaguely recognizable to me from my near-constant consumption of celebrity gossip.

Reed motions to two young guys on the couch smoking pot—a strawberry blondie with piercings and tattoos and a dark-haired hottie with striking, cobalt blue eyes—and they stride over to Reed and bro-hug him.

"Hey, man," the dark-haired hottie says to Reed, hugging him.

"How was Dallas?" Reed asks.

"Fucking awesome," dark-haired-hottie says. "Great crowd. It still gives me chills every time an entire arena sings along to a song I wrote." He grins adorably.

Reed pats his cheek. "Get used to it, Baby Dino. Where are the other guys?"

"Around here somewhere. Probably passed out. It's been a long-ass day."

Reed addresses our small group. "Everyone, this is Dean Masterson and C-Bomb from Red Card Riot. RCR is playing tomorrow night at the MGM Grand—lemme know if any of you want tickets to the show."

Will and Carmen instantly leap at the offer, thanking Reed profusely, while I jump up and down, tugging on Josh's arm.

Josh laughs at my exuberance. "Looks like Kat's in for sure. But I'm not sure what the fuck we've got going on tomorrow night—I'm in town for this thing with my brother." Josh looks at Will and Carmen. "If it turns out I can't go, can Kat go with you guys?"

Oh. It didn't occur to me we might be tied up tomorrow night with our mission to take down The Club, whatever the heck that means. "Oh, no, Josh, that's okay," I mumble. "I wouldn't go without you."

"Of course, you would. You can't miss seeing RCR—and from the VIP section, no less."

"Fuck the VIP section," Reed says. "I'll take you backstage, Kat. You can watch the show from there."

"Really?" I say. "Wow."

"Thanks, man," Josh says.

"No problem, bro. Just text me when you know who's going tomorrow," Reed says. "Jonas, Henn, whoever's in your group. Just lemme know. Speaking of which, where's Henn? I miss that little fucker."

"I called him. He's still working," Josh says. "He said he might be able to break free tomorrow night, depending on how the work thing goes. It's all really up in the air."

"Okay, lemme know. So, Dean," Reed says to the dark-haired hottie, "2Real's been writing songs for his debut album. Wait 'til you hear what this guy writes. Fucking brilliant. Game-changing. I'm not exaggerating. You're gonna wanna get in on this. I was thinking you two might set up a writing sesh when you're back in L.A. after the tour? I have a feeling if you guys lock yourselves into a room together for a day, a number one hit's gonna come out of it."

"Sure," Dean says. "I'd love to."

"Sick," Will says, his face bursting with excitement. "Looking forward to it."

The two guys exchange numbers.

"You guys just did *SNL,* right?" Will asks.

"Yeah. Last week. Surreal," Dean says.

"Were you shitting your pants the whole time?"

Dean laughs. "Totally."

Everyone laughs.

"I'd totally shit my pants, too, no doubt about it," Will says.

"Well, then, you'd better invest in some fucking Depends, 2Real," Reed says. "Because you'll be doing *SNL* one of these days, too—sooner rather than later, I predict."

Will pulls Carmen into him. "That'd be so fucking insane." His face is on fire.

"There's no doubt in my mind," Carmen says, nuzzling into him.

Josh begins chatting comfortably with the RCR boys and Will about music and the tour, but I'm completely mute. It's totally out of character for me, but I can't seem to think of anything witty to say, so I figure I'd better not talk at all. How did I get here? Red Card Riot's hit "Shaynee" was playing in the taxi on the way to Reed's club, and now two members of the band are standing here, swigging beers and chatting amiably with Josh about their show in Dallas earlier tonight? It takes a lot to make me speechless, but, by God, I am.

Josh puts his arm around me. "Are you okay, PG?"

"Yeah. Why?"

"You're awfully quiet."

"I'm just... stunned."

He laughs. "How 'bout a drink?"

I nod, though I'm already feeling extremely buzzed, truth be told.

"A martini?"

I shake my head. "Surprise me," I say. "I love surprises."

He winks. "My kinda girl."

After Josh leaves, I unabashedly eavesdrop on Will's conversation with Dean and C-Bomb. They're talking about their musical influences with incredible passion. God, I wish my youngest brother, Dax, were here. Listening to these guys talk would be his dream come true.

After a moment, my eyes drift to Carmen and I notice she looks a little bit lost.

I move to her and put my arm around her shoulder. "Hey, Carmen. Is this party as overwhelming to you as it is to me?"

Carmen twists her mouth adorably. "I feel like a deer in headlights," she admits. "It wasn't too long ago I was watching Will perform at a local club for fifty people."

"Have you and Will been together a long time?"

She nods. "About two years. What about you and Josh?"

"Oh, we're not a couple. This is just our first night out."

"Seriously? Wow. I would have guessed you've been together forever."

I laugh. "That's funny."

I glance across the suite at Josh—he's deep in concentration, making some sort of complicated concoction at the bar—and my skin buzzes at the mere sight of him.

Carmen rests her cheek on my shoulder in the most adorably affectionate way, making me think of Sarah again.

"Carmen, you remind me so much of my best friend, Sarah, it's uncanny."

"I do?"

I nod. "She's the best. Gorgeous, funny, super-duper smart. Weird." I laugh. "The sweetest girl you'll ever meet."

"Well, thanks. It sounds like you've just given me a huge compliment."

"Definitely."

Josh returns with two glasses and hands me a red-colored drink.

"What is it?" I ask, sniffing it. "You looked like you were busy building an atomic bomb over there."

"It's an original creation. I call it a Kiss," he says, a cocky grin spreading across his face.

"Oh, really? I've never had one of those—at least not from you," I say.

"I figured you were dying to taste a Kiss from me, though." He winks. "So I decided to make your dreams come true."

I smirk. "Gee, thanks. What's exactly in a Kiss from Josh Faraday?"

"All sorts of stuff to make your toes tingle and your face go numb. Try it."

I take a long, slow sip. "Whoa, it's strong," I say. "And delicious. Kinda curls my toes, actually."

"That about sums up a Kiss from Josh Faraday: toe-curling."

I motion to his cup. "Is that what you're having, too?"

"No, I made myself something totally different—I call it The Terrorist." He takes a sip from his cup. "It really socks a punch. Honestly, it'll probably knock me off my feet—might even be the death of me. But something tells me it's gonna be well worth the pain."

## Chapter 18

*Kat*

After downing two Kisses from Josh Faraday, I've suddenly got a freaking fantabulous idea. "Let's go for a swim, Joshie Woshie."

"Yesssssssssssss, Kitty Kat," he says. Without hesitation, he rips off his jacket and begins unzipping his pants while I frenetically pull my mini-dress over my head and kick off my shoes.

I throw my dress over the back of a lounge chair, adrenaline coursing through my veins (along with the booze), and stand with my hands on my hips like Wonder Woman in front of Josh, wearing nothing but a G-string, belly ring, black-lace push-up bra, and a smile. "Hey, Playboy," I coo. I wink and pucker my lips at him.

He stops what he's doing and freezes, his eyes fixed on me. "Whoa."

I shake my ass, honk my boobs like they're horns on the handlebars of a little girl's bike, and cannonball into the pool with a humongous splash. When my face breaks the surface of the water, I'm treated to the hilarious vision of Josh furiously kicking off his shoes and peeling off his pants like they're on fire.

"Come on, Playboy," I catcall to him. "That's as fast as you can move, you pansy-ass?"

There's a huge splashing noise to my right. And then another. And another. Sounds like I've started a trend. I glance toward the splashing—it's two guys and a girl I recognize from a sitcom—and then my eyes drift back to Josh. He's just now in the process of removing his button-down shirt... to reveal... holy motherfucking shit on a fucking stick. Wow. Holy Washboard Abs, Batman. Holy Pecs. Holy Biceps. Holy Hot Damn. Josh Faraday is unexpectedly a freaking god among men.

Good lord. I knew I felt hard muscles underneath his designer suit when we were dirty dancing. And I knew the dude regularly climbs rocks and mountains with his brother. But I never could have predicted... *this*—this walking temple of masculine perfection. For the love of all things holy, Cameron Fucking Schulz is a professional athlete and his body doesn't hold a freaking candle to Josh's. Josh is a living sculpture. Ripped and perfectly proportioned. Lean in all the right places and buffed out where it counts. Holy hell.

And speaking of buffed out where it counts, Jesus Christ, those little white briefs can't hide the extremely large package he's got between his legs. Holy hell, I'm swooning.

And on top of all that, oh my God, as if all that goodness weren't enough to hurtle a woman into instant orgasm, the man is absolutely riddled with the sexiest tattoos I've ever seen, too. How the hell did I not know he was covered in ink until now? His chest is emblazoned boldly with the swirling word "GRACE" and the word "OVERCOME" is inked across his lower abs, right above the waistband of his tighty-whities. When he pivots to throw his shirt onto a nearby chair, a tattoo I can't make out flashes quickly on his left side—I think I saw a tree? And when he turns the other way, oh my God, to top it all off, there's a fire-breathing dragon covering his right bicep.

A dragon?

Oh, jeez.

I'm pretty sure I told Josh dragons are top of the list of "social suicide" tattoos, along with YOLO and barbed wire and girlfriend tattoos. Why the hell did I say all that? I was just talking out my butt—babbling off the top of my head. Sometimes I'm too snarky for my own good.

Well, damn, just one look at him and it's obvious my made-up rules were meant to be broken. This boy could sport a YOLO tattoo framed by barbed wire wrapped around a fire-breathing dragon's neck and stamped with an ex-girlfriend's name and he'd make it all look sexy as hell. Hot daaaaaaaa-yam, this is a sexy man. My skin's bursting into scorching flames just looking at him, even though I'm standing in cool water up to my chest.

Josh grins at me from the ledge of the pool, obviously enjoying the expression on my face. "Why are you looking at me like that,

Kat?" He pats his rock-hard abs and snaps the waist of his briefs playfully, just below his "OVERCOME" tattoo. "Haven't you ever seen a guy in his undies before?"

There's a rippling commotion just behind him and a loud squeal, but I'm too fixated on Josh's exquisite body to take my eyes off him. Fuck the bet. Fuck the application. I'm gonna have drunken sex with this gorgeous man right now and come like a freight train. Right fucking now. In the bathroom. Or in one of the back bedrooms of the suite. Or, hell, right here in this goddamned swimming pool, if need be. Hell yeah. That's the plan. We'll just pretend we're hugging and cuddling in the water and all these drunk, high people around us will never effing know I'm having the orgasm of my life.

"Josh Faraday, you better get your gorgeous ass—" I begin, but I stop.

*Holy shitballs.*

Isabel Randolph just waltzed right up to the edge of the pool! Oh my God. She's even more beautiful in person than on the big screen. I feel faint. How is this my life right now?

"Reed!" Isabel says, waving happily toward the swimming pool, her eyes focused immediately to my right.

I glance to my side and Reed's standing just a few feet away from me in the pool, holding a drink. When did he get into the pool? And, hey, he looks mighty fine, I must say.

"Hey, Isabel, you came," Reed replies, smiling broadly. "Awesome to see you."

"Wouldn't have missed it. Hey, Josh," Isabel says, turning her attention to Josh a couple feet away from her on the ledge of the pool. She kisses him on both cheeks and then unabashedly looks him up and down. "Wow. You're looking awfully... *fit.*"

Josh opens his mouth to reply, but before he can say a damned word, his face pales like he's seen a freaking ghost.

"Josh Faraday," a blonde woman says, emerging from the milling crowd and sauntering toward him and Isabel. "I had no idea you'd be here." She squeals. "I don't see you for seven long years, and now, out of nowhere, I get to see you *twice* in two weeks—*and both times without a stitch of clothes on*?" She giggles gleefully. "I guess there's a God, after all."

## Chapter 19

*Josh*

I feel physically ill.

I look at Kat in the pool and her face is a mixture of rage and... well, no, nothing else. Just rage. Shit. I look at Reed in the pool and he grimaces at me like I just got pounded in the face with a sledgehammer.

Jen takes another step forward, advancing on me like she's gonna hug me, so I do the only thing my drunken brain can come up with to save myself: I cannonball into the pool.

The minute I emerge from my splash-landing—or is it a crash-landing?—I throw my hands up at Reed. "What the fuck, man?" I ask, my voice low but intense.

Reed throws his hands up in mimicry of my posture. "You didn't tell me you were gonna be in Vegas this week, Faraday—how the fuck was I supposed to know?" he says, matching my energetic whisper. "I invited Isabel to the RCR concert when we saw her last week in New York. You should have told me then you were gonna be in Vegas if you didn't want to see—"

"I didn't know I'd be here—it came up last minute. Why didn't you at least tell me Jen was coming tonight? Jesus, Reed. Help a brother out."

"I didn't even know Jen was coming—I didn't even know *Isabel* was coming. She said she'd *try,* and that's the last I heard." He lowers his voice to barely above a whisper. "And I sure as fuck didn't know she'd bring *Jen*, man." Reed glances furtively at Kat.

"Fuck," I say. "Not good, man."

"It's your own damned fault," Reed says. "Play with crazy, you're gonna get crazy-burned."

I turn to Kat, ready to apologize or assure her or laugh with her—hell if I know where her head is at right now—and the expression on her face makes it clear she's pissed (though about what, I'm not sure).

"Kat, listen," I begin. "I—"

There's a loud splashing noise right behind me. Jesus, no. I wheel around, hoping my gut is wrong. But it's not wrong, unfortunately—Jen just jumped into the pool in her bra and underpants, giggling and squealing like she's auditioning for *Girls Gone Wild.*

I grunt in frustration and lunge over to Kat. "Kat, I'm not even *remotely* interested in her. I told you that—"

"Josh!" Jen says wading up to me, her jaw-dropping tits on bodacious display in her see-through electric-blue bra. "Isabel didn't tell me you were coming to see RCR, too. *Awesome*." She puts her hand on my arm and leans into me like she's gonna kiss me.

I jerk my arm and lurch back from her violently, toward Kat.

"Jen, I'm here with someone." I motion to Kat. "I'm on a date."

Jen's face instantly turns to ice. "Oh." She clenches her jaw. She blatantly looks Kat up and down. "So are you gonna introduce me to your *date*? Unless, of course, you don't know her name?"

I feel physically sick. "No need to be—"

"Actually, he doesn't know my name," Kat spits at Jen. "He hasn't asked me for it and I haven't supplied it, despite the fact that we were just about to fuck in this pool." She glares at me sideways and then flashes a sweet smile at Jen. "I'm Kat." She puts out her hand.

Jen takes Kat's hand like she's picking up trash from the side of the road. "Jen." Jen looks Kat up and down again. "A Vegas girl, I presume?" Her nostrils flare. "When in Rome, I guess, huh, Josh? Charming."

Kat turns her demonic eyes on me, full-force. "Oh, so your name is *Josh*, is it? Did I hear that right? Or did she call you *Jess*?"

I don't reply. Well, not with my vocal chords. My dick certainly seems to be replying, loud and clear. Yeah, my dick's always had a thing for crazy, it's true—not to mention a perfect pair of tits. Not to mention *two* perfect pairs of tits, all of them glistening wet and covered in barely-there see-through bras.

Kat stares Jen down, smiling the whole time. "You know what, Jen? I think you just saved me from doing something really *dumb*."

She's spitting nails through that beauty-queen smile of hers. "This guy here—Josh or Jess, whatever his name is—won't stop talking about some woman he banged in New York last week."

Jen's face lights up. What the fuck is Kat doing to me right now? Is she clinically insane?

"Yeah, he keeps going on and on about how this New York girl was a horrible fuck, that the whole thing was totally meaningless to him, how he was so fucking shitfaced drunk he doesn't even remember it—'oh, it was such a *huge* mistake, blah, blah, blah—she was such a fucking airhead'—I mean, how chicken-shit is that? Why the hell did he bang that poor girl if she was such a horror show? What a fucking douche."

Jen's brief elation from a moment ago is long gone. Now she looks like she was just whacked across the face with a two-by-four.

This is one of the most uncomfortable moments of my life. Jen looks like she's gonna cry—which makes me feel like the biggest prick on the planet—and Kat, the demon-queen herself, is glaring at me like she's readying her blowtorch, a Hershey bar, some graham crackers, and a very sharp knife.

"And here I was stupidly about to give the guy more of the same," Kat continues, on a roll. "Just some meaningless, shitfaced sex he won't even remember tomorrow. Ha! Well, fuck that shit."

Without warning, Kat heaves herself out of the pool and glowers at Jen from the ledge, her incredible body dripping wet and on full, glorious display.

"He's all yours, Jen. Maybe you'll have more luck than the poor girl he burned through in New York last week—whoever the hell she was." She flashes me a rage-filled smile. "Bye-bye, Jess. Or Josh. Whatever your name is. Have fun in Vegas, asshole—when in Rome." With that, she struts over to the nearby lounge chair, grabs her sparkling dress, and waltzes toward the open French doors leading back into the suite.

A man has never leaped out of a swimming pool so fucking fast in his entire life.

"Kat," I yell after her. "Wait."

But she doesn't wait. Hell no, she doesn't, because she's a goddamned terrorist.

She marches straight through the French doors, into the suite, and toward the front doors, her incredible ass-cheeks shuddering with each ground-quaking march of her long, toned legs. On her way to the front door, she makes a pit stop at C-Bomb sitting on the couch. She bends over and whispers something to him, her tits falling out of her bra and into his face as she does. I'm just about to leap across the room and tackle him when he nods and hands her his drink—which looks to be straight whiskey or Scotch. She throws the whole drink back in one fluid motion and hands the empty glass back to him. "Thanks, son, I owe you one," she says, patting him on the head.

"Any time," he says, smirking and looking right at her chest.

"Kat," I say, my blood pounding in my ears.

She completely ignores me. She puffs out her fucking incredible chest and marches haughtily toward the front door of the suite, her ass-cheeks bouncing with each determined stomp.

Jesus Christ. This woman is gonna be the death of me.

"Kat, wait," I say, running to catch up to her. But she ignores me again. Jesus, the girl's having a *bona fide* tantrum—but she's so fucking hot while she's doing it, I truly don't mind.

"Kat, what the fuck are you doing?" I call to her.

She swings open the heavy front door of the suite and marches right through it, toward the private elevator at the end of a long hallway, her sequined dress in her hand, her wet body glistening under the hallway lights.

"*Kat*," I say, making my way through the doors. She's halfway down the hall. "Wait. I'm coming with you and I can't go down there in my fucking underwear."

She stops on a dime.

Oh, *that's* what made her finally stop? Another peek at my nearly naked body? Well, good to know.

She whips around to look at me, and, instantly, her gaze falls right on my dick. My very, very hard dick.

Her mouth drops open. "Wow," she says, her eyes not wavering from my crotch.

I look down. My soaking wet briefs are completely see-through. I might as well be completely naked right now.

She opens her mouth and closes it again. "Wow," she says again, her eyes fixated on my hard-on beneath my see-through briefs.

My dick twitches under her gaze and hardens even more. "Just stay put," I say. "Okay? I'm gonna get my clothes from inside and come right back. I'm coming with you."

"No," she says, her hand on her hip. "Fuck that shit."

I laugh. "Fuck *what* shit? What the fuck does that mean?" I ask.

"Did you see how she talked to me? 'A Vegas girl, I presume?' Ha! I'm not gonna stay here and get treated like scum on the bottom of her fucking shoe." She whips back around and marches toward the elevator at the end of the hall again.

"Kat, *wait*. You're drunk. You can't go alone."

"Yes, I can."

"You don't even have your fucking shoes."

She stops short and looks down at her feet like she truly had no idea she's shoe-less. "Well, hmmph. I don't need no stinkin' shoes."

I laugh. She's so fucking adorable. "You said you never get jealous," I say. "What happened to that, hmm? 'I never get jealous unless the guy is mine in the first place.' Remember that?"

"Yeah, well." She sniffs the air and wobbles in place. "I guess I changed my motherfucking mind. So sue me, fucker."

I laugh. "Nice language."

"Girls can't say fuck? Fuck, fuck, fuck."

I laugh again. "Kat, you're acting fucking crazy."

Her face changes from pissed to hurt on a dime. "Why'd you fuck *her* of all people, Josh?" She wipes her eyes. "She's so *mean*. So... snooty. What were you thinking?"

"What was I *thinking*?" I shrug. "Not a whole lot."

"Why'd you fuck such a mean, mean girl? I hate mean girls."

I'm utterly confused. "You want me to have meaningless sex with only nice girls?"

She ignores me. "And why'd you let her keep thinking you were interested in her after New York, huh? She obviously thought there was some sort of open invitation afterwards."

"No. I told her I wasn't interested."

"No, you didn't. No frickin' way. Or if you did, you didn't make it clear enough. Total douche move, Josh Faraday."

"What are you talking about? What's a total douche move?"

She waggles her finger at me. "I should have known with that whole 'Mickey Mouse roller coaster' thing. *Douchey.* I should have listened to my Scooby Doo senses."

"What the *fuck* are you talking about? It's douche-y that I had sex with Jen?"

"No. That you had sex with a girl who obviously wants a relationship and then left her hanging. *That's* douche-y."

"Oh, and I assume you sat Cameron Schulz down right after you fucked him and told him he has zero chance with you?"

"Well, not then and there, no. I'm not *that* heartless. But, yeah, I told him later when he called, very clearly, that I wasn't feeling it. But maybe, now that I think about it, that was a mistake on my part. Maybe I should have said yes when he asked to see me again because a) he's not a douche, and b) I don't know if I've mentioned this but *he's the shortstop for the goddamned Mariners*!"

I roll my eyes. "Gimme a fucking break. You'd rather scratch your eyes out than go out with that tool again—unless, of course, you suddenly have a huge craving for Shirley Temples."

"Maybe I do," she seethes. "Maybe that's exactly what I want right now, come to think about it—a nice, sweet guy who actually *respects* women and doesn't fuck any mean bitch who happens to have a great rack—and, did I mention?—who happens to be the shortstop for the goddamned fucking Mariners!"

"I respect women," I say lamely.

"Maybe this is exactly the wake-up call I needed," she huffs. She waves her arms at me in a bizarre little frenzy like she's a magician on meth trying to make me disappear, and then she turns back around and begins stomping away from me again.

"*Goddammit, Kat*," I say. "Stop."

She stops and whirls around, glaring at me.

"What are we fighting about?" I ask earnestly. "I'm totally confused."

She doesn't reply. She whirls away from me, *again,* and saunters away, once again mesmerizing me with the stomping motion of her incredible ass.

"Kat," I bellow. "You're a fucking train wreck. Chill the fuck out and listen to me."

She turns back around to face me and crosses her arms over her spectacular chest. "*What*?"

I know we're supposedly in the middle of a heated conversation right now—maybe even a fight—about *what* I'm not entirely sure because I can't figure out exactly what I've done wrong and why she's reacting this way—but the truth is I can't stop looking at her insane body. It's as gorgeous as her face. She's perfection from the top of her head to the bottom of her feet. Jesus. She's not an eleven like I previously thought—she's a fucking *twenty—way* hotter than Bridgette, and Bridgette's a fucking supermodel, for fuck's sake.

"*What*?" Kat repeats, tapping her toe.

I swallow hard. "You were gonna fuck me in the pool?"

"What?" She scoffs. "*No*. You wish."

"You told Jen we were just about to fuck in the pool."

She rolls her eyes. "I just *said* that to piss off your nasty little bitch of a fuck buddy. I'd never be just another ride on your freaking 'Mickey Mouse roller coaster.' Hell no. I'm officially done with that. Starting now." Those perfect tits of hers are rising and falling sharply with her rage. Fuck, she's turning me on so much, I can't think straight.

"What the fuck are you so pissed about?" I ask. "I told you I fucked Jen in New York and you didn't give a shit. I didn't know she was gonna be here tonight—I wasn't the one who invited her. So what the fuck's made you so goddamned mad?"

She presses her lips together, her cheeks rising with color.

I chuckle. "Oh man." I smile broadly, realization descending upon me. "You're so *jealous,* you can't see straight," I say. "Miss I'd-Only-Be-Jealous-If-You-Were-My-Boyfriend is so fucking jealous, she's about to explode." I take a cautious step toward her and she takes a step back like a skittish pony. "Aw, come on, Party Girl. Tell the truth. You're jealous as shit." I smirk. "Come on, babe. We're telling the truth tonight, remember—we're playing the honesty-game?"

"Well, one of us is, anyway," she says, taking another step back. "And one of us is full of shit. I'll leave it to you to decide which of us is which."

I laugh. "You're insane right now. Certifiably insane." I bite my lip. "But I guess that's what jealousy will do to a woman, huh?"

She scowls.

"You were totally gonna fuck me in the pool just now, and you know it."

She shakes her head, but her eyes tell me I'm right.

"You wanna talk about who's full of shit? You don't give a shit about my stupid application—that's all an act. All you care about is feeling my hard cock deep inside you—nice and deep, making you come like I did in the club, only even harder." I take another slow step toward her, and to my surprise, she doesn't back up this time. Oh shit, her nipples are hard little pebbles behind her skimpy lace bra. "Aw, poor little Party Girl," I coo at her. "You wanna fuck me so bad, just thinking about my hard cock inside you is making you drip down your thigh." I point.

She jerks her head down to look between her thighs. "*No*. That's just water from the pool, you sicko."

I laugh. "Oh no, it's not. It's your juices. You're dripping wet for me, aching for me so bad it hurts."

"Screw you," she mutters. She wheels around and marches emphatically down the hallway toward the private elevator, throwing her sequined dress over her head as she goes. She gets tangled in her dress briefly while it's over her head and walks smack into the wall with a loud thud.

I grimace for her. "Ouch. You okay, babe?"

She bounces off the wall and wobbles for a moment in place and then yanks her dress firmly over her head and onto her tight little frame. "I'm *fine*," she says emphatically. She pulls her wet hair out from the back of her dress and smooths her dress over her hips, her face the picture of pure defiance.

I laugh. She's so fucking cute right now, she's killing me.

"It's not funny," she huffs.

"I'm going back into Reed's suite to get my clothes and your shoes and purse and then we're going back to our hotel and we're gonna fuck."

Her lips part with surprise.

"No more terrorist bullshit," I say firmly. "No more demanding my fucking application. I'm gonna fuck you and make you come so hard, you're gonna cry. If you think you're dripping down your thigh now, just wait 'til I get through with you." I begin to turn cautiously away from her, not sure if my skittish pony is gonna stay or run, and she bangs the call button for the elevator, flashing me blazing eyes.

"Don't do it, Kat," I say. "*Wait here*."

"You're not my boyfriend—and I'm obviously not your

girlfriend any more than *Jen* is. And, yes, I *do* demand your application before you can do a goddamned thing to me—even *kiss* me. So there." She sticks out her tongue.

"Real mature," I say, my heart suddenly pounding. Shit. She can't really be serious about going down to the casino floor without me, can she? "I mean it, Kat. Stay here. I can't go down there like this." I motion to my wet briefs.

"Hmmph."

The doors to the private elevator open and she glares at me, her eyes on fire.

"Kat. I can't go down into the casino wearing nothing but wet underwear and a hard dick. Don't go."

She sticks her tongue out again.

I roll my eyes. "Kat, I promised Jonas I wouldn't leave your side tonight. Please stop acting like a fucking toddler."

She steps inside the elevator, smirking. "Sucks to be you. Hopefully, your crazy-ass brother won't beat your ass too hard for breaking your promise to him." She waves. "*Ciao, motherfucker.*"

"Kat. *Stop.* Don't you dare fucking leave me right now."

Her pout turns into a diabolical smile. "'Don't you dare'? Ha! Just a tip, *Jess*," she says. "Never use that threat with me—it'll backfire every freaking time." The doors begin closing. "I *hate* that, Jess. I really do." She waves as the doors close on her smug face and, just like that, she's gone.

"Goddammit, Stubborn Kat!" I scream out loud in the empty hallway. I make a long, exasperated sound like a pot about to boil, and then I turn and sprint back into Reed's suite (which isn't a pleasant thing to do with a raging hard-on, I gotta say), muttering words like "terrorist" and "fucking" and "crazy" and "bullshit" and "so fucking hot I wanna punch a goddamned wall" to myself as I go.

# Chapter 20

*Kat*

Oh shit. Why did I just do that? What came over me? I never get jealous, ever, unless I'm in a committed relationship—and even then it's an extremely rare emotion for me to feel. And here I was, ready to rip that bitch's pretty little head off and cut off Josh's balls and smash them between two graham crackers. Am I just ugly drunk? That's gotta be it. Why do I care who Josh slept with last week? I did the exact same thing, didn't I?

*No, I didn't.* I didn't sleep with the meanest little *bitch* in the whole, wide world and then *obviously* leave the door open for her afterwards to think there was even a snowball's chance in hell for more of the same. Jen looked awfully happy to see Josh—when she saw him, she certainly didn't look like she thought she'd been rejected by him a few days before.

My head is reeling. I can only assume my brain has short-circuited from sexual frustration and seething jealousy. And who could blame me after what I witnessed tonight? Goddammit, Josh is literally the hottest man I've ever laid eyes on, by far. Jesus Christ, I had no idea what he was hiding under his suit. I practically climaxed at the sight of him standing in that damned hallway with that ridiculous dick of his. Oh my God, I could see every detail of it, every ridge and bulge—the tip, the shaft, his balls, that little vein—all of it as plain as day under the wet fabric of his briefs. Good lord, he'd gag me with that thing. Maybe even kill me. But what a way to go. My clit is throbbing mercilessly just thinking about it. If I had my vibrator right now, it'd take me less than a minute to give myself the biggest orgasm of my life.

The elevator arrives at the lobby floor and the doors open onto the hotel's bustling casino. Wow, it's closing in on dawn and this place is still jumping.

What the hell is happening to me right now? I feel completely out of control. Like, literally *insane.* I can't even remember half of what I just said to Josh in that hallway. Why the hell did I rip into him like that? I honestly didn't care when he told me about his New York screw earlier tonight—I *really* didn't—but I suppose *hearing* about her and *seeing* her are two different things. When he told me about fucking some faceless blast from his past, I didn't have to stare at her perfect boobs and tiny waist and get hit with her snooty I'm-better-than-you-rich-bitch glare. And I didn't have to imagine Josh thrusting his enormous dick into her petite little body and ripping her in two or pressing his magnificent muscles and tattooed skin against her, making her scream his name.

A repulsive image suddenly flickers across my brain: Josh naked with a gigantic hard-on and *Jen,* not me, down on her knees, taking his enormous dick into her mouth. Oh my God, I'm gonna barf. That should be me, goddammit! I throw my hands over my face, stuffing back tears. *That should be me.*

Why am I reacting like this? Josh isn't my boyfriend. Whatever I've been starting to feel about him, I'd better back it the fuck up and cool my jets. This guy's not even remotely interested in having a committed relationship, not with me or anyone. And, frankly, neither am I. I'm single and loving it. Hell yeah, I am. *Loving it!*

There's a craps table a few feet away so I drift over to it like a drunk driver following headlights on the freeway, my bare feet shuffling along the dirty casino carpet as I walk. I peek over at the game just in time to see a handsome gray-haired man roll a seven and crap out.

My eyes are burning. There's a lump in my throat.

I think I might have just embarrassed myself in that hallway.

I acted like a toddler.

Not to mention a terrorist, just like Josh said—a jealous, pissy, bitchy little terrorist. And a mean girl. That's right, I said it. I was every bit as mean to that bitch as she was to me in the first place. Maybe even meaner. Right now she's probably crying to her bestie—*Isabel Effing Randolph, for crying out loud!*—about how she doesn't understand what Josh could possibly see in a mean bitch like me.

And she's right. But that bitch started it, goddammit! '*Charming, Josh,*' she said, looking me up and down. Who could blame me for tearing into her? If Sarah were here she'd tell me what I did was justifiable bitchicide.

I just can't understand what Josh ever saw in a girl like that. Is he *really* that shallow? I'm not exactly an endless reservoir of deep thoughts, I'll admit, but I'm not human plankton like that girl. And, even more importantly, I'm *nice.* Or, okay, I'm not *mean* (not normally, anyway)—although, okay, yes, I have a bit of a bitchy streak, a wee bit of a temper—and it certainly came out tonight. But I'm not flat-out *mean* (not usually). Sarah always says I have a heart of gold, doesn't she? And Sarah's a fantastic judge of character.

Seriously, if Josh is interested in a girl like Jen, even for one night, just because she has an incredible body—which, holy hell, she sure does, oh my effing God, that was quite a body on her—then he truly must be the diehard playboy I pegged him for right from the start. And that thought makes me feel... What does it make me feel? I can't identify it.

*Rejected.*

Yeah. That's it. I feel rejected more than anything else—even more than jealous.

And that's just plain stupid.

But I can't help it.

All night long—or, actually, even before coming to Vegas—I've been feeling like Josh and I have some sort of special connection, something with potential to turn into something serious. Something maybe even beautiful. And now I can't help thinking that's exactly what Jen thought she had with Josh, too. Maybe Josh makes every girl feel like girlfriend-material, simply because he's so damned gorgeous and charming? Jen was clearly clueless about the way Josh really felt about her—am I equally clueless, too?

The shooter at the craps table rolls a nine, and everyone breathes a sigh of relief.

Goddammit, why don't I have my purse or phone? Or at least my effing shoes? Classic Kat. I cross my arms in a huff and wobble in place with the effort.

Shit. I feel kinda bad for how hard I punched that mean girl in the teeth, even though she was a total bitch. Did I really have to go *quite* that nuclear on her ass? Couldn't I maybe have just thrown a cherry bomb at her? Or maybe even, like, a dart? I put some horrible words into Josh's mouth—words that probably shattered her heart, if, indeed, she's got one buried underneath those spectacular breasts.

Jeez. Maybe I don't have a heart of gold, after all, no matter what Sarah says.

I wipe my eyes. They're suddenly burning like crazy. I can't seem to swallow that huge lump in my throat. Maybe I'm just a bitch through and through.

"Kat."

I turn around. It's Josh, holding my shoes and purse and looking incredibly relieved to see me.

Without even thinking about it, I throw my arms around his neck and squeeze—and he encircles me in his strong arms.

He kisses me on the cheek. And then the ear. And then the neck. I brush my lips against his jawline, aching for him to kiss me like I've never been kissed before.

But he doesn't.

He pushes a large swath of wet hair off my cheek. "What the fuck is wrong with you? You went fucking psycho on me."

I shake my head.

"Come on, Kat. Talking lets the feelings out."

"I'm just drunk," I say, squeezing him with all my might. "Ignore me—I'm not acting like myself. Just, please, forget this ever happened. I'm not mean, I swear."

"Forget this ever happened? Highly unlikely," he says. "A man doesn't soon forget the sight of a bare ass like yours marching down a hallway." He nuzzles his nose into mine but, again, he doesn't kiss me, not that I can blame him.

I kiss his cheek. And then his ear.

He shudders at the touch of my lips.

"Josh," I whisper, my heart aching. I want him so bad, it hurts.

After a moment, Josh pulls back from me and looks deep into my eyes, rubbing my cheeks with his thumbs. "I guess this settles it, huh?—you really *do* have a vagina."

I smile. "That wasn't clear to you when you stuck your fingers inside it on the dance floor?"

"Could have been smoke and mirrors—you never know." He

pushes more wet hair off my face. "You just kicked Jen's ass so fucking hard. Oh my God. You absolutely decimated that girl."

"I should have warned you—I've got a bit of a temper."

"You did warn me. I just didn't realize you meant you were a trained fucking assassin. *Jesus*."

"I shouldn't have done that to her. She's a bitch, but she didn't deserve that. It's just that I was just so effing—"

"*Jealous*," he says, finishing my sentence for me. "Just so effing *jealous*."

I exhale and nod. "Yeah."

He holds my face in his hands. "Well, you're in luck. Because I happen to be a sick fuck and I thoroughly enjoyed watching you go batshit crazy with jealousy over me."

"You did?"

"Oh yeah," he says. "It gave me a raging hard-on, you might have noticed."

I grin. "Oh, you had a hard-on? Hmm. I didn't notice."

He laughs. "Or maybe I just had a raging hard-on from ogling your smokin' hot body. Jesus, Kat. You're fucking incredible."

"You're pretty incredible yourself," I say.

There's a long beat.

"You still sticking with your stupid jihad?" he asks. "Or are you ready to let me take you back to our hotel and make all your dreams come true?"

"*Jihad*," I say, swallowing hard. Damn, it pains me to say that. I wish he could understand what I'm really saying to him. At this point, it's not about his application anymore. *I want him.* And I won't settle for getting anything less than of all of him now.

Josh looks genuinely disappointed. "It's not fair, you know. You don't have an application to give me in return."

"If I did, I'd give it to you," I say.

He mulls that over for a moment. "I thought you only get jealous with boyfriends."

Something in the way he just said that makes my heart race. "It was the truth when I said it. I'm sorry. This has never happened to me before."

He touches the cleft in my chin for a long moment and I close my eyes at his sensuous touch.

After a moment, he removes his finger and slowly licks the indentation in my chin with a languid flicker of his tongue.

My knees buckle and my clit zings. I stick out my tongue, yearning for his warm tongue to intertwine with mine, but he pulls back. I let out a shaky breath. Holy shitballs, that was sexy.

"You hungry?" he asks softly. "Suicide-bombing can really work up an appetite."

I shift my weight. Blood is flooding into my crotch. "Yeah, I'm starving."

He looks at his watch. "We're supposed to meet up with our *Ocean's Eleven* crew in just a few hours—no sense sleeping before then, right? Let's go back to our hotel and grab some breakfast, maybe gamble a little—we can crash after we meet with everyone."

"Yeah, sounds good. 'Sleep when you're dead,' right?"

"'Go big or go home,'" he says, smirking.

"YOLO."

Josh touches the cleft in my chin again, his sapphire eyes sparkling at me. "That's right, baby—you only live once. So don't fuck it up." He pauses, his eyes looking deeply into mine. "What am I gonna do with you, Kat?" he whispers. "Huh? You're a goddamned runaway train."

I shrug and wipe my eyes. "I know. I'm off the tracks."

He exhales softly and slips his hand in mine. "Come on, Madame Terrorist. Let's get you back to the hotel and get some food into you before you pass out—or, God forbid, injure some more innocent bystanders."

# Chapter 21

*Josh*

Kat's drunk but beautiful head is resting on my shoulder as we sit in the back of the taxi, heading to our hotel. I grab her hand and look out the window at the pre-dawn zombies shuffling down The Strip. My eyelids are beginning to feel heavy. My head is beginning to pound. And yet I feel like I'm walking on air, sitting here next to Kat, holding her hand.

"Who's Grace?" Kat suddenly asks.

"What?"

"The tattoo on your chest. You've got the dragon on you arm, so I can only assume the tattoo on your chest is the ever-regrettable ex-girlfriend-tattoo."

"'Grace' isn't a person," I answer smoothly, like I always do. I don't give a shit how "honest" I said I'd be with her—I don't bare my soul about that particular tattoo to anyone, and certainly not to a woman I'm interested in. If Emma taught me anything, it's that laying myself completely bare to a woman is a colossally bad idea. "It's a reference to the phrase, 'But for the grace of God go I,'" I continue. "It's just a simple way of reminding myself to be humble and not take anything for granted—something I regularly need to be reminded of, it seems."

She absorbs that for a moment. "No ex-girlfriend tattoo anywhere?"

"Nope."

"You've got ex-girlfriends, though, right?"

"Sure."

"Anything that lasted more than a month?"

I scoff. "My longest relationship lasted three years."

"Wow. What was her name?"

"Why?"

"Just curious."

"Emma."

She squints. "You don't have a current girlfriend, right?"

"I already told you I fucked Jen in New York last week. I wouldn't have done that if I had a current girlfriend—and I most certainly wouldn't be sitting here with you."

She smiles. "Just checking."

I squeeze her hand. "I'm not a cheater," I say.

She nods. "Good to know." She touches the tips of my fingers. "Okay, so no to girlfriend tattoos; yes to dragons. How about YOLO wrapped in barbed wire?"

"Oh, great idea for my next drunken mistake."

She laughs. "Please don't."

"What do you care? You're not the one who's gonna have to look at it for the rest of your life."

There's an awkward pause. That came out kinda weird. Shit. Now I feel like I should say, "Unless, of course, it turns out you *are* the one who's gonna have to look at it for the rest of your life." But then that would be an even weirder thing to say. Shit. I look out the car window, my mind racing. When it comes to Kat, I keep finding myself saying shit I shouldn't say and having thoughts I never, ever have.

"So what's the deal with the dragon on your arm?" she asks, thankfully filling the awkward silence.

I clear my throat. "Ah. That was my very first drunken tattoo, though certainly not my last. I'm kinda known for drunken tattoos, actually. It's sort of a thing with me and my friends."

She laughs. "Can't wait to see your collection up close some time."

"Oh, you will."

My heart is pounding in my ears.

"So what's the deal with the dragon?" she asks.

"Ah, the dragon. I'd love to tell you I got it for some profound and intellectual reason—dragons have all sorts of meaning and symbolism, especially in Asia—but since you and I have agreed to play the honesty-game, I'll tell you the truth: I stumbled into a tattoo parlor in Bangkok, drunk and high as a kite, and thought, 'Dude. A dragon would be so rad.'"

She laughs.

"Reed got a tattoo that night, too—but not a dragon. His is way, way cooler than mine, actually—which isn't surprising, since he's way cooler than me."

"Reed was in Bangkok with you?"

"Yeah. After my first year of college, I traveled the whole summer with Jonas, all over the place, and for a short bit of our trip, some of my buddies joined us."

"You like to travel?" she asks.

"I love it. You?"

"I haven't done a lot of it, but I've loved it when I've gotten the chance. My parents took the whole family to Mexico for their anniversary when I was a teenager. And then we went on a Caribbean cruise for Christmas a couple years later. That was super fun."

I make a face.

"You don't like the Caribbean?"

"I don't like cruises—unless, you know, you're talking about a private yacht. That's the only way to travel by sea."

She scoffs. "Oh, well. Who doesn't demand a private yacht when traveling by sea? Duh."

I cringe.

"It's not like I have stock in a cruise line or anything," she sniffs. "I was just saying I was happy to get to go somewhere out of the country, that's all, like most normal people would be. And, by the way, my dad's a pharmacist and my mom has her own little interior designer company, so it was a really big deal for them to take five kids on a week-long cruise."

I feel my cheeks burning. "I'm sorry," I say. "That was really snobby and out-of-touch of me to say. Sometimes my inner douchebag oozes out. Please forgive me."

But she's not done with me yet. "I guess you better get another tattoo to remind yourself to be humble, huh? Because the 'Grace' one doesn't seem to be doing the trick."

There's a really long pause, during which I feel like my tongue is literally tied into knots along with my stomach. She looks out the window of the cab, apparently gathering herself, her cheeks bursting with color, and I stare at her profile, marveling at her beauty. How is it possible she keeps getting more and more attractive to me? Usually, a beautiful woman like Kat becomes less and less physically attractive the more I get to know her. I mean, with someone like Kat, you'd think there'd be only one way to go from here, right? But, nope, I'm more and more drawn to her with each passing minute.

"I'm sorry," I say earnestly. "I'm a total douchebag sometimes. I know this about myself. Please always call me on it. So few people in my life do."

"Oh, I will."

"Obviously."

"What's that supposed to mean?"

"Exactly what you think it means: that you will *obviously* call me on my shit. No more, no less. That's all it means."

"Oh. Yeah, well, that's true. I will."

"Jesus. You're insane."

"Sorry," she says. "I can't even blame you for being out of touch, honestly. I mean, how are you supposed to know what's normal? Just look at your effing shoes, for crying out loud. How much did those things cost?"

I look down at my shoes.

"More than a thousand bucks?" she asks.

I flash her an annoyed look.

"I thought so." She shakes her head. "You never stood a chance."

"Again, you lick my balls and punch 'em at the same time."

She laughs.

For a moment, we look out the window at the rat-haired horror shows dragging their sorry asses down The Strip in the pre-dawn light.

"Oh, look at that poor girl," I say pointing to a young woman who unintentionally looks like an extra in the *Thriller* video.

"Poor baby," Kat says. "Doing the Walk of Shame in *Vegas* is like reaching the Super Bowl in the sport." She shakes her head. "I've done the walk of shame a time or two myself—but never in *Vegas.* I've got my *standards,* for crying out loud."

I laugh.

"To be honest, it always pisses me off that people say women are doing a 'walk of shame,' but they never say that about guys. I mean it takes two to tango, right?"

"Absolutely." I look out the window. "I've definitely done my share of shame-walking." I scoff. "I've done my share of everything, actually. I was a bit out of control for a while."

"But not anymore?"

"Not anymore."

"Was The Club part of your out-of-control phase?" she asks.

Goddammit. I hate that she knows about The Club. There's no other circumstance in which a woman I'm interested in would know about that. "No," I say. "The Club was just a short vacation from my adult responsibilities. I did that *way* after my out-of-control phase. It was just a blip. No more or less."

"And now it's over—the blip, I mean?"

"Yeah, now it's over."

"Until the next blip."

I don't reply—but she's pegged me right. Surely, another blip's coming at some point. When your brother is Jonas—and you're his only lifeline—losing your shit for more than a blip here or there just isn't an option.

"Tell me the story of why you got your 'grace' tattoo," she says. "Were you drunk and high in Thailand for that one, too?"

I look out the window of the cab. "No, I got that particular tattoo in L.A. when I was stone-cold sober," I say. "I was twenty-three and recently out of school—it took me a little while to graduate—and I decided it was time to stop throwing my life away on total and complete bullshit and start living a life that my..." I swallow hard. "That *I* could be proud of." I shrug. "I decided to start living up to my name. So I decided to open a satellite office of Faraday & Sons and stop destroying myself, and the rest is history."

"And did you?"

"Yeah, I opened the L.A. office about the time Jonas took over the main Seattle office."

"No, I mean, did you stop destroying yourself? Did you start living a life you could be proud of?"

"Oh." I run my hand through my hair. "Mostly. A few slip-ups now and again over the years." I look into her gorgeous blue eyes. "But, yeah. By and large."

Another long pause.

"Isn't Thailand one of those countries where they could put you in jail and throw away the key if you get caught with drugs?"

"Yeah. Why?"

"You said you were drunk and high as a kite in Thailand."

"Oh. Yeah. Well. I thought I was invincible back then. Or maybe I didn't care if I wasn't. Actually, it's funny you say that. I've got a pretty hairy story about that night. I'll tell it to you some time, maybe."

There's a long beat.

"Josh, I know what happened to your parents," she says. "Sarah told me. I'm really sorry."

I'm stunned. I had no idea Kat knew about my parents. What the fuck? She knows about The Club *and* my parents? Fuck.

"It was a long time ago," I respond stiffly.

She doesn't press me, thankfully, but she's clearly looking at me with sympathy in her eyes. Shit. I don't have any desire to be the Poor Little Rich Boy in anyone's eyes, least of all Kat's.

"No worries," I add. I squeeze her hand to reassure her and she squeezes back.

Our taxi pulls up in front of our hotel and I help Kat out of the car. She's pretty wobbly.

"You okay?" I ask, holding her arm.

"I'm fan-fucking-tastic. Just a little car sick, I think. I'll be fine once I eat something."

We walk toward the front doors of our mammoth hotel.

"Do you need to put on some dry undies before we eat? My briefs are still wet—I think my dick is getting chafed."

"Oh, well, we don't want that," she says. "Yeah, I could use a change, too. Let's run up to our rooms and meet at that Americana restaurant on the far side of the casino in fifteen."

"You aren't gonna pass out on your bed and not come back down, are you?" I ask.

"Not a chance. I'm the Party Girl, remember? I'm a machine."

"Atta girl," I say. "But I'd better walk you up to your room, just to make sure you get there safely."

"You mean so you can have *sex* with me," she says coyly, batting her eyelashes. "I know your game, Playboy."

"Kat, I'm not gonna fuck you for the first time at six in the morning after a long-ass night of partying when you're obviously drunk off your ass and, no offense, look like road kill."

She scowls at me.

"Oh, wait, scratch all that. I forgot we're playing the honesty-game here. The truth is I'd totally fuck you, despite all that, for sure—but I'm most definitely *not* gonna fuck you 'til you've dropped your ridiculous demands."

She makes a "good luck with that" face.

"Hey, you're the one who made The Rules, PG. I'm merely enforcing them."

She pauses, considering something. "Well, how about this? What if we fuck without any kissing?" she asks. "Would that be a loophole?"

I laugh. The woman's trying to find a loophole from her own bullshit? Clearly, she's a heartbeat away from caving completely. "You're not in any shape to negotiate on the bet, PG. You made your demands, and now you have to live with them. The only way out now is to concede. There's no middle ground."

She scowls yet again.

I suppress the urge to laugh out loud at her expression. She's such a bullshitter, this girl. She wants me so bad, she's about to pull her hair out. Time to turn up the heat.

"Plus, I happen to like kissing when I fuck," I say nonchalantly. "I like it a lot. Every variety of it."

She stops walking abruptly and puts her arms out like she's trying to balance herself on a log.

Oh man, she's drunk. Her eyes are half-mast. Her hair's matted against her head. Her eye makeup is smudged. And she's still fucking gorgeous.

"Look, here's the thing you're obviously not getting about me, Party Girl: I've been exercising superhuman patience my whole fucking life. You think you're gonna wear me down? *Nothing* fucking wears me down—I've got the patience of a fucking saint. I've been the fixer my whole life—and nothing ruffles me. As far as I'm concerned, there's a time and place for everything—including fucking the one and only Party Girl with a Hyphen—and until the right time for that bit of awesomeness presents itself, I'll just wait and be patient, let you drip down your thighs 'til you're begging me for it."

She's speechless.

I can't suppress my laughter anymore. She's too fucking cute. "Come on, PG. Let me get you to your room to change." I grab her limp arm and usher her toward the hotel again, but after three more steps, she stops short and hunches over.

"Kat?"

She nods and puts her hand to her mouth. "Yeah. I'm fine." She takes two more steps and stops again, grabbing her stomach.

"Kat?" I grab her shoulders? "Are you okay?"

"I'm fine. I think I just need to—"

Without warning, she bends over and barfs—all over the sidewalk—and all over my two-thousand-dollar shoes.

## Chapter 22

*Kat*

I slowly open my eyes. I don't feel great, but it definitely could have been a *lot* worse. When Josh brought me to my room after I barfed all over him, he helped me shower—in my bra and undies, I noticed—ordered me chicken noodle soup from room service, and made me drink a bunch of Gatorade and take four Ibuprofen before finally tucking me into bed. I have to admit, I kinda swooned at how attentive and sweet he was, even through my queasiness.

I look at the clock. Three o'clock. Wow, I slept a full seven hours. I grab my phone and look at my emails. Damn. I've got two messages from my boss, attaching documents that require my attention. Obviously, I'm gonna have to head back to Seattle soon or risk losing my job. My work is piling up and I've already used up all my vacation days this year. Hmm. Maybe there's a way for me to finagle this.

I forward my boss's email to my co-worker Hannah, asking her if maybe she's willing to help a sistah out?

Hannah's email reply is immediate. "Of course, baby. I got you. Any time."

"Thanks, baby. You know I'll return the favor."

"You've helped me with a thousand pitches, girl. And I still owe you big time for helping me with the politician who sent the dick pic to the teenager."

"You don't owe me a damned thing," I write. "And if you do, then helping me with this pitch puts you way ahead, for sure."

"Where are you? Still in Vegas?" Hannah writes.

"Yeah. And currently hung over. Partied all night. You won't believe who I partied with."

"Who?"

"RED CARD RIOT!"

"WTF!!!!!! Are you serious?"

"Serious. LMFAO," I write.

"Cray," Hannah writes.

"Probs going to their concert tonight, too. And watching from backstage!!!!!"

"No way! Double cray. Are they hot?"

"Totes. But really young. Just wee little baybays."

"Oooooh, you could do the Mrs. Robinson thing. That'd be hot."

"That's not one of my fantasies, actually. But, trust me, I've got plenty of others."

"Oh, I know you do. LOL," Hannah writes.

"Thanks again, girl. You're a great friend."

"Takes one to know one. Speaking of which, say hi to Sarah. How's she feeling?"

"She's great. Breaking news: she's in luuuuuurve."

"Awesome! With that guy she went to Belize with?"

"Yup. And he's in luuuuuuuurve with her, too."

"Aw." Hanna attaches a heart emoji. "I'm jelly." She attaches a green-faced emoji.

"Me, too." I exhale wistfully. "Okay, gotta go," I write. "Just woke up. Gotta get some food in this sad-sack body."

"By all means. Partying requires fuel. Have fun."

"Thanks again for the assist."

"No worries. Have an extra drink for me. Or two or three."

"Thanks, Hannah Banana Montana Milliken."

"LOL. Any time, Kitty Kat."

"Meow."

"Mwah."

Phew. Catastrophe averted. At least for now. I have no doubt Hannah will style me—the woman's damn good at PR—and that ought to buy me at least a little time. But, clearly, I can't stay out here in Las Vegas forever. Sooner or later, the jig's gonna be up. I just wish I knew how long Operation *Ocean's Eleven* was going to last (and what my part in it might be).

I scour the rest of my emails. Nothing important. I move on to my texts.

There's a text from Sarah. "Hey, Kitty Kat. What happened with you and Josh last night? Did you have fun? Winky winky boom boom? Jonas and I are heading out to Henderson to meet Oksana the Pimpstress right now. Kerzoinks! I just pissed my pants a little bit writing that. Okay, well, just wanted to check in and say hi and get all the juicy deets about last night. You're probably sleeping, knowing you. Hope you didn't barf, girl. But if you did, I hope you didn't barf on Josh. But if you did, I hope Josh held your hair for you, since I wasn't there to do it like usual. See you later when we get back. IF WE GET BACK." She attaches a scared-face emoji. "If I don't come back, just know I loved you with all my heart and soul. Oh, and, just in case, I hereby bequeath you my One Direction albums."

I tap out my reply. "Hey, girl. Just woke up. Yes, I barfed. Yes, Josh held my hair. He showered me and Gatoraded me, too, and then put me to bed." I attach a blushing emoji. "Don't say 'IF we get back.' NOT FUNNY. I love you, too, with all my heart and soul, and then some. It's probably too late for you to get this now, but be super-duper careful with the pimpstress. Don't leave Jonas' side. See you when you get back. Can't wait to hear all about it." I attach an ear emoji. "And I don't want your stinkin' 1D albums, you tweener. If I did, though, does this mean you're 'bequeathing me' (WTF??) your entire laptop? Sorry to look a gift horse in the mouth, but I'm not sure I know how to extract the digital files off your laptop. Heehee. Love you, girl. Meow. Xoxo."

My next text is from Josh from an hour ago. "You up yet, PG?"

I type a reply. "Hi, PB. Just woke up."

His reply is instantaneous. "You feeling like death warmed over?"

"No, I feel pretty fab. Can you talk?"

My phone rings. "Hey," his smooth voice says. I hear slot machines ringing and people cheering in the background.

"Thanks for putting me to bed and taking such good care of me. Sorry I barfed on your fancy shoes."

"I hated those shoes anyway. Total douchebag-shoes."

"I was thinking of getting something to eat before Jonas and Sarah get back from meeting the Pimpstress Extraordinaire. Do you know if they're back yet?"

"Not yet. I saw them before they left. They were both wearing matching platinum bracelets engraved with each other's names."

"What? Oh my God."

"You should have seen them, Kat. Seriously, they can't get enough of each other. They're pretty cute."

My heart flips over in my chest. "Wow. Good for them."

There's a long beat.

Josh clears his throat. "So did you get any sleep?"

"A ton. How about you?"

"A couple hours at most. Henn and I are down in the casino playing craps, waiting for Jonas and Sarah to come back."

"Okay, I'll get dressed and come on down."

"No. I don't want you walking around alone. Text me when you're ready to come down here."

"Will do."

I jump in the shower and wash my hair and lather my body from head to toe. And when I'm done with the functional aspects of my shower, I grab the showerhead and stick it between my legs, positioning the strong stream of water right on my clit. My body's reaction to the vibrating water is extreme and instantaneous. Whoa, oh yeah, I'm ready to go.

I close my eyes and begin touching myself, trying to duplicate the precise way Josh touched me when we "danced" at Reed's club. God, that was hot. So *fucking* hot.

Oh, I'm already pulsing like crazy.

My fingers massage and rub, working round and round.

I imagine the ridges and ripples of Josh's abs, the incredible muscles on his arms, that tight "V" on either side of his lower pelvis, his tattoos, and, the crowning glory, that incredible hard-on I saw hiding beneath his wet briefs.

Oh, I'm especially sensitive to touch right now. Getting myself off today is gonna be as easy as falling off a greasy log.

I begin moaning softly.

Oh, I'm right on the cusp.

I imagine the outline of Josh's hard dick in his wet briefs, and then I fantasize about it sliding inside me, thrusting in and out of me, over and over.

His lips are on mine, devouring me. His hands are touching my naked body. He's whispering in my ear, calling me his Party Girl with a Hyphen.

Oh yeah. My skin is beginning to prickle like I've got a chill, always a deliciously disorienting sensation under hot steaming water.

I imagine the cocky expression on Josh's face when he accused me of dripping down my thigh with desire for him—*which I was*. Oh, God, yes, I was.

I'm rocked with a massive orgasm that makes my insides twist and shudder.

"Fuck," I blurt. "Oh my God."

Pleasure is vibrating between my legs and throughout my abdomen.

Oh boy. That was a nice one.

I return the showerhead to its holder and lean into the shower wall for a moment.

I've never wanted a man this much in all my life.

Damn.

What have I done? How the hell am I gonna get myself out of this pickle I've created? Never in a million years did I think it would take this long to wear Josh down. I figured he'd throw me some nominal, flirtatious resistance and then give me what I want, the way all other men do, to be perfectly honest. *Goddammit*. I feel like stomping my foot in frustration.

I get out of the shower and dry off with one of the thick, white towels on the nearby shelf and quickly check my texts again—I stayed in the shower longer than I intended to—and, oopsies, there's a group text from Jonas, telling Henn, Josh and me to meet him and Sarah up in his suite in ten minutes. Oh, crap. I better get a move on.

I quickly dial Josh. He picks right up.

"Did you see Jonas' text?" I ask.

"Yeah, I just got it a minute ago. Henn and I are on our way to your room to get you. We don't want you walking up to their suite alone. See you in five."

## Chapter 23

*Josh*

It's official. Sarah Fucking Cruz is the biggest badass I've ever met. She took a naked selfie in the bad guys' bathroom and emailed it to them right then and there? She must have ice in her veins. Ha! Well, I guess Kat's not the only terrorist in our group. Holy shit.

"And then," Sarah continues, beaming, "*both* of them opened my email right on the spot."

"Now *that's* the way to do it, Sarah Cruz! Who's the fucking genius now?" Henn shouts, scrambling to his laptop.

I glance over at Jonas in the far corner, intending to share a look of celebration with him, but his jaw is clenched and his eyes are blue chips of granite.

"Bingo," Henn says after a brief moment of studying his screen. "You did it, Sarah. We're in. I've got Oksana's computer and that guy's phone. Holy shit. Jackpot."

"She's a fucking assassin," I whisper to Kat.

"Birds of a feather flock together." She winks.

I chuckle.

"Oh my God," Henn says, staring intently at his computer screen. "The bastard forwarded your email to another computer and opened your photo there, too." He makes a sound of extreme joy. "Brilliant, Sarah." He clicks a button on his keyboard and, all of a sudden, his cheeks suddenly turn bright red.

"So, Henn?" Sarah asks, her cheeks flushing every bit as much as Henn's.

Henn jerks his head up from his screen, his cheeks blazing. "Yes?"

"So now what?" Sarah asks.

"Well, um," Henn says. He swallows hard. Oh yeah, my boy's definitely been thrown for a loop by something on his screen. Henn clears his throat. "I'll snoop around both computers and this Max guy's phone and see what I can find. And then we wait for them to hopefully access their mainframe and bank accounts. I imagine we won't have to wait too long."

"Can you delete that photo?" Jonas asks, his voice tight. "Can you find it and erase it everywhere?"

"Um, sure, no problem," Henn says quickly, his face turning an even darker shade of red. "I can delete it right now, if you want me to. I've got total access."

Oh, well, that answers that question: Henn's looking at the selfie Sarah sent to Oksana and Max. Ha! Poor Henn never did know how to keep a poker face.

"Yeah, but if you delete that photo off their computers now, won't that tip them off?" Kat asks.

"Yeah," Henn says. "If that photo magically disappears, this Max dude is gonna know something's up for sure—and if he designed their tech like he says, then he's a badass motherfucker of epic proportions and we don't want to do anything to tip him off."

"Well, then, don't delete it. I don't want to give them any reason whatsoever to be suspicious," Sarah says. She juts her chin at Jonas.

"I agree," Henn says. He winces at Jonas like he's expecting to get punched.

Jonas exhales and crosses his arms over his chest, his brand new engraved bracelet gleaming on his wrist. Oh man, he's in full serial-killer mode right now, though I don't understand why. What did he expect Sarah to do? It was do or die time and she *did*. If she were my girl, I'd be kissing her from head to toe right now, telling her she's a fucking genius. Seriously, my brother is the dumbest (smartest) guy I know.

"God, Sarah," Kat says, laughing. "First the solo-boob shot and now this. You're quite the exhibitionist, aren't you?"

"A 'boob shot?" I ask. "Oh my goodness, tell us more, Sarah Cruz."

Sarah blushes. "Just a little sexting with this really hot guy I met online." She looks at Jonas, but he remains stone-faced. "A hot guy who *used* to have a sense of humor," she continues. "It's no big deal—all the kids are doing it these days."

Jesus. My brother's being a total prick. I gotta help this poor girl out. "And all the politicians," I add.

"And athletes," Henn says.

"And housewives," Kat adds.

"And grandmas," I say.

"And some priests, too," Henn adds, and everyone (except Jonas) laughs.

Kat beams a smile at me and I wink back at her.

"Sarah, you picked the perfect bait for your email," Kat says, swigging from a water bottle. "No matter how smart or powerful or rich a guy might be, he's got the same Kryptonite as every other man throughout history." She raises one eyebrow at me. "*Naked boobs.*"

I return the eyebrow-raise. "Are we really that simple?" I ask.

"Yes," Kat says. "You really are."

I laugh.

"Never underestimate the power of porn," Henn says.

"That's catchy," Kat says. "The porn industry should adopt that for a billboard campaign."

"I don't think the porn industry needs help with their marketing," Henn says.

I look over at Jonas again, hoping he's eased up on the psycho-killer bullshit, but he's still channeling Ted Bundy over there. Shit. Poor Sarah. A woman's got to be superhuman to put up with my fucking brother, I swear to God—or maybe just a masochist.

"That was really quick thinking on your feet, Sarah," I say. "You went in there hoping to harpoon a baby whale, and you wound up landing Moby Dick. Great job." I raise my eyebrows pointedly at Jonas. "Right, bro? *Aren't you proud of her?*" I say.

Jonas scowls at me, the bastard.

"I was scared; I'm not gonna lie," Sarah says. "My hands were shaking like crazy the whole time I was in there. But there was no way I was gonna leave that building without implanting that virus, no matter what. There was too much at stake."

"You're such a badass, Sarah," Kat says.

Jonas exhales and uncrosses his arms and Sarah shoots him a look that says, "Screw you, motherfucker." Ah, well, maybe little Miss Sarah Cruz is gonna be able to handle my brother, after all.

"Hey, guys," Henn says, engrossed with something on his screen.

"Holy shit. Oksana's going into her bank account right now—that Henderson Bank we were scouting out before?" He stares at the screen for another ten seconds. "Sha-zam. She just typed in her password. Ha! I got it." He shakes his head. "Oh man, I love technology."

"So what do we do?" Sarah asks.

"We wait a few minutes for her to log off, and then we go in and snoop around."

"Sounds like the perfect time for me to fill drink orders," I say, heading to the bar. "Party Girl with a Hyphen?"

"Club soda, please."

"You sure you don't want a little hair of the dog?"

She shakes her head, grimacing. "I'm sure."

Damn, she's cute. "I'll join you. My liver could probably use a little break."

"We're really not living up to our nicknames, you know," she says.

"I won't tell if you won't."

I get everyone else's drink orders, and just as I'm passing a glass of champagne to Sarah, Henn calls us over to his computer screen. "She's logged off," he announces. "Let's go in."

We all gather around Henn's computer, bursting with anticipation.

"Well, she's already deposited your checks—one hundred eighty thousand big ones," Henn says. "I bet that boils your blood, huh, Jonas?"

Jonas grunts.

"And she just transferred half of it into her savings account. Hmm," Henn says, sounding perplexed.

"What?" Sarah asks, her eyes bugging out.

"Even after today's deposit, Oksana's got only about half a million total in these two accounts." He furrows his brow.

"Hmm," I say.

"Hmm, indeed," Henn agrees. "Chump change. These must be Oksana's personal accounts—definitely not The Club's main accounts."

"Damn," Sarah says. "So how do we find the big money?"

Jonas walks away from the group to the other side of the room, apparently mulling things over.

"We just have to wait for them to log into their main bank accounts," Henn says. "It could be five minutes, five hours, five days—who knows?"

I glance at Kat and something's made her visibly anxious all of a sudden, though I have no idea what it was.

"But I guarantee they'll lead us there sooner or later," Henn continues. "And in the meantime, I'll take a nice, long gander around their files and data, make copies of everything, see if there's anything of interest. Oh, and I'll listen to Max's voicemails, too. That's so cool you got Max's phone, Sarah." He sips his beer. "Dang, there's a lot to do."

I exhale loudly, drawing everyone's attention, including Kat's. "Well, it looks like poor Henn's gonna be working through the night again, going through all this stuff." I pull out my phone, intending to text Reed about those RCR tickets. "What do you say, Party Girl with a Hyphen—you wanna paint Sin City red with me again?"

"I'd actually like to help Henn, if that's okay," Kat says.

I'm blown away. She'd rather stay here and help Henn with his hacking shit than watch the RCR concert from backstage?

"I'm kind of excited about all this. I have a strong motivation to want to bury these guys," she adds. She looks at Sarah and her facial expression bursts with protectiveness. "Would that be okay with you, Henn? Or would I be in your way?"

My heart is racing and my skin is buzzing. I wouldn't have predicted Kat turning down backstage tickets at the Garden Arena to help Henn hack into The Club—not in a million years.

"No, that'd be awesome," Henn says. "But only if you really want to. I mean Josh and Jonas are *paying* me to do this, so . . ."

"Could you use my help, too?" I ask.

Henn's face lights up. "Yeah. That'd be great."

"Okay, then. I'll order us room service and the three of us will get to work."

"Make that the four of us," Sarah says. "I'll stick around and help, too. I'm pretty motivated to bury these guys, too."

We all look at Jonas. Obviously, this is his cue to say, "Me, too." Or better yet, "No, baby, lemme take you out to celebrate how you kicked the bad guys' asses today." But Jonas doesn't say either of those things. Of course not. Because he's an imbecile—a socially inept imbecile. Instead, my stupid serial-killer-moron of a dumbshit-brother just stands in the corner, silently sipping his beer. Well, I guess I'll just have to give the fucker a little push.

"Nah," I say. "You two kids should go out and *celebrate*." I look at Jonas pointedly. "Or stay *in* and celebrate, whatever floats your boat. Either way, *definitely celebrate*—you both kicked ass today."

Jonas' eyes flicker with sudden understanding of what I'm trying to tell him. He looks at Sarah, but he's already blown it—she's looking away, gritting her teeth. Oh shit. She looks like she's ready to join Kat in roasting some testicle s'mores.

I grin at Sarah, trying to charm her into forgiving my stupid brother. "The three of us will move our party down to my suite and let you two crazy kids swing on the chandeliers up here."

Jonas takes a long, slow sip of his beer, staring at Sarah—and she's flashing him the most adorable look of defiance I've ever seen. Well, actually, she's flashing him the *second* most adorable look of defiance I've ever seen—the first being the look Kat flashed me last night when she stood in that hallway in her skimpy undies, dripping wet, absolutely crazed with jealousy, banging on the call button for the elevator.

Jonas drains his beer and puts the bottle down—a good start—but then the moron doesn't cross the room and take Sarah into his arms. *Dumbshit.* Does he have fucking eyes? Or half a brain? Clearly, that's all Sarah wants him to do—take her into his arms and give her a kiss. I always say, when it comes to women, especially an angry one, just about any problem can be solved with a fucking awesome kiss.

Jonas crosses his arms over his chest and stares at Sarah.

I lean into Kat. "I feel like I'm watching Wimbledon."

She nods. "I think it's Jonas' serve."

I snicker.

"What do you say, baby?" Jonas finally says. I nod enthusiastically. Definitely a good start.

But Sarah doesn't reply. She juts her chin at him, her eyes on fire. She's such a cutie, I don't know how he's resisting her right now.

"You up for a little celebration tonight?" Jonas asks.

I hold my breath. How could she possibly resist him? He's clearly at least trying to turn on the charm. But Sarah shrugs and looks away.

"Why doesn't he just walk over to her and *kiss* her?" Kat whispers to me.

"Maybe she's told him kissing is off limits—maybe she's a fucking terrorist on a jihad," I whisper back.

Kat scoffs. "Or maybe she's just a frickin' *genius*."

"Or maybe she's painted herself into a corner she doesn't know how to get herself out of," I say.

Kat grunts.

"I think we should celebrate," Jonas says.

Sarah shrugs again. Oh man, she's holding firm.

"She definitely learned that stonewalling thing from her best friend," I whisper.

"Hmmph."

"Aw, come on, baby," Jonas says, grinning at Sarah. "You wanna have a little fun?"

"There it is," I whisper. "Game, set, match."

"Not so fast," Kat whispers. "Not gonna be that easy."

"Twenty bucks says she lays down her weapon right here."

"You're on. She'll hold out for at *least* two more asks. Trust me."

"*Maybe*," Sarah says.

"See?" I whisper. "He's got her."

Kat puts up a finger, as if to say, "Wait for it."

"And maybe *not*," Sarah adds, pursing her lips.

Kat puts out her hand. "Pay up."

Jonas mocks Sarah's pout. "What if I said *please*?"

"Double or nothing?" I whisper. "Next ask."

"You're on, fool," Kat replies.

Sarah's trying to suppress a smile. "Then I'd say *possibly*."

"Ha!" I whisper. "Pay up."

Kat puts up her finger.

"But not *probably*," Sarah says.

"Fuck," I say.

Kat puts out her palm again and I lay forty bucks in it, rolling my eyes.

"What if I said pretty please?" Jonas asks, smiling broadly.

"Double or nothing again?" Kat whispers.

I shake my head and Kat giggles.

Sarah shrugs again.

"Jesus. Glad I didn't make another bet," I whisper. "She's as stubborn as you."

"What if I said pretty please *and* that we can do whatever you want, anything at all, you name it?" Jonas asks.

"Okay, whoa. I think he's overdoing it," I whisper to Kat.

She giggles. "No, he's doing the bare minimum."

"*Anything at all*?" Sarah asks.

"Don't do it," I whisper to Kat.

"He will," Kat says.

"*Anything at all*," Jonas confirms.

Kat giggles. "Sucker."

"Pussy," I say.

"But sweet," she responds.

Sarah touches the platinum bracelet on her wrist. "You'll be at my mercy completely?"

Jonas squints and bites his lip, considering.

"Don't do it," I whisper.

"He will."

Jonas still hasn't replied.

"Hang tough, man," I whisper. "Fight the good fight."

"He's toast," Kat replies.

"Stand strong," I whisper.

"He's a goner."

"Well? Will you be at my mercy or not?" Sarah prods him. "What do you say?"

"He says yes," Kat says.

"Definitely," I agree.

"Hmm." Jonas walks slowly toward Sarah like she's pulling him on a string. "What do I say?" he says softly. When he reaches Sarah, he takes her face in his hands and whispers to her, but I can't make out what he's saying. Clearly, whatever it is, he's saying it with passion.

"Really, you should owe me at least a hundred bucks," Kat whispers. "Are you always this stupid, or just when it comes to women?"

"How was I supposed to know Sarah's a terrorist like you?"

"Who do you think taught her all her tricks?" Kat says.

We both giggle.

Jonas and Sarah are whispering to each other and kissing like they're the only two people in the room.

"Hey, PG," I say, leaning into Kat. "Why'd you look like you were gonna have a stroke when Henn said it might take five days before he's able to crack The Club's system?"

She waves me off. "Oh nothing."

"Tell me. You looked like you were gonna throw up right then."

"Which isn't an unusual look for me, unfortunately." She shoots me an adorable smile. "Sorry about your shoes again."

I chuckle. "No worries. What's going on?"

She rolls her eyes. "I just, you know, I've got a job. Bills to pay. I don't have enough vacation days to cover me staying in Vegas that much longer. If it takes five days for us to complete this 'mission,' whatever the heck it is, I'll probably have to quit my job. Or maybe take an unpaid leave, if they'll let me, I dunno. But it's okay. Wild horses couldn't drag me away if Sarah needs me here. It's a no-brainer. Don't worry about it."

## Chapter 24

*Kat*

By the time the second round of room service arrives at Josh's suite, Henn, Josh, and I have been extracting and analyzing information off the bad guys' computers and phone for almost five hours straight.

"Woot!" I squeal when the room service guy spreads the plates of goodies on a glass table in the middle of the suite. "Now this is my idea of heaven on earth."

We all gather around the table, drooling at the decadent food in front of us.

"Yummalicious," I say, rubbing my hands together with glee. "Everything looks so tantalizing, it's hard to decide where to start."

"That's exactly what women say when they throw themselves at me," Henn says. "*Where. To. Start*?"

I laugh.

Henn considers the various plates of dessert in front of him. "It's a no-brainer—chocolate cake is the clear entry-point."

"Careful. Chocolate cake is a gateway drug," Josh says.

"I'll risk it," Henn says.

"I like the way you think, Henn. YOLO, right?" I shoot Josh a wink and he smiles.

"Slide that plate between us, Kitty Kat," Henn says. "We'll share."

I hand Henn a fork and slide the cake plate between us. "Josh? You wanna succumb to death by chocolate with us?"

"Nah, I'm a cheesecake man, through and through. Send that bad boy down here."

Henn slides the cheesecake across the table toward Josh.

"Hey, Josh, shoot that apple pie over to papa," Henn says, a huge bite of chocolate cake stuffed in his mouth.

"Here you go, papa," Josh says.

"Oh no, did they forget the ice cream?" I ask. "Please, God, no."

"It's right here," Henn says, shoving the bowl of ice cream at me. "Save your prayers for world hunger or curing cancer."

"Or Seahawks games," Josh adds.

I laugh.

When our eating frenzy has slowed down a bit, we lean back in our chairs, patting our stomachs.

"That hit the spot," I say. "Thinking so hard really works up an appetite. Who knew?"

Henn laughs.

"I don't know how you do it day after day, Henn," I say. "Just a few hours of thinking hard and my brain hurts."

"It's not thinking hard for Henn. Like I keep saying, he's a fucking genius," Josh says.

"Thanks, man."

"So what's next, boss?" Josh asks.

"We send all the data we've extracted through translation software and hope whatever comes out the other side leads us to our next rabbits to chase."

"How long 'til you crack into their system, you think?" Josh asks.

"There's no way to know for sure, but I'm guessing just a couple days. Maybe four or five, outside."

My stomach turns over and my chest tightens. Damn. I'm definitely gonna have a problem keeping my job if this takes much longer than another day or two. I glance up at Josh and he's staring at me intently. I half-smile at him, but I'm suddenly wracked with anxiety.

"I tell you one thing, though," Henn says. "Having you guys helping me out tonight sure sped things up a ton. Probably shaved a couple days off."

"It was amazing watching you work," I say.

"Yeah, that's what all the pretty girls say, Kitty Kat."

I laugh. "I'm sure they do, Henny."

"Actually, no, they don't. That was humor borne of pain."

"That's all humor is," Josh says. "The flipside of pain."

"Hey, no deep conversations allowed here," I say. "Only superficial banter, please. And cake."

"Amen," Josh says. "No argument from me."

"Henn, I can't imagine why girls aren't tackling you to the ground as you walk down the sidewalk," I say. "You're obviously the total package."

"Why, thank you."

"Which means whatever's not working for you can be traced to whatever you're doing or *not* doing to get their attention. What's your go-to move to close the deal, if you know what I mean?"

"No, I don't know what you mean. That's the problem. *I have no idea what you mean.*"

I shoot a worried look at Josh. "The patient is flatlining, doctor. We need the crash cart."

Josh laughs. "He's too nice—that's the problem," Josh says. "Just dick it up a little bit, Henn, and women will be elbowing each other in the earholes to get to you, I guarantee you."

"*'Dick it up'*?" I repeat.

"Absolutely. There's a time and place for nice and sensitive and sweet—and a time and place for dicking it up. And something tells me Henn needs to introduce more dick into his repertoire."

"*That's* your advice for attracting women? 'Dick it up'?"

"Absolutely." He winks at Henn. "Trust me, man. Just throw a big ol' steaming pile of 'I don't give a fuck' on every woman who crosses your path for the next month, and you'll have to beat the babes off with a stick."

"Sorry, Josh," Henn says. "No offense, but your advice is utterly worthless to me. When *you* dick it up, I'm sure women wanna birth your babies—but if I were to dick it up even a little bit, women would just call me a dick and walk away."

"That's not true, man," Josh says. "When it comes to women, certain things are tried and true, no matter who you are."

I sit back in my chair, smirking at Josh. "Please, oh wise and powerful one, tell us *more* nuggets of wisdom about how any man, no matter who he is, can bag a babe."

"I'd be glad to. Well, for one thing, women *think* they wanna be chased—that's what all the movies and books tell 'em they want—but they don't. Not really."

"We *don't*?" I ask. "Huh. Fascinating."

"It's true. You chase a woman too hard, she thinks you're desperate—and women *can't stand desperate*." He grins at me. "That's rule number one. If you do the equivalent of driving to her house and holding a boom box over your head, you might as well hand her your dick and balls in a Ziplock baggie, too, 'cause you're not gonna need 'em any more." He leans back, looking at me with smoldering eyes. "You always gotta leave her wondering, keep her guessing—at least a little bit." He winks at me. "That's how to keep her wanting more."

I lean forward, my eyes locked on his. "Oh, so, for instance, if a guy's got a business trip to New York for a whole freaking week, then he should just text brief messages to a woman like, 'Hey' and 'What's up?'—just enough to let the babe feel like he's thinking about her but brief and superficial enough to keep her wondering if he's even interested at all?"

Josh grins broadly. "*Exactly*. Let her wonder if you give a shit or not. Keep her off-balance. And then just sit back and watch her eat out of the palm of your hand the next time she sees you."

"Hardly," I say.

"Dude. What the fuck are you two talking about?" Henn asks.

Josh ignores him. "But you have to be wary. Because she's a demon spawn and she'll start fucking with you—doing shit like demanding to see something you've never shown *anyone,* something that's none of her fucking business—all while acting like what she's asking for is perfectly reasonable and that *you're* the crazy one if you say no."

"Interesting. Maybe she's not playing head games, though—ever think of that? Maybe you're reading the situation wrong, completely misunderstanding her motivations."

"No, that's just bullshit justification for sociopathic behavior."

"*Sociopathic*?"

"Borderline."

"Wow."

"The bottom line is that she's just a goddamned terrorist—which means that on principle alone, you must never, ever *give in to her unreasonable demands*. You just gotta keep your eye on the prize—the big picture—and stay strong."

"What the fuck are you two talking about?" Henn asks.

"And the big picture is . . .?" I ask, completely ignoring Henn. "Pray tell?"

"You don't know?"

I shake my head. "No, I don't."

"Well, if you haven't figured it out by now, then I can't help you."

I squint at Josh. "So that's the sum total of your advice on how to bag a babe, huh? Dick it up, dig in your heels, don't act desperate, and keep your eye on the prize?"

"Yeah, pretty much. That and *always* wear cologne. Women are highly sensory creatures. You gotta overwhelm all their senses—sight, sound, smell, touch. It's primal." One side of his mouth tilts up.

"Okay, this I understand," Henn says. "Wear cologne. That's something I can actually do."

"Well, as long as it's the *right* cologne, yes," I say. "Wear the wrong cologne, and you're sunk. The wrong cologne is worse than no cologne at all."

That cocky grin isn't going anywhere. "Oh really? Well, what about mine, for instance? Right or wrong?"

I hate to give him the satisfaction, but the truth is the truth. "Very, very *right*." I say. I inhale deeply as if I'm taking in his scent from across the table.

Josh barks the name of his cologne at Henn. "Write that down, man. You heard the woman—she likes my cologne *a lot*." He licks his lips, assessing me. "Actually, you know what, Henn? If you're gonna get advice on how to bag a babe from anyone, you should get it from Kat. She's probably the world's foremost expert."

I narrow my eyes. What does that mean? Did he just call me a slut? Or does he think I'm bisexual? "No, I think Josh has lots and lots more experience bagging *babes* than me."

Josh rolls his eyes. "Testy, testy. Jeez. What I mean is that you're a babe, so best to ask you. Actually, you're the best of both worlds. You've got a *vagina* (so I'm told—I'm still not sure I believe it) *and* you've got four brothers, too. So as a woman *and* an honorary dude, you can give our beloved Henny the female *and* male perspectives on babe-baggery. Shit, with those credentials, you could probably teach a Learning Annex seminar on the subject, maybe even a twelve-week course."

I smile broadly. "Thank you for recognizing my expertise."

Josh nods. "Plus, you're demonic as hell. If he's gonna learn the ropes, best if he learns from an instructor who blows shit up, rather than one who plays by the rules. No one ever learned a damned thing from following The Rules. Ever. Am I right?"

I shoot him my most demonic look. "Well, actually, yeah, we're definitely in agreement about that."

Josh grins.

"Well, all right, then." I turn my attention to Henn, popping up from my chair. "Get up, Henny. We're gonna role-play." I let my eyes drift suggestively to Josh. "One of my very favorite things to do, actually." I wink.

The smoldering look on Josh's face tells me he understands my meaning just fine.

"Come on, Henn. Get up."

Henn stands warily.

"Okay. We're at a bar. You see me from across the room. You're interested in me. Go."

"*Go*?"

"Yeah, go. Do what you'd normally do when you see a babe at a bar."

"You want me to do what I usually do when I see a really pretty girl at a bar?"

"Correct."

Henn shrugs, beelines to the front door of the suite, opens the door, and leaves the room. Josh and I look at each other and burst out laughing. After a beat, there's a soft knock at the front door and Josh strides to it, still laughing.

"Thanks," Henn says, re-entering the room. "Damn door locked behind me."

I'm laughing so hard, I'm crying. "Oh, Henny, you're hilare."

"I think maybe my strategy needs a little fine-tuning," Henn says.

"Just a little," I agree. "Okay, so approach me. Come on. Pretend I'm a girl you're interested in."

"Well, that's not hard to do," he mutters.

"Come on. Just be yourself."

Henn stares at me for a long minute and then throws up his

hands. "I have no fucking idea what to do." He plops himself into a chair.

"Don't overthink it. The truth is, it doesn't actually matter what you say to a woman—it's all in your attitude. You know how in public speaking, they say to imagine your audience naked?"

"Yeah. You're saying I should imagine you naked? Oops. Too late. I just did." His face turns bright red. "Confession time: that wasn't the first time I've done that. Sorry."

I laugh. "No, no, no. Don't imagine the babe naked—you'll get too flustered. Instead, just imagine your dick is so big, it drags on the ground." I glance at Josh pointedly and he shoots me a naughty smile.

"Do you have any advice that's a bit more *concrete* than that?" Henn asks. "Imagining my dick is dragging on the ground seems a bit *esoteric*."

I laugh. "Okay, I've got a great rule of thumb for you," I say. "Every time you open your mouth to talk to a woman you're interested in—a *babe* you wanna bag—ask yourself this question: 'Is what I'm about to say more or less likely to get me a blowjob?' If the answer is yes, then say it—but if the answer is no, then shut the fuck up."

Josh bursts out laughing.

"Whoa," Henn says.

"Words to live by," Josh says. "Did one of your brothers come up with that little gem?"

"No. That's all me."

"Damn," Josh says. "I think we just discovered who of the three of us is the *real* fucking genius. *Damn*."

"If all men knew that one simple rule," I continue, "the world would be a much happier place."

"Fuck yeah," Josh agrees. "For everyone." He spreads his legs and reaches under the table, presumably adjusting his dick in his pants. "What other tips you got, Madame Professor? I must admit, I'm finding your lesson plan highly educational."

"That's it. I'm done talking. Now it's time for Henny to learn through *doing*. Come on, Henny. Get up. It's role-play time."

Henn scowls at me.

"Oh, come on. This is for your own good. Try to pick me up, using all the advice I just gave you."

Henn grimaces.

"Get up. Come on," I say.

Henn begrudgingly stands.

"Okay. We're in a bar. I'm a babe you're interested in bagging. *Go*."

"Bars aren't really my thing, actually. I have a lot more success at places like, you know, Starbucks. Gimme a woman with a laptop in Starbucks, preferably a cute little brunette with glasses, and I'm Don Juan."

"Okay. Fine. We're in Starbucks. I've got a laptop. *Go*."

"Brown hair and glasses?"

"You bet. Now *go*."

"Well, is your laptop a Mac or a PC?"

I make a face. "Whichever. That's not important. *Go*."

"Not *important*? Are you *mad*?"

"Okay, fine." I roll my eyes. "A Mac. Now, *go*."

"Can you be more specific, please? What model? A Mac Book Pro? Or a Mac Book Air? And how many gigabytes of memory?"

"Holy Filibuster, Batman!" I shout.

Josh laughs.

"No more stalling, Henn," I say. "Come on. *Gooooooooooo*."

"*Fine*." He closes his eyes briefly, and when he opens them, he's clearly got his Casanova face on. "Um. Oh, hi there, pretty brunette lady with glasses. I'm Hennessy. I was wondering, is your name 'Wi Fi' by any chance?"

I make a face. "Is my name '*Wi Fi*'?" I ask, not comprehending his meaning.

"Yeah, because I really feel a *connection* to you."

We all laugh together.

"I told you, I have no idea," Henn says, smiling shyly. "The initial approach is the hardest thing for me."

"You just have to act like it's a foregone conclusion," Josh says. "Make her think it's her lucky day you've graced her with your attention."

I roll my eyes. "Oh, this I gotta see. Show us how you do it, Playboy."

"Oh, you wanna see how I do it, huh?"

"Hell yeah. Razzle-dazzle us, Playboy."

He smirks. "You sure you can handle it?"

"Pretty sure."

"Okay, I'll show you the Playboy razzle-dazzle, but I gotta warn you, even in role-play, it's gonna make you wanna sleep with me."

"I'll risk it."

"Just sayin'—you've been warned."

"I'll risk it," I say again.

"I think you should sign a waiver first."

I roll my eyes. "Just give it to me already."

"That's exactly what you'll say after I show you the Playboy razzle-dazzle."

I laugh. "We'll see about that. Come on."

"Fine. But we're at a bar, not Starbucks. At least let me play on my home turf."

"Okay," I say. "We're at a bar. *Go.*"

Josh slowly gets up from his chair and sidles up to me, taking his sweet time.

"Hey, beautiful," he says smoothly. "I'm Josh." He puts out his hand.

I take his hand. "Hi, I'm Kat."

He leans into me, close enough for me to get a whiff of his cologne, and my knees instantly go weak.

He whispers softly into my ear. "What are you drinking, Kat?"

My clit zings. "A mojito," I choke out.

He turns to Henn. "Hey, bartender, another mojito for the gorgeous lady with the sexy little cleft in her chin." He looks at me and levels me with a dark blue smolder that makes my clit pound like a jackhammer. "You ready to get out of here, sweetheart? Because I'm in the mood to make you feel so fucking good," he whispers, almost inaudibly, skimming his hand down my arm. "Before you answer, you should know: I've got a huge dick and I know exactly how to use it to make you scream. All you need to decide is whether you wanna have the night of your life."

There's a long beat during which I feel warm wetness literally ooze into the crotch of my panties.

"What do you say, honey? You ready to go?"

I nod.

"Let's go."

He holds out his hand and I take it.

All of a sudden, I want one thing: for Josh to pull me out the door and straight to my room. But, instead, Josh releases my hand and turns to Henn, smiling.

"Badah-bing-badah-boom," he says. "Easy peasy. Now you try it. Just like that."

"Ummmmmmmm," Henn says. "Could you be serious, please? I actually wanna know what you do, no kidding around."

"I wasn't kidding around. That's what I do."

Henn laughs. "Come on, Josh."

Josh whips his attention onto me. "Kat, in all seriousness—would that have worked on you if I did it just like that?"

"In all seriousness?" I say. Oh man, my heart is racing out of my chest. "*Hell yes*."

"See?" Josh says. He shrugs. "Success with babe-baggery is all about confidence. Everything else is secondary." He sits back down, a cocky grin on his face. "Thank you, Kat." He winks. "You're excellent at role-play—not surprisingly."

I sit back down, flustered.

"It always boils down to confidence," Josh says. "Am I right, Madame Professor?"

"Yeah," I say, struggling to regain my composure. Oh shit. There's a deep, dull ache in my abdomen that won't go away. I clear my throat. "But don't forget, Josh, getting the babe hooked on the line is only the first step—then you've actually got to be able to *deliver* on all that bravado or else you're sunk." I shoot Josh a smart-ass look that, hopefully, says, "You're full of shit."

Josh's eyes are brimming with confidence. "Well, duh. It goes without saying a guy's gotta be able to deliver on everything he promises—that's where true confidence comes from, being able to walk the walk." He winks. "'Under-promise and over-perform,' I always say. And believe me, I just under-promised on what I can perform."

Oh holy hell. I can't breathe.

"So let's start simple, then," Josh says to Henn. "The first step is being able to kiss a woman like a boss. For women, kissing is everything—you gotta be able to curl her toes, man. From there, all good things will come to you. Kiss a woman right, she'll be begging you for more. Am I right, Madame Professor?"

I shoot Josh a pointed look. "Yep. No doubt about it. Begging."

Josh bites his lip.

"Well, no sweat, guys. Because I happen to be a fantastic kisser."

"Really?" I ask, surprised.

"Yup."

"*Fantastic*?"

"Well, okay, maybe not *fantastic.* But pretty damned good."

"What's your technique?"

"My *technique*? Well, I can't *describe* it. It's a show-me-don't-tell-me kind of thing."

"Well, you gotta give me something to work with here, Henny. How else am I gonna be able to give you feedback?"

"I can't describe it," Henn says, shrugging his shoulders. "You'll just have to trust me."

"Try explaining it to me, Henn," I say. "Josh is right—that first kiss can make or break you—lead you to the Promised Land or sink you like a stone." I flash Josh a smart-ass look. "You gotta get it right."

Josh squints at me. "Yeah, Kat's right. But that's only because women sometimes place ridiculous importance on what should be a simple kiss—irrational, ridiculous, stupid importance—when they should just chill out and go with the flow and stop acting like a fucking terrorist."

"Jesus, Josh," Henn says.

Josh's eyes are locked with mine. I squint at him, and he returns the gesture.

"Why don't you just *show* her, bro?" Josh says, still looking at me. "That's the simplest way for us to approach this."

My face involuntarily morphs into a "what the fuck" look.

"You don't mind, do you, Kat?" Josh asks evenly.

"You mean... you want me to . . .?" Henn asks.

"Yeah, why not?" Josh says. "Unless, of course, Kat's gonna require you to reveal all your secrets in order to kiss her?"

I narrow my eyes at Josh and then whip my head to look at Henn. "I think it's a great idea for you to kiss me. How else are we gonna know if you've got the right technique?"

Henn's face is bright red. "I don't think this is such a good idea, guys."

"Why the fuck not?" I say. I look at Josh with defiance. "It's just for instructional purposes, right? No big deal." Josh isn't really gonna let me kiss another man in his presence, is he—even if it's just Henn? Even if it's just for "instructional purposes"?

"I agree," Josh says, clenching his jaw.

I open my mouth, horrified. What the *fuck*? He's gotta be bluffing.

"The woman obviously places a shit-ton of importance on kissing," Josh continues. "So I'm sure her feedback will be invaluable to you." His eyes are searing holes into my flesh.

There's no way he's gonna let me go through with this, right?

"No, it's too weird," Henn says. "I mean, you two guys are a couple... right?"

"Josh and me?" I say through gritted teeth. "Noooo. Josh and I haven't even kissed—and we've mutually decided we're not going to. Ever. We just don't see eye to eye on certain things."

Josh swallows hard, his eyes burning. "Kat's right. We're never going to kiss because she's a fucking terrorist who takes some sort of sick pleasure in holding men hostage for ransom she has no business demanding."

"What am I missing here?" Henn asks. "What's going on with you two?"

"Nothing's going on, like I said. Josh and I are just friends—friends who don't tell each other everything, and therefore don't kiss."

Henn looks confused. "You require someone to tell you 'everything' just to *kiss* you? What does that mean?"

"Nothing. Not *everything.* Just certain things." I clear my throat. "Things I'd tell if the situation were reversed."

Henn and Josh exchange a look.

I look down, color rising in my cheeks. Is Josh really gonna watch me kiss another man?

"Go ahead, Henn," Josh says. "*YOLO.*"

I swivel my head up to look at Josh. He looks like he wants to kill me right now—right after he fucks the living hell out of me.

Well, if he's not gonna stop me, then I'm not gonna stop me, either.

Is Josh really not gonna stop me?

I look at Josh. He's glaring at me. I look at Henn. He looks utterly confused.

"Okay, Henn," I say. "Gimme your best kiss. I'll critique you from the field. And, Josh, you watch closely from the nose-bleed seats so you can give Henn your feedback, too."

Josh doesn't reply.

"Did you hear me, Josh? I want you to watch Henn kiss me—watch *closely*."

"I heard you, Madame Terrorist."

Henn looks at Josh, seemingly for permission.

"Go ahead," Josh says. "Kiss her. She's all yours." He exhales and leans back in his chair, crossing his arms over his chest.

He's really not gonna stop me? Goddammit! I feel like stomping my feet, I'm so mad. Doesn't he realize this whole thing's not about his stupid application anymore? We're way beyond that now. Now it's about something more—something bigger.

"Kat?" Henn asks. "Are you okay?"

I wipe my eyes, emotion threatening. I don't look at Josh—I can't. I'm afraid if I do, my eyes will betray every last thought bouncing around in my head. I want him. I want him so bad, I'm aching. But I want all of him. Not just his lips or his very large dick. I want to know what's hiding beneath his Happy Josh mask. "Yeah, I'm fine. Let's do this," I say.

"You're sure you're cool with it?" Henn asks me.

"Yeah. I'm sure." I stand. "I can't think of a single reason not to."

I can feel Josh's eyes on me, but I don't look at him.

Henn stands slowly.

"And you're cool, Josh?"

"Yup."

My chest is tight. I still can't look at Josh. "Okay," I say. "Gimme your top-of-the-line smooch, Henny. Hit me with your best shot."

Henn takes a slow step toward me. "You're sure?"

"I'm sure." I put my finger up. "Just for instructional purposes, though."

"Yeah, I know." Henn exhales. "Should I go brush my teeth first? Have a mint?"

"Did you eat onions or garlic recently?"

"No. Chocolate cake, apple pie, cheesecake, ice cream. Oh, and tiramisu."

"We're good, then."

He exhales and shakes out his arms. "Whew. Okay."

Henn takes another step toward me. And then another. But then he stops. He glances at Josh—but since I can't bring myself to look at Josh's face right now, I have no idea what Henn is seeing over there. Whatever it is, Henn obviously feels emboldened by it, because he turns back to me and takes another step, bridging the final gap between our bodies.

Henn cups my face gently in his palms and leans forward.

I close my eyes and, within half a second, Henn's soft, warm lips meet mine, gently at first—as if he's introducing himself to me—and after a few seconds, coax my mouth open with surprising confidence and skill. He slides his tongue into my mouth, instantly leading my tongue into a sensuous, languid, swirling motion—until, after one last flicker of his tongue, his lips guide mine closed and he retreats.

Henn's lips leave mine. Kiss over.

Holy shitballs.

I open my eyes to find Henn staring at me, his eyes wide and face red.

I glance at Josh, my cheeks suddenly blazing with heat, and my breath catches at the ferocious expression on his face. I don't know Josh well enough to understand exactly what emotion he's telegraphing right now—is that anger, arousal, jealousy... or something else? Whatever it is, it's clear to me the man is feeling something fueled by a shit-ton of testosterone.

"I... That was... um . . ." I stammer. "Wow, Henn." I swallow hard. "I don't think you need... any... instruction whatsoever."

## Chapter 25
*Josh*

Jesus Christ. Enough, already. When will this torturous kiss between Henn and Kat end? *Enough.* Well, now I know: I'm dealing with a fucking monster. A gorgeous, twisted, evil, sexy fucking monster. I didn't think she'd actually go *through* with it. What the fuck is she thinking? Poor Henn's never gonna recover from this goddamned kiss. I'm only watching it, and she's scarring me for life.

After what seems like forever, Henn and Kat *finally* break away from their kiss, and Kat's eyes instantly dart to me. I steel myself, expecting her to smile like the vicious shark she is—like the prehistoric *killing* machine she is—but the look on her face absolutely floors me. Her eyes aren't blazing with smart-ass defiance, no—they're glistening with something else... *Hurt.*

Henn hasn't stopped staring at Kat since they broke apart from their kiss, even though she's looking at me. Jesus, the poor guy looks like he just stumbled out of a hookah lounge.

Clearly, I've got to say something to smooth things out here, even though I'm literally trembling in my seat with adrenaline.

"Awesome, Henn," I say. "You nailed it man—or should I say *her*?"

Kat's face contorts into unbridled disgust.

Henn fidgets and takes a step back.

"I watched your technique carefully, man," I continue breezily, "looking for any chink in your armor. But I couldn't find a damned thing to critique. *You* should be giving *me* pointers, man."

"Yeah, you slayed it, Henn," Kat adds, her voice tight. Her mouth smiles, but her eyes don't. "All I've got is praise, baby."

I stand abruptly. "Well, I think I'm gonna hit the sack. I'm pretty wiped."

Kat stands. "Me, too. Unless you still need some more help, Henn?"

"No, I'm good. I can take it from here." He looks at his watch and clears his throat. "Wow, it's almost three. I'm gonna get another Americano and start going through the first batch of stuff that's been processed through translation software." He looks at his three laptops sprawled on the table. "Should I move my shit to my room and work there?"

"Nah, no worries. Stay put. I'm just gonna crash. Gimme your room key, man. I'll crash in your room." My eyes flicker briefly to Kat to get a read on her—to see if maybe she's toying with the idea of letting me "crash" in her room for the night—and I'm met with blue eyes of steel. My eyes dart back to Henn. "What's your room number again, man?"

"1836."

"Okay, well, nighty night, man." I slide Henn's key-card into my pocket. "Don't drink too many Americanos. That shit'll kill you." I start moving toward the front door of the suite. "Come on, Kat. I'll walk you to your room."

"No need."

"I promised Jonas I wouldn't leave you alone while we're here in Vegas, unless you're safely in your room."

She clenches her jaw. "Well, we wouldn't want you to break a promise to Jonas, would we?"

"Thanks again for all the help tonight, guys," Henn says. "You cut my workload down by hours."

"Any time, bro. We're all in this together."

Kat hugs Henn and kisses him on the cheek. "You're amazing, Henn—a fucking genius."

"So I've been told."

"And thanks for the kiss," she says. "I know it was for instructional purposes only, but it was a really, really lovely kiss."

"Really?"

"Yeah. One for the memory book."

"Hang on a sec, Kat," I say. I quickly gather my toiletries and a change of clothes from the bedroom and stuff everything into a small duffel bag. "Okay. See you in the morning, Henn. Do you need anything from your room?"

"No. I'll call down to the front desk for a toothbrush. I'm fine."

"Okay. Good night, man."

I silently guide Kat through the front door of the suite.

"It's all fun and games 'til someone gets hurt," I mutter the second the door closes behind us.

"I couldn't agree more," she says, gritting her teeth.

"Didn't look like you gave a shit about someone getting hurt a minute ago," I reply.

She whips around to face me, her eyes blazing. "What the *fuck* is wrong with you?" she asks.

"I could say the same thing to you. Are you a complete sociopath?"

"What? You're the one who offered me up like I was a wench at a pirate-bride auction."

"Ha! I didn't think you'd actually *do* it. I hope you're happy now. You've ruined that boy."

"*I've* ruined him? You're the one who threw me at him! And now you're all pissy because I did exactly what you told me to do?" she seethes. "Who's the sociopath now?"

I throw up my hands in frustration.

"It looks like I'm not the only one who's a suicide bomber, huh?" she says. "Looks like you're willing to blow yourself up to win every bit as much as I am."

She's right about that. Fuck. I'm a fucking suicide bomber, goddammit. What's happening to me? Kat's driving me certifiably insane.

Wordlessly, I grab her arm and pull her to the elevators—I'm gonna drag her to her room and ditch her sorry ass there, let her think about what she just did to poor Henn—what she just did to me, goddammit—but when the doors open, something overtakes me. This woman makes me fucking crazy. I can't get enough of her, even when she pisses me off.

I pull her inside the elevator, drop my duffel bag, and slam her against the fucking wall, pressing my hard-on into her and kissing her neck.

She moans loudly. "Yes," she breathes.

"Stop torturing me," I say, groping her breasts. "No more fucking games."

She throws her head back and lifts her leg around my waist, guiding my hard-on into her crotch. I grind into her, pinning her hands above her head, licking and kissing her face, her ears, her chin—but not her lips. Fuck no, not her lips. There's no fucking way.

The doors open. We're on her floor. I pick up the duffel and drag her out of the elevator roughly and into the hallway, but we don't make it more than a few steps before I'm attacking her again. Goddamn this woman. I pin her to the wall again, just outside the elevator, and unbutton her jeans, sliding my hand inside her pants. She cries out as my fingers slide into her pussy. Oh God, she's so wet. My dick is throbbing mercilessly. I can't stand this anymore. I've got to have her. "You're evil," I say, sliding my fingers in and out of her. "You're so fucking evil."

She moans loudly as my fingers fuck her furiously.

She begins pawing at the front of my jeans, trying to unbutton my fly.

"I've got to have you," I growl. "Fuck this shit, Kat. Come on."

"Yes," she says. "Do it. Come on."

The nearby elevator dings.

I pull my hand out of her pants and leap back from her, shaking with my arousal, and a small group of forty-something women tumble out of the elevator, laughing hysterically.

"Which way?" I mumble. "I forget your room number."

She points. "2715."

I grab her arm and yank her toward her room, my cock throbbing, my nostrils flaring. "No more bullshit. I'm fucking you right now. This is over right now."

"Why didn't you stop me?" she asks as I drag her down the hallway.

"Because I didn't think you were gonna actually go through with it."

"I thought for sure you were gonna stop me."

We've reached her room. "Gimme your key. I'm fucking you right now."

She exhales. Something in her eyes has shifted. "No, wait." She swallows hard. "Why didn't you stop me?" Her eyes are glistening with obvious hurt. "I thought you wouldn't be able to stand seeing another man kiss me—even Henn."

My heart squeezes. She looks authentically hurt.

"Kat," I say, shocked at the genuine emotion on her face.

"I thought you'd stop me." She wipes her watering eyes.

Oh, shit. I've fucked up here, haven't I? I've really fucked up.

"I just..." I begin, my head reeling. "I thought we were in a... battle to the death... I was... just trying to force your hand."

Why does she look like she's about to cry?

Kat wipes her eyes again. "I'm tired of battling to the death, Josh," she says softly, exhaling. "Or maybe I'm just plain tired." She motions to her room. "You wanna fuck me, but you don't wanna take off your mask. Sorry, but I'm not interested."

I'm speechless.

She exhales a long breath. "I'm just gonna get some sleep tonight. I'm totally sleep deprived."

"What? No. Let me come in with you."

"Why? What's the point?" Her blue eyes have steeled over. "Thanks for walking me to my room." She turns to swipe her key-card in the lock.

"Kat, wait." I grab her arm.

She freezes.

My pulse is pounding in my ears. How did we go from attacking each other in the elevator to this? What just happened?

"I'm sorry, Kat," I say. "I... thought you'd back down. I was just... I didn't understand. I didn't know it would hurt your feelings."

She stares at me, apparently waiting for me to continue.

But I don't. I don't know what else to say.

"I think I just need a short break from the game—or maybe I just need a little sleep. Either way, I just wanna crash."

"Kat, wait," I say, squeezing her arm gently. "Let me come in. Talk to me."

She shakes her head. "Why won't you just tell me what's in your application? How bad can it really be? I'm clearly not Snow White—I'm sure I'll understand. What's the big deal at this point?"

I don't reply.

"Is it S&M, Josh? Is that what you're into? Because I wouldn't care."

"Just, please. Enough. Stop pushing for this. It's gonna backfire. Trust me. It's gonna backfire and we won't be able to stuff that genie back into the bottle."

"But if I give in now where would we go from there?" She wipes her eyes again. "I admit I've fucked this up. Okay? I've taken it too far, created a no-win situation—I admit that." Her eyes water. "But it is what it is. And now I can't figure out an endgame besides seeing it through to the bitter end. If I don't insist on it now, then it'll always be this big 'thing' between us. I'll always wonder what the hell you're hiding from me."

I swallow hard. "It's not that big a deal, okay? It's really not. It's just that I don't talk about certain things," I say softly. "I'm not always Happy Josh, okay? I'm not always what I seem. And you reading that application would force me to spill my guts to you in a way... I'm not willing to do."

She twists her mouth. "I never spill my guts, either, Josh. I hate spilling my guts, believe me. But if I had an application, I'd give it to you," she says softly. "I really would, Josh. I'd spill my guts to you, if the situation were reversed."

"Easy for you to say. The situation's not reversed."

"But if it were, I'd tell you my secrets." Her lip is trembling.

I can't formulate a reply. She's breaking my heart. I don't understand what's happening. I haven't even kissed this goddamned girl and I feel like she's got a stranglehold on my fucking heart.

I shake my head, at a loss. I'm stuck between a rock and a hard place. She says if she gives in and quits the battle, she'd never trust me? But it works the same way on my end, doesn't it? If I tuck my dick and balls between my legs and give her what she wants, if I act like a pussy-whipped little puss who can be manipulated into doing puppy tricks for her, where the fuck could we possibly go from there? We'd be doomed.

"I'm not gonna give it to you," I say evenly. "If you wanna get with me, then get with me. If you don't, then don't. That application shouldn't have anything to do with it, either way."

Her eyes are unreadable to me. She sighs. "I think maybe we should just concentrate on saving the world for a bit, okay? Things have gotten out of control. That's my fault, not yours. I'm sorry about that." Her eyes suddenly flood with tears. "I think we should just take a break on battling to the death for a while—concentrate on saving the world."

"Kat. Wait. Let me come in. Not to fuck you. Just to be with you. Just to sleep next to you."

“Josh, we’re obviously two suicide bombers on opposing missions—both of us stubborn as hell. We’re not a good combination.” She opens her door. “Thanks for walking me to my room. I appreciate it.” She slips inside her room, and her voice travels through the gap in the door, just before it closes. “I’m sorry, Josh. Good night.”

## Chapter 26

*Kat*

"Well, to summarize," Henn begins, "we're dealing with some big shit here, fellas. Like, oh my fucking God." He cracks a huge smile. "Totally awesome."

We're all gathered around the table in the early afternoon light of Jonas and Sarah's suite to hear the latest on what Henn's uncovered about The Club—much of it, apparently, after Josh and I left the suite last night around 3:00 a.m.

Josh slipped into our meeting after me, looking groggy and bleary-eyed, and took a seat at the table next to me, nodding curtly as he sat down, his face tight and his eyes unreadable.

"Just tell me—were you able to get into The Club's system?" Jonas asks Henn.

"No, not yet. Wherever it is, it's buried deep, deep, deep in the web, way deep. But I'm getting close. I've got lots of breadcrumbs to follow. I'm hot on their trail, fellas. And very pretty ladies." He smiles at me and winks at Sarah.

"You should have seen how Henn figures things out," I say, pointedly not looking at Josh to my left. "He's a techno-Sherlock Holmes."

"The man's a fucking genius," Josh adds. He puts his right arm across the back of my chair as he speaks, but I lean forward in my chair to avoid letting his arm cradle my back. Just one touch and I'll melt. And I don't feel like melting right now.

Josh exhales with frustration, but I don't look at him.

"What do we know so far?" Jonas asks.

Henn launches into telling Jonas and Sarah what he (and Josh and I) discovered last night: namely, that The Club's operations are way bigger than any of us expected.

"What about a member list? Any luck on that?" Sarah asks.

My phone buzzes with an incoming text and I take a quick peek. Shoot. It's from my boss. This isn't gonna be good. I've been putting her off for days.

I open the message:

"Kat!" my boss writes. "Wow, wow, wow! Just got the signed contract and full retainer from this new client of yours! Holy crap! Biggest up-front retainer we've ever landed, by far. I know you're in meetings all day on your new account (!), but call me ASAP. I want to hear all the details. If you need me to fly to Las Vegas to help you with *anything* just say the word. Fantastic work! Of course, take as long as you need out there. Just check in occasionally to give me an update so we can manage our workload internally. Keep up the great work! We'll drink champagne when you get back!"

I keep reading and re-reading the email, not comprehending what my eyes are seeing and feeling like I've slipped into some sort of gap in the space-time continuum. Did I take acid and not remember? Have I been roofied? What the *hell* is she talking about?

I look at Josh, but he's listening intently to whatever Henn's saying.

"The identity of that über VIP guy seems like something we'd better nail down," Henn is saying. "His emails are double encrypted, but I cracked an email from Oksana to Max forwarding one of the über VIP guy's emails—and the guy said shit like 'my security personnel will post outside the door.' He's got security personnel? And they 'post' outside doors? Like, who the fuck says that?"

"A rock star?" Sarah suggests. "Guys like that always have bodyguards."

"No," Henn says. "Not based on what I've seen."

"Yeah, I know plenty of rock stars with bodyguards—and they don't talk like that," Josh says.

"I'll keep working on it," Henn says. "Okay, so are you guys ready for your minds to be officially blown?"

"You mean there's *more*?" Sarah asks.

"Oh yeah. The next part is what makes this so much fun." Henn looks at me. "I figured this next part out right after you left last night."

I look at the group apologetically. "I finally had to get some sleep."

"That's what happens when you don't subsist on a diet of caffeine and nicotine," Henn says.

"Did you leave to get some sleep, too?" Jonas asks Josh, flashing him a knowing look.

"Yeah, I couldn't keep up with Henn, either," Josh says. "I think I left around the time Kat left." He glances at me, his eyes full of apology. "Maybe just a little bit later."

It suddenly hits me like a thunderbolt: *Josh*. Whatever my boss was just babbling about in her email, it was Josh's doing.

I ask Henn a question absentmindedly, requesting clarification on something, but my mind is shifting into frenetic overdrive. There's no doubt in my mind: Josh contacted my boss and requested my personal "PR services" out here in Las Vegas.

"Oh my God," Josh mumbles in response to something Henn just said, his entire body stiffening next to me. He pulls his hand away from the back of my chair and rubs his eyes like he's blown away by something. Uh oh. I wasn't paying attention. What did I just miss?

"What?" I ask, my stomach twisting with dread.

"They're funding the Ukrainian separatists," Josh answers, his face draining of color.

I don't have the faintest idea what the hell that means.

"Which means Oksana's funding Putin through the back door," Jonas adds, as if that would make things clearer for me.

But it doesn't. Ukrainian separatists? Putin? Who's Putin? That sounds familiar, but I forget. Wait, isn't he that Russian guy? Obviously, I just missed something major when my brain was fixated on my boss' email.

"You guys, break it down for me," I say. "Sorry."

"Okay, back in the day, there was the U.S.S.R., right?" Jonas says. "Then it got broken up into all these pieces—Russia and Ukraine and the Baltic states. Well, now Putin wants to put all the pieces of mother Russia back together again, to resurrect the former empire—and he wants the diamond of his new Soviet Union to be Ukraine."

"And is Ukraine down with that plan?" I ask, wishing I'd paid more attention in my political science class in college. I honestly don't even know exactly where Ukraine is, to be honest.

"No, not the official government," Jonas says. "But there's a faction within Ukraine—the *separatists*—and they want to *separate* from their government and go along with Putin's reunification plan. So the separatists have waged armed conflicts with their own government, funded by the Russians."

Jonas and Josh exchange a look of extreme anxiety.

"Holy shitballs," I say softly, even though, honestly, I'm still not one hundred percent sure I get it. Whatever's happening, though, it's obviously holy-shitballs-worthy.

"Yeah, most definitely," Henn says. "Well said."

"We've got to find out who Mr. Bigwig VIP is," Jonas blurts. "We need to know who all the heavy hitters are. You said congressmen are involved in this shit, right?"

"Yup," Henn says.

"That could be really, really bad," Josh says, his body stiff and tight next to mine. His face looks ashen.

"Seriously. 'Oh, hi, constituents. Please re-elect me,'" Henn says, putting on his best congressman-voice. "'I added more police to our streets, got a library built, and voted to increase the minimum wage. Oh, *and* I paid a whole bunch of money to a Ukrainian prostitution and weapons ring to fund the reunification of the Soviet Union. Can I count on your vote during the next election?'"

Oooooh, I totally get it now. Leave it to Henn to explain things in terms I can easily understand. Ooph. Holy shitballs, indeed. This is a big deal.

"This is too big for us to handle on our own," Sarah declares emphatically. "We've got to hand this over to the FBI." Her eyes widen. "Or the CIA? I don't even know which one. I mean, jeez, I'm a first-year law student at U Dub." She shakes her head. "This is like, a matter of international significance—and that's not even an exaggeration."

Henn talks for a while, explaining how he plans to obtain the bad guys' passwords and banking information, all with the goal of uncovering data we can use to convince the good guys to take immediate action—and, suddenly, I feel like a round hole in a square peg. What the heckity-heck am I doing here? How can I possibly help with all this? I know what value everyone else in this room brings to our *Ocean's Eleven* crew, but what on earth is my role?

When Henn finishes talking, Sarah leaps out of her chair like a woman possessed.

"Henn, I'm your new best friend," she says.

She explains she's gonna write a kick-ass report with supporting documentation which we'll submit to the authorities and we all agree enthusiastically with her plan.

"Kat," Sarah says sharply at the end of her passionate speech, her eyes like lasers.

"Yes, ma'am." My heart's beating out of my chest. My brain is in overload. I keep thinking "Holy shitballs" on an endless loop.

"For each and every criminal count, I'm gonna need a piece of supporting evidence—something to show them we're not making this stuff up," Sarah says, looking at me. She's in full ass-kicking mode now. "I'll tell you exactly what kind of thing I'm looking for, and then you'll go digging through whatever Henn's been able to find so far to get it for me. You'll be my research assistant."

"I can do that," I say, my stomach churning. But what I'm thinking is, "*Holy shitballs.*"

"That's good," Jonas says. "And Josh and I will powwow and figure out our best strategy for the hand-off. I agree—we're going to have to turn this over to *someone*—but to whom? That's the question. If we put it in the wrong hands, we might just buy ourselves an even bigger enemy than The Club."

"What does that mean?" I ask, the hairs on my arms standing up.

"It sounds like there are plenty of powerful people on that client list who wouldn't want this scandal to see the light of day," Jonas says.

Josh puts his arm around my shoulders and I lean into him, shaking. This whole thing is making my head spin and my stomach churn. "Holy shitballs," I say under my breath.

"It's all gonna come down to the money," Jonas says. "Money talks."

"I agree," Josh says, pulling me into him.

"Henn, that's top priority, okay?" Jonas says. "Track the money. Get access to it."

"Roger," Henn says. "Shouldn't take me more than a couple days."

"We can do this," Sarah says. "Look at the talent in this room.

We don't need no stinkin' George Clooney and Brad Pitt and Matt Damon."

"Yeah, but I sure wish we had that Chinese acrobat guy," Henn says. "He was cool."

Finally, someone in this room who speaks my freaking language.

"The one they stuffed into the little box?" I ask. "I loved him."

Henn beams a smile at me that instantly calms my raging nerves. "Yeah, he was rad."

"Yen. Wasn't that his name?"

"Oh *yeah.* Good memory, Kat." He taps his temple. "Brains *and* beauty."

I return his beaming smile. Thank God for Henny.

"Hey, guys, sorry to interrupt your profound musings, but I'm kind of getting tunnel vision here," Sarah says. "There's a lot to do and I wanna get started right away."

"Sure thing," I say (even though I'm thinking "holy shitballs"). "Whatever you need, boss."

"Hey, Sarah," Henn says. "One more thing. What do you wanna do about Dr. Evil's text to you?"

Sarah's face turns bright red.

"I'm monitoring his phone, remember?" Henn says, motioning to his laptop. "'I'm not a patient man.' What was *that* all about?"

## Chapter 27

*Kat*

Sarah sputters and stammers for a moment, clearly incapable of responding to Henn's question, so Jonas grabs her hand and speaks for her, telling the group about how Max demanded a "freebie" from Sarah yesterday at The Club's offices and then followed up with a creepy-skeevy text demanding she come through.

"What should I do?" Sarah asks the group, obviously wracked with anxiety. "Ignore him? Answer him? Hide?"

"Ignore him and hide," Jonas says firmly. "I don't want you saying a fucking thing to that motherfucker."

"I agree," Josh says, clenching his jaw. "Ignore him and hide."

Finally, something I know a shit-ton about. *Men.*

"No," I say emphatically, straightening up in my chair. "*Answer* him and hide. Ignoring him will piss him off, and we don't want to piss that guy off. We want to keep him calm and confident and predictable."

There's a brief silence while everyone mulls over what I've just said.

"Dr. Evil's real boner isn't for Sarah—it's for Jonas," I continue.

"Jesus, Kat," Jonas says, grimacing. "Please don't say it that way."

I can feel Josh's eyes trained on me, and suddenly, I feel emboldened. I might not be the sharpest knife in the drawer when it comes to brainiac stuff like hacking and world politics and legal research and figuring out how to take down a global crime syndicate, but when it comes to men and PR, I'm flippin' Einstein, peeps.

"Not *sexually*," I say. "He's got an *alpha-male* boner for you, Jonas. This is all about a beta silverback wanting to knock off the obvious alpha. He wants what you've got so he can *win*. Hence, his Jonas-boner."

"For Chrissakes, *please* stop saying that," Jonas says.

"So how should I reply to him, then?" Sarah asks.

"We have to keep him off your back and convince him you're motivated solely by greed and absolutely *not* by loyalty to Jonas," I say. "The more he thinks your interests are the same as his, the safer you'll be. You've got to keep him trusting you. If you ignore him, he'll start getting paranoid."

Sarah looks at Jonas and he nods like he's in agreement with everything I've said—and when I glance at Josh, he nods encouragingly, a smile dancing on his lips—so I forge ahead. "Tell Max not to text—Jonas is monitoring your phone," I say, "and he's just on the cusp of giving you another humongous check. That way, you play right into his egomania and also appeal to his greed. No matter how much he wants his little freebie to satisfy his Jonas-boner—"

"Okay, Kat, that's enough," Jonas cautions.

"—he won't insist on it at the risk of sabotaging the scam. We'll just make Jonas out to be the bad guy and let Sarah sound like she's doing her best to manage him and keep the money rolling in."

Everyone's staring at me, but no one's saying a word.

I glance at Josh again and the look on his face right now is unmistakable: I've surprised him.

I shrug. "What? There are two things I know well in this life—PR and men."

Josh laughs a full-throated laugh and beams a heart-stopping smile at me, quite obviously thoroughly impressed.

"Nice," Henn says, grinning broadly at me.

"Hey, I might be *dumb*," I say, "but I'm not *blonde*."

Everyone laughs and so do I—but the way Josh is laughing and smiling is making me do more than laugh; it's making me sizzle and pop like Rice Krispies in milk.

Josh grabs my hand and squeezes it, his eyes blazing at me. "Does everyone agree with Kat on this? Because I most certainly do."

Everyone expresses enthusiastic agreement with everything I've said, and I feel myself swell with pride.

Josh leans into my ear, still squeezing my hand. "I do believe this little fishy just went for a swim in the river." He kisses the top of my hand.

I look at him quizzically and he smiles broadly.

"Trust me, I won't," Sarah is saying in response to something Jonas just said. "Now that I know that creep's out there watching me, I have no desire to leave the suite ever again. I've got to hunker down and write my report, anyway. This is going to be a huge job." Sarah shakes her head. "This is so crazy."

"It's totally insane," Henn agrees, exhaling happily. "Isn't it *awesome?*"

Henn and Sarah begin chatting about their strategy for gathering the mountain of data and documents Sarah needs for her report and my attention drifts to Josh. He's staring right at me, his eyes smoldering.

"Hey, Josh," I whisper. "Can I talk to you for a minute over there?"

"My pleasure."

We move to a sitting area in the corner of the suite, away from the rest of the group.

"What's up, Party Girl with a Hyphen?" Josh asks. He leans back in his chair, making himself comfortable.

"I got a really interesting email from my boss a little while ago," I say.

"Oh yeah?" he asks. "What'd it say?"

"It seems I've somehow managed to secure a huge new account for my firm—an account I've apparently been working on while I've been here in Vegas, all while getting shitfaced and barfing on your shoes—an account that's so big and important and *lucrative* my boss told me to 'stay in Vegas as long as needed.'"

"Wow. Sounds like a big account. Congratulations."

"What did you do, Josh?"

He bites his lip. "Not a whole lot. I just picked up the phone and called a friend, that's all."

"Josh, what's going on?"

He smiles broadly. "It seems one of the owners of the hottest nightclub in Las Vegas, a good friend of mine—a guy named Reed?—remember him?—well, Reed met you the other night and you two got to talking and you wound up blowing him away with a thousand amazing ideas for raising the visibility and branding for his club. And now, understandably, he wants *you* personally, and only *you,* to work on a massive PR campaign for his club all month. He's redoing *all* the branding, at your suggestion, which is a huge job. Of course, he understands what a major inconvenience it is, having your personal, undivided attention for so long all the way out here in Vegas, so he was very happy to pay a ridiculous premium for your exclusive services—up front."

I'm speechless.

"Pretty straightforward." He beams a huge smile at me.

"But... is there an actual campaign? Something I actually have to *do* in exchange for this payment?"

"Well, there's no actual PR campaign," he says. "But, yes, you have to *do* something in exchange for the payment. Of course."

I raise an eyebrow. "And what would that be?" I feel heat rising in my cheeks.

"Well, *obviously*, you've gotta help us topple the Evil Empire and save the world." He shrugs. "You're a fucking PR-genius, Kat. If I didn't already know that about you, you sure proved it in spades a minute ago."

I blush.

He puts his hand on my knee and leans forward like he's gonna kiss me, and my breathing catches in my throat. He leans closer, his eyes burning, and I close my eyes, bracing myself for his warm lips against mine. But, nope. No kiss. Instead, I feel the sensation of his fingertip pressing lightly against the cleft in my chin.

I open my eyes.

His blue eyes have darkened.

"We all need you here, Kat—you just proved that. And speaking for myself personally, I have no desire to save the world without my Party Girl with a Hyphen by my side."

## Chapter 28

*Kat*

For hours and hours, Sarah and I have worked alongside Henn, gathering and assembling evidence for Sarah's report while Josh and Jonas have worked tirelessly on the other side of the room, researching, analyzing, and formulating the big-picture strategy for whatever the heck we're finally gonna do with the report when it's done.

"Dudes, I'm turning into a pumpkin," Henn finally declares, his face the picture of total exhaustion. "I can't uncross my eyes."

"Go crash, Henny," Sarah says. "You've already given us plenty of stuff to work with for the rest of the night."

"I won't sleep too long. There's still an ass-load worth of shit to do. I just need a power nap."

"Hey, Americanos and Red Bulls can only stave off the physical needs of the human body for so long," Sarah says.

"I'll see you pretty ladies later." He stumbles away, bleary-eyed.

"What about you, Kitty Kat?" Sarah asks. "You need a break?"

"Hell no," I answer. "I'm an evidence-assembling machine. Just give me another task and I'm on it."

"Coolio Iglesias," Sarah says. "Let's turn on some music—that always helps me get my second wind." She flips through her music library on her laptop. "Oh, *yes*. My girl, Audra Mae—now there's a voice that inspires greatness." She presses play on a song and a freaking hurricane of a female voice blasts me and jolts me back awake.

"Who's this?" I ask. "Oh my God. She's incredible."

"Audra Mae and the Almighty Sound," Sarah says. "'The Real Thing.'"

"Holy shitballs," I say. "I'm gonna make this my ringtone. I've got goose bumps."

We listen to the song all the way through, and when it ends, I want to hear it again.

"Play it on a loop, Sarah," I say. "I'm already addicted. Gah!"

"Right? I know. She sings right from her soul." She glances at Josh and Jonas across the room, their noses buried in Jonas' laptop. "Hey, how are you boys doing over there? You've been going nonstop for hours."

"Just coming up with a foolproof plan to fuck the bad guys up the ass, baby," Jonas mutters, typing something on his keyboard.

"Jonas, your eyes are bugging out of your head—maybe you should take a short break—like, go work out or something?" Sarah says.

"There's no time for that," Jonas says, not taking his eyes off his screen. "I'm on a mission from God here, baby."

Sarah begins to say something more, but Jonas cuts her off.

"*Because I love my baby more than life itself.*"

Sarah takes in a sharp breath. "Holy crappola," she whispers.

"Holy shitballs," I reply, my heart racing vicariously for her. "Is that the first time?"

She shakes her head. "No, but definitely the first time in front of other people."

"Aw." I grab her hand. "Our little boy is growing up."

Sarah smiles broadly. "That gorgeous man never ceases to surprise me."

"I could say the same thing about that gorgeous man's brother," I say.

I stare at Josh for a long beat. He's wearing jeans and a T-shirt today, a rarity for the ever-fashionable Playboy, and he looks hot as freaking hell. Jesus God, everything about that man—from his taut muscles to the slight wave of his dark hair to his sly smile, even the dragon on his bicep peeking out from his short sleeve—is drawing me to him uncontrollably.

But, damn, he's stubborn. And guarded, too—deceptively so. He comes off as so open and easygoing, but he's hiding darkness under there, I can feel it. I try to imagine Josh fucking me in a bunny suit, but that doesn't ring true. More than likely, he's into S&M, right? He's gotta be some kind of a dom—into whips and chains and butt plugs. I imagine myself calling him "master" in a doggie collar and my clit pulses. I could work with that. Or, whoa, wait, maybe he's a *sub*? Holy Not What I'm Hoping For, Batman. Not at all. That's the thing—it could be *anything.* It's killing me not knowing.

"Kat?" Sarah says.

"Sorry," I say. "Got distracted."

Sarah gives me a document and asks me to scour it for any references to international money transfers.

"Sure thing," I say. But the words on the page are beginning to blur. My head is bobbing on my neck like I'm a drowsy truck driver. I didn't even study this hard in college, for crying out loud.

For the hundredth time tonight, I glance over at Josh across the room. He's engaged in an animated conversation with Jonas about... What the heck are those two jabbering about now?—I strain to listen over the music on Sarah's laptop—oh, which NFL quarterback is the greatest of all time. Well, that's an easy one: *Joe Montana*. Everyone knows that. Duh. Surely, my dad, mom, and three out of four of my brothers would say the same thing.

"It's a no-brainer," Josh says. "*Joe Montana.*"

I smile broadly to myself. Josh would fit right in with my family.

"That's the conventional answer," Jonas says. "But I'd argue Peyton Manning has recently overtaken the top spot."

I roll my eyes. Well, that's plain ridiculous.

"No way," Josh says from across the room. "That's fucking ridiculous."

I smile to myself again. Great minds think alike.

Jonas keeps arguing his (ridiculous) position until, suddenly, without warning, Josh reaches up, midsentence, and flicks Jonas' forehead with his index finger.

Jonas abruptly stops talking and puts his hand on his forehead. "*Ow.*"

For a short beat, it's not clear if Jonas is gonna throttle Josh or laugh uncontrollably, but then Jonas' features contort into unmistakable amusement and he lets out a belly laugh, causing Josh to burst out laughing, too. All tension averted, Josh leans back, spreads his legs, and shifts his dick in his pants.

"Dumbshit," Josh mutters, shaking his head.

Jonas chuckles.

"*Peyton Manning.*"

"Sorry," Jonas says, still laughing.

"You should be, bro—you fucking should be."

The boys laugh together a bit more and then finally refocus their attention on Jonas' laptop.

My jaw is hanging open.

My chest is tight.

My pulse is pounding in my ears.

I can't take my eyes off Josh, though all he's doing is staring at a laptop.

Audra Mae is singing from Sarah's laptop into my ear, and suddenly, I realize her lyrics were written for me—for this moment. *I want Josh.* And I'm coming for him, just like Audra Mae is coming for her man in the song.

Josh had better watch the fuck out.

Forget what I said about wanting to take a break from our battle to the death. That was before this moment—before Josh correctly named Joe Montana as the all-time best NFL quarterback of all time. Before Josh defended his (correct) position with a perfectly timed forehead-flick, expertly diffusing potential tension with humor. Before he shifted his donkey-dick in his pants for the umpteenth time, making my crotch burn and my pulse race. Before Audra Mae and the Almighty Sound entered the room and belted out my own feelings into my ear. And, most of all, that was before Josh Faraday paid some ungodly amount of money to my boss so I can continue saving the world here in Las Vegas with him *and* keep my job in Seattle, too. "*And speaking for myself personally, I have no desire to save the world without my Party Girl with a Hyphen by my side,*" Josh said. Holy hell, I get goose bumps just thinking about him saying those words to me.

*I want him. I want him. I want him.*

And not just sexually, either—I'm way past simply wanting to bang Josh now (though God knows I want to bang him more than I want to breathe). I want Josh to be *mine*—in every conceivable way. I want his body. I want his heart. I want his soul. *And, goddammit, I want his secrets, too.*

Josh says I've been demanding something from him that I can't or won't give him in return? Well, he's got a point about that, actually. But what if I *did* unexpectedly have something to give him in return for his secrets? What if I had secrets of my own to give him—and what if I turned the tables on him and gave them to him *first*?

"*If I had an application, I'd give it to you,*" I told Josh last night outside my room after the Henn-kissing debacle.

"*Easy for you to say*," Josh replied. "*You don't have one*."

But what if I *did*? That would change everything, wouldn't it?

"Hey, Sarah," I whisper, leaning into her shoulder.

"Hmm?"

"Do you happen to have a copy of an old Club application lying around?"

Sarah pauses what she's doing and looks up. "Um. No, all the applications I had were on my laptop that got stolen."

"And Henn hasn't been able to access member applications yet?"

"Not yet." She puts down the document she's reading with sudden emphasis and looks at me like I've suggested we try to sneak up on the President of the United States and give him a wedgie. "Katherine Morgan, even if we *could* get our hands on Josh's application, you absolutely can't read it without his permission."

I roll my eyes. "I know that. Jeez. Gimme some credit."

Sarah's looking at me like she doesn't buy a word of my bullshit.

I pause. "Okay, yes, I'd read that effing application in a heartbeat if I could get my grubby little hands on it," I say.

Sarah laughs. "I know."

"But I'm not trying to get Josh's application through Henn—I wanna get it directly from Josh. And to do that, I need to see the questions he answered—the questions everyone answers when applying to The Club."

Sarah presses her lips together. "Why?"

I ignore her question. "Do you remember the questions?"

"They're burned into my gray matter for eternity. *Why* do you want them?"

"Would you email them to me, exactly the way they're worded on a standard application?"

Sarah smirks. "Are you by any chance planning to write *answers* to these questions, my dearest friend?"

A smile spreads across my face. "Why, yes, that is the plan, my lovely, darling friend."

"Oh my, my, my. Are you gonna apply to the *Josh Faraday Club,* by any chance?" She shoots me a naughty smile.

"Ooooh, I like that, Sarah. Why, *yes*, I do believe I am," I say slowly, my skin tingling.

"Did Josh *ask* you to apply to his club?"

"No. He has no idea. This is gonna be a surprise—or more like a *blindside*." I glance furtively across the room at Josh. He and Jonas are chatting calmly about something on Jonas' laptop. "This is gonna be a diabolical tactic to get two suicide bombers to finally lay down their bombs and make nice—very, very *nice*."

"Well, I'm sure it'll work like gangbusters. The day Kat Morgan can't get a man to bend to her mighty will, the rest of us might as well crawl into bunkers and await the End of Days."

"I'm not so sure this time, to be honest. Josh is the hardest nut to crack I've ever encountered. The Most Stubborn Man in the World."

"So he's the male version of you, then?"

I nod slowly, not taking my eyes off Josh across the room.

Sarah laughs. "Well, that's a scary combination. Definitely sounds *explosive*."

"That's what we are—even against our mutual interests." I begin to say something more but wind up yawning, instead.

"Aw, honey, you better get some sleep," Sarah says. "You look like you're gonna pass out."

"Yeah, I'm about to fall over."

I get up and stretch.

"Oh, are you heading out, Kat?" Josh asks, his head whipping up from his work.

"Yeah," I say. "I've gotta get some sleep—I'm about to crash and burn."

"I'll walk you to your room. Hold on just a sec." He turns to confer with Jonas about something.

"Enjoy getting blown to bits, girl," Sarah whispers. "*Ka-boom*."

"Nah. There are no explosions on the agenda tonight," I say. "Tonight, I'm gonna get good and rested so I can write my application to The Josh Faraday Club first thing tomorrow."

Sarah smiles at me suggestively. "I'll send you those questions ASAP."

"Thanks. I appreciate it. I'm gonna start working on my 'application' the minute I wake up."

Sarah doesn't reply. Something across the room has grabbed her attention. I glance across the room. Oh. Correction. *Someone* has grabbed Sarah's attention. Oh my, that's quite a look Jonas is giving Sarah right now—it's downright primal.

"I'll send those questions to you as soon as I can, Kitty Kat," Sarah says absently, not taking her eyes off her smoldering boyfriend. "Something tells me my hunky monkey boyfriend is gonna distract me from writing those questions for you for at least the next few hours."

## Chapter 29

*Josh*

My phone beeps with an incoming text, waking me from a dead sleep. Jesus. Is it night or day? My body clock is totally fucked up.

I grab my phone and check the screen with one eye. Shit. *Jennifer LeMonde.*

"Hey, Josh," Jen's text says. "I'm still waiting on that phone call you promised me. I'm available now."

Fuck. When I sprinted back into Reed's suite the other night to grab my clothes and Kat's stuff, I practically bowled Jen over.

"Did you really say all that stuff about me?" Jen asked, marching behind me in a huff as I grabbed my clothes off a nearby lounge chair. "You think I'm an 'airhead'?"

"No, I don't think you're an airhead," I said, even though I think she's an airhead. "I'm sorry, Jen," I continued. "I'd love to explain everything to you, but I've gotta run right now. I'll call you later. I never called you an airhead, I swear. Kat put words into my mouth."

"Wait," Jen said as I gathered my clothes up, frantic about where Kat might have stumbled off to with no shoes, purse or phone, wandering around all by herself in a fucking casino at the break of dawn. "I need to talk to you."

"I'll call you later, Jen. I promise," I said. "But right now I gotta go."

"Do you promise to call me?" Jen asked.

"Yeah."

And then I promptly didn't call her. Because I've been busy. And obsessed with Kat. And because... I'm... a dick.

Fuck.

I press the button to place a call to Jen, despite the fact that every fiber in my body revolts against the idea.

She picks up immediately. "Hi," Jen says stiffly. "So nice to finally hear from you."

"Hi, Jen," I say. "I'm sorry I didn't call sooner. I've been really busy."

"Mmm hmm. You still in Vegas?"

"Yeah. You?"

"I'm at the airport now. Heading to New York. My mom's got a show opening tomorrow night."

"You mean on Broadway?"

"Yeah."

"I didn't know your mom did live theatre."

"She doesn't. This is her first time. She's shitting a brick."

"Well, I hope she breaks a leg. How was the RCR concert the other night?"

"Great." She exhales. "So did you say all that stuff about me or not?"

"No."

"None of it?"

"Well, I said we had meaningless sex, which we did, as I'm sure you'll agree." I pause, waiting for her to agree, but she doesn't. "Jen," I continue, flustered, "Kat knew I was with you in New York when she said all that shit. She was just mind-fucking you for the purpose of fucking with me."

There's a beat.

"Well, then, she's an even bigger bitch than I thought," Jen says coldly.

"Yeah, she tore you a new one, for sure. I'm sorry about that. Kat can be pretty intense. She was just jealous."

"Why'd you tell her about our night in New York in the first place? I take it you didn't just meet her in Las Vegas?"

"Yeah, I met her before."

"Is she your girlfriend?"

"No, she's not my girlfriend. It's kinda hard to explain what she is."

Jen snickers. "Well, it's interesting you told her about me. That wasn't very nice of you." I can hear her smiling across the phone line. "No wonder she was jealous."

Shit. This is totally backfiring on me.

Jen's voice shifts into full flirt mode. "So, hey, enough about The Jealous Bitch. Why don't you come to New York with me? I'll take you to the premier of my mom's show and to the after-party and—"

I take a deep breath. "Jen, no. That's what I'm calling to tell you. I thought we were on the same page last week in New York—both of us just having some meaningless, drunken fun. I'm sorry if you were up for something different than that." I clear my throat, suddenly extremely uncomfortable. "I should have been clearer with you, Jen. I'm not looking for a relationship. I'm sorry if I... misled you."

Oh my God. I'm suddenly realizing something: Kat might have had a point the other night when she called me a douche. It's distinctly possible I didn't make my intentions clear enough to Jen last week—even though I could plainly see the girl was way more into me than any casual hook-up ought to be. And, if I'm really digging deep into the honesty bin, I probably left things way too open-ended with Jen, just like Kat said I did, simply because I didn't want to hurt her feelings... or... actually, because I didn't want to deal with her feelings at all.

"Josh," Jen says. "I'm not looking for anything *deep* from you. Let's just hang out and see if—"

My phone buzzes with an incoming text and I pull back to see who it's from.

"*I hit the motherlode,*" Henn writes. "*All hands on deck!*"

"Oh, shit. I gotta go, Jen," I blurt, pressing the phone back into my ear. "Something really important just came up. Sorry. Gotta go."

"What?"

"Look, Jen, I'm sorry about the other night at the party. Kat's got a bit of a temper, it turns out." The image of Kat stomping like a toddler down the hallway, dripping wet, barefoot, her incredible ass-cheeks hanging out of her black G-string, pops into my mind. "She put words into my mouth. I absolutely didn't call you an airhead. That's what I wanted to tell you—and also that I'm not at all interested in a relationship. I'm sorry to cut this short, but I really gotta go."

## Chapter 30

*Kat*

I take a deep breath. I've got a full flock of butterflies flapping around in my stomach. Our *Ocean's Eleven* crew is scheduled to meet at ten to head over to the Las Vegas branch of the FBI, Sarah's report in hand, and by God, I'm determined to give Josh my application before then. I take another deep breath, turn up the volume on the Audra Mae and the Almighty Sound song I'm now officially addicted to ("The Real Thing"), thanks to Sarah, and place my hands on my keyboard. Here goes nothing.

"The following is my application to The Josh Faraday Club," I type onto my screen. "All answers will be one hundred percent honest. (And bee tee dubs, some of this stuff is kind of personal, so please keep it in confidence.)"

*Name?*

"Katherine Ulla Morgan," I write. "But everyone just calls me Kat." I take a deep breath. I never tell anyone about this. I can't believe I'm writing this. "I'm named after my dad's mother Katherine and my mom's Swedish grandmother Ulla. Pretty name, huh? *Katherine Ulla Morgan.* Yeah, it's pretty until you realize my initials spell 'KUM.' Let me repeat that, in case you're not understanding the full implication: my initials spell the word 'KUM' *and I have four brothers*. Which means that, in addition to being called Kat and Kitty Kat my whole life, I've also been called charming things like... wait for it... Kum Shot, Jizz, Splooge, Pecker-Snot, Man-Yogurt, Dick-Spit, Schlong-Juice, Jerk-Sauce, and, oh, so many more clever and classy things only boys would ever dream up.

"The only one of my brothers who's never joined in on the semen-infused nicknaming is my oldest brother, Colby—and I'm pretty sure I know why. As family lore goes, my clueless mother had originally wanted to give Baby Colby her grandfather's name as his middle name, but thanks to a family tradition on my dad's side (whereby the first-born son is given the middle name of Edwin), Colby narrowly escaped being named Colby *Ulysses* Morgan. And so, perhaps in adherence to the philosophy 'But for the grace of God go I'—a philosophy you've expressed a strong affinity for, too—Colby's always stuck to calling me 'Kumquat.' (As a side note, my second oldest brother Ryan ultimately wound up with the dreaded 'Ulysses' moniker as his middle name, but being called 'RUM' and 'Bacardi' and... wait for it... 'Captain Morgan' hasn't exactly scarred him for life.)

"So, there you have it. I'm KUM. What you choose to do with the truth about my name is entirely up to you. But be warned: if you're suddenly feeling an irresistible urge to call me Cream-of-Sum-Yung-Guy or Baby-Gravy or Protein-Milkshake, you won't be the first. There's literally no semen-related name you could sling at me that I haven't already been called a hundred times in the 'comfort' of my own home or in the hallways of middle school (where, for three long years, we were most unfortunately required to mark our full initials onto the hem of our P. E. shorts).

"Beginning in high school (when I thankfully was no longer required to display 'KUM' on my P. E. shorts anymore), I started lying and saying my middle name is Ella. And to this day, I never tell anyone the truth about my middle name, just in case they're apt to put two and two together and start calling me Nut-Butter or Trouser-Juice or Man-Chowder or Spunk.

"Why, you might wonder, am I telling *you* of all people my KUM-tastic secret after all this time? I'm not entirely sure. All I know is that, judging by the way Sarah and Jonas have benefitted from playing the honesty-game right from the start, I'm eager to give the game a whirl, too. With you."

*Age?*

"24," I type.

*Provide a brief physical description of yourself.*

I stare at my computer screen for a moment. Josh is already quite familiar with almost every square inch of me—I mean, jeez, the man has seen me throw a tantrum in my underwear and shoved his fingers up my wahoo on a dance floor. But, still, I might as well answer the question.

"I have blonde hair, blue eyes, and a VAGINA," I write, giggling to myself.

*With this application, you will be required to submit three recent photographs of yourself to your intake agent. Please include the following: one headshot, one full-body shot revealing your physique, and one shot wearing something you'd typically wear out in a public location. These photographs shall be maintained under the strictest confidentiality.*

I pull out my phone and take a selfie-headshot, crossing my eyes and puckering my lips. Next, I strip off my clothes and stand in front of the full-length mirror in my hotel room and snap a quick shot of myself in my bra and undies—a sight he's already well acquainted with. And, for my last required shot—"something I'd typically wear in a public location"—I throw on my sequined dress from the other night, kneel at the toilet and pretend to be barfing into it while holding my phone above my head and snapping a photo.

"I'm attaching all three required photos with this application," I write. "Enjoy!"

*Please sign the enclosed waiver describing the requisite background check, medical physical, and blood test, which you must complete as a condition of membership.*

"If you want to do background and credit checks on me, knock yourself out. But if you don't want to expend the effort, let me tell you exactly what you'd find out: I've never been convicted of a crime (though I've broken the law a time or two and not gotten caught, heehee); I've got two credit cards, one of which is maxed out (and which I'm planning to pay off with my craps winnings); I'm paid up and current on my rent at my apartment; I'm one payment behind on my car loan (which I'm also going to pay off with my gambling winnings); and I've been employed at the same PR firm for almost two years.

"The last time I checked, my credit score was around 660, which is decent but not stupendous. It's possible it's gone down slightly recently because of that missed car payment. I swear to God, I'm normally really responsible when it comes to paying my bills, I really am, but when my place was trashed by The Club, there were several things I needed to replace and I just didn't have enough cash to go around for all that stuff plus my car payment, too. I was planning to make a double payment this month (because I'm supposed to get a raise when I hit my two-year anniversary at work), but now, thanks to you and Jonas (and some lucky dice!), I can pay off the whole car loan in one fell swoop. (Thank you so much!)

"You know, writing this makes me realize I haven't adequately thanked you for that craps money. I think I was just sort of stunned and also maybe a little uncomfortable with how easily I took it from you. I probably shouldn't have said yes so fast, if at all, but I couldn't stop myself. Not having a car payment or that Visa bill hanging over my head every month is going to be so effing amazing, I can't begin to tell you. So thank you again, very, very much. I'm really grateful. And thank you also for arranging everything so I could stay here in Las Vegas to save the world with our *Ocean's Eleven* crew *and* keep my job. Your generosity is truly mindboggling, Josh. I've never met anyone with such a big and generous heart. The way you take care of everyone around you, including me, is admirable and beyond attractive and sexy. I want you to know I'm grateful and blown away by your incredible thoughtfulness. Thank you.

"Okay, back to the application. What would you learn about me if you called my ex-boyfriends? Well, probably that I'm a wee bit crazy (sorry!), overly dramatic at times (sorry again!), and stubborn (news flash!). But I can also be bighearted, especially with the people I care about, devoted to my friends and family, funny, and outlandishly serious about having fun. (I think maybe I've got a little Jekyll and Hyde thing going on?)

"You'd also find out I've had only three serious boyfriends in my life—one in high school and two in college. Besides those three 'serious' boyfriends, I've also had other 'relationships' that have lasted anywhere from one night to, oh, about three or four months maximum, but, for purposes of this application, I'm only gonna bother telling you about the three boys I've cared enough about to bring them home to meet my family:

"My first serious boyfriend was in high school—a guy named Kade. Kade was two years older than me and oh man did I love, love, looooooooooooooove him. Holy shitballs, I loved that boy. I used to write 'Kat + Kade' on all my notebooks and practice writing my signature using his last name. Kade was the star quarterback on my high school's football team, and when he went away to college on a scholarship, he decided he needed to have the 'full college experience,' which, roughly translated, meant he didn't want to be tied down by having a sixteen-year-old girlfriend pining for him back home. Of course, my adult self realizes that was absolutely the best decision for both of us, but at the time I didn't think my heart would survive the horrible pain.

"My second serious boyfriend was Nate. I met him at a fraternity party in college. He was sweet and funny and completely in love with me from day one. He was also smart and athletic and a truly good person. He wanted to become a doctor and work with Doctors Without Borders, not even kidding. And on top of all that, the boy was objectively perfect-looking, too (one of those can't-find-a-bad-angle types). Plus, he was head over heels in love with me, which I found an attractive trait in a boyfriend. Oh my God, how Nate worshipped me. He always talked about how the second he saw me, he just *knew* we were meant for each other. 'It was love at first sight,' he would always tell people, and I always wondered if he noticed I never said, 'For me, too.'

"The truth was I didn't love Nate the way he loved me, and I knew it in my bones. I never felt that thunderbolt he felt when he saw me, though I was physically attracted to him (because, like I say, he was objectively gorgeous). Maybe I should have listened to my gut and cut ties with Nate sooner, but I was young and I kept thinking the passion would come. It had to, right? Nate was perfect in every way. And sure enough, as time went by, I loved him more and more. I truly adored him for the wonderful guy he was, how funny he was, how endlessly thoughtful and sweet and good. But I never, ever fell in love with Nate. And I knew it. I didn't practice writing my name using his last name. I never ached for him when we were apart—hell, I didn't even *think* about him when we were apart, to be perfectly honest. I never got butterflies when we held hands or kissed or had sex, though all were exceedingly pleasant. And I most certainly didn't feel an ounce of jealousy at the thought of him with another girl. Not an ounce. And yet Nate made it abundantly clear he lived to make me smile, yearned to touch me every chance he got, dreamed about me, and for sure envisioned me as his future wife.

"Why didn't I feel what Nate felt for me? To this day, I have no fucking idea. But for a long time, I truly thought things would change and I'd come to my senses and fall head over heels. 'When you like a flower, you pick it,' my mom always says. 'When you love a flower, you water it and let it grow.' So I figured I'd just keep watering our flower and soon my feelings would morph and ignite into the kind of life-or-death passion I'd always dreamed of experiencing. But they didn't. I guess some things just can't be forced, no matter how much you water them.

"Finally, about a year into our relationship, I was at a party with friends where I met a guy who made my panties burst into flames in a way I'd never felt with Nate, not even once. Honestly, the guy took my breath away with just a glance. It was like he'd cast a spell on me and my lady-parts. I'd never experienced full-body lust like that before. I didn't know my body was even capable of getting that dripping wet—and that was just from *looking* at the guy. I could only imagine what would happen if I actually got to touch him.

"It took all my self-restraint not to cheat on Nate that very night (because believe me, my *vagina* desperately wanted to do it), but I didn't. Instead, I nutted up and sat Nate down the next morning and I broke it off with him as gently as I could (and then went out and banged the shit out of that hot guy from the party four nights later on our second date).

"To say I broke Nate's heart is an understatement. Even as I'm writing this, I'm crying at the memory of the look on his face when I told him I wasn't in love with him. To this day, I've never felt more like a shitty person than when I told that beautiful, sweet, loving boy I didn't want to be his girlfriend anymore for no other reason than 'I dunno why.'

"Now and again, I'll get an occasional email from Nate, asking me how I'm doing, if I'm happy, asking if I'm married, and I always feel like crying when I have to reply honestly to him, 'I'm really great, Nate. Still single. How are you?' I know he's hoping one of these times I'll write, 'I was an idiot. Please take me back.' But I'm never even remotely tempted to write those words. And, honestly, I hate myself for it.

"I tried to be in love with Nate. I really did. But, apparently, passion isn't something you can force. If it were, I swear I'd be passionately in love with that boy to this very day—because he so deserved that.

"My third serious boyfriend was the one who shattered my heart into a million tiny pieces. Garrett Bennett. Or as I like to refer to him, The Asshole.

"I met Garrett on the first day of my junior year. I was walking to class with Sarah when Garrett beelined right to me from across a large lawn and asked me out, saying I was the most beautiful girl he'd ever seen and if I didn't say yes to a date, I'd ruin his life. Well, to say my panties were wet at the sight of him is an understatement. The boy had an animal magnetism I'd never encountered before. So, of course, I said hell yes.

"On our first date, Garrett took me to a really nice restaurant, the nicest restaurant I'd ever been to, actually. Not the burgers and fries I'd been expecting. As it turned out, his dad was a senator and his mom some sort of philanthropist-lady who organized trips to Africa through her church. And the dude played on the freaking golf team at our school. (Who *does* that?) He seemed sort of fancy to me, but in a good way.

"But it wasn't his swankiness that made me like him that night. Our conversation flowed easily and I laughed a lot. He was hysterically funny. (And did I mention he made my panties wet?) Actually, wait, let me amend the statement that he was hysterically funny. I'm not really sure if that's true, in retrospect. The guy could have recited the phone book that night and I would have giggled like a fucking idiot. I was just instantly smitten. It was Nate, but in reverse. In fact, more than once during dinner, I thought, *So this is what Nate felt!* If you'd asked me that night, 'Do you believe in love at first sight?', I would have shrieked, 'Yes!'

"So, anyway, when Garrett asked me to come back to his place after dinner, I said *yes, yes, yes.* I'd only intended to make out with him, to tell you the truth, because honestly, up until then, I'd never had first-date sex or even a one-night stand. (Even that guy I banged after breaking up with Nate lasted two months.) Plus, Garrett had made a few comments during dinner that made it clear he'd come from an extremely conservative religious background, unlike me (organized religion is pretty much nonexistent in my household—as long as I'm dumping my entire life's story on you, might as well hit you with religion, too), so I didn't think first-date sex would be in the cards with a guy like that. But one thing led to another and another, pretty damned quickly, actually, and soon, Garrett and I were at his place having headboard-banging sex like nothing I'd ever experienced before.

"This kind of sex was a revelation to me. Before Garrett, I'd never had such uninhibited, wild sex. Even sex with the after-Nate guy wasn't nearly as explosive as sex with Garrett Bennett. Our chemistry was off the freaking charts. I felt like I could be as wild as I wanted to be with him, like there were no limits—and that opened up a whole new side to myself I didn't even know existed. I'd been giving myself orgasms for years before then, and I'd had orgasms during oral with guys, but this was the first time I had orgasms during sex with a guy—during actual intercourse—and it was like, wow, wow, wow, wow.

"I was immediately addicted, as you can probably imagine. I could never get enough. I wanted more, more, more, every chance I got. And so, from that day forward, for the better part of the next seven months, I banged Garrett as much as possible, which wasn't as much as I would have liked (because, as he kept telling me, golf is an extremely time-consuming sport, especially for someone trying to go pro).

"But suffice it to say we had a ton of sex. But we also had lots and lots of conversations, too, mostly in bed, during which I told him pretty much every honest thought I had about anything and everything, never holding back. For some reason, the uninhibited sex made me feel uninhibited in all ways, like I could tell Garrett anything. No topic was off limits, and I just babbled and babbled.

"In some very big ways, it was obvious Garrett and I came from strikingly different backgrounds and families, but it didn't matter. I just always felt like Garrett totally "got" me and secretly saw the world the way I did, despite his parents' expectations about what and who he was 'supposed' to be.

"Honestly, I felt like I'd met my perfect match—my soul mate, if you will (a phrase I've since banished from my vocabulary). We never said 'I love you' to each other, because Garrett made it obvious he didn't feel comfortable with saying 'trite' words like that—but that was fine with me. I knew in my heart how we both felt—so I didn't need to hear the stupid, trite words.

"About six months into our relationship, I invited Garrett to meet my family and, much to my thrill, he said yes. I was super nervous about it because Garrett meeting my family was a pretty big deal to me, but, much to my relief, everyone in my family wound up loving him to pieces. Well, everyone except my oldest brother Colby, who despised Garrett almost instantly. 'What the fuck is wrong with you, Kumquat?' he said. 'Can't you see he's using you?'

"I couldn't believe my ears. I felt completely offended and hurt, like Colby was telling me I wasn't good enough for a guy like Garrett from a fancy family with a senator-dad. 'No, honey,' Colby said. 'He's a loser—not even close to good enough for you. He's completely full of shit.' Well, I lost it. I told Colby I was gonna marry Garrett one day and it's too bad he wouldn't be invited to my wedding and until he learned to say something nice about my future husband he could just forget he had a fucking sister. (Full disclosure: I'm sort of overly dramatic sometimes when I get mad.) Colby said, 'Don't worry, Kumquat, I'll be there to pick up your pieces when he breaks your heart.'

"I was pissed as hell at Colby, especially since everyone else loved Garrett the way I did. But Colby's comments did make me wonder why Garrett never brought me home to meet his family. But Garrett just kept finding excuses, telling me his dad (the senator) was traveling, or his mom was getting a facelift or bringing school supplies to underprivileged youth in Guatemala or some other rich-person-helping-the-world thing like that—and it just never worked out.

"Finally, about eight months into our relationship, I was supposed to go to a concert with Sarah for her birthday, but she came down with the stomach flu. So I decided to use the opportunity to give Garrett a sexy surprise at his apartment.

"When Garrett opened his apartment door, I clutched my trench coat, intending to rip it open and flash him my birthday suit underneath, when I glimpsed a beautiful brunette over his shoulder inside his apartment. She was sitting at a candlelit table-for-two, a vase of red roses at its center—something Garrett had never once set up for me. Even from a distance, I could see a large, sparkling cross around her neck. And when she moved her hand to her mouth in surprise, something twinkled brightly on her finger in the candlelight.

"Instantly, every doubt and concern I'd stuffed down and

reasoned away for months—and every single word Colby had said to me—came slamming into me full-force. In a flash, I knew that pretty, demure girl in Garrett's apartment was his girlfriend—and maybe even his fiancée if I was reading that flash on her hand correctly—and I knew with every fiber of my being that he'd already said those three little 'trite' words to her, the ones I'd longed to hear him say to me. Motherfucker.

"When I tore out of there, sobbing, Garrett followed me, explaining to the back of my head that Maggie's father was some lah-de-dah über-wealthy businessman who'd invented air freight or some shit like that and she was a really sweet girl from his church back home and well-connected and, he said with utmost reverence, *Maggie was saving herself for marriage.* At that last statement, I whirled around to face Garrett, my mouth hanging open, my heart shattering. 'Are you calling me a slut?' I asked. He didn't reply, which was reply enough. 'I thought you *loved* me,' I said, wiping away the hot tears streaming down my cheeks. 'I thought you wanted to marry me one day.' And do you know what that motherfucker did? He chuckled at the thought of marrying me. And then he said, 'Come on, Kat, you're a great girl—super fun—*but you're just not marriage material.*'"

I sit and stare at the screen for a minute, tears streaming down my cheeks. Man, those words from Garrett still cut me to the core. I wipe my tears and place my fingers on my keyboard again, but I can't see well enough to type yet. I can't believe I'm letting The Asshole get to me, even to this day. But I can't help it. The pain of getting blindsided like that never fully goes away, I guess.

"I've never told anyone (except Sarah) what The Asshole said to me that night," I finally type. "I've always been too embarrassed and ashamed, I guess. I didn't even tell Colby what Garrett said. All I told him was, 'You were right.'

"And yet now I'm telling you," I write. "Why? Honestly, I don't fucking know."

I have to stop typing for another minute. I'm too emotional. Why the hell am I baring my obviously pathetic soul to Josh like this? Is getting his stupid application really this frickin' important to me?

No, it's not. I don't care about his application right now. Writing this to Josh isn't about me getting his stupid application anymore. This is about something much bigger than that.

I wipe my eyes again. I'm veering way off track here. Have I even answered this particular question yet? I'm not sure. I re-read the question at the top of the page again. Oh yes.

"So that's pretty much the story of my ex-boyfriends," I write. "Besides those three guys, I've dated plenty of guys for a few months here or there and had sex with a truckload besides that, as I've mentioned, but no one serious enough to bring home."

I glance up at the question I'm supposedly answering again. Oh, yes. Okay.

"As far as blood tests," I write, "I'll submit to any kind of testing you require (as long as it doesn't involve math). But in the interest of saving time, let me just tell you what the testing would reveal: I'm clean. About two months ago, when I went in to get a new prescription of birth control pills, I got tested. And even though I'm on the pill, I insist on condoms every single time I have sex, no exceptions, unless I'm in a committed relationship and the guy's been tested. (But, hey, like I say, if you require formal medical testing before my application can be approved, then I'll sign or do whatever you request.)"

*Sexual orientation? Please choose from the following options: Straight, homosexual, bisexual, pansexual, other?*

"Straight. But in the interest of full disclosure, I should inform you I made out with a girl during my senior year in college. It's a long story that can be summarized as follows: Truth or Dare combined with Ecstasy combined with a pervy boyfriend (hers) can lead a girl to do anything once. I can honestly say the experience didn't cause me to question my sexual orientation whatsoever. In fact, it wasn't nearly as hot as it sounds, I'm sorry to say. But, regardless, I'm definitely straight."

*Do any of your sexual fantasies include violence of any nature? If so, please describe in detail.*

I sit and think. Well, jeez. I have lots and lots of fantasies, for sure, some of them pretty darn elaborate, but do any of them involve actual *violence*? No.

I place my hands on the keyboard and begin typing. "I have lots and lots of fantasies—it's kind of a *thing* with me," I write. "And not a single one of them involves actual violence. However, a couple of my fantasies involve the *threat* of violence, but only as a backdrop to setting the scene. For instance, I've got a bodyguard fantasy that only makes sense if there are bad guys coming to get me, or else why the heck do I have a bodyguard? (And to answer the question that's just popped into your head, no, I didn't have sex with any of the bodyguards Jonas hired to protect me from The Club.)"

I smirk to myself. Sure, I *almost* had sex with Derek the Bodyguard, but Josh doesn't need to know that.

I begin typing again.

"The threat of violence is also prevalent in another one of my fantasies, one in which I'm held captive by a sex-slave-master. The sex-slave master absconds with me one night and forces me to be his slave, but he never actually hurts me. And, also, in regards to violence, a second sex-slave-master comes to steal me away from the first, but my original captor fights the other bad guy to the death and protects me (which kinda turns this scenario into yet another bodyguard fantasy, doesn't it?)."

I stare at my screen. Holy What the Fuck Am I Doing, Batman? I can't write all this shit to Josh. He's gonna think I'm a freaking loon, which I am. I've never told anyone about the elaborate, imaginary pornos bouncing around in my head. What if Josh reads all this and decides I'm too much of a freak? Or worse, that, based on this stuff, we're not sexually compatible? That would be pretty soul crushing.

I let my fingers hover over my keyboard again, trying to decide what to do.

Fuck it. Better to be completely honest and get rejected for who I really am than to hide myself and make him like me. Like my new favorite singer, Audra Mae, said in her powerful song, better to be The Real Thing, for better or worse.

*Are you a current practitioner of BDSM and/or does BDSM interest you? If so, describe in explicit detail.*

"I am not a current practitioner of BDSM," I write. "As I've described above, the idea of being tied up as part of my 'captive' fantasy interests me—although, I should tell you, I'm not turned on by the idea of being physically harmed in any way."

Shit. I hope that last part's not a deal-breaker with Josh. Goddamn, I wish I knew what Josh wrote in his freaking application.

*Payment and Membership Terms. Please choose from the*

*following options: One Year Membership, $250,000 USD; Monthly Membership, $30,000 USD. All payments are non-refundable. No exceptions.*

"I'd like a one-month membership, please," I write. "I don't have $30,000 to pay you for your services, unfortunately—but, hopefully, you'll find it in your heart to waive your membership fee (or maybe accept services in lieu of payment, heehee?)."

*Please provide a detailed explanation about what compelled you to seek membership in The (Josh Faraday) Club.*

"I wanna get in your pants."

I chuckle to myself. That'd be funny if I left it at that. But I'm not going for funny. I'm going for full-scale nuclear decimation of this man.

"Remember how you accused me of dripping down my thigh in that hallway after Reed's party?" I write. "And remember how I scoffed and said it was just pool water trickling down my leg? Well, I lied. I *was* dripping down my thigh for you, just like you said. Before witnessing your muscled, tattooed body in that hallway, I was already quite fond of masturbation, I must admit—but ever since I saw you in that hallway, Josh, I've taken self-love to an art form. I want you so badly I'm in pain, desperate to feel your hard-on sliding deep inside me.

"But I'm not gonna give in to my desire for you without seeing your motherfucking application first. Why? Because it's not about the application anymore, Josh. It's about something bigger than that. I don't want Happy Josh. I want Real Josh. And I'm willing to show you the real Katherine Ulla Morgan to get him.

*Please provide a detailed statement regarding your sexual preferences. To maximize your experience in The Club, please be as explicit, detailed, and honest as possible. Please do not self-censor, in any fashion.*

"Well, I feel like I've already answered this one. I want to read your application, word for word, without censorship of any kind, and then I want you to do whatever freaky things you've asked for in your application to me, exactly as described. I want to be your Mickey Mouse roller coaster, Josh—and I want you to be mine. Come on, Josh. *YOLO*. I've told you my secrets. Now it's time for you to tell me yours."

## Chapter 31

*Josh*

"We really need to talk to your boss," Jonas says to the FBI agent sitting across the table from us.

"Yeah, well, that's not gonna happen. I'm who you get."

"I'm Jonas Faraday," Jonas says smoothly. "And this is my brother, Josh."

I nod at the guy.

"We run Faraday & Sons in Seattle, L.A. and New York," Jonas continues. "We'd like to talk to the head of this office."

The kid shrugs. "I'm the only one available to talk to you, sir. Sorry."

"How long have you been an agent?" Kat asks.

The guy shifts his attention to Kat in all her blonde glory and his entire demeanor detours from "stop wasting my time, bastard" to "I'd love to help in any way I can."

"Four months," he replies, his mouth relaxing into a semi-smile.

"Did you go to Quantico for training like they show in the movies?" Kat asks.

"Yeah."

"Wow. That's cool. So what's your assignment? All I know about the FBI is what I saw in *Silence of the Lambs.*" Oh my God, Kat's in full terrorist mode. I can't help but smirk in admiration.

The agent's smile broadens. "Well, new agents are assigned to run background checks for the first year, mostly. And, of course, I'm the lucky guy who gets to talk to all the nice people such as yourselves who come in off the streets of Las Vegas to report the crime of the century."

"Everyone's gotta start somewhere," Kat says breezily. She

leans forward like she's telling a dirty secret. "So here's the thing, Agent Sheffield. I've come here today off the streets of Las Vegas to report the crime of the century."

He laughs.

Kat's face turns serious. "Actually, I'm not kidding. I'm here to report the crime of the century."

He props his hand under his chin, obviously enthralled by the mere sight of her, as any man would be. "What's your name?"

"Katherine Morgan. But you can call me Kat."

"Kat," he repeats. "I tell you what. You guys file your report with me and I promise I'll take a long look at it within the next two weeks—maybe even a week. And, if I see something there, I'll most certainly investigate further."

"Thank you, Special Agent Sheffield," Kat says, biting her lip seductively. "I really appreciate that." She bats her eyelashes. "What's your first name?"

"Eric."

"*Special Agent Eric*," she purrs. "The thing is, this is an urgent matter—this is a career-making kind of case for an agent such as yourself, I swear to God."

Holy shit. I feel like standing up and slow-clapping right now. She's blatantly flirting to get Eric to read Sarah's report—anyone could see that, even him—and yet, she's so damned gorgeous and charming and unapologetic in her sensuality, he obviously doesn't care if he's being used.

"Henn," Sarah interjects. "Will you please play Special Agent Sheffield that voicemail we have cued up?"

"Yes, ma'am." Henn presses a button on his computer and a gruff male voice speaking Ukrainian fills the room.

"Yuri Navolska," Sarah says. "About a minute after leaving that message, he sliced the external jugular vein in my neck and stabbed me in the ribcage, causing me to fall back and crack my skull on a sink ledge."

I've suddenly got chills over my entire body, imagining that violence being inflicted on poor Sarah. I glance at Jonas and he's clenching his jaw.

"If you need to see the scars on my head and torso, I'll show you," Sarah continues.

"No, that's okay. I believe you."

"Please," Kat pleads. "These guys tried to kill my best friend. Just give us a couple hours of your time."

Agent Eric sighs. "You've got more voicemails besides this one?"

"Several," Henn says. "About all kinds of nasty stuff. Maksim Belenko's a really bad dude—prostitution, weapons, drugs, money laundering."

"Okay," Eric says. He nods definitively. "Let's dig in. We'll go through the report together, page by page, and if it's everything you say it is, I'll take this to my boss today."

Kat leaps up from her chair and gives Eric a big hug while Sarah and Henn take seats on either side of Agent Eric, their determination and excitement apparent.

I watch Kat for a long beat.

She's obviously incredible to look at, but, watching her right now, it's clear she's much more than a gorgeous face (and slamming body). She's a fucking force of nature. Smart as hell. Brilliant at reading people. Savvy. The most determined woman I've ever met. Which reminds me, what the hell is the email she sent me before we left for the FBI offices? God only knows what that little terrorist is up to now.

"I sent you an email, Playboy," Kat said coyly about twenty minutes before we left our hotel. "Read it when you can."

"Sure thing, PG," I said.

But just then, Jonas asked me to research something about the jurisdiction of the DEA, and I got completely sidetracked.

I guess now would be a good time to read it, whatever it is—Sarah, Henn, Jonas, and Kat are busy talking about Sarah's report, and I certainly don't have anything to contribute to their conversation, eye candy that I am.

I quickly pull my laptop from its case and click into my email inbox. I scroll for a moment until I find Kat's email from two hours ago. The subject line says, "*Please read this.*" There's no text in the body of the message, just a Word document and three photo files attached. I click on Kat's attached Word document and instantly have a fucking heart attack, followed immediately by a fucking boner.

"*The following is my application to The Josh Faraday Club*," the document says. "*All answers will be one hundred percent honest. (And, bee tee dubs, some of this stuff is kind of personal, so please keep it in confidence.)*"

"Oh my God," I blurt. I look up. Sarah, Henn, Jonas and Eric are absorbed in Sarah's report—but Kat's looking right at me, looking like she's holding her breath.

*She knows I'm reading it.*

I feel my face turn completely red.

Kat smiles a wicked smile, motions to my computer like she's saying, "Get back to work, asshole," and then slowly, ever so slowly, returns her attention to the group.

I look back down at my screen, my heart beating out of my chest, and continue to read:

". . . *my initials spell KUM... Kum Shot, Jizz, Splooge, Pecker-Snot, Man-Yogurt, Dick-Spit, Jizz, Schlong-Juice, Jerk-Sauce*," she writes, and I put my hand over my mouth to keep from bursting out laughing.

". . . *I have blonde hair, blue eyes, and a VAGINA,*" she writes.

This time, I laugh out loud. I can't stop myself.

I look up at Kat, chuckling. She's already been watching me intently, biting the tip of her finger nervously. I shake my head at her, nonverbally calling her evil. She nods, a smart-ass expression on her face.

". . . *I'm attaching all three required photos with this application. Enjoy!*"

I click into her first attached image. A silly headshot. She's making a fishy-face and crossing her eyes, and yet, even making this ridiculous face, she's gorgeous as hell.

Photo number two. Jesus Christ. The body that mesmerized me the other night when it was stomping down that hallway, dripping wet.

I glance up at her.

Her chest is rising and falling visibly, mirroring mine.

I look back at my screen. Photo number three: something she'd 'typically wear out in public.' I click on the image and laugh out loud again. She's pretending to pray to the porcelain gods, wearing her sparkly dress from the other night.

Jesus Christ.

She truly is the female version of me. Anything for a laugh.

What the fuck am I gonna do about this girl? It suddenly dawns on me, full-force: I'm powerless to resist her. I've been thinking all along I've got the upper hand with her, but I've been kidding myself. At the end of the day, she's gonna get whatever she wants, eventually, from me and anyone else—no one could possibly resist her—and I know it. It's inevitable. She's fucking gravity. Death. Taxes. I feel like I'm hurtling in slow motion toward a brick wall, but I can't stop myself.

I look down at my screen again and continue reading, my pulse pounding in my ears.

Aw, shit. My heart breaks for this Nate guy.

I keep reading.

And reading.

Motherfucker.

*Garrett Bennett.*

I grit my teeth. I feel the vein in my neck bulging. I wanna kill this fucker. I wanna hunt him down and rip him limb from limb. What kind of motherfucking asshole does that to a girl—any girl?—but especially one as awesome as Kat? He called my girl a slut? Said she's not 'marriage material' just because she likes sex a whole lot? He's the one who taught her how to like it so much, after all, didn't he?—and he certainly reaped the benefits of her newfound sexual prowess. And then he turned it around on her and burned her at the stake for it? I feel literally homicidal right now, I really do. Having a live wire in the bedroom is every guy's fantasy, and this guy made Kat feel like shit about it? If that motherfucker were here right now, I think it's safe to say I'd be going to prison for what I'd do to him on federal property.

I keep reading, my blood boiling, my heart clanging in my ears.

*"I want to read your application, word for word, without censorship of any kind, and then I want you to do whatever freaky things you've asked for in your application to me, exactly as described. I want to be your Mickey Mouse roller coaster, Josh—and I want you to be mine. Come on, Josh. YOLO. I've told you my secrets. Now it's time for you to tell me yours."*

Holy fucking shit.

"So what do you want me to do?" Agent Eric asks, thumbing through the exhibit log.

"We want a meeting in D.C. within the next two days with power players at the FBI, CIA, and Secret Service," Jonas says.

They continue talking, but I can't follow their conversation. The words on my computer screen are calling to me like a siren—drawing me in like a drug.

I read the entire application again from start to finish, my mind racing, my heart variously racing and breaking, my blood boiling, and, most of all, my cock throbbing the whole time. And when I'm done reading it for the third time, I close my eyes, trying to figure out what the fuck to do. I've never wanted a woman so much in all my life. She's a force of a nature. How am I supposed to resist a fucking tornado? A tsunami? An earthquake? I can't.

"You're not bullshitting me? You can do it?" Agent Eric asks Henn.

"We can do it," Henn says.

"Then I'll vouch for you with my boss," Eric says. "I'll do everything in my power."

I breathe deeply, trying to control my racing thoughts and hard dick. What the fuck am I gonna do? I gotta give her my application, don't I? Shit. Yeah, I do. I wouldn't have believed it possible, but I'm gonna do it. There's no other logical conclusion to this story. The woman just bared her entire soul to me, not just her sexual history. If I don't at least give her my stupid application in return, then I truly am the sociopath she accused me of being. Not to mention a fucking pussy. And an asshole.

"Hey, Agent Sheffield," Sarah says. "I've got a favor to ask of you. You do background checks, right?"

"Yeah," Eric replies. "Every day."

I'm instantly pulled away from my thoughts about Kat. I don't recall a "favor" being part of the strategy Jonas and I cooked up for today's meeting. What the fuck is Sarah talking about?

"I'd like you to find two people for me," Sarah continues.

I look at Jonas as if to say, "What the fuck is she talking about?" and he shakes his head, totally at a loss.

"This isn't a demand," Sarah continues. "It's just a personal favor. But it's really important."

I look at Kat and shoot her the same "What the fuck is she talking about?" look I just flashed Jonas. Kat shrugs, clearly as in the dark as the rest of us.

"Who are the two people?" Eric asks.

"The first is a woman named Mariela from Venezuela."

# Chapter 32
*Josh*

The room warps and buckles. Did Sarah just say she wants Agent Eric to find *Mariela from Venezuela*? My brain can't process what I'm hearing.

I look at Jonas. His face looks exactly the way I feel: blindsided.

If Jonas has told Sarah about Mariela, then he's surely told her about Mom, too. Does that mean he's told her *everything*?

"I don't know her last name," Sarah continues calmly, "but she worked for Joseph and Grace Faraday in Seattle during the years from...I'm guessing 1984 to around 1991."

What the fuck is happening right now? I feel like Sarah just punched me in the balls. I glance at Jonas again. He's got his hands over his face. Good idea. I do the same.

"In 1991, Grace Faraday was murdered in her home . . ." Sarah continues, and the minute she says Mom's name this second time, I suddenly realize she just revealed the true meaning of my "Grace" tattoo to Kat.

I steal a quick look at Kat, and her eyes tell me she's already put two and two together. *She knows.* Oh, fuck. I seriously can't do this. Enough with the honesty-game. It's too much. I put my hands over my face again. I'm shaking.

"Hang on," Eric says. "Could you repeat all that?"

Sarah repeats everything again slowly, including Mom's name, yet again, just in case Kat didn't catch it the first two times. "Grace Faraday," Sarah says. "She was murdered in her home... We need you to find *Mariela*—and if she's not alive, then her children."

"Okay. That sounds doable," Agent Eric says.

Am I hearing that right? This FBI guy is gonna track down Mariela?

I look across the room at Jonas. He looks like he's in total shock.

"Awesome, Eric," Sarah says. "Thank you. And there's one more woman, too. I don't know her first name—but her maiden name was *Westbrook*."

Oh Jesus Christ.

Jonas and I exchange a look of pure astonishment. This is beyond insanity. Sarah's asking the FBI guy to find Mariela *and* Miss Westbrook? Well, that settles it beyond a doubt: Jonas has told Sarah literally every little thing about his life, and therefore mine: Mom, Mariela, Miss Westbrook, Dad, The Lunacy. Holy fuck. I never thought I'd see the day. Haven't we always said no one needs to know about all that—that it's best if these things remain between us?

"Miss Westbrook was a teacher in Seattle in probably 1992," Sarah continues, "and then she married a guy in the Navy named Santorini who was later stationed in San Diego."

"What do these two women have to do with The Club?" Eric asks.

"Absolutely nothing," Sarah says. She gazes at Jonas in a way I've never seen anyone look at him before—with so much tenderness my heart stops vicariously for him. "This would be a personal favor to me," Sarah says, not taking her eyes off Jonas. "I don't have the resources to find these ladies by myself without having their full names, but I think you can do it."

"Shouldn't be a problem."

"Thank you. I'm gonna need this information as soon as possible, please."

"I'll do my best."

I can't stop staring at Sarah—at the way she's looking at Jonas. I've never seen anyone look at him like that. Shit, I've never seen anyone look at *me* like that.

My eyes are burning. I've suddenly got a lump in my throat. Holy shit. What's happening to me right now? I'm about to lose complete control. I swallow hard and steal a quick look at Kat. Her eyes are glistening and her face is red.

I cover my face with my hands again, too overwhelmed to look at her anymore. I can't process this. It's too much.

I honestly never thought Jonas would find a woman he'd tell about Mom and Dad and The Lunacy, too. And I certainly never thought, if he did, that woman would nonetheless look at him like Sarah's looking at Jonas right now. I swallow hard, forcing my emotions down again. I'm so happy for my brother right now, and so fucking relieved for myself, I feel like crying, which is a fucking crazy thought. Holy shit. Jonas is gonna be happy. Sarah loves him, warts and all. I swallow hard again. This is fucking incredible.

But wait.

My joy for my brother is suddenly derailed by an overwhelming sense of panic for myself.

*Kat.*

*She knows too much.* She knows things I never tell anyone—things I don't want her to know. In the taxi after Reed's party, Kat already told me she knows about my parents, thanks to Jonas telling Sarah. "It happened a long time ago," I said breezily, dodging the subject like I always do. But now she knows I'm not quite as unscathed by everything as I let on—that my tattoos aren't just quippy doodles on my skin or youthful, drunken attempts at being profound. Now she knows my skin is inked with my life's greatest sorrow.

*She knows.*

And yet.

Kat gave me her "application" to "The Josh Faraday Club," didn't she—even though she knows I'm more scarred than I let on? She did it because she wants to see the scars, whatever they are.

"What's the name of the school where Miss Westbrook worked in Seattle, Jonas?" Sarah asks Jonas. "That might be helpful for Eric to know for his search."

There's a beat. Jonas isn't answering her. He looks like a deer in headlights.

*Aw, Jonas.*

"St. Francis Academy," I say, answering for my brother.

Jonas flashes me a grateful smile and I grin at him. Some things will never change.

"Okay. I'll do my best," Eric says.

"Thank you," Sarah says. She puts her arm around Jonas' back and squeezes him tightly, and he leans into her, completely at ease in her tender embrace.

"Okay," Agent Eric says. "I'll go talk to my boss right now. I'll give you guys a call later." He nods at Kat, reassuring her in particular. "I promise I'll give it my all."

"I know you will, Eric," Kat purrs. She shifts her eyes to me and leaves them there. Oh my God, she's looking at me like she sees right through me—like my invisible shield has somehow vanished and I'm laid bare for her. "*I have full faith in you,*" Kat says.

# Chapter 33

*Josh*

"Henn, pass the ketchup," I say, but I can barely concentrate on my burger.

Our meeting at the FBI was un-fucking-believable in countless ways, not the least of which is the fact that Kat's application to The Josh Faraday Club is burning a hole in my proverbial pocket. And heart. And dick.

"You crushed it, Kat," Jonas says. "You were amazing."

"Absolutely," Sarah agrees.

Henn passes the ketchup to me. "Who's the fucking genius now?" he says. "Damn, girl." He puts his fist up and she bumps it with hers, a huge smile on her gorgeous face.

*Kat fantasizes about me while masturbating?*

"To Kat," Sarah says, raising her beer, and the rest of us hold up our beers in Kat's honor, too. "You're the reason Eric started taking us seriously," Sarah says. "No doubt about it."

"Aw, thanks," Kat says. "But it was definitely a team effort."

We all raise our glasses again and drink to "the team."

*She wants to feel my hard-on sliding deep inside her?*

I clear my throat. "So how are we gonna get the money, Henn?" I ask, pointedly not looking at Kat. Shit, I'm hard as a rock right now. If I look at her, I'm not gonna be able to stop myself from grabbing her and kissing the hell out of her right here and now, in front of everyone. "I thought you said most of those accounts are set up for in-person transfer only." Fuck. I can't stop imagining Kat masturbating.

*Ever since I saw you in that hallway,* she wrote, *I've taken self-love to an art form.*

I shift in my chair, trying to relieve the throbbing of my dick in my pants, but it's no use.

"They are," Henn says. "Which, obviously, means we're going to transfer the money in-person." He pauses, shooting Kat a meaningful look. "Hello, Oksana Belenko."

Kat grimaces sharply. "Oh, I dunno—" she begins.

"You'll be fine," Henn says. "I'll set you up with a passport and a driver's license—"

"I don't know if I can—" Kat says, sputtering.

"You *can*," Henn says. "Today proved that. Indubitably. Don't worry, Kitty Kat." He touches the top of her hand. "I'll hack into each account and shave thirty years off Oksana's age—they won't even question you're her for a second. And then I'll walk into each and every bank with you, right by your side."

"But will she be safe?" Sarah asks.

"I'll make sure of it," Henn says.

"So will I," I add.

At my words, Kat's eyes flicker to me and my cock hardens even more. The right thing to do is pull her aside and kiss her for the first time in private—but I'm not sure I can wait.

A waitress walks by and Kat flags her. "Double Patron shots all around, please." When the waitress leaves, Kat lets out a long exhale. "Okay, I'll do it."

"Kat, are you sure?" Sarah asks. "You don't have to do this."

"Yes, I do. This ain't no casino heist, fellas—and very pretty lady." She winks at Sarah. "This is about taking these guys down so they can't hurt you ever again, Sarah. It's a no-brainer."

Holy shit. She's blowing my mind today—first, with the FBI guy, and then with her application, and now with this. She's willing to impersonate Oksana Belenko to steal The Club's money? I wouldn't have thought it possible when we first started on this bizarre adventure, but Kat's turned out to be every bit as valuable to the team as any of us—far more valuable than me, actually.

"We'll create an offshore account," Jonas is saying to the group. "And funnel everything into it at the last possible moment."

"*Two* offshore accounts," I say pointedly. "I think we're gonna have to take a little *finder's fee* on the deal—don't you think, bro? Maybe one percent?"

A light bulb goes off on Jonas' face—as usual, my brother can read my mind.

"Fuck yeah," Jonas says. "Great idea. Yeah, five and a half mill sounds about right for our commission. Kat and Henn, you guys will each get a cool mill off the top. You've both earned it."

I nod emphatically. A million each is exactly what I'd had in mind.

"Are you *serious*?" Kat squeals. "You're gonna give me a *million* dollars?"

"You deserve it," Jonas says.

Kat squeals again and leaps up to hug Jonas, jiggling her tight little body with excitement, and then moves on to kiss Sarah full on the mouth.

Oh, Jesus. That's it. I give up. I've got to kiss this woman right now. Waiting 'til we're alone is a fucking pipe dream. Whatever she wants, yes, I'll do it. I don't fucking care anymore. She told me her shit, I'll tell her mine. I've got to have her, no matter the price.

Kat's done kissing Sarah and now it's my turn. She bends down, obviously intending to chastely kiss my cheek—but I stand abruptly, grab her face, pull her sexy little body firmly into mine, and devour her lips. My tongue slides inside her mouth and instantly leads hers into sensual movement.

Kat yelps with surprise and throws her arms around my neck, her tongue responding to my entreaties with extreme enthusiasm.

I press myself into her even harder, suddenly overcome with so much arousal, I can barely stand, and she runs her hands through my hair.

Oh, God, I'm light-headed. Every nerve ending in my body is in overload, surging with pleasure and relief. Oh, God, yes, she tastes incredible, better than I'd even imagined. And she smells fucking amazing. Our tongues swirling and intertwining feel electrically charged. Oh my fuck, if we were alone in my room the way I'd originally planned to finally kiss her, her clothes would already be off and my cock inside her. It's just that good.

But, shit, we're not alone.

Fuck.

Contrary to every primal urge coursing through my body, my lips release hers.

She pulls away from me, her lips red and her eyes smoldering.

I clutch my chest and smile at her. "I feel like I've been waiting a lifetime to do that," I say softly.

"Why the hell did you wait so long, Playboy?" Kat breathes, pressing herself into my hard-on.

"Gee, I wonder why." I press my forehead against hers, grinning broadly.

"So does this mean you're finally gonna tell me?" Kat says.

I nod. "You win," I whisper, almost inaudibly. "God help me, you little terrorist, you win."

Kat laughs and sits back down, grinning from ear to ear, a living portrait of victory, but when she sees Henn's face across the table, her face instantly falls.

"Oh, Henny. I'm sorry," she says.

Henn shakes his head. "No, it's great. You're both the best." He swallows hard. "Indubitably." He tries to smile.

"Hey, Henn—" I say.

"No, really." He waves me away. "I'm good."

But, clearly, he's not good. Not good at all.

Kat gets up from her seat next to mine and works her way around the table to Henn. She grabs his shoulders emphatically and stares into his eyes. "You're the best. I'm proud to call you my friend." She kisses him on the cheek.

But he's clearly heartbroken.

*Shit.*

The waitress arrives with the tequila shots Kat ordered and Sarah leads the charge on raising our drinks in the air. "To the Party Girl with a Heart of Gold and the Hacker," Sarah says, clearly trying to cheer Henn up. "A couple of *mill-ion-aires.*"

"Here, here," I say.

"Yeah, well, let's not put the cart before the horse," Kat says, putting down her empty shot glass. "There's still the little matter of actually getting the money."

"Oh, we'll get it—don't you worry," Henn says.

I grab Kat's hand under the table and squeeze it and she leans into me.

"Those fuckers almost killed you, baby," Jonas is saying to Sarah. "They owe you a shitload more than three million bucks. Plus, you've been our fearless George Clooney through all this—you deserve it."

"One hundred percent," I say.

"No, I can't—"

"Sure you can," I say.

"Absolutely," Kat adds. She returns my hand-squeeze under the table and leans right into my body.

"But what about you, Josh? Don't you want some of the money?" Sarah asks.

I laugh. "Hell no."

"But you've been helping us from minute one—"

"Of course, I have. I wouldn't have it any other way." I smile at Jonas and he grins.

"Just don't make a decision about the money yet," Jonas says to Sarah. "Think about it for a little while."

Kat puts her hand on my thigh under the table and my cock twitches violently.

"*I want you so badly I'm in pain*," she wrote to me. Jesus Fucking Christ. I can't wait another minute to fuck her.

"So, Henn, how quickly do you think you can—" Sarah abruptly stops talking.

Some dude in a suit has just walked up to our table.

Sarah looks ashen.

Jonas looks like he's about to commit murder.

Oh, Jesus. Shit. This dude's got to be Max—the creep who demanded a "freebie" from Sarah. No wonder Jonas looks like he's about to kill the fucker—I wanna kill him myself. I look at Kat and her eyes are bugging out of her head.

"What do you want?" Jonas spits out, putting his arm protectively around Sarah. He looks like a rabid Doberman pinscher on a leash.

"Hello, Mr. Faraday," the guy says smoothly. "Sarah." He glances at the rest of the table for show, but it's clear he doesn't give a shit about anyone but Sarah.

"I hope you're still enjoying your stay here in Las Vegas?" the guy asks.

"What the fuck do you want?" Jonas asks.

"I had some business in the hotel—what a coincidence to run into you."

The expression on Jonas' face makes me release Kat's hand under the table, just in case I need to leap up and fight this fucker.

"Hi, Max," Sarah says, her voice shaky. "Yeah, that's one helluva coincidence. Hey, everybody, this is Max—a friend of mine. These are some friends of Jonas' who met us in Vegas to party—Jonas' brother Josh, Josh's girlfriend Kayley, and his roommate from college, Scott."

Max barely acknowledges the rest of us. "I just need to steal you for a couple minutes, Sarah." He puts his hand out like he's expecting Sarah to take it.

"No," Jonas says, pulling Sarah into him.

"Hey, guys," Sarah says to the group. "Could you all excuse us for a few minutes?"

I look at Jonas, unsure whether we should leave him and Sarah alone with this asshat or not. "Um... ," I say.

Jonas nods at me, signaling it's okay for us to go.

I flash Jonas a look asking him if he's sure, and he nods again.

"Sure," I say slowly. "Come on, Kayley. Scott. Let's go roll some dice." The three of us get up from the table and walk toward the front door of the restaurant—but just inside the front doors, we stop and watch Jonas and Sarah for a long moment, assuring ourselves they're gonna be safe if we leave, and when it seems certain the guy is here to flap his gums and nothing more, we slip outside the restaurant and enter the bustling casino.

"Whoa, that guy was exactly like I pictured him," Henn says. "Talk about Dr. Evil."

My eyes lock with Kat's. She smiles broadly at me.

"Did you see Jonas' face?" Henn asks. "That Max dude's about to become hash browns, man."

I can't wait another minute. I grab Kat's hand and pull her toward the elevators on the far side of the casino.

"Hey, boss," Henn says behind me. "The craps tables are this way, man."

"You're gonna have to play on your own for a little while, Henn," I say over my shoulder.

"Oh," I hear Henn say behind me. "Gotcha." He sounds crestfallen. And I'm intellectually sorry about that, I really am—because I love that fucking genius like a brother—but right now, the only thing I care about is finally getting to experience the motherfucking force of nature that is Katherine Ulla Morgan from the inside-out.

"Are you taking me to read your application?" Kat whispers, clutching my hand.

I don't reply. We've reached the elevators and I bang on the call button. Now that I've kissed her, I'm about to explode with my pent-up sexual desire. I'm a dam about to break.

"Are you taking me to read your application?" Kat repeats, her voice barely controlled excitement.

I turn to face her. "No. I'm taking you to my room where I'm going to fuck the living shit out of you," I say evenly. "And *then* I'll give you my goddamned motherfucking application."

She clamps her lips together, shocked.

I grunt with frustration and lean in to whisper into her ear. "And I swear to God, you little terrorist, you better not say another goddamned fucking word about that motherfucking application until after I'm through fucking you. You'll get what you want, I swear to fucking God, because it's clear to me now you're as inevitable as goddamned gravity, but first things first I'm gonna get inside that tight little body of yours and fuck you 'til you're screaming my name."

## Chapter 34

*Kat*

The elevator arrives and Josh pulls me inside, his chest heaving, his eyes blazing. An orchestral version of "Take on Me" by A-ha greets us in the enclosed space.

The doors begin closing and Josh lunges at me, making my clit zing with anticipation—but just before the doors slide shut, a hand stops their progress and an elderly couple steps into the elevator car.

Josh leans abruptly away from me, clasps his hands in front of his crotch, and looks down at the floor of the elevator.

I straighten up, feeling light-headed and weak-kneed.

"Hello," the lady says. She's got silver hair and she's wearing a simple sundress.

"Hello," I say brightly to the woman and her husband, trying to distract attention away from Josh and his pained expression.

"Are you two having fun?" the woman asks.

"Definitely. You?"

"Oh, yes. We always have fun in Vegas. We play the slots and see a show—always a good time."

"Have you been winning?"

The lady laughs. "No."

I look at Josh. His head is bowed. His hands are still clasped in front of his pants.

"What show did you see this time?" I ask, my heart racing.

Josh shifts his weight next to me.

"Blue Man Group," the woman replies, her eyes darting to Josh and back to me. "What have you been up to, honey?"

"Oh," I say. "Nothing much. The usual Vegas stuff—a little craps, *Cirque Du Soleil,* plotting to overthrow the evil empire and save the world, bringing a stubborn man to his knees—you know, blah, blah, blah."

The woman chuckles.

The older couple's floor dings and they step out, and the minute they're gone, Josh leans toward me aggressively, like he's gonna fuck me right here and now. But a dad with two young kids in swim gear immediately gets onto the elevator, causing Josh to step back and clasp his hands in front of his crotch again.

"We're going *up,*" Josh barks out, his eyes like lasers.

"Oh, whoops, thanks," the dad says, putting his arm out to stop the elevator doors from closing. "Come on, guys, step out," the dad says, glaring at Josh. "Daddy messed up. We've gotta go *down* to get to the pool. Sorry about that, folks."

"No problem—have fun," Josh says, obviously trying to make amends for how loudly he just barked at the guy.

Wow. I've never seen Josh look more like his brother than he does in this moment. If this is how Jonas looks at Sarah on a regular basis, then it's no wonder she's suddenly been acting like a cat in heat.

The dad and his kids step off the elevator and the doors close behind them—and Josh freaking *attacks* me. His lips are on mine. His hands are all over me, exploring my breasts and ass and back. Oh lordy, he smells so fucking good. His tongue is sensual and confident, his lips utterly delicious. His hand moves confidently between my legs, under my sundress, right to the crotch of my panties, where his fingers confidently stroke me. I pull back slightly and grip the bulge in his pants as his fingers slide over the fabric covering my clit.

"Oh my God, Kat," he murmurs as I vigorously stroke the hardness under his slacks.

"I'm *dying,*" I breathe, my body bursting into flames.

The elevator doors open and we tumble out together, still kissing and groping each other. We bang into the wall with a loud thud but keep going, both of us moaning and laughing at the same time as we work our way down the short hallway toward Josh's room.

"You have a condom?" I mumble into his lips. Oh my God, my body's already beginning to warp and twist from deep inside.

"Mmm hmm."

We're a frantic tumble of lips and fingers and limbs, hurtling together voraciously toward Josh's suite, until—*boom*!—our writhing bodies literally crash into a cart filled with towels and cleaning supplies right outside Josh's room.

"No," Josh growls. "No, no, no."

He grabs my hand and yanks me into his suite, a low rumble simmering in his throat—and, yep, sure enough, a maid is in the bedroom across the large suite, tucking a sheet.

"We don't need cleaning service today," Josh shouts at the poor woman across the large suite, making her freeze mid-tuck.

"Oh, I'm sorry, sir," she says. "I was just finishing up this—"

"Thank you," Josh says, his tone adamant. "You can go. *Please*."

The maid looks flustered. "Yes, sir." She exits the bedroom and heads toward the front door.

"Thank you so much," Josh says, obviously trying to soften his tone.

"Do you want clean towels before I—"

"*Nope*. We're good. Thank you so much." He squeezes my hand.

The woman presses her lips together and beelines out the front door as fast as her short legs will carry her, obviously surmising exactly what we've barreled into Josh's hotel room to do.

"Oh my fucking God," Josh says the moment the door shuts behind the woman. He hastily reaches behind my back and unzips my dress. "I've waited my entire life to get inside you, Katherine Ulla Morgan." He kisses my neck and peels my dress off my shoulders. "Nothing's gonna stop me now—this hotel could crumble to the fucking ground and they'd find me under the rubble, my dick still hard and inside you."

I laugh.

He pulls my unzipped dress down past my torso, over my hips, to the floor, sliding his palms along my bare skin as he goes, and before I even know what's happening, my dress and bra are on the floor, his tongue is in my mouth, my nipples are rock hard, and he's backing me against a nearby table, his hard-on behind his pants grinding into my crotch.

His mouth leaves mine and devours my neck, collarbone, breasts, nipples. He bites my left nipple and sucks on it feverishly, and I throw my head back, my entire body convulsing and bursting into flames at his mouth's voracious assault. Holy shit, this feels incredible. I can't remember the last time I wanted a man this bad, if ever.

He kisses my stomach, swirling his tongue around the piercing on my belly button, and then moves on to my hips and pelvis, his lips and tongue giving me goose bumps of pure pleasure. I grab and pull feverishly at the collar of his shirt, wordlessly begging him to take off his clothes so I can press my body against his nakedness, but he ignores my implicit request, abruptly kneeling down and leveling his mouth with my crotch. "I couldn't hear you well enough when you came on the dance floor—the music was too loud. I wanna hear every little sound you make when you come."

*Oh.* I shudder with arousal.

He slides my G-string off my hips, his fingertips caressing my hipbones, his warm lips laying soft kisses on the flesh just below my belly button. When he suddenly and fervently pulls my pelvis into his face, my entire lower abdomen tightens sharply and begins to burn.

"So fucking gorgeous," he murmurs, his warm, wet tongue swirling around the perimeter of my crotch. I grip the table behind me, bracing myself for the delectable moment when his tongue is finally gonna land right where I want it most. Oh God, I'm desperate for him to take my throbbing clit into his mouth and suck on it like a lollipop.

He's getting closer and closer to ground zero, but he's drawing it out, teasing me, sending me into a frenzy. I prop my left thigh onto his shoulder, straining my pelvis toward him, jerking like a dog in heat. I grab his head and yank his hair and he moans into my crotch, puffing warm air onto my sensitive flesh.

Finally, after what seems like forever, his warm tongue flickers onto my clit and begins lapping at me voraciously, eliciting a sound from me like I've just placed my hand on a hot stove. I press myself into him violently, desperately, jolting, gripping the table behind me, my pelvis jerking rhythmically with the hungry movements of his lips and tongue.

"Oh, hell yeah," I breathe. "Fuck, that's good."

Oh God, I'm beginning to clench forcefully from deep inside. This is incredible. This man right here gets the job done right.

"You taste so fucking good," he growls from between my legs. "So *fucking* good."

As his mouth continues working my tip, he slides his fingers deep inside me—and that's all my body needs to release forcefully. In an instant, pleasure is slamming into me like a hurricane—I'm twisting, warping, shuddering around his fingers, all the while grasping urgently at his head between my legs. "Josh," I sputter. "Oh my God, *yes*." I claw at him, gasping, gripping the hair on the back of his head, his ears, cheeks, neck, yanking at the fabric of his shirt—doing whatever it takes to survive the brutality of the pleasure I'm experiencing.

Josh abruptly takes my thigh off his shoulder and stands up to his full height, his eyes blazing like blue coals. He licks his glistening lips and begins slowly unbuttoning his shirt, his eyes never leaving mine. I'm dripping down my thighs with my arousal, jerking my pelvis in anticipation of the delicious fucking I'm about to take. Oh my God. My clit is vibrating with a low, insistent hum, rippling with faint aftershocks from my orgasm.

As Josh continues unbuttoning his shirt, I reach down and stroke the bulge in his pants, reveling in the delectable hardness of him against my fingertips. I can't think straight. All I can do is *want*.

He peels off his shirt and tosses it onto the floor and I'm treated to the same panty-soaking view of his muscled, tattooed torso I beheld in the hallway after Reed's party. Only this time, he's even sexier than he was to me then, if that's possible.

"Oh my God," I whisper, ogling him. "Oh my *God*."

Josh flashes a cocky grin. "I know, but feel free to call me *Josh*."

Even through my intense arousal, I laugh.

"Oh man, I'm gonna fuck you so hard, Party Girl," he growls. "I'm gonna fuck you *and* your fucking Hyphen, baby."

I semi-chuckle—my brain knows that was funny—but I'm too wound up to laugh. I can barely stand, I'm so frickin' aroused.

I run my hands over the "Grace" tattoo on his muscled chest, convulsing with excitement as I do, and then across his "OVERCOME" tattoo scrolling across his ripped lower abs. Oh God, I'm beginning to feel desperate for him.

He leans forward and kisses me, caressing my breast as he does, and I reach down hungrily to unfasten his pants.

I open his belt and zipper and quickly open the front of his pants.

His humongous bulge is trapped inside simple white briefs. I yank feverishly on his underwear and he pulls them off.

I look down at his naked body and convulse with pleasure at the sight of him. Holy fuckballs, he's the sexiest man alive.

Josh embraces me and I melt into his arms, shaking with excitement.

His lips are on mine, his tongue in my mouth, his hands on my back. He gropes my ass and skims his fingers inside my ass crack and I moan involuntarily. Oh God, I'm losing my fucking mind with anticipation.

"Fuck me already," I say. "*Please.*"

I pull back from him and grasp his shaft, twitching with arousal as I do—and at my eager touch, Josh grips the back of my hair, pulls my head back and leans right into my face.

"You've been torturing me—so now I'm torturing you."

He kisses me deeply, still gripping my hair, making my knees buckle.

"I like hearing you beg," he breathes. "As you should."

I'm reeling. I can't think straight. I feel like I'm losing hold of my sanity. Why won't he do it already? I've already waited far too long.

"Please," I beg.

He smiles wickedly. "Oh my God, the things I'm gonna do to you," he whispers, almost to himself. He grabs his pants off the floor, fishes into his pocket, and pulls out a foil packet. Ten seconds later, he looks up from rolling the condom onto his erection, growls, turns me around abruptly and guides my shuddering body to the nearby table.

Good lord, I can't remember the last time a man turned me on this much. I'm non-functional—his for the taking, any which way he pleases. I've quite literally never been this turned-on before.

"You want me, Kat?" he whispers into my ear, pulling my backside into him and reaching around to grope my breasts. "Because I'm gonna fuck you so hard you'll forget all about that fucking application."

"Please," I gasp.

Without warning, he slaps my ass and I yelp with surprise. "You know why I just did that?"

"Because I'm a fucking terrorist."

"That's right, baby." He growls with pleasure.

His fingers move to my crotch and massage my clit rhythmically as he glowers over me from behind.

I moan loudly. "Fuck me."

"Oh, say it again."

"Fuck me."

"Beg me for it," he growls, grinding his dick into my back and working my clit with fervor.

Oh, yeah, I'm liking this. He's good at this. "*Please*," I breathe.

"Please what?"

"*Please fuck me*." Oh my God, he's working my clit better than any battery-operated-boyfriend ever could.

"Admit you've touched yourself just like this, dreaming about sucking my hard cock."

How'd he know that? "Yes," I breathe. "Every fucking day."

"Now beg me to fuck you one more time. And maybe I will."

Oh good lord. I'm so turned on, I'm gonna come before he's even entered me.

"Fuck me," I say between teeth gritted. This is too much. I'm going fucking insane with anticipation. "*Please* fuck me, Josh. *Please*." I'm shuddering, trembling, dripping with arousal. My head is spinning. My clit's on fire. I can't wait another minute.

"You're gonna come for me first," he growls, his fingers working me into a frenzy.

At his words, my skin begins prickling like I've got a sudden chill. "Oh, shit," I say. "*Yes*. I'm about to come. Oh fuck. It's gonna be a big one." I grip the table. "Oh, Jesus."

He puts his lips right against my ear, his fingers still working me. "That's right," he whispers, his breath tickling my ear. "Beg me."

"Fuck me now," I gasp. "Please."

He slaps my ass again and I yelp with excitement.

"My little terrorist," he says, his voice low and taut. "I'm torturing you because you've been so, so bad."

I've never been treated this way. Men usually act like I'm their pretty, precious trophy—a prize to be won and worshipped. Nate certainly never spoke to me this way, not even once, and Garrett never said a frickin' word during sex beyond growling like a bear. Sure, occasional guys have talked dirty to me during sex, but this... this thing Josh is doing to me... this is a whole new level—and it's turning me on like crazy.

"Please," I whimper, sweat beading on my brow.

"Bad girl." He slaps my ass again and, immediately, a massive orgasm slams into me, wrenching my insides like a towel being wrung out to dry.

He growls with pleasure. "Oh my God, you're so fucking hot, baby."

He sticks his fingers deep inside me again, making me cry out at the sensation, and the next thing I know, his hard cock is finally, mercifully sliding deep inside me, deep, deep, deep inside me, filling me to the brim and then some.

Josh makes a sound of pure pleasure and that's enough to push me over the edge.

"Oh, *fuck*," I say, my body clenching forcefully around his hardness.

I'm absolutely shocked—I've never had back-to-back orgasms like this, and I've certainly never had an orgasm triggered solely by the sensation of a man entering me, either. Holy shitballs, I'm being turned inside out.

"Fuck, oh my God. Fuck," I say as warm waves of pleasure grip me.

I lay my palms on the table in front of me, steadying myself as my body tightens and ripples and warps around Josh, this time even harder than the last time. "Oh, Jesus," I choke out. Oh my God, his cock is absolutely enormous inside me—if he misused that thing, he'd surely rip me in two. But, oh my God, no, he's not misusing it—he's using it exceptionally well. I'm clenching so furiously around his cock, I can't breathe.

Josh lets out a low moan as his dick burrows into me all the freaking way—balls deep, baby—and then he grips my hips from behind and leads my body into rhythmic movement with his.

"You're perfect," he whispers into my ear, his hands groping every inch of my body voraciously. "Jesus Fucking Christ, you're fucking incredible."

His thrusts are becoming more and more intense. I gasp with excitement and reach up over my shoulder to grab his cheek and pull him into me.

"You feel so good," he murmurs into my ear, cupping my breasts in his large hands. He kisses my neck, pinches my nipples, fucking me all the while in rhythmic thrusts. "You're so fucking wet and tight," he growls. "You feel so good."

Good God, I can't think. I'm overwhelmed with pleasure.

"You feel so fucking good," he whispers into my ear again, pumping rhythmically inside me. "You've got a magic pussy, baby."

Oh Jesus. I've never been treated like this before—never been fucked so well and with such glorious dirty-talk, too. Oh my God, I'm losing my freaking mind.

I slam myself into him as best I can on wobbly legs, moaning and grunting as I do. I'm riding his cock as hard as I can, losing complete control. I'm a rubber band about to snap. I reach down and touch the spot where his cock is sliding in and out of me, then let my fingers wander to his balls and feel them swinging and slamming to and fro against me as he thrusts. The sensation makes me shudder with pleasure.

"You're gorgeous," he whispers into my ear, his fingers working my clit as he thrusts. His free hand finds its way to my mouth and I suck voraciously on his fingers.

He makes a strangled sound. Oh, he's ramping up hard. I can feel it.

He pulls his finger out of my mouth and abruptly bends me over the table, pushing on my back and forcing my sweaty chest into the glass.

"You liked torturing me, didn't you?" he growls.

"Yes," I breathe.

He slaps my ass harder than ever and my body jerks with pleasure.

"Tell me you're sorry for what you did."

"I'm not sorry," I say.

He spanks me again.

I inhale sharply, and that hand-on-a-hot-stove sound escapes my lips again.

"Oh, yeah, that's it," Josh says, apparently already keyed into my body's cues. "Here it comes, baby. Come for me."

A couple more spanks and deep thrusts and I climax again, gasping as I do—and a moment later, Josh jerks with what seems like a massive orgasm, too.

When my body stops warping and clenching, and Josh seems to

have finished coming behind me, I sprawl myself onto the table, completely spent, soaking in sweat and shaking with my exertion.

Oh my God. That was the best sex of my entire life. I never wanted it to end. And, holy shitballs, I wanna do it again as soon as humanly possible.

"Holy That Was Even Better Than I Expected, Batman," I finally say, my sweaty cheek resting against the glass table. "Daaaaaay-am."

Josh laughs and slaps my ass, hard, but I barely flinch.

"Hell yeah, it was, Batman—or, shit, wait, are you Robin?" He chuckles. "Dude, I just realized—were Batman and Robin *gay*?"

"I think they were just really, really, *really* close friends."

Josh pulls out of me and turns my limp body around to face him. "You're amazing," he says simply, looking into my eyes with surprising tenderness. "I had pretty high expectations for fucking the Party Girl with a Hyphen, I gotta admit, and it was even better than I'd fantasized."

He cups my face in his palms and kisses me—and I melt into him, returning his kiss passionately, my heart racing. For several minutes, we kiss and kiss and kiss, making up for lost time, I suppose, our mouths consuming each other voraciously, my sweaty breasts smashed into his muscled chest, my arms wrapped firmly around his neck.

"Best ever," he whispers.

"Ditto," I whisper. I don't know if he's saying this to me as a figure of speech, but I'm being literal. That was quite literally the best sex of my life. "I feel high right now," I say. "Like I could jump out a five-story building and fly."

Josh laughs. "'I am a golden god.'"

"*Almost Famous,*" I quip, easily identifying the source of his quote.

Josh beams a smile at me. "We can add that to your list of dude-like qualities: 'can identify movie quotes.'"

I laugh. "Yeah, I'm pretty damned good at it, actually."

"You're good at everything," he says tenderly. He sighs and strokes my hair. "You're amazing—like a drug. I feel totally buzzed right now. Jesus."

I blush.

"I loved your application, by the way. Best gift I've ever gotten." He smirks. "And utterly diabolical of you, I must say—brilliant strategic maneuver. I couldn't resist you after that."

"So does that mean I'm a shoe-in to get approved for the Josh Faraday Club?"

"Oh, you're a shoe-in, for sure, baby. Fuck yes. But the approval process takes a bit of time, you should know, so you gotta be patient. I suggest we order some room service while we wait for round two of the review process—that motherfucker Max interrupted my burger and fries and I'm hangry as hell about it."

I laugh. "Oh, really? Is that how this is gonna go down? You're just gonna keep fucking me 'til I forget all about your application?"

"Yeah, that's pretty much the plan."

"That wasn't the deal," I say, narrowing my eyes. "The deal was you kiss me, you give me the application."

"No, the deal was I kiss you; I *fuck* you; I give you the application. I've kissed you. I've fucked you—and now I'm gonna fuck you again and again (all part of the *approval* process, baby)—and *then* I'm gonna give you my application."

A wave of anxiety floods me. "Josh, you aren't really gonna try to weasel out of giving it to me, are you?"

He flashes me a megawatt smile. "Of course not. I never go back on my word. That's something you should know about me right up front." He touches my thigh. "My promise is ironclad."

I exhale in relief.

"Don't worry, PG, the review process will continue only as long as we're in this hotel room together. Just give me this little bubble of time to fuck you without that shit hanging over my head—and when we leave this hotel room, the review process will be complete, your membership will be approved, and that stupid application will be all yours."

I make a face.

"Aw, come on, PG. I kiss you; I fuck you; I give you my application. That was the deal. Remember? You said kissing you would lead to immediate fuckery. I'm just taking you at your word."

I glare at him. I'm not sure that was the deal. But sex with Josh is so freakin' good, I'm not feeling the urge to argue with him.

"Don't fight me on it, baby, just enjoy the ride." He snickers.

"*YOLO*, right? Wasn't that the super-cool thing you told me to say as much as possible?"

I roll my eyes.

"YOLO, Kat. *YOOOOOOOLO.*"

With that, he pulls the condom off his dick, slaps my ass yet again, and heads into the bathroom—giving me my first ever view of his beautiful bare ass... which, much to my shock (and squealing delight), is stamped across its left cheek with four tiny, but unmistakable, letters.

## Chapter 35

*Kat*

"What the fuckity, Josh? You didn't feel the slightest urge to mention the 'YOLO' tattoo on your ass cheek when I was going on and on about how 'YOLO' tattoos are social suicide?"

We're sitting in our underwear on Josh's bed, macking down on double cheeseburgers, fries, and Moscow mules from room service, laughing hysterically and involuntarily wiggling our bodies to the beat of the disco song blaring on Josh's laptop ("You Dropped a Bomb on Me" by The Gap Band, which Josh says is now his official theme song).

"How the heck did you manage to keep quiet about your tattoo? That must have taken Herculean willpower."

"Meh, I figured it'd be best for you to find out about it exactly the way you did—by seeing my ass in all its glory after I'd fucked you." He smiles wickedly. "So much more fun than just *telling* you about it. Am I right?" He chomps a French fry.

I laugh. "Why the *hell* do you have 'YOLO' stamped on your ass cheek, Josh? It's inexcusable. Seriously, if I had any self-respect whatsoever, I'd grab my shit and go."

He laughs. "I lost a bet." He takes a big bite of his burger.

"What?" I shriek.

"I lost a bet," he mumbles, his mouth full of burger.

"Well, what was the freaking bet?"

He finishes chewing. "See, that's the thing. I don't remember exactly."

"What?" I shriek. "You got 'YOLO' tattooed onto your ass-cheek and you don't even know *why*?"

"Well, I know *why*—generally speaking. The bet was over a

quote from *Happy Gilmore*. I just can't remember *which* quote we were arguing over."

I smack my forehead with my palm. "Please tell me you're kidding. You got YOLO inked onto your ass over a quote from *Happy Gilmore*?"

Josh laughs and turns off the blaring disco song. He looks at his laptop for a moment, searching for something. "Oh, this is a good one. Listen to this—Jonas turned me on to these guys." An acoustic guitar suddenly fills the room. "X Ambassadors. 'Renegades.'"

"Yeah, great song," I say. "You were about to tell me how *Happy Gilmore* led to your tragic ass-tattoo."

He shrugs. "It's embarrassing."

"All the more reason to tell me."

He rolls his eyes. "It was when I was at UCLA, when I lived in my fraternity house. A group of us used to say 'YOLO' all the time, laughing our asses off about it, thinking we totally made it up. And, hell, maybe we did, for all I know—several years later, Zac Efron got 'YOLO' tattooed on his hand and my friends and I texted each other like crazy about it, like, 'Did you see Zac Efron stole our thing, man? We came up with that years ago!' And, then Drake claimed he invented it in a song, and Reed was like, 'Yeah, that's 'cause the fucker came to my house for a fucking party and we were all saying it!'"

I laugh. "You guys started a trend."

"That's what cool kids do, baby." He winks.

"But that doesn't excuse you getting it stamped onto your ass, Josh Faraday. That's just inexcusable. Seriously."

He chuckles.

"Please explain this horrifying tragedy to me."

He laughs gleefully. "Well, like I say, 'YOLO' was kind of a thing with my friends and me, but only because we thought it was super douchey and hilarious and stupid. And one night at the house I was drinking beer with Henn and Reed and a few other guys and we were throwing out movie quotes and guessing the movie, as one does, and Henn threw out some quote from *Happy Gilmore*. I was like, 'Dude, no, you've got it wrong.' And he was like, 'No, dude, I have it exactly right.' And I was like, 'No, no, man, it's *this*.' And he was like, 'No, man, it's definitely this other thing.' And I was like, 'I love you, man, like a brother, but you're wrong as shit.' So we went around and around, both of us positive we were one-hundred-percent right, until finally Reed said, 'Okay, dudes, put your money where your mouth is. Whoever's wrong has to get 'YOLO' inked onto his ass.' Well, everyone in the room lost his shit. For some reason, that was the funniest idea we'd ever heard. So, of course, I was like, 'Hell yeah. I'm in, motherfucker.' Because the chance to saddle Henn with a fucking 'YOLO' tattoo, and on his *ass cheek* no less, for eternity, was too good to pass up. And I guess Henn was thinking the same exact thing about me, so he was like, 'Boo-fucking-yah.' So we shook on it and then Reed put on a DVD of *Happy Gilmore* and found the scene with the quote, whatever it was, and, *motherfucker*, Henn was exactly right."

For a long beat, I'm laughing too hard to speak and Josh is right there with me.

"That's just... insane," I finally choke out. "What a horrible, horrible reason to get YOLO stamped on your ass."

"Could there possibly be a good reason?"

I consider. "Yes. If Make-A-Wish called and asked you to do it for some poor kid with cancer. That's literally the only defensible reason to get a 'YOLO' tattoo anywhere on your body."

Josh laughs. "But, see, the thing is I never go back on my word—no matter what. We went out that very night to a tattoo place in Hollywood and I did it." He chuckles to himself, seemingly at a memory. "Henn and Reed were laughing so hard the whole time, they wound up on the floor of the place, sobbing like little girls."

"Well, I hope it was worth it," I say. "Because you've got that horrible thing *forever,* Josh."

He shrugs. "Meh, there's no such thing as forever. Skin's just temporary—we're all gonna die, right? Sooner or later, maybe sooner. And, yeah, it was totally worth it—in fact, it turned out to be a very good thing."

"How could a 'YOLO' tattoo on your ass possibly turn out to be a good thing?"

"Because it's a constant reminder to me of something I don't wanna forget." He considers his words for a moment. "I was so fucking sure I was right about that damned quote—and I was dead fucking wrong. So I guess that stupid tattoo reminds me not to get too cocky or comfortable in life—no matter how much I think my shit doesn't stink, I could always be dead wrong." All joviality in his demeanor is gone. He swigs his drink.

His face has turned dark. I bite the inside of my cheek, unsure how to respond.

"And, hey, either way, it's a good story, right?" he adds. He's obviously trying to lighten things up again. "So that's always a win in my book."

"Oh, yeah, it's definitely a good story," I agree. "And a very telling one, too."

"Telling? In what way?"

"About you as a person."

"Oh yeah? Pray tell—what does my YOLO ass-tattoo tell you about me as a person? Besides the fact that I'm a total dumbshit, of course."

I chuckle. "It tells me plenty of stuff—some of it kind of deep."

He raises his eyebrows. "Well, this ought to be good."

I take a long sip of my drink, gathering my thoughts. "Well, okay, they're not *all* deep and profound things—some are kind of, you know, online-profile-ish."

"Tell me all of it."

"Okay. Well, you were in a fraternity, obviously."

He nods.

"And you're fun."

"I am."

"You're a guy who'll do frickin' anything for a laugh."

He makes a face like that's patently obvious.

"You're an extremely loyal friend."

"I am. Extremely."

"You're a man of your word," I continue. "That's pretty deep and profound, I'd say."

He nods decisively. "I am most definitely a man of my word."

"Unless you've promised to give a girl your application to The Club after you kiss her."

He rolls his eyes. "Patience, little terrorist. It's coming. The review process is just a bit lengthier than you realized. Kiss, fuck, application, I told you—we're still in the 'fuck' stage of the proceedings. What else?"

I make a stern face about the application, but he looks so adorably charming, I melt. "Well, you like to party—or at least you did back then."

He holds up his drink, making it clear this observation is still accurate and I return the gesture. We clink our glasses and take giant swigs of our drinks.

"What else?" he asks.

"You like dumb comedies like *Happy Gilmore*," I reply.

He laughs. "Definitely. Oh shit. *Please* tell me you like dumb comedies. I should have mentioned that's a bit of a deal-breaker with me. No movies with subtitles, please."

"Of course, I love dumb comedies," I say. "*Duh.* I have four brothers, remember? Until I went off to college, I didn't know televisions were capable of showing anything besides dumb comedies, football, and my mom's HGTV."

Josh laughs. "I really should have asked you about your movie preferences before I fucked you. I got lucky, but it could have gone horribly wrong for me." He grins. "So what are some of your favorite dumb comedies? *Anchorman*?"

I nod enthusiastically. "'I love Scotch. Scotchy, Scotch, Scotch,'" I say, doing my best Ron Burgundy impression. "'Here it goes down—down into my belly.'"

Josh belly laughs. "'I'm kind of a big deal.'"

I giggle.

"So what's at the tippy-top of your list of favorites?" he asks.

"Well, in the modern era I'd have to say *Twenty-One Jump Street* is pretty damned high on the list."

"Ah, good one. 'Hey, hey, stop fuckin' with Korean Jesus! He ain't got time for your problems! He busy—with Korean shit!'" Josh shouts, doing his best Ice Cube impression.

I laugh hysterically. "'Chemistry's the one with the shapes and shit, right?'" I reply, doing my best stoned Channing Tatum.

"'Did you just say you have the right to *be* an attorney?'" Josh adds, laughing his ass off.

"'You *do* have the right to be an attorney, if you want to,'" I reply, and Josh laughs his ass off.

"'You have the right to... suck my dick, motherfucker!'" he says.

Oh, jeez. We're laughing so hard we can't breathe.

"Oh my God, Kat—you're a dude, through and through," Josh finally says, beaming at me. "A really, really hot dude with a tight, wet, magic pussy."

I bite my lip. Man, I love this boy's dirty mouth.

"So what about a classic?" he asks. His face is glowing.

"Hmm. I'd have to go with *Zoolander*."

He shoots me the "Blue Steel" male-model face Ben Stiller made famous in that movie.

"Blue steel!" we both shout at the same time.

"Oh my God, Josh," I say. "You're the first person I've ever seen make 'Blue Steel' look *good*."

He laughs. "So is that it? Is that everything you've figured out about me from my deep and profound 'YOLO' ass-tattoo?"

"Oh no, there's more." I look at him sideways. "You clearly have a bit of an evil streak."

"No, I don't. Not at all. We're talking about *me,* not *you*, remember?"

"Ha, ha."

"Really, though, I don't have a mean bone in my body."

"Ha! You were willing to tag poor Henn's ass for the rest of his life, for nothing but stupid yucks."

Josh looks wildly offended. "How the fuck does that make *me* evil? Henn was willing to do the exact same thing to me—and, in fact, he *did* do it to me. That makes Henn way more evil than me."

"But Henn was *right*."

"But I didn't know that. Actually, the most heinous person of all was Reed. He's the one who came up with the diabolical idea in the first place, just for his sick pleasure, the prick."

"Yeah, that was pretty evil."

There's a beat as we both sip our drinks, smiling broadly at each other. My skin is buzzing with electricity.

"What else can you tell about me, Party Girl? I like this game."

"Well, you've got an extraordinarily beautiful ass. Perhaps the most beautiful ass I've ever seen."

"Thank you. Back at you. Especially when it's stomping furiously down a hallway in nothing but a G-string."

"Oh, you liked that, did you?"

"I liked that a lot."

"I could tell." I wink. "Your wet undies were completely see-through, you may recall."

He licks his lips. "You wanted me so bad," he says, "you were losing your fucking mind—not to mention dripping down your legs."

I smirk, but I don't deny it.

"So tell me more, PG. More, more, more."

"Well..." I trail off. "Besides the fact that you have a beautiful ass?"

"Besides that. Something deep and profound."

"Okay. Well . . ." I twist my mouth. "You seem to be ... kind of... I don't know the word. I took Philosophy 101, but I forget it all. *Fatalistic*?"

"I think that's when someone believes their fate is, like, written in the stars—outside their control. Is that what you mean?"

"No. That's not it. Well, maybe, sort of."

"Because I *am* fatalistic to some degree. I think some things are beyond our control—like a brick wall you're hurtling toward whether you like it or not. Nothing you can do about it."

"Well, jeez. That's kind of a bummer."

"Not necessarily. Some brick walls feel fucking awesome when you crash into them." His eyes flicker. "Some brick walls are worth the pain."

I blush.

"What about you—do you believe in fate?"

I shake my head. "No. I believe in kicking ass."

He smirks. "So, then, what did you mean to say?"

"What is it when someone thinks nothing matters? That everything is kind of pointless in the end?"

"I think that's nihilism. I'd have to ask Jonas, though. But, of course, I'd never do that because then he'd talk my ear off about fucking philosophy for an hour and then I'd have to kill myself, which would be a major bummer."

"Oh. Well, I wouldn't have been able to come up with the word 'nihilism' if my life depended on it. I must have meant something else. I dunno."

"Is that what you think of me? That I don't think anything matters?"

"No. Of course not. I know things matter to you."

He shifts his position on the bed. “Because I definitely think some things matter. A man’s word. Friends. A man’s family—whatever’s left of it, anyway.” A shadow briefly crosses his face. “It’s just that so *few* things really matter, there’s no sense getting too worked up about much. Getting a stupid ass-tattoo? Who gives a shit, you know? Like I say, in the end we’re all gonna die anyway, might as well just enjoy the ride and not sweat the small stuff.”

“So maybe your YOLO tattoo isn’t really a reminder to you not to get too cocky or comfortable, after all,” I say tentatively. “Maybe, it’s more something to help you remember the few things that actually matter to you.”

There’s a long beat.

“What about your other tattoos?” I ask, suddenly uncomfortable with the silence. I wasn’t trying to get all deep—it kind of happened by accident. “Did you get your other tattoos in tribute to the few things that matter—or because we’re all gonna die, anyway?”

He makes a face. “Some of each, depending on the tattoo.”

“When did you get the one for your mom?” I ask.

“When I was twenty, I think.”

“She died when you were seven?”

He nods.

“Why did you tell me it means ‘But for the Grace of God I go’ rather than telling me it’s your mom’s name?”

He shrugs. “I never tell people about my mom.”

“Why not?”

“Why are you asking me so many questions?”

“Because I gave you my application and you still owe me yours.”

He makes an annoyed face. “When I was really young, I used to tell people about her whenever anyone asked. Jonas and I had to see a therapist when we were kids and I used to just talk and talk and talk. Blah, blah, blaaaah. But when I was a teenager, I noticed every time I told people, I felt *worse,* not better. Telling people made them look at me funny—like there was something wrong with me because my mom was murdered—like, I dunno, all of a sudden, they thought every time I laughed I was full of shit. And then, after my dad died, and everything that happened with Jonas, I just shut the fuck up completely. From then on, talking about Mom just opened the floodgates to questions about my dad, which meant I'd pretty much be talking about Jonas and all his shit. And I realized I don't need anyone scrutinizing my face as I'm talking for telltale signs that I'm 'laughing through the pain.'"

I bite my lip.

He exhales. "New topic. Have you always been this way?"

"What way? Annoying?"

"No. So fucking *orgasmic*."

"Oh." I make a face like he just gave me whiplash. "Wow, that was a sudden shift in topic."

He forges right ahead. "I've never been with a woman who has orgasms so easily and often as you do." He smirks and bites into a fry. "I'm already addicted to making you come. Best game ever."

I feel a surge of pure elation, but I don't reply.

"Jesus, if I could come that many times in a row, I'd never leave my room. You must masturbate all the time."

I blush.

"Oh, come on. Cat got your tongue, Kitty Kat? You wrote me that awesome application and now you're gonna get all shy on me?"

"It's different to write all that stuff down than to talk about it, face-to-face."

"Aw, come on, PG." He shoots me an incredibly charming look. "It's just me, remember? Honesty-game. How often do you masturbate?"

I feel my cheeks blazing.

"Come on, Kat. Honesty-game, baby."

I sigh audibly. "Every day, pretty much. I try not to let a day go by without having an orgasm."

"*Nice*."

"An orgasm a day keeps the blues away."

"I love it. When did you discover your motor runs so hot?"

My cheeks are hot. "Growing up, my brothers always talked about sex and jerking off as easily as talking about the weather. When I was, like, twelve or thirteen, I asked my oldest brother, Colby, if girls jerk off and got off, too, just like boys, and he said, 'Sure they do—of course—it's just a bit harder to tell.' He was so matter of fact about it, like it was no big deal. He made me feel like one of the guys, like it was perfectly natural and not shameful or weird. So later that day I put the showerhead between my legs and left it there on the massage setting, and within a few minutes, I had my very first orgasm. And I *loved* it. I mean, I was like, 'Oh my God, that was the best feeling ever.' So then every single time I took a shower, I just made it a habit to give myself an orgasm, along with washing my hair and shaving my legs—just a part of my routine. And soon, I was getting off twice in one shower. And then I started reading romance novels as a teen and touching myself and getting myself off... I dunno. I just got really good at it." I shrug and take a huge bite of my burger.

Josh's eyes are boring holes into my face.

"What?" I ask.

"You're incredible," he says. "The hottest woman alive. Do you have any idea how hot you are?"

"Honesty-game?" I ask.

He smirks. "Of course."

"Yeah, I think I'm pretty hot." I giggle and take a bite of a French fry.

He laughs. "Yes, you are, Madame Terrorist. Most definitely."

"Do you know how hot you are?" I ask.

"Honesty-game?"

I nod.

"Yeah, I think I'm pretty hot."

We both laugh.

"So when you masturbate, what's your weapon of choice?" he asks, swigging his drink.

"Why do you wanna know all this?"

"I'm collecting intel for future use. Plus, it's just plain turning me on."

I make a face. "Well, recently, the thing I like to use the most while touching myself is the memory of this one really hot guy with a huge dick, standing in a hallway, dripping wet in his tighty-whities, every detail of his hard-on clearly visible beneath his wet briefs."

Josh grins. "Wow, that's quite a coincidence, because, recently, I've been partial to jacking off to memories of this one incredibly hot terrorist, stomping down a hallway in her bra and G-string, her bare ass-cheeks quaking with fury as she goes."

I laugh.

"So tell me exactly how you like to masturbate. What works best for you? Lying down? Shower? Toys? Fingers?"

All of a sudden, my clit is tingling. "*Why*?"

"Because I wanna know. It'll help me get you off to know exactly what you like."

"It's hard to explain."

"Ah. Show me don't tell me?"

I nod. There's a beat. I know exactly what he wants me to say. My heart is pounding in my ears. I bite my lip. "Would you like to watch me do it some time?" I ask softly.

He nods, his eyes smoldering. "I thought you'd never ask."

My cheeks flush. I swallow hard. Why is this turning me on so much?

"But, first, tell me about it." He licks his lips. "I wanna hear you tell me."

I bite the tip of my finger. "Well, I really like to do it in the shower, with my fingers. I also have a vibe—a Rabbit. That does the trick the quickest, but sometimes I don't want quick. Sometimes I like to take my time, let it build and build until I get myself off so hard I have a backache the next day."

He exhales slowly. "This conversation is turning me the fuck on."

"I can see that." I glance down at his huge erection behind his briefs.

"Have you ever used a Sybian?" he asks.

"A what? A *Sybian*?"

He nods.

"No, I have no idea what that is."

He looks aghast. "No idea?"

I shake my head.

He takes a huge swig of his drink, clearly energized by whatever grand idea has just popped into his head. "Oh shit. You're gonna be epic on a Sybian."

"What is it?" I ask.

His eyes are absolutely blazing with excitement. His dick is rock hard in his briefs. "I'd rather show you than tell you," he says. He grabs his laptop off the nightstand, turns off the music, and begins searching the Internet for a moment. "Bingo," he says after a minute.

"Oh, PG, we're gonna have some fun tonight." He smiles broadly at me. "You trust me?"

"In what context?"

He furrows his brow, obviously offended by my question. "In any context."

"I'll answer that question after I've read your application."

"Bullshit. You trust me."

I shrug. "I've been wrong before."

"You're not wrong this time."

Goose bumps erupt all over my skin. I nod.

Elation floods his face. "Excellent." He grabs his phone and punches out a phone number on his screen, evil-laughing with glee as he does. "Yeah, hey," he says into the phone. "I'm looking to rent a Sybian tonight, as soon as possible?" He pauses to let someone on the other end of the line speak. "No, tomorrow won't work—it's gotta be tonight. Right *now.* I want it delivered to my hotel room within the next thirty minutes." Josh says the name of the hotel and pauses to let the person on the other end of the line speak. "Listen, dude. I don't care if someone else reserved it. That's not my problem. I want it and I'll make you an offer you can't refuse. What's your usual rate for rental and delivery of a Sybian for one night?" He pauses. "Okay, piece of cake. I'll pay you ten times that, in cash, *if* you get it to my hotel room within the next thirty minutes." Josh smiles broadly and winks at me. "Yeah, I thought so." He repeats the name of the hotel and gives the guy his room number. "Thirty minutes or less, I'll pay ten times your usual rate. If it's here within an hour, I'll pay only five times as much," he says. "Any longer than that, I'll pay three times your usual rate, as long as it's here by midnight." He smirks. "Yeah, okay, see you soon."

When Josh hangs up the phone, I'm staring at him, dumbfounded. What the hell did I just agree to?

Josh rubs his hands together. "Oh, Party Girl. You're in for such a treat. And so am I. Shit. I can't wait to see this. I've never been with a woman who gets off like you do. This is gonna be fucking amazing."

"You've never been with a woman who gets off like me? Really?"

"Really—and, trust me, women get off with me—I've got a magic cock—but you're something special. A fucking unicorn."

"Seriously?"

"You know you are."

"No, I don't. How would I know that? I have no basis of comparison. I'm not the one who sleeps with women."

"Ha! That's right—you've only slept with *one* woman." He winks.

I roll my eyes. "I didn't *sleep* with her. I just *made out* with her."

"What, exactly, is the difference between making out and sex when there's no dick involved?"

I think for a minute. "I'm not sure. But we definitely just made out."

"Well, did you two just kiss and kind of grope each other outside your clothes?"

I blush.

"Holy shit. More than that?"

I don't reply.

"Did you go down on her?"

"*No.*"

"She went down on you?"

I blush again. "*No.* Just kissing and heavy petting. But we weren't in our clothes." I clear my throat. "Stop looking at me like that."

Josh bites his lip. "I'm not looking at you like anything. Tell me all about it."

"No."

"Honesty-game."

"Screw that. So far, the honesty-game has been me spilling my guts to you and getting nothing from you in return."

He grins. "Now you see how it feels."

I roll my eyes.

"Come on, PG. Gimme a little dirt about your lesbo-encounter. Look how hard you're making me." He motions to the bulge behind his briefs.

I feel myself blushing like crazy. "My friend was just trying to drive her boyfriend crazy. They'd had a fight and he was being an ass and she was trying to make him lose his shit. We were just being, you know, naughty, trying to get him riled up. It was pretty hot, actually. He sat there and watched us."

"Ah, so that's what turned you on, huh? Having him watch?"

My cheeks are absolutely blazing. "Yeah. I guess so."

Josh's boner is absolutely huge behind his briefs—and the look of arousal on his face is unmistakable.

"Did the boyfriend join in after a bit?"

My heart is racing. "I think I'll wait to answer that question 'til after I've seen your application. The honesty-game only gets you so much when it's a one-way street. Speaking of which, I do believe it's time you gimme that damned application."

"I kiss you; I fuck you; I give you my application—I told you. We're still in the I-fuck-you portion of our program." He lies back onto the pillows on the bed, smirking, and puts his arms behind his head—revealing tattoos on the undersides of his biceps that say "Welcome to" on one arm and "the Gun Show" on the other.

"Oh, Jesus, Josh, no," I say, rolling my eyes. "No, no, no. Those are even worse than freaking 'YOLO'!"

He laughs.

"You're hopeless." I hit my forehead with my palm. "Oh my God. What am I gonna do with you?"

He's laughing his ass off. "I told you. Drunken tattoos are kind of my *thing*. These bad boys were a dare." He flexes his bicep and kisses it.

"Josh. *No*."

"Kat. *Yes*. I had to—I had no choice. Reed 'double-dared' me, Kat. What else was I supposed to do?"

I laugh. "Holy hell. From here on out, you're gonna check with me before you even walk past a tattoo parlor. Do you understand me?"

He laughs. "Thanks, Mom."

I twist my mouth. "You're joking, but that shit wouldn't have happened if you'd had an ounce of fucking parental supervision in your life. You're just an overgrown child."

He shrugs. "Yeah, probably. I haven't had a parent since I was seventeen."

"You've never had anyone tell you to stop acting like an idiot, have you? Everyone around you just double-dares you and goads you on."

"Pretty much."

"Well, jeez." I shake my head. "Call me before you do anything else involving ink on your body. Do you hear me? You're a freakin' train wreck, Josh Faraday. You need someone to slap you occasionally."

He belly laughs. "I know—I totally do." He's beaming at me.

I roll my eyes. "That shit would so not fly in my house. My mom would have whipped you the fuck into shape. Jesus God."

He laughs.

"So what's the deal with your other tattoos? What other monstrosities am I gonna find on you?"

"No other monstrosities. Everything else is meaningful."

"What's the story of 'OVERCOME'?"

He takes a long sip of his drink. "Sorry, I don't tell anyone the truth about that one."

"No?"

He shakes his head.

"What do you say when people ask you?"

"I just say it means, you know, 'keep your chin up' or 'rise above' or some other inspirational sound-bite like that."

"But that's not true?"

"Well, yeah, it's *true*. But that's too simplistic to be the whole truth."

"What's the whole truth, then?" My heart is suddenly clanging wildly.

He looks at me with hard eyes for so long, I'm not sure if he's ever going to answer my question. "I never tell anyone the whole truth about that particular tattoo."

I bite my lip. "Well, gosh, I never tell anyone my initials spell *KUM*." I flash him my most charming smile. "*And* I never tell anyone I made out with a woman. *Or* about Garrett Asshole Bennett calling me a slut." I feel my cheeks burning. "And I *never* tell anyone about poor, sweet Nate and how I broke his heart." I frown. Even saying his name makes me feel literally sick with guilt.

Josh looks unimpressed.

"Aw, come on, Josh. I already know the truth about your 'Grace' and 'YOLO' tattoos, so why not go balls-deep and tell me about the rest of them, too?"

Josh exhales. "Yeah, but I never would have told you the true meaning of 'Grace.' Sarah spilled the beans for me, against my will."

I purse my lips. What more can I do? I can't force the guy to open up to me.

Josh takes a deep breath. "Shit." He looks up at the ceiling like he's trying to make a decision.

I wait, my skin buzzing.

Josh looks at me with sparkling eyes. "Goddamn you, Kat. I really can't resist a woman who uses the phrase 'balls-deep.'"

I grin.

He sighs audibly. "I got my 'OVERCOME' tattoo so I'd see it every single day and feel inspired to keep going, no matter how much I sometimes just wanna lie down and say 'I can't fucking do it anymore.'"

I wait again.

"You sure you wanna hear the whole fucking thing?"

I nod. "Honesty-game."

"Okay. Here it is. Honesty-game." He exhales loudly. "I got it because sometimes, it's all too much. Sometimes, I wanna just... you know... escape."

I nod, encouraging him to keep talking.

"I got it because my mom was slaughtered while I was sitting at a fucking football game with my dad. Because my poor brother was so traumatized by what he witnessed that day, he still hasn't recovered." His voice cracks.

He pauses, collecting himself.

I nod again.

"I got it because my dad killed himself by blowing his brains out, and made sure poor Jonas would find him." His voice cracks again. "I got it because my dad offed himself without saying goodbye to me or leaving me even a goddamned fucking note." He swallows hard. "I got it because Jonas drove himself off a fucking bridge that same day, and if he'd succeeded in offing himself, I would have joined him at the bottom of that bridge." He looks at me with blazing eyes.

I nod again. My skin is electrified.

"You want more? Because I got more."

I don't even hesitate in my reply. "I want it all, Josh."

His eyes are on fire. His chest is heaving. "I got it because, after the thing with my dad, my brother was in a fucking mental institution for almost a full year, totally and completely losing his shit—he didn't even look like himself, Kat. There was nothing I could do to help him. No joke I could tell to make him laugh. No words of wisdom to make it all better. So I went away to college or else I was gonna fucking kill myself, I swear to God—I was right on the verge—and I joined a fraternity and lived in the loudest, most chaotic house I could fucking find and got shit-faced half the time and high the other half and made friends who saved my fucking life. And from there on out, I've been Happy Josh all the live-long fucking day."

My heart is racing. I swallow hard.

His voice becomes low and quiet. "I got it because sometimes I get so fucking tired of being the sane brother, the one who always rises above, the one you can always count on, the *happy* one, I just lose my fucking shit, Kat. I lose it. And then I go on a bender of one kind or another until I get whatever crazy fucking shit out of my system—and then I go back to being Happy Fucking Josh just like I always am—just like Jonas needs me to be."

I swallow hard, trying to alleviate the lump in my throat.

I wait, but Josh doesn't say anything else.

He clears his throat. "Will you excuse me for a minute?" he says abruptly.

Without waiting for my reply, Josh gets off the bed, beelines to the bathroom, and disappears.

I sit for about a minute, staring at the closed door, trembling, swallowing hard.

And then a dam breaks inside me and I burst into tears.

## Chapter 36

*Kat*

For ten minutes, I sit and wait for Josh to come out of the bathroom. And in that time, I manage to regain control of my emotions. I'm calm again. My eyes are dry.

I switch the song on Josh's laptop to Audra Mae (my new favorite) singing "The River." And then, I sit and wait.

Josh comes out of the bathroom and sits back down on the bed, positioning himself exactly the way he was before he left the room.

I open my mouth to speak, but he cuts me off.

"So, PG, I have yet to discover a single tattoo on you," he says, his voice light and bright. "And, believe me, I've conducted an extremely thorough search."

I shift my position on the bed. My heart feels like it's gonna hurtle out of my chest. I put my hands over my face, collecting myself. I didn't expect him to come back in here and pretend he never said any of that stuff to me. I was steeling myself to hold back my tears while he continued pouring his heart out to me. I didn't expect him to come back in here like nothing happened.

"Ever thought of getting a tattoo?" he asks, his voice tight, his eyes pleading with me to play along.

I can't concentrate. I don't know what to do—how to react. "Um," I stutter, "I have one, actually."

"You do? Where?" His eyes are warming, reverting to the way they always look.

I pivot my body and lift my hair, revealing a tiny scorpion on the nape of my neck. "I'm a Scorpio."

"Whoa. Sexy. Can't believe I missed that. So are you into astrology? Or you just really like being a Scorpio?"

"Yeah, I love astrology. I've read a bunch of books on it."

There's a beat. His chest is rising and falling visibly. He bites his lip.

"Um, I wanna get a second one," I say, still not sure how I'm supposed to proceed here. "But I've just never been able to decide on something that would be meaningful enough—something I'd want 'til the end of time."

"Well, that's silly. There's no such thing as ''til the end of time.' Just get what you like right now. That's all we have, no matter what story we tell ourselves to make us feel better."

There's a long beat. Damn. He's kinda dark.

His eyes flicker. "I don't wanna sit here and talk about my fucking feelings all night long, okay? Just forget I ever said all that shit to you, okay? Don't ask me about it—just put it out of your head, okay? Please."

"Okay. I'm sorry."

"What are you sorry about?"

"For... I dunno. Forcing you to spill your guts if you didn't want to."

"You didn't force anything. I'm a grown-ass man." He pauses a long time. "I shouldn't have told you all that. I'm sorry."

"No need to apologize. I'm a grown-ass woman. I told you in my application—I want to know the real you. I don't want Happy Josh. I want Real Josh."

He stares at me for a long beat. "So, as far as a second tattoo for you goes, my advice is don't overthink it. My brother always thinks his ink has to make some earth-shattering statement about the meaning of life." He scoffs. "But you can waste half your life trying to be all deep and profound all the time. The bottom line is we're all gonna die—so who gives a shit if you die with 'YOLO' stamped on your ass or not?"

My stomach is somersaulting. This is not the fun-loving Josh I've come to know.

He motions to my half-eaten plate of food. "You done with that, PG?"

I nod.

He grabs the half-eaten burger off my plate and polishes it off and then clears my plate of all leftover French fries, too. "You want another drink?"

"Thanks."

He gets up and puts our empty plates on a table and then moves behind the bar, his glorious body on full, dazzling display. "So, okay," he says, opening a bottle. "Where the fuck can I find this Garrett Bennett fuckwad? Because I swear to God I wanna hunt him down and beat the fucking shit out of him."

I don't reply. He suddenly looks different to me.

"Stop looking at me like that," Josh says, his jaw pulsing. "See? This is exactly why I don't talk about any of this shit. Now you're looking at me funny. I don't like it."

"I'm not looking at you funny."

He scoffs. "This is the real me, Kat." He motions to his bare torso. "What you see is what you get—a wise and powerful man with a huge cock."

There's a long beat.

Josh clenches his jaw. "So, back to Garrett Asshole Bennett. Why do you care if that guy said you aren't 'marriage material,' Kat? He was obviously a total prick."

I swallow hard. I've never talked about Garrett Asshole Bennett with anyone. I've always been too ashamed at what an idiot I was. I open and close my mouth, struggling to find words.

"What does it matter what some total douchebag said about you?" Josh persists. He pours something into two glasses on the bar. "You're awesome, Kat. A beast. He was obviously dead wrong about you."

My heart is pounding in my ears. Did Josh just indirectly call me *marriage material*?

"It just freaks me out how utterly *clueless* I was. I was ready to give my heart to a guy who thought I was a slut."

"That reflects poorly on him—not on you. You trusted him. He took advantage of you. He was a shit. A cruel, heartless, self-loathing, small-minded, small-dicked little shit."

"It's okay. In the end, it was probably a good life lesson."

"What was the lesson?"

I consider my words. "I think Garrett Bennett is my 'YOLO' tattoo. I was one hundred percent sure of something, and I turned out to be dead wrong." I shrug, trying to come across like it's no big deal. "Good thing to remember."

He looks pained. "That douche deserves to get the shit kicked out of him," he says between gritted teeth.

There's a loud knock at the door and Josh is instantly distracted. A wide grin spreads across his face. "Oh, damn. Looks like talking about our fucking feelings will have to wait, thank God." He suddenly slaps his face—really hard—leaving a bright red mark.

"What the hell?" I gasp.

Josh chuckles and slips around the bar toward the front door, a wide smile on his striking face. "I do believe your chariot has arrived, Party Girl."

## Chapter 37
*Kat*

Josh hands the delivery guy a huge wad of cash and gleefully turns back around, a large, hefty-looking cardboard box in his arms, an evil gleam in his eye.

At the look of trepidation on my face, he laughs. "Don't worry, PG. You're gonna love it."

"What is it?"

"You'll see."

He places the box on the edge of the bed, opens the flaps, and peeks inside. "Come to papa," he says, his dick visibly hardening in his briefs.

He pulls out a tarp-looking thing and spreads it on top of the bed.

"Oh, jeez," I say. "Am I about to star in an episode of *Dexter*?"

Josh chuckles.

"Why the heck do we need a freaking *tarp*?"

"Because things can sometimes get a bit messy." He winks.

"Huh?" I say.

But Josh doesn't elaborate.

"Did you write about this machine in your application to The Club?" I ask.

He scoffs. "*No*. Don't think about that stupid application right now. Just live in the moment, Kat. Just enjoy the *ride*." He snickers. "Literally and figuratively."

"What the fuck is this thing?"

Josh reaches into the box and pulls out a little black machine—a little half-domed box-machine, about a foot long and wide and high, attached to a black power cord and a small control box. Basically, the thing looks like a curved saddle with a power cord.

"It's an orgasm machine," Josh says simply. "It was designed to give a woman the most powerful orgasm she's ever experienced—over and over and over again—for as long as she can stand it." He places the Sybian in the middle of the bed on top of the tarp. "This baby's about to rock your world, Kitty Kat." He smiles greedily. "And, therefore, mine."

I survey the contraption for a moment, utterly fascinated. "So I sit on top of it?"

"Yeah, ride it, cowgirl."

My lower abdomen is beginning to burn and tighten with anticipation.

He points at a flesh-colored strip of prickled rubber on top of the machine, at the apex of the half dome. "This rubber strip here presses against your clit, giving you as much vibration as you can handle—I think the highest setting is something like a small jet engine or something, literally." He laughs. "And then the second stimulation is... Hang on." He reaches into the box, rummages around, and pulls out a clear bag filled with hygienically sealed, flesh-colored dildos, complete with veiny shafts and mushroom tips.

My eyes go wide. "Whoa."

"Pick whichever cock you want," he explains, holding up the bag of dildos of varying sizes. "And then it rotates inside you, hitting your G-spot over and over, while the vibration on the pad blasts your clit."

A dull ache is beginning to burn painfully in my lower abdomen. "This thing looks pretty intense."

"Yeah. It is. Are you game to try it?"

My nipples are hardening. My crotch is filling up with blood. My clit is fluttering and zinging in my panties. "Um. Yeah?"

"Excellent." He sits down on the edge of the bed, his face blazing, and pats the empty spot next to him. 'Okay, PG. Pick your dick."

I sit next to Josh on the bed and he hands me the clear bag of vacuum-sealed dildos. I look through them for a moment, studying each one carefully, my heart racing. There are several varieties to choose from, including a double-pronged dildo thing clearly intended to slide up two holes at once.

"Yeesh," I say, holding up the double-duty dildo. "This one looks interesting."

He grins. "I think you'd better start with something slightly less ambitious for your first ride at the rodeo. Maybe next time for that one."

"Yeah, definitely next time." I roll my eyes and he laughs. I rummage around again and pull out a detailed rubber finger, complete with a knuckle and nail bed. "Wowza." I hold it under Josh's chin like I'm tickling him. "Coochie coo."

Josh laughs. "That's probably a good choice, seeing as this is your first time out. Good entry-level dildo."

"Hell no, I need something more than a freakin' *finger*. I want a *cock*, man. Come on." I rummage through the bag again and finally hold up a big, fat dildo with a thick shaft and bulging tip. "How about this one?" I say.

"Whoa, that's pretty big for your first time," he says. "You sure you don't want to start a little smaller, maybe get used to the rotation first?"

"No way. I like big cock, baby."

His eyes ignite. "Oh yeah?"

"The bigger the better." I blush like a virginal schoolgirl. I'm talking a good game—but this whole situation is way outside my comfort zone. I've never done anything like this. "Have you done this before?" I ask. "I mean, you know, rented an 'orgasm machine' for someone?"

"No." He smiles like that's a stupid question. "I've seen women riding Sybians online, of course—you know, in porn and on Howard Stern or whatever—but I've never rented one for a woman—though I've always fantasized about doing it." His eyes light up. "Especially with a woman like you."

I feel my entire face turning beet red. "And what kind of woman am I again?" If he's calling me a slut, I swear to God I'm gonna—

"Hot as the fucking hinges of hell," Josh replies.

Oh. My inner voice shuts the hell up.

There's a beat.

"Ready, babe?"

My chest is tight.

Before I can reply, Josh bends down and takes my nipple into his mouth.

Instantly, my body bursts into flames. Oh God, forget the

machine. I want him—I want him inside me.

But Josh pulls back. "Okay, cowgirl," he says, his eyes sparkling. "Time to ride."

I nod. My cheeks are hot.

"Go pee while I attach your dildo and get everything all set up for you."

"I don't have to pee."

"Try. You need to void your bladder completely before you get on this thing. It's gonna make you feel like you're gonna piss yourself, even though you're not. You gotta be able to relax completely for it to work its magic."

"Lovely," I say, scrunching up my face.

"Oh, it will be," he says, his blue eyes sparkling wickedly. "Trust me."

## Chapter 38

*Kat*

I come out of the bathroom.

Josh has attached the dildo to the machine, plugged the power cord into the wall, and laid the control box neatly in front of the box on the bed. He turns to look at me, his face ablaze.

"Come here, babe," he coos. He holds out his hand and I pad across the room toward him, my skin zipping and zapping with anticipation.

When I reach him, he takes my hand, pulls me into him, and begins kissing me.

"This is a big-time fantasy of mine," he says into my lips. "Thank you."

"My pleasure," I say—though my mind is reeling. I really don't know what I've gotten myself into—and whether this truly will be my "pleasure" or not. I've never let a man watch me masturbate before in any form, let alone on a machine with a jet engine.

His fingers slip inside my undies and into my wetness. "This is gonna be epic," he says, kissing my neck. He snaps the waistband of my G-string. "Take these motherfuckers off, baby."

I pull my undies down, shuddering with anticipation, and stand before him naked, my clit throbbing under his gaze.

"You're gorgeous," he says, his eyes smoldering. "You ready?"

I nod.

"Climb on, cowgirl."

"Are you gonna show me how to work the controls first?" I ask.

"Oh, no." He grins. "*You're* not gonna work the controls—*I'm* gonna work them."

"*You're* gonna work the controls?" I ask, my eyes wide. "No, I'd feel much more comfortable working them for myself."

"Nope. I gotta be in control, Kat." His jaw muscles pulse. "That way, you can lose yourself completely. No thinking required. You'll just go on the ride of your life." He strokes my hair like I'm a puppy. "I'll take care of you, babe, I promise. No worries."

"What if it's too much? Too fast? Too strong?"

"Then I'll slow it down."

There's a long beat.

"You can trust me. It'll be fucking amazing."

I exhale. "You'll be careful with me? You'll listen to whatever I say?"

"Of course." He smiles. "Always."

"Okay."

"The vibe on your clit and the rotation of the dildo run completely independently of each other, each of them on a separate control dial. So we'll start really slow—one stimulation at a time and on the lowest setting. And then we can work our way up higher and higher on the first stimulation—we'll start with the dildo—and then we'll add vibe if you're liking it—nice and slow to start, and we'll work our way up to *The Exorcism*. Whatever you can handle."

"Oh, Jesus," I say, hopping back. "No *Exorcism*."

He laughs.

"I'm serious, Josh. No *Exorcism*. Save letting me get possessed by Satan for the second date."

He chuckles.

"I'm relieved you find that funny. I still haven't read your application, you may recall. Please tell me Satanism isn't something that turns you on."

He rolls his eyes. "No, Satanism doesn't turn me on. What kind of pervert do you think I am?"

"Dude, I have no idea what kind of pervert you are. That's the whole point of me wanting to see your application."

"All in good time, PG. All in good fucking time. In the meantime, have a seat on this bad boy so we can make any necessary adjustments before we get started."

"Adjustments?"

"We have to make sure the vibe is perfectly flush with your clit when you're sitting completely upright. You don't wanna have to lean forward to get your clit stimulated, or else the dildo won't hit your G-spot at the right angle. And that's where the money is—hitting your G-Spot." He smiles devilishly. "A woman who has clit orgasms *loves* sex—but a woman who gets G-spot orgasms *can't live without it for a single fucking day*."

I stand staring at him, speechless for a moment. I've never heard a man talk this way. I feel like, up until this moment, I've slept with a whole bunch of boys. But Josh is a real man.

Josh motions gallantly to the machine. "Your chariot awaits, m'lady. Hop on."

I can't believe I'm doing this. I'm about to let Josh watch me masturbate on a jet engine?

"Do me a favor," I say. "Take off your briefs. I wanna be able to see your hard-on while I ride."

A broad smile spreads across his face. "My pleasure." He wordlessly removes his briefs, revealing his massive hard-on. "Climb aboard, my lady," he says softly, motioning to the machine.

My crotch is aching and burning. My nipples feel like bullets. My chest is tight. "Honestly, I'd rather climb aboard your cock right now," I whisper.

His cock twitches. "All in good time. That's coming next. Now get on, babe. This is a total fantasy for me; you have no idea."

I crawl onto the bed and straddle the machine on my knees, hovering my crotch just above the tip of the huge dildo, contemplating how the hell to lower myself onto it. Now that it's positioned right at my entrance, it seems a helluva lot bigger than it did a moment ago.

"Wait. Hang on," he says.

I freeze with the dildo positioned right against my entrance.

He bounds over to a duffel bag in the corner and comes back with a condom packet and a bottle of lube. He opens the packet and lays the rolled-up condom on top of the opened wrapper on the corner of the bed—out of the way but clearly at the ready—and then he squeezes some lube into his hand and spreads a huge mess of it all over the dildo, then across the prickly rubber pad intended for my clit, and then he reaches between my legs and covers my clit and hole and lips in slickness, making me shudder and moan softly at his touch. Without missing a beat, he squirts another big glob of lube into his palm and matter-of-factly slathers his hard-on with lube.

I'm suddenly overwhelmed with sexual excitement. "Okay to sit now?" I ask, my voice tight.

"Yeah." His voice sounds as excited as the way I feel: totally turned-on.

I lower myself slowly, taking the dildo into me, and position myself gingerly into the saddle. "Whoa," I say, shifting around and getting acclimated. "This thing's *huge*."

"You want a smaller one?"

"No, no, this is good." I take a deep breath, willing my body to relax around the rubber inside me. "Ooph. It's big, though. Just gimme a second. Damn."

"You okay?"

"Yeah. I get off the hardest when I feel totally filled up. Just give me a second to relax."

His cock twitches. "This is so fucking hot." He exhales.

I take another deep breath and my body relaxes and absorbs the dildo completely.

"Okay, I feel good," I say. "Whew."

"All right, lemme check the fit." He bends down and carefully assesses the contact point between the machine and my clit. "Yup, looks good," he says. He touches my clit gently, making me twitch. "Keep your clit perfectly flush with this rubber strip for maximum pleasure. Okay? No need to lean forward. It's all adjusted perfectly."

I'm already twitching and shuddering with anticipation. I nod.

"Sit back, Kat. The key is letting that cock hit your G-spot over and over. That's where the money's at, baby."

I sit back.

"Good. Does it feel like your clit is flush with the pad when you sit back like that?"

"Yep."

"The more upright you sit, the more G-spot stimulation you'll get—and that's what we're really going after. *G-spot*—not clit, contrary to popular belief."

I nod. "Silly rabbit, clits are for kids."

He laughs. "You're so fucking hilarious." He looks me up and down for a moment, his eyes devouring me, his erection straining.

"Um. Josh? Hello? I'm kinda sitting here with a big, fat dildo up my wahoo?"

He laughs. "Okay, PG. Here we go." He kneels in front of me on the bed, his hard-on massive, and strokes the curve of my hip for a moment, making me shudder. "I'll start with the dildo first, rotating on low, no vibe at all yet, just so you can get used to the motion inside you. Okay?"

I nod and let out a shaky breath. "Please be careful with me."

He touches my hair. "You're in good hands, baby."

I nod again.

Josh sits on the bed next to me and picks up the control box like a kid with an X-box. "You ready, babe?"

I nod.

The machine comes to life, humming loudly, and the dildo begins rotating slowly inside me, swiping repeatedly at a pinpoint location. "Oh," I say, taken aback at the sudden sensation. "Wow. That's amazing." I lean forward instinctively, trying to relieve the pressure already building inside me.

"No, don't lean forward," Josh reminds me. "You can lean back, but never forward. Go against instinct. Don't try to relieve the pressure. Push through it."

I lean back, as instructed. "Wooh," I say, the sensation making my skin prick. "Wow. That's really nice. Whoa."

A beaming smile spreads across Josh's face. "You like that, babe?"

I nod and take a deep breath, trying to steady myself.

"That's the lowest setting—just rotation, no vibration."

"Oh," I say again. "Wow. That's hitting me exactly right. It's like magic. Wow."

"This thing is engineered to do nothing but give you orgasms," Josh says. "Just tell me when you're comfortable, and I'll increase the speed of rotation a bit."

Wooh, this thing is igniting me with no clit stimulation whatsoever, just the swipe... swipe... swipe of the dildo inside me, rotating round and round, hitting my G-spot at the exact right spot with each revolution. It's amazing, really, like nothing I've felt before. So precise. I moan softly. "Oh, God, I like this," I say, my voice beginning to quaver. My skin suddenly erupts with goose bumps. There's suddenly a strange pressure in my ears.

"Wooh," I say softly. "Oh boy."

"Ready for faster?"

I take a deep breath and nod.

Josh twists a dial on the control box and the rotation inside me palpably increases in speed. Swipe, swipe, swipe, the dildo goes, quite a bit faster than before, hitting my G-spot in rapid succession with only a fraction of a second in between each swipe.

"Oh, Jesus," I say. I let out a very loud moan. The wall of my vagina contracts sharply and doesn't release. It just keeps tightening. "Ooph," I say. Something huge is building inside me. I've never felt anything quite like this before. "Holy shit," I say. I begin to lean forward, aching to relieve the pressure.

"No. Don't lean forward. *Back*."

I lean back.

"Good. Now start humping it, babe," Josh says. "Move your hips like you're on top of me, fucking the shit out of me, trying to get yourself off."

I comply, and it's like I've been struck by lightning. My body begins squeezing and clenching fiercely, winding tighter and tighter.

"Yeah, that's it," Josh says. He's begun stroking himself with his free hand. "Oh my God. So hot. Just like that, babe."

I look at Josh, the way he's jerking himself off, the totally perverted look on his face, and my entire body bursts into a ball of flames.

I move my hips forward and back with increased enthusiasm, imagining I'm fucking him, and he growls his approval. "Nice," he says, his hand stroking his shaft fervently. "Oh, Kat. You're killing me right now. You're so fucking hot."

The movement of my hips, combined with the rotation of the dildo and the sight of Josh jacking off—and especially the look on his face—are all conspiring to turn me into something inhuman. Oh, jeez, I'm about to turn into a freaking werewolf. I'm sweating. My skin is rippling all over. My heart is leaping out of my chest.

Josh twists the dial again.

*Swipe-swipe-swipe-swipe-swipe-swipe-swipe-swipe-swipe-swipe,* the machine says, a perfect frenzy of precise stimulation.

Holy shitballs. Jesus fucking Christ. Oh my God.

I make a sound like a wild boar that's just been struck by a hunter's crossbow.

"Holy shit," I gasp. The pleasure is too much to bear. I have to relieve the pressure somehow. I lean back and fondle my breasts and pinch my nipples and throw my head back, grinding my hips voraciously into the machine, growling like a maimed beast. I'm completely swept away by the outrageous sensation inside my body. I literally bite my fingers, my knuckles, grab at my hair, claw at my face, looking for relief from the painful pleasure.

"I'm pushing it higher," Josh chokes out, and the machine buzzes louder.

The dildo is raging inside me now, whacking the shit out of me from the inside. I look down, expecting to see my abdomen visibly zigging and zagging and lurching with the insane rotation of the dildo inside me, like how that alien bursts out of that guy in *Alien,* but all I see is my usual belly and pelvis.

"Oh, Jesus," I whimper.

I'm howling like a trapped animal, fucking the shit out of the machine, sweating like a pig. I'm in pain now. Horrible, brutal pain. And it feels so good.

The entirety of my skin suddenly pricks with goose bumps, exactly like I'm about to throw up—and a strange numbing feeling overtakes my feet. That's something new. What the hell is that? "Oh, shit," I say. "I'm gonna come." I roar. "Oh fuck. It's coming." I dry heave. Whoa, that's new, too.

My toes curl and I let out a weird screeching sound.

"I'm turning on the vibe now, along with the rotation," Josh whispers, his hand working his shaft furiously.

A low vibration hits my clit and, instantly, my body hurtles into some sort of a seizure, warping and clenching and twisting so violently, I feel like I'm gonna lose control of my bowels. My eyelids flutter and my eyeballs roll into the back of my head. I dry heave again.

I shriek. "Oh my fucking... *fuck*!"

My entire body wracks with the most intense orgasm of my life. It's indescribable. I feel like I'm being possessed by a fucking demon.

But rather than give me relief, Josh increases the vibration on my clit.

I can't control myself. I feel like I'm being electrocuted.

I begin releasing strangled expletives at the top of my lungs as my body is slammed by orgasm after orgasm without reprieve. Is this one long, continuous, unending climax, or multiple ones stacked one on top of each other? I can't tell. The pleasure doesn't end. My body's in some sort of trance, warping and wrenching, buckling and undulating, over and over, without relief. I feel like I'm gonna barf or burst into tears or piss all over myself. Or all of the above.

I make yet another sound I've never heard myself make before, and, all of a sudden, I feel warm fluid gushing out of me and pooling underneath me in the saddle. Was that pee? Well, if it was, I don't even care. I just keep humping the saddle furiously, shrieking, my head thrown back, sweat pouring down my face and trickling down my breasts, my body creating a loud slapping noise as my flesh pounds furiously into the wet saddle over and over.

I manage a glance at Josh and he looks enraptured.

The vibe and rotation both increase together and I shriek.

I run my hands over my face, through my hair, bite my fingers, moaning with pleasure and pain. All of a sudden, I feel Josh's lips on my hard nipples, sucking me. He's licking up the sweat off my neck, kissing me furiously.

"I want you to suck my cock," he growls.

I nod. "No. Yes, yes."

He rises to his feet on the bed, bends his legs to lower his dick to the right height for my face, and shoves his hard-on in front of my face. But instead of shoving it into my mouth, he unexpectedly stops and places his wet tip on my chin, right on my little indentation.

"Oh yeah," he says, running his hands through my hair. "Look up at me."

I can barely follow his command. I'm about to come again.

He growls. "Been wanting to do that since I first saw that little cleft in your chin."

Before I can reply, he slides his hard-on from my chin into my mouth, and I instantly begin sucking on him voraciously, moaning loudly as I do.

This is insane pleasure. My body and mouth are both filled up with cocks, my clit is vibrating, his hands are running through my hair. I swirl my tongue against the little hole at his tip, and he growls loudly, grabbing furiously at the back of my head.

My eyes roll back into my head again.

I'm dizzy.

A strange vertigo overtakes me, a kind of tunnel vision. I feel like I'm literally gonna keel over. A blast of white light bursts in front of my eyes and momentarily dances in my field of vision, as if I've just come inside after being in the brightest light and my eyes haven't yet adjusted.

I bat Josh's hand forcefully and pull my mouth off his hard-on.

"I can't," I sputter.

Josh drops down to the control box in a flash and the machine instantly stops humming. The vibration stops. The dildo stops moving.

The machine comes to a complete stop—and yet I'm still twitching and gasping like a freshly caught fish.

Without hesitation, Josh leaps behind me on the bed, roughly lifts my pelvis off the dildo, pushes me forward onto my hands and knees over the machine, and begins furiously licking and suckling my pussy from behind, lapping up the fluid that's literally dripping out of me.

I shudder and moan at the sensation of his tongue and mouth slurping and sucking and lapping at my sensitive folds and creases, at how passionately he's eating me.

"Are you on the pill?" he grunts.

"Yes. Do it."

"Are you clean?"

"Yes. Do it."

"I'm clean."

"Do it."

He plows into me without hesitation, all the way, and proceeds to fuck the motherfucking shit out of me.

I cry out with pleasure as a bone-rattling climax hurtles through me, yet again.

I'm delirious. Out of my head. Aching for him to tear me clean apart.

His fingers reach around me to my clit as he pounds me, and, all of a sudden, I'm blinded. Literally. All I can see is a white light. Then yellow. Pink. Holy shit. My abdomen twists. I feel like I'm gonna throw up. My toes curl. My skin pricks. I dry heave again.

Warm fluid suddenly gushes out of me the way it did on the

machine a few minutes ago and spurts down my thighs. Oh, Jesus. I can't see. I literally can't function. I think I'm gonna black out.

Josh grips the back of my hair and comes so hard inside me, I can feel his cum shooting into me.

Holy... Something-Something, Batman. Fucking hell. I'm so fucked up right now, I can't even come up with a clever Batman quip. Fucking fucky fuck. Holy fuck. Fuck. That's about all I got. Holy Fuck, Batman. Fuck you.

Josh scoops me up into his arms from behind, kisses my neck, and fondles my sweaty breasts. I can't return his affection. I can't move. I'm an inanimate object in his arms. A floppy, spineless, sweaty blow-up doll.

I feel his lips against my ear, his hands in my sweaty hair. "You're the hottest woman alive, Katherine Ulla Morgan," he says, kissing my ear. "My fantasy in every fucking way. Holy fucking shit."

## Chapter 39

*Josh*

Kat shifts in my arms in her sleep and I freeze.

I'm freaking out.

I never, ever have sex without a condom. Ever. It's my cardinal rule and I never break it. *Ever*. No matter the woman. No matter how hot she is. No matter how hot the sex promises to be. I didn't even go bareback with Emma, and we were together for three fucking years. What the *fuck* was I thinking doing it with Kat?

I look at Kat's sleeping face, my heart racing. What if we just made an accidental Faraday? I can't stop hearing my dad's voice, ringing in my head: "'Don't you dare let me catch either of you making an accidental Faraday with a woman unworthy of our name or I'll get the last laugh on that gold digger's ass and disown the fuck out of you faster than she can demand a paternity test.'" How many times did I endure hearing Dad say those fucking words to Jonas and me? Way too many times to count. It was his fucking mantra.

I study Kat's sleeping face again. Even asleep, even without animation to her features, she's utter perfection. That cleft in her chin slays me. Her eyebrows. Her lips.

Adrenaline floods me.

Who gives a fuck what Dad said? Kat's not a gold digger—and Dad's no longer here to disown me even if she were. So what if Kat and I fucked up and made an accidental Faraday? It's none of his fucking business, either way. And, anyway, it was well worth the fucking risk. I smile to myself. Best sex of my fucking life. In the international sport of fucking, this woman just took the gold *and* silver medals. And when I fuck her for a third time, which I plan to do as soon as she wakes up, she'll no doubt snag the bronze medal, too. The woman's got superpowers or something. She's a fucking fembot is what she is. Oh my God. That's it. *Katherine Ulla Morgan is a fucking fembot.*

I'm screwed. Doomed. I smile to myself again. But what a way to go.

Kat shifts in my arms in her sleep and I freeze again. Oh my God. I'm acting like a complete lunatic right now. A total and complete lunatic. I'm acting like fucking Jonas is what I'm doing, letting my mind run uncontrollably. I need to get a fucking grip.

Kat shifts again and a lock of her blonde hair falls into my face.

I breathe in her scent.

Damn, she smells good.

I lift the sheet up and stare at her sleeping body for a moment. I take in the curve of her breasts as she breathes in and out slowly. Her waxed pussy. Her flat belly with her sexy little belly-ring. Her long, toned legs. Her bright blue toenails. Oh my fuck, she's a drug.

I put the sheet back down and gaze at her sleeping face for the hundredth time.

She's so fucking gorgeous, I could look at her all day and never get tired of her face. Her nose. Her lips. Her cheeks. All of it, gorgeous. I can't find a single flaw with this woman. Well, physically, anyway. She's certainly flawed as hell otherwise, that's for fucking sure. First off, she's jealous as fucking hell—something I normally *hate* in a woman. But wait a second. Is that really a flaw when it comes to Kat? Because, holy shit, I kinda like that about her. It's a nice change from how Emma never gave a shit, no matter what I did or what woman practically threw herself at me right in front of her. I thought it meant Emma was somehow more evolved than the average woman, somehow *enlightened*—smarter than me. Of course, in retrospect, now I know it just meant she didn't give a shit.

But enough about Emma. I don't give a shit about her right now. I can't believe I even let my mind wander to her when I've got a woman like Kat in my bed. Speaking of which, I just thought of another flaw. She's stubborn. So fucking stubborn I want to throttle her. But, wait. I like that about her, too. I want things my way, of course—but I wanna *work* for it. Otherwise, I get bored. And there's no such thing as getting bored with Kat, is there? Jesus God, no.

And, in Kat's defense, she's not just jealous and stubborn. She's also ridiculously funny. And smart. Not a brainiac in the traditional sense, maybe, but who the fuck needs book smarts? Bah. Overrated. Just look at Jonas. Smart as hell and the biggest dumbshit I know. Kat's the kind of smart I care about: witty, clever, intuitive, and sassy. Oh God, is she ever sassy. And, on top of all that, she's got a heart of gold underneath all that gorgeousness. It's buried deep underneath a thick outer layer of evil, maybe, but it's there, for sure, buried nice and deep. The way she loves Sarah—the way she doesn't even think twice about her own safety when it comes to protecting Sarah and going after the bad guys for her... man, that shit knocks me out. And, damn, she sure does love her family, too. I've never met a girl from a happy family before. It makes her fascinating to me.

And oh my God, who am I kidding about all that shit, anyway? She could be fucking Attila the Hun from the orphanage across the street and I'd still be infatuated with her after what I just experienced. Holy motherfucking shit, can this woman fuck. I've never seen anything like her. I seriously wanna murder that Garrett Something-or-Other guy—what the fuck was his name? Slut-shaming motherfucker. He sure didn't mind Kat being a slut when he was banging her against his headboard, did he? Fucking asshole cocksucking fuckwad. He must have a very tiny dick, that's all I can say. Asswipe.

Because this woman can suck a dick and ride a cock and come like a fucking tornado. And I don't know any man, other than that fucking douchebag, who'd even *think* of putting a woman down for any of that. Hell no.

Kat stirs again and her eyes flutter open. She smiles and my heart skips a beat.

"Hey," she says softly. "I drifted off."

"No worries. I enjoyed watching you sleep."

"Well, that's not creepy or anything."

"Let me clarify: I enjoyed lifting up the sheet and ogling your naked body while you slept."

"Oh. Okay, I feel better now." She stretches. "Wooh. Every single muscle in my body is sore. Wow. That was intense."

She puts her arms around me and I follow her lead, pulling her into me. We lie nose to nose for a long moment.

"I had some sort of *episode*," she says.

"Sure looked that way. Damn."

"Dude. I went blind. Like, lights were flashing before my eyes. I saw white, then pink, then yellow. And then everything went black. I thought I was dying or being beamed up by aliens."

"Cool."

"Weird," she says.

"Awesome," I say.

"That's never happened to me before. I think I might have had an aneurysm."

"Have you ever squirted before?"

"Is that what I did? I *squirted*? I've never heard that term before."

"You've *never* heard of squirting? Jesus, woman, have you been living under a sexual rock without access to wifi?"

She shrugs.

"Yeah. It's totally a thing. Watch some Internet porn some time, dude. It's kind of like the brass ring of porn."

"Huh."

"You don't watch *porn*?"

"No. It bores me. I like erotic novels a lot. That's my porn. I love them."

"Ah. Yet again, you prove you've got a vagina."

"Dude, if your dick sliding into a warm, tight, wet hole between my legs didn't prove that well enough, then I'm done."

"Could have been smoke and mirrors, you never know."

She laughs.

"I like your warm, tight, wet hole, by the way. I like it a lot."

"Aw, thank you." She puts her hand on her heart like she's accepting an Academy Award. "What a lovely thing to say."

I laugh.

"I kinda surmised you liked my warm, wet hole when you sucked on it like a kitten getting the last drops of milk out of a baby bottle," she adds.

"Holy shit, Kat. That was so fucking hot."

She giggles. "Best ever, fo shizzle ba dizzles."

"Best ever really?"

"Mmm hmm. That's for damn sure. Feel free to help yourself to my warm, wet hole any ol' time you like. Jesus God, that was good. Seriously, that right there was the absolute most amazing sexual experience of my life."

I'm electrified. I push my body into hers and nuzzle my nose into her cheek. "You're so fucking sexy, Kat. I feel like an addict and you're my drug."

She kisses me. "Me, too."

"And the way you rode that Sybian? That memory will stay with me for the rest of my days."

She giggles. "That machine was something else. No wonder it's big in porn."

"Yeah, but that's the thing. I've seen it a million times in porn, and it never does *that* to anyone. Not even close. Jesus. I knew you'd get off on it, but I could never have predicted *that*. It was like you got electrocuted."

"It was incredible. If I owned one of those things, I'd never leave my house."

"If you owned one of those things, *I'd* never leave your house. You wouldn't need an alarm clock. I'd sit in the corner of your room yelling, 'Wake up, Kat! It's Sybian time again!'"

She smiles, but then she pauses, apparently considering something. "I need to tell you something, Josh. I never have sex without a condom—well, unless I'm in a committed relationship and we've both been tested. I don't go without protection casually."

"I was just now freaking out about the same thing. I never do it, either."

"You're sure you're clean?" she asks.

"I'm positive. Just had my annual physical. You?"

"Yeah, I'm sure. One hundred percent. I was tested two months ago when I went on the pill, and I've used condoms every single time since then."

I exhale, totally relieved. "Okay. Well, then I think we should—" I'm interrupted by my phone ringing on my nightstand. "Hang on," I say, turning onto my back and reaching for my phone. I look at the screen. It's Jonas.

"Hey, bro," I say.

Instantly, just by the sound of Jonas' breathing across the phone line, I can tell he's agitated about something.

"Agent Eric just called," Jonas says stiffly. "The feds want a meeting with Sarah and me in Washington *tomorrow*."

"Holy shit." I sit up from Kat, my heart leaping out of my chest. "So are you and Sarah gonna catch a flight tonight?"

"Yeah, I already booked a red-eye. We're packing up now."

"Wow." I run my hand through my hair. "This is big."

"What still needs to be done before Henn can make those bank transfers?" Jonas asks.

I look at Kat. She looks anxious.

I think for a minute. "Um. Henn said he needs to take Kat's passport photo and make her an 'Oksana Belenko' passport. But he said that won't take long."

"Okay, good. I don't know how fast this thing's gonna move once Sarah and I have that meeting. You three need to be ready to make those money transfers as early as tomorrow, just in case."

"We'll be ready."

"Can you come up to my room?" Jonas asks. "I need to talk to you before I leave." He lets out a loud breath. "There's something I need to bounce off you."

"Sure thing, bro. Don't stress. Whatever it is, we'll figure it out. Let me hop in the shower and come right up. Hang on a sec." I pull the phone away from my face and address Kat. "Jonas and Sarah are leaving in an hour for the airport—they're going to D.C. to meet the feds tomorrow. You wanna head up to their room with me?"

Kat's eyes go as wide as saucers. She nods.

I put the phone back to my mouth. "Kat and I will jump in the shower and be there as soon as possible. I'll call Henn and tell him to join us, too."

"Kat's with you?"

"Yeah."

"And the two of you need to hop in the shower?"

I can't help grinning broadly. "Yep."

"I knew you two were fucking! Why have you guys been so secretive about it?"

I ignore the question. "So we'll be up there in fifteen, okay?"

"You like her?"

I look at Kat's gorgeous face. She looks anxious. "Mmm hmm," I answer.

"Awesome. Okay, see you in a few. Oh, and hey, Josh, I need to talk to you privately when you get up here—without the girls overhearing us, okay?"

"Cool. Whatever it is, we'll figure it out."

Jonas lets out a long breath. "Thanks, Josh. See you soon."

"You bet. So, hey, wait, how'd it go with Max after the rest of us left the restaurant? He was like a fucking James Bond villain with metal teeth."

"No, he's a villain from *Die Hard.*"

I laugh. "*Exactly*. Oh my God, yes."

"That's what Sarah says."

"So what happened after we left?"

"Nothing. We just swung our dicks around for a bit. I called him motherfucker like twenty times and told him not to even look at Sarah and he stomped away like a butt-hurt little baby."

"Good."

"Motherfucker."

"Pussy-ass bitch." I pause. "Hey, Jonas, now that I've seen the guy, I have a weird feeling about him—a really bad feeling. Don't underestimate him. The dude looks like he has no soul."

Jonas makes a sound of agreement. "Hence the reason I wanna talk to you privately before Sarah and I head to the airport. I'm thinking no loose ends."

"Yeah, I follow you, bro," I say. "I agree."

"I just wanna talk it through. Make sure I'm not missing anything."

"Gotcha. I'm thinking the fucker from the bathroom at U Dub, too."

Jonas' breathing hitches on the other end of the line. "You've read my mind."

"It's not hard to do. You're kind of a simpleton."

Jonas laughs. "Okay, motherfucker, stop fucking the shit out of Kat for a goddamned minute and get up here. There's a lot to talk about before Sarah and I head out."

"I'd only stop that particular activity for you, bro, just so you know."

"Good times?"

"The best of times. Oh my fucking God."

"Excellent."

"Kat and I will see you in a few."

"Okay. Call Henn."

"Will do."

I hang up with Jonas.

"What's going on?" Kat asks, her eyes bugging out.

I explain everything Jonas and I talked about (other than Jonas' desire to leave no loose ends). "So, hey, let's hop in the shower real quick and head up to their room," I say.

Kat's face ignites. "Oh, so we're gonna finally leave this room, huh?"

"Yeah, we gotta get the crew together to talk about . . ." I trail off. My heart lurches into my mouth. Oh shit. That's right. I kiss her. I fuck her. *I give her my application.* Shit. The jig is up.

"You promised you wouldn't leave this room without giving me that application," Kat says evenly.

I exhale a long, exasperated breath.

"You promised," she says.

"Yeah, I know. But Jonas and Sarah have to go to the airport within the hour and there's a ton of stuff we all need to figure out before they go. There's no time for our little game—not right now. We've gotta press the 'pause' button 'til they leave."

Kat throws up her hands in frustration. "Seriously?"

"Just 'til they leave."

She's fuming.

"Babe, we gotta save the world right now."

She exhales with exasperation. "*Fine*. Goddammit. I'll press the 'pause' button. But only because I love Sarah so much and I wanna take those assholes down as much as anyone. But the minute they leave for the airport, you're gonna give me that goddamned application."

I take a deep breath. My pulse is pounding in my ears. Shit. Things have been going so well between us. I don't want to fuck things up.

"Is it on your laptop?" she asks.

I nod.

"Email it to me right now."

I shake my head. "No way. The deal was you get to *read* it—you don't get to *have* it."

She rolls her eyes. "Then I suggest you bring your frickin' laptop with you to Jonas and Sarah's suite so you can hand it over to me the *minute* they leave."

I don't respond. I guess some part of me was hoping that, after I finally fucked her, Kat would say, "To hell with the stupid application. It doesn't matter anymore."

Kat touches my chest and goose bumps erupt on my body. "Josh, listen to me. My initials spell KUM. I grew up being called Kum Shot and Jizz. A guy I thought I *loved* turned out to have a fucking fiancée and told me I'm a slut." She smiles, but there's no mistaking the insecurity in her eyes. "Not to mention the fact that I just sucked your gigantic dick while riding an orgasm machine and then came so hard I went momentarily blind." She shoots me an adorable grin. "And you're nervous about sharing some stupid sex club application with me?" She strokes my face. "Holy Nothing Can Shock Me Now, Batman."

I close my eyes. She kisses me gently.

"Holy Give Me Some Credit, Batman," she whispers, continuing to kiss me.

I return her kiss. My dick is hardening. But, shit, there's no time. My brother's waiting. I pull away.

She puts her finger under my chin and kisses my lips gently. "Holy *YOLO*, Batman."

I smile at her. What man could resist her? I tried my mighty best, I really did, but even I couldn't pull it off. "Okay," I say. "A promise is a promise. The minute Jonas and Sarah leave, I'll hand it over. I give you my solemn word as a Faraday."

## Chapter 40

*Josh*

The five of us have gone over Jonas and Sarah's talking points for the big meeting in Washington tomorrow, twice, and Henn has walked us through the logistics of how our very own "Oksana Belenko" is gonna get The Club's approximately five hundred fifty-four million bucks transferred out of the bad guys' twelve bank accounts. During the whole conversation, every one of us has looked on anxiously, but none more than Kat—which is understandable, considering she's the one who's gonna have to waltz into each and every bank and commit large-scale bank fraud.

I wish I could do the job for her, I really do. In fact, I've pushed Henn to come up with some way to transfer the money that doesn't rely on Kat, but he keeps telling me there's no other way: the accounts are all in Oksana's name and the majority of them require in-person transfers for amounts over a million bucks. Henn and I went around and around, but there's no alternative. We can't do it without Kat.

"Don't worry, Kitty Kat," Henn says. "I promise. It's gonna go like clockwork. I've rigged it so the banks will think you're Oksana, no questions asked, and I've also figured out a way to block the bad guys' access to the Internet on their devices during the whole time we're in the banks, just in case they try to check their accounts while we're in the middle of things."

Kat bites her lip. "Thanks, Henny."

"We'll both be right by your side," I say, taking her hand in mine. She leans into my shoulder and I kiss the top of her head. "I'll be right there with you, PG," I whisper. "Every step of the way."

"Okay, so are you three good?" Jonas asks.

"Yeah, we're good," I say. "Are you two good?"

Jonas and Sarah look at each other. "Do you have any questions, baby?" Jonas asks.

Sarah shakes her head. "No, no questions. But I do have a comment: holy crappola—I'm shitting a brick."

Jonas laughs and kisses her forehead. "No need for brick-shitting. Your report is gonna do all our talking for us."

Sarah takes a deep breath. "God help me if I wind up on some government watch-list after all this."

"Don't worry. They wouldn't be meeting us in the first place if they didn't take your report seriously."

Sarah nods and exhales.

Jonas looks at me. "Josh, can I talk to you for just a second?"

"Sure, bro."

"Do you mind, baby? I just gotta talk to Josh for a quick second, and then we'll head out."

"No worries. I'll chat with Kitty Kat."

Jonas and I get up and Sarah and Kat instantly launch into a rapid-fire conversation behind our backs.

"You two want me to join you or... ?" Henn asks us.

Jonas looks at me for my input.

I nod.

"Yeah," Jonas says. "Thanks, Henn. We could definitely use your brain."

The three of us move to a sitting area on the other side of the suite, far enough away that the girls won't overhear us.

Jonas looks nervously across the room. "There's not a lot of time, so lemme cut to the chase. I want Max and the Ukrainian Travolta dead." He clenches his jaw.

Henn doesn't seem the slightest bit surprised. "Shouldn't be hard to persuade the feds to do it for you. The feds are gonna want them dead, too."

"How do you figure?"

"Well, dude. Come on. The Secretary of Defense is one of The Club's biggest clients? Not good. They'll do whatever the fuck you ask them to do to keep that quiet and make sure this deal goes off without a hitch. Offing a couple Ukrainian separatists is a small price to bury that particular bit of information."

"'Ukrainian separatists' isn't really sexy enough," I say. "I don't think the average person watching the news understands all that."

"True," Henn says. "Good point."

"I think we need something easily digestible for the masses—something the media will pick up on and run with—something the feds can feed to them that they won't even question."

We're all silent for a beat.

"Terrorists?" I say.

"*Yes*," Henn says. "The media can spin that 'til the end of fucking time. They'll eat that shit up."

"Yeah, but *Ukrainian* terrorists? Americans don't even know where Ukraine is," I say.

"That's true." Henn says.

"*Russian* terrorists?" Jonas says.

"Yeah," Henn says. "'A Russian terrorist cell.'"

"Ha! Perfect," I say. "You're a fucking genius."

"So I've been told," Henn says.

"I like it," Jonas says, nodding. He looks deep in thought.

"It's actually eerily perfect," Henn says. "It's got all the bogeyman buzzwords at once, tied up in a neat little package. The news stations will have themselves a field day, whipping everyone into a frenzy, which means the feds will have a free pass to do whatever they need to do in plain sight—all in the name of protecting us all from a huge terrorist threat.'" Henn nods emphatically. "It's brillz."

"What if those two fuckers die in a shoot-out during a raid on the 'terrorists' compound'?" I ask. "That's pretty sexy, isn't it?"

"Perfecto," Henn says. "Maybe those two fuckers 'pulled weapons on officers' during the raid? That'd be the cleanest for the feds and best for us, too—no way to trace anything back to us. Simple. Effective. Believable. The feds save the world. We have nothing to do with it. Great mega-story for the news outlets. It's a win-win-win."

Jonas nods. "Thanks, guys." He looks emboldened. "I think that might work if I sell it right."

Henn scrunches up his face, thinking. "Lemme see if I can't get you a little insurance to help you out, big guy. Maybe I can dig up some more shit on the Secretary of Defense. Some compromising photos or whatnot. Kiddie porn on his computer. A dick pic he sent to a minor? I'm sure there's something. There's always something with these guys. A little insurance would be a good thing to have in your pocket in case the feds balk about taking those two guys out as part of the deal. "

"Thanks, Henn," Jonas says. "Yeah, insurance would be awesome."

"Cool. No problem."

"Is that everything, bro?" I ask.

Jonas looks at his watch. "Just one more quick thing. What about Oksana? Does she pull a weapon during the shoot-out or not?"

We all ponder the question for a moment, pursing our lips.

"The more people 'pulled weapons on officers' and didn't make it out alive, the less believable the whole thing is," Henn says. "Plus, women are much less likely to pull a weapon, statistically speaking. We don't wanna raise any suspicion that anything's hinky."

Jonas clenches his jaw. "Did you uncover anything whatsoever to suggest Oksana had something to do with the hit on Sarah?"

"Or maybe knew about it beforehand?" I ask, my jaw clenching in sympathy with my brother's. I want these fuckers dead every bit as much as he does.

Henn shakes his head. "Everything I've seen tells me Max ordered the hit and the Ukrainian Travolta carried it out. All evidence is that Oksana's a pimpstress and a loyalist to mother Russia, but not a stone-cold killer. Max is the head of the snake. Indubitably."

Jonas looks deep in thought.

I touch my brother's shoulder. "I vote you be the God of the *New* Testament, Jonas—show the perfect measure of force and mercy."

Jonas runs his hands through his hair. "Fuck. I dunno." He exhales. "I'll think about it on the plane some more."

"Okay. Follow your gut." I hug him. "Be safe, bro." I kiss him on the side of his neck.

"You, too," Jonas says. He kisses my cheek. "Be careful in the banks, guys. Please."

"We will."

"Take extra good care of Kat." He looks across the room at Sarah. She's chatting and giggling happily with Kat. "My girl can't live without her."

I stare at Kat across the room, my heart suddenly bursting in my chest. "I won't let anything happen to her, bro."

"We'll keep her safe, big guy," Henn says.

Jonas hugs Henn. "You're a fucking genius, man. I can never thank you enough for all you've done."

"Hey, man. We're family now."

They slap each other's backs and when they pull apart, Jonas looks determined.

"You got this," I say. "You're a fucking beast, bro."

"Fuck yeah," Jonas says.

"Fuck yeah," I reply.

"Fuck yeah," Henn echoes. "Wow, I feel so *masculated* right now. Is this how you guys feel every fucking day? Wow."

We all laugh.

I look at my watch. "Okay, bro. You better get your ass to the airport. Keep us posted. We'll be ready all day tomorrow. Just give us the word and we'll head to the banks."

Our threesome walks over to the girls, and after the five of us have completed every possible permutation of hugging and whispered goodbyes, Jonas and Sarah waltz out the door, bags in hand and determined expressions on their faces.

"Good luck saving the world, guys!" Kat shouts to their backs.

"Holy crappolaaaaaaaaaaa!" Sarah shouts, just as the door closes behind her.

They're gone.

Henn, Kat, and I look at each other in a shared daze for a long moment.

"Holy shitballs," Kat finally says.

"Big shit going down in little China," Henn says.

"Or little Ukraine," I add.

"Shit just got real," Henn says.

"Fo shizzle pops," Kat says.

Henn exhales, filling his cheeks with air like a blowfish. "Welp." He looks at Kat. "I guess we'd better take your photo for your Oksana passport, huh? If Jonas and Sarah call upon us to save the world tomorrow, we'd best be ready."

# Chapter 41
*Josh*

"Okay, Kitty Kat," Henn says, his eyes bugging out. "There's nothing to stress about. I've already shaved years off Oksana's age on all the banks' systems and I'm gonna swap your photo for Oksana's on the accounts using photo identification. Tonight, I'm gonna check and recheck all the passwords and codes on every account, too, just to make sure everything goes off without a hitch tomorrow. Oh, and I'm gonna infect the bad guys' devices with malware to block their wifi at the flip of a switch too—just on the off chance they try to log into their accounts while we're in the middle of making the transfers."

"How many Americanos have you had today, Henny?" Kat asks.

"Why does everyone always ask me that?" He chuckles. "So are you ready to get your photo taken, Oksana?" He motions to the door of Jonas and Sarah's suite. "I think we should head down to the casino and look for a white wall as a background."

Kat steals a glance at me, and there's no mistaking what she's thinking about."Sure thing," she says tentatively, still looking at me. "How long do you need me?"

"Just a few minutes. Shouldn't take long once we find a good backdrop."

"Is there any hacker-stuff you could do first, before taking my photo? Maybe for about an hour?"

"Um. Sure. I can certainly work on my malware for a while. And I've got a little research on the Secretary of Defense to do for Jonas."

"In that case, how about we split up for a bit? You guys do whatever while I stay here in the suite and do a little personal reading? It won't take too long."

"Cool," Henn says. "Actually, I could use to blow off a little steam for a bit before I get to work, if you guys don't mind. You wanna roll the dice with me, boss?"

"Yeah," I say slowly, my stomach clenching. "I gotta talk to Kat first, though. I'll catch up with you in a bit."

"Cool. See you soon. Just text me when you're ready to meet up."

The minute Henn leaves, I take Kat's face in my hands and kiss her. And then I kiss her again. And again. And again. All I wanna do is kiss her one last time before my application potentially fucks everything up—but before I know it, my clothes are off and so are hers and she's on top of me on the bed, riding me, screaming my name, humping me exactly the way she rode that Sybian—and I'm underneath her, guiding her smooth hips, groping her hot little ass, mesmerized by the way her tits are bouncing, by the little cleft in her chin, the way her blonde hair falls around her shoulders, and wondering how the fuck I'm letting myself have sex without a condom *again* (even though it feels so, so fucking good).

When we're done, we hop in the shower, neither of us speaking.

Clearly, that was a detour neither of us expected or planned. We're like fucking dynamite, the two of us. A nuclear reaction.

"You're on the pill, right?" I ask.

"Yep. Still on the pill since the last time I told you."

"Sorry. Just double-checking."

She smiles. "Sorry. Ask me as many times as you need. Yes, I'm on the pill."

"I'm sorry. My dad used to put the fear of God into me about having sex without a condom. I've never done it before. I'm just paranoid."

"You've never had sex without a condom before?"

I shake my head.

"Not even with girlfriends?"

"Never. You're my first."

I lather her up under the hot water for a moment.

"So you've literally *never* felt sex without a rubber before me? Not once?"

I shake my head again—and then I grin broadly. "It feels fucking *amazing.*"

She grins broadly. "Yeah, I bet it does. Jeez, Josh. No wonder you think I'm amazing. Ha!"

I kiss her. "You are," I say. "It's not just that."

She throws her arms around me and kisses me. "God, I'm addicted to you."

"Me, too. You're a drug."

I take my sweet time in the shower with her, washing her, touching her. And then, what the fuck, why not? I get down on my knees and eat her out, too, bringing her to a climax that has her pulling on my hair like it's on fucking fire.

When we're done, we dry ourselves off with the fluffy white towels and get dressed quietly, a sense of doom descending upon me. The jig is up. There's nowhere else to run. I've got to give it to her now.

"Can I make you a drink, PG?"

"Sure. Surprise me," she says.

"My kind of girl," I reply. My voice is casual, relaxed. But it's an act. My stomach is tight. My pulse is pounding in my ears.

I bring her the drink. "An old fashioned," I say.

"Oh, you hipster." She notices my empty hands. "You didn't make one for yourself?"

"I don't wanna be here when you read my application," I say. "I'm gonna go down to the casino and meet Henn."

"Oh. Okay. Suit yourself."

There's a long pause. I stand, rooted to my spot, my hand in my pocket.

"Now would be when you *finally* give me your application, Josh," she says.

I exhale. "I know."

There's another long pause. I'm waiting for her to say, "Don't worry about it. I don't care what it says." But she doesn't. She just stares at me, smiling like a wolf.

"Okay," I finally say. I grab my laptop from the table, click into my PDF-formatted application, and lay the laptop on her lap. "Here you go, Madame Terrorist," I say. "Enjoy."

"Thank you kindly," she says.

"Text me when you're done so I can come get you. I don't want you to be alone out there—now more than ever. I didn't like the looks of that Max guy."

She nods. "I promise."

I take a deep breath. "Okay. Well. Happy reading."

"Thank you."

I linger briefly, hoping she'll say never mind. But she doesn't.

I bite the inside of my cheek for minute. "Okay, well, bye."

"Bye." She shoots me a clipped wave.

I return her wave and stride to the front door of the suite, my heart pulsing in my ears. Just before I leave, I turn back around. Kat's settling herself into her chair. She takes a swig of her old fashioned and leans into the screen, biting her lip.

The hair on the back of my neck stands up. This is it—the brick wall I've been hurtling toward without brakes since I first laid eyes on that beautiful terrorist. And now the damned wall is finally here, an inch from my fucking nose, and there's nowhere to turn.

I take a deep breath, open the door, and quietly slip into the hallway.

The door closes behind me.

I close my eyes.

*Crash.*

## Acknowledgments

This book is for The Love Monkeys, my devoted and wonderful readers. Thank you for loving my characters as much as I do—and, therefore, loving me.

## Author Biography

*USA Today* bestselling author Lauren Rowe lives in San Diego, California, where, in addition to writing books, she performs with her dance/party band at events all over Southern California, writes songs, takes embarrassing snapshots of her ever-patient Boston terrier, Buster, spends time with her family, and narrates audiobooks. To find out about Lauren's upcoming releases and giveaways, sign up for Lauren's emails at www.LaurenRoweBooks.com. Lauren loves to hear from readers! Send Lauren an email from her website, follow her on Twitter @laurenrowebooks, and/or come by her Facebook page by searching Facebook for "Lauren Rowe author." (The actual Facebook link is:

https://www.facebook.com/pages/Lauren-Rowe/1498285267074016).

## Additional Books by Lauren Rowe

All books by Lauren Rowe are available in ebook, paperback, and audiobook formats.

**The Club Series (The Faraday Brothers Books)**

*The Club Series* is seven books about two brothers, Jonas and Josh Faraday, and the feisty, fierce, smart, funny women who eventually take complete ownership of their hearts: Sarah Cruz and Kat Morgan. *The Club Series* books are to be read in order*, as follows:

-*The Club* #1 (Jonas and Sarah)

-*The Reclamation* #2 (Jonas and Sarah)

-*The Redemption* #3 (Jonas and Sarah)

-*The Culmination* #4 (Jonas and Sarah with Josh and Kat)*

*Note Lauren intended *The Club Series* to be read in order, 1-7. However, some readers have preferred skipping over book four and heading straight to Josh and Kat's story in *The Infatuation* (Book #5) and then looping back around after Book 7 to read Book 4. This is perfectly fine because *The Culmination* is set three years after the end of the series. It's up to individual preference if you prefer chronological storytelling, go for it. If you wish to read the books as Lauren intended, then read in order 1-4.

-*The Infatuation* #5 (Josh and Kat, Part I)

-*The Revelation* #6 (Josh and Kat, Part II)

-*The Consummation* #7 (Josh and Kat, Part III)

In *The Consummation* (The Club #7), we meet Kat Morgan's family, including her four brothers, Colby, Ryan, Keane, and Dax. If you wish to read more about the Morgans, check out The Morgan Brothers Books. A series of complete standalones, they are set in the same universe as *The Club Series* with numerous cross-over scenes and characters. You do *not* need to read *The Club Series* first to enjoy The Morgan Brothers Books. **And all Morgan Brothers books are standalones to be read in *any* order.**

**The Morgan Brothers Books:**

Enjoy the Morgan Brothers books before or after or alongside *The Club Series,* in any order:

1. *Hero.* Coming March 12, 2018! This is the epic love story of heroic firefighter, **Colby Morgan,** Kat Morgan's oldest brother. After the worst catastrophe of Colby Morgan's life, will physical therapist Lydia save him… or will he save her? This story takes place alongside Josh and Kat's love story from books 5 to 7 of *The Club Series* and also parallel to Ryan Morgan's love story in *Captain.*

2. *Captain.* A steamy, funny, heartfelt, heart-palpitating insta-love-to-enemies-to-lovers romance. This is the love story of tattooed sex god, **Ryan Morgan**, and the woman he'd move heaven and earth to claim. Note this story takes place alongside *Hero* and The Josh and Kat books from *The Club Series* (Books 5-7). For fans of *The Club Series,* this book brings back not only Josh Faraday and Kat Morgan and the entire Morgan family, but we also get to see in detail Jonas Faraday and Sarah Cruz, Henn and Hannah, and Josh's friend, the music mogul, Reed Rivers, too.

3. *Ball Peen Hammer.* A steamy, hilarious enemies-to-friends-to-lovers romantic comedy. This is the story of cocky as hell male stripper, **Keane Morgan**, and the sassy, smart young woman who brings him to his knees on a road trip. The story begins after *Hero* and *Captain* in time but is intended to be read as a true standalone in *any* order.

4. *Rock Star.* Do you love rock star romances? Then you'll want to read the love story of the youngest Morgan brother, **Dax Morgan,** and the woman who rocked his world, coming in 2018 (TBA)! Note Dax's story is set in time after *Ball Peen Hammer*. Please sign up for Lauren's newsletter at www.laurenrowebooks.com to make sure you don't miss any news about this release and all other upcoming releases and giveaways and behind the scenes scoops!

5. If you've started Lauren's books with The Morgan Brothers Books and you're intrigued about the Morgan brothers' feisty and fabulous sister, **Kat Morgan** (aka The Party Girl) and the sexy billionaire who falls head over heels for her, then it's time to enter the addicting world of the internationally bestselling series, *The Club Series.* Seven books about two brothers (**Jonas Faraday** and **Josh Faraday**) and the witty, sassy women who bring them to their knees (**Sarah Cruz** and **Kat Morgan**), *The Club Series* has been translated all over the world and hit multiple bestseller lists. Find out why readers call it one of their favorite series of all time, addicting, and unforgettable! The series begins with the story of Jonas and Sarah and ends with the story of Josh and Kat.

**Does Lauren have standalone books outside the Faraday-Morgan universe? Yes! They are:**

1. *Countdown to Killing Kurtis* – This is a sexy psychological thriller with twists and turns, dark humor, and an unconventional love story (not a traditional romance). When a seemingly naive Marilyn-Monroe-wanna-be from Texas discovers her porno-king husband has thwarted her lifelong Hollywood dreams, she hatches a surefire plan to kill him in exactly one year, in order to fulfill what she swears is her sacred destiny.

2. *Misadventures on the Night Shift* – a sexy, funny, scorching bad-boy-rock-star romance with a hint of angst. This is a quick read and Lauren's steamiest book by far, but filled with

Lauren's trademark heart, wit, and depth of emotion and character development. Part of Waterhouse Press's Misadventures series featuring standalone works by a roster of kick-ass authors. Look for the first round of Misadventures books, including Lauren's, in fall 2017. For more, visit misadventures.com.

3. *Misadventures of a College Girl* – a sexy, funny romance with tons of heart, wit, steam, and truly unforgettable characters. Part of Waterhouse Press's Misadventures series featuring standalone works by a roster of kick-ass authors. Look for the first second of Misadventures books, including Lauren's, in spring 2018. For more visit misadventures.com.

4. Look for Lauren's third *Misadventures* title, coming in 2018.

Be sure to sign up for Lauren's newsletter at www.laurenrowe books.com to make sure you don't miss any news about releases and giveaways. Also, join Lauren on Facebook on her page and in her group, Lauren Rowe Books! And if you're an audiobook lover, all of Lauren's books are available in that format, too, narrated or co-narrated by Lauren Rowe, so check them out!

Lightning Source UK Ltd.
Milton Keynes UK
UKHW010604010519
341862UK00002B/676/P

9 780986 309182